Messages
to
Jake

Laura Ann Neuleo

LAURA ANN NEULEO

Cover design by Shannan Garrett-Cooper.

Map illustrated by Josh Lewis.

The characters and events portrayed in this book are fictitious. Any similarity to real persons, living or dead, is coincidental and not intended by the author.

*To my mom who, on an April day when I was on the brink of losing my income to COVID-19, asked me,
"How's Jake?"*

LAURA ANN NEULEO

CONTENTS

PREFACE

This is a work of fiction inspired, in part, by my experience as a Peace Corps Volunteer in Panama. Certain places and all people are fictitious. In the 'A Note from the Author' section at the end of this novel, I've included details about scenes based on real life.

LAURA ANN NEULEO

ACKNOWLEDGMENTS

Messages to Jake wouldn't be what it is today without the unwavering support and guidance of my family and friends.

I appreciate everyone who cheered me on and handled my hermit ways with grace during my eight months of writing and editing. There are five people in particular who I'd like to give special recognition to.

To my mom, Terrie, who sparked the idea for *Messages to Jake*. She helped me brainstorm the storyline in its early stages, was my cheerleader when I doubted myself, and my 'Comma Momma' during the proofreading phase.

To my dad, Cliff, and my stepmom, Paula. They read and re-read my manuscript with enthusiasm, thought of creative workarounds for plot holes, and encouraged me to expand on pivotal scenes.

To Penny Owen, who encouraged me to write a book. She taught me the important lesson of less being more. Her selfless guidance and generous coaching helped turn *Messages to Jake* into a more powerful story.

To Robert Webber, who poured his heart and experience into countless pages of invaluable editing notes. His honesty and keen perception of human behavior offered an added layer of depth to the characters and story.

Finally, while I'm grateful for the input and insight of all those who read *Messages to Jake* before it was published, I take full responsibility for its content and any errors or misrepresentations. I recognize that writing about Panamanian culture as a white woman who grew up in the United States comes with the risk of unintentional inaccuracies. I have the utmost respect for the Emberá and Latino people in Panama, and I'm forever on the journey of learning from people with different backgrounds than mine.

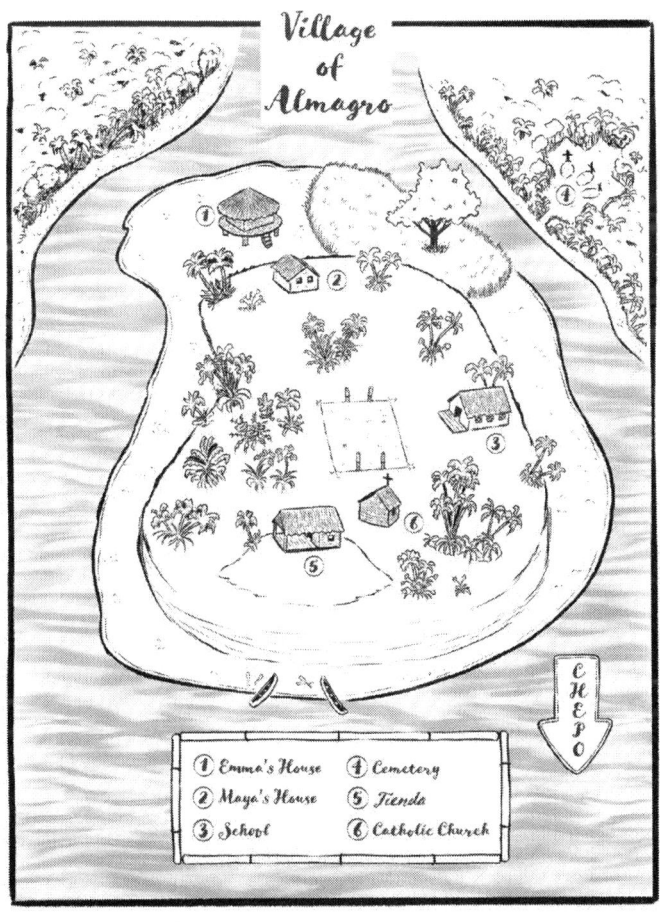

LAURA ANN NEULEO

CHAPTER 1

Emma ~ Present

J uice trickled down Emma's wrist and dripped onto her *paruma* skirt as a worm squirmed beside the knife in her mango. She felt the tickle of a bee-like insect burrowing into her scalp. Pulling her fingers through her hair, she untangled it starting at the root, working her way to the tips, knowing this particular species wouldn't sting her. Moments like these, as parrots dropped debris from the branches above her hammock, she tried to remember when her Panamanian life became familiar.

Chuleta wagged her tail against the worn hammock, watching minnows nibble grass along the river's edge. Shades of brown streaked her white and beige fur from drying mud.

Or rather, drying clay.

Emma had made the mistake of referring to clay as mud when she first arrived in Almagro. She was told— and reminded in the months that followed—that the

Spanish name 'Almagro' was derived from the Arabic word for 'red clay'. The caveat was that red was brown and the clay was dirt. Oftentimes, the villagers in her community had twice as many theories about how their ancestors decided on Almagro's name as fish they caught in the river. But sometimes, they agreed it was from the sunset casting hues on Almagro's sunbaked shore.

A dugout canoe rocked upstream. Emma waved at the man, admiring the balance it took for him to stand in the hollowed-out log to greet her, but the canoe was too far away to make out who he was. Even if she wasn't home, though, she knew anyone in her Peace Corps village would recognize her.

"Yes!" a voice shouted, sending leaves falling into Emma's lap as parrots flew to higher branches.

Emma closed her eyes. She had a longer morning alone than usual. Time was abundant in Almagro, but the villagers made sure she didn't spend too much of it by herself—especially since she didn't have a husband.

"Andre*yes*!" she said, turning in her hammock and matching the boy's enthusiasm with a grin.

With momentum from running down the hill, Andrés launched into the side of her hammock, laughing as Emma swung her arm away to keep the knife from hitting him.

She already knew the outcome but asked him in English anyway. "How are you?"

He crawled into her hammock, smearing a muddy handprint on her leg in the process. "Yes!" he said. Giggling, he sprinted up the hammock's rope to reach for a mango.

Emma sighed and resorted to Spanish. "Don't pick the green ones."

Mango leaves revealed Andrés' smile in rhythm with the breeze. He swung his leg over a branch and looked down at her. "Yes!"

Emma studied Andrés' skinny limbs, blemished skin, and bulging stomach. Between fruit trees, fish, and crops, food wasn't in short supply in Almagro when the weather cooperated. Parasites weren't, either. She had gotten better at guessing the children's ages in her village of two hundred residents which, despite being in the same province as Panama City, was tucked in the jungle without roads, electricity, or running water. To an American's eye, Andrés looked three or four. To her trained eye, he looked just like the six-year-old he was.

"Andrés." Emma eyed him as he plopped down across from her in the hammock, a green mango in hand.

He shook his head, grinning. "Andre*yes.*"

Andre*yes* was the nickname Emma had given Andrés, since he only ever said 'yes' in her English class. She responded to him with scrunched eyebrows, which fueled his laughter. He reached for her knife, grabbing it by the blade. Emma knew better than to correct him; he learned to use a machete on his third birthday.

Emma heard a splash and turned towards the river. A jagged circle of light danced on an otherwise solid shadow of a canoe. With a thin, wooden *palanca* stick twice the length of his body, Hugo pushed the canoe onshore, mere feet away from her. Chuleta leapt into it, jumping over its hand-carved wooden benches as she raced up and down its center to greet him.

"It's got a hole," Hugo said, grinning as he stepped into the water. He slid his finger through the worn opening at the front of the canoe. As he tinkered with it, he stole glances at Emma. She knew it was the perfect scenario for him, and he didn't intend to fix his canoe; the hole originated with the tree trunk he pulled from the river as a teenager thirty years ago.

Emma smiled and rubbed a sticky hand against her *paruma*. "One of these days you'll get it fixed."

"Maybe." He straightened up. "You look extra beautiful today."

With skill gained from twelve months of practice, Emma balanced a smile with muted enthusiasm. The villagers did well by choosing Hugo as their mayor. He was hardworking, thoughtful, and had more patience than Emma would have liked, considering it was channeled into him waiting for her to accept him as her husband. Never mind that she was half his age and the Peace Corps discouraged relationships with community members; the villagers insisted that Emma needed a husband—and soon. But in a village so small, Hugo was the only man without a wife.

"It must be the red on your *paruma*," he said. "You're keeping our culture alive by wearing it, and the colors are repaying you with their beauty."

A mango peel escaped Andrés' grip, falling into Emma's lap. "A beautiful skirt to match a beautiful culture," she said, picking the peel off her *paruma* and tossing it into the tall grass near them.

Her eyes fell on a path leading into the jungle close to where the peel landed. As she stared at the tips of bent grass, she remembered the first time she noticed the path forming. It happened in the afternoon a few weeks back as she scraped overcooked rice out of a pot.

Aware of her silence, she turned back to Hugo.

Had he noticed her staring at the path? He was still studying her face—a relief, for once. Then again, even if he had followed her stare, would he have seen what she did? The path was subtle; only a person living beside it would notice.

Or so she hoped.

Hugo kept smiling. "Maybe someday the others will wear them too."

"It would be nice." She meant it but doubted it, given that only a few of the villagers had indigenous Emberá roots. Despite their differences, the Emberá and Latinos in Almagro worked well together. A Latina woman in the village wearing a *paruma* was a different story, though. Emma couldn't understand why; *parumas* were stunning. Her favorite ones had flowers with bright green, yellow, and purple patterns. On sunny days they dried in under an hour. But after washing them in the river, she enjoyed leaving them in the sun twice as long to enjoy the colorful fabric on her clothesline.

"Hugo yes!" Andrés held up a mango pit with its fibers sucked clean of meat.

Hugo looked at Emma, nodding towards Andrés. "Don't you want children?"

Emma sighed, thankful Hugo had reached for a tilapia beneath the bench in his canoe. She decided to humor him for the third time that week since he'd leave after he gifted her the fish, just like always.

"Maybe someday."

"It doesn't have to be someday, you know. We could get married."

She smiled at him. "Thank you for the tilapia." She pulled herself out of the hammock and brushed tree debris off her t-shirt. Andrés' laugh pierced the air as the hammock swung back and forth.

Hugo rubbed his head. "Maybe you'll change your mind. *Si Dios quiere.*"

God willing. But Emma preferred the literal translation, 'If God wants.' It was a phrase in Almagro that served as both a motivator and an excuse, a reason to have hope and to judge. It was why Emma didn't have a boyfriend and why she may never have one, if life turned out that way.

CHAPTER 2

Emma ~ Present

Emma's name echoed across the soccer field before she was halfway up the hill. Shading her eyes, she scanned Maya's thatched roof, looking for lumps draped over its peak. The lumps waved at her before ducking behind palm leaves, shouting Emma's whereabouts to kids in the soccer field behind them.

No doubt, children frequented Maya's roof because they wanted to know what Emma was up to. But just as much, Emma's stilt house was one of only four in the village built in Emberá style.

And as such, it was a looker.

Six-foot tree trunks supported her circular floor—the height served as a deterrent for animals and to keep her house from flooding, should a storm ever hit Almagro as big as legend had it. Unlike traditional Emberá homes which weren't enclosed, the villagers had built a single, square room in the center of Emma's floor to serve as her bedroom, complete with custom-made walls level with her forehead. A steep, thatched roof towered over her house, including her railing-free wraparound balcony.

Of the three building sites the villagers had shown her, Emma chose the backside of Almagro because it was one of the only places on the island hidden from the *tienda's* view, Almagro's only store. The villagers miscalculated Emma; they didn't believe she'd choose such a remote location. Emma had miscalculated too; within days of moving into her home, she discovered the disadvantages of Maya having an unobstructed view of it.

"Your shirt's clinging to your ribs." Maya leaned out of her porch hammock, running a finger along her lower lip. Her hot pink nail polish glistened with a fresh coat of drying paint. "It's because you don't eat the brains, you know."

Fish brains. It was a source of minerals or libido, depending on the day and person. Emma forced a smile. Under normal circumstances, she wouldn't have stopped to chat. But then she thought of Rosa.

"How's your mom feeling?"

"Resting, what else?" Maya rolled her eyes. "I swear she's faking it so I'll do all the chores." She pulled a shirt off the clothesline, exposing her self-pierced bellybutton.

"She's lucky to have you."

"They don't all say that."

Emma couldn't argue with that. Gossip was woven into the daily life of villagers in Almagro. Most of it wasn't harmful—or, at least, not intentionally so. But Maya made Emma uneasy. Perhaps it was because the villagers knew when Emma lit a candle in the middle of the night to relieve herself, or how many days had passed since she last swept her balcony. All because of Maya's watchful eye.

And yet a part of Emma felt bad for Maya. Maya's family was often in the forefront of Almagro's gossip. Rosa only had two children—Maya, now in her early twenties, and Andrés, born just six years ago. In a community where double-digit family sizes were common, the villagers had determined, in unsubtle ways, that Maya made Rosa infertile. But once Rosa became pregnant with Andrés, the villagers concluded that it was as clear as truth—Rosa and her husband had withheld from intercourse because Maya spent too much time at home.

Andrés ran onto the porch, swinging around a post that leaned over the hill. A fallen bamboo railing laid beside it, rotting into the dirt floor. "Yes, Emma! Yes, Maya!"

"That's sister to you," Maya said, swatting a mosquito on her arm.

Andrés stuck out his tongue and grabbed Emma's hand, pulling her towards the soccer field. Emma consciously smiled and scrunched her eyes at Maya as a goodbye, like she did naturally with the rest of the villagers.

Squealing ensued when the kids saw Andrés approaching the soccer field with Emma in tow. Barefoot, they ran across dirt that made up one-fifth the size of a real soccer field. They circled around trying to hug her. All of them, all at the same time.

Emma returned the hugs, remembering how when she first arrived in Almagro, the kids used to hold down her hands to snatch strands of her hair. They had never seen anything like it they'd say, as they stretched out her brown curls.

Emma freed her leg and kicked the soccer ball. "Let's get this game started!"

She ran across the muddy field, her flip flops slipping on pebbles. Meanwhile, the kids dashed around her barefoot, their calloused feet immune to hazards that would've bedridden her.

"Emma, watch!" María leaned back on her heel, digging it into the mud as she slid towards the ball.

"Good one!"

It was a good one. María skidded three feet, triggering envy among the kids. All of them, that was, except Andrés. While the kids tried to beat María's skid, Andrés patted her on the back. They would have been labeled the cutest couple in Almagro if it weren't for María being taller than Andrés by the whopping girth of a full-grown pineapple. In six-year-old fashion, María and Andrés didn't notice.

María tugged at Emma's t-shirt, mud weighing down her naturally straight black hair. "Teacher Emma!"

The rest of the kids joined in. "Teacher Emma! Teacher Emma!"

Knowing the kids wanted to practice English, Emma lifted her hands above her head, putting on an imaginary hat. Cheering, the kids stopped their soccer game mid-kick. Their heads spun around as Emma swooshed her hand in the air, waiting to see where her invisible wand would land.

"House!" they shouted, eyeing Carla's mud home.

"Excellent." She repeated the word 'house' so they could practice its pronunciation.

Emma tried not to have favorites in the village, but Carla was like a mom to her. She waved at the house. Stocky ankles filled the space where the cloth door didn't reach the ground, so she knew Carla was watching them through a hole in the fabric. Emma remembered the time she asked Carla if she would prefer a solid door. Carla could barely speak through her laughter. 'There's nothing private happening here anymore. Given the choice between a thirteenth kid or ventilation, a cloth door is what you get.'

Feeling the children tug at her *paruma*, Emma waved her arm again. Her finger landed on a structure at the far end of the soccer field—the place that had prompted her outing.

The kids pointed with her. "Store!"

"That's right," she said, giving them high fives.

Almagro's *tienda* sat on a small plateau, sticking up from the village's main plateau. Given its viewpoint over the rest of the village, it was the most precious land in town.

Knowing there was another stop to make before reaching the *tienda*, Emma shouted, "Last one!" and kicked the ball into the goal, marked by two bamboo posts that never knew a net.

She then set her eyes on Abuela, who puttered in front of the wooden church. At eighty-three years old, Abuela was one of the oldest villagers in Almagro and the second-best source of gossip, after the *tienda*. She was also the youngest and first female mayor in Almagro, elected at just nineteen years old. When her husband died eleven years ago, the villagers began taking care of her, whispering among themselves about how sorry they felt for her since she never had children. Equipped with years of leadership, feminist ways, and the priest's blessing, Abuela leaned into her faith, shaping it into a version that was unique to Almagro. And as her age increased, so did her particularities.

As Emma approached the church, she studied its perimeter. A small hill leading to the top of the plateau divided the church and *tienda*, with Mateo, the store owner, owning all of it. Abuela insisted that the church sat beneath the plateau, on flat ground. But Mateo maintained that the church's altar stole a few feet of his sloped land. To the rest of the villagers, the truth was in the Virgin Mary who sat on the bamboo altar inside the church, offerings to her often sliding off and adorning the dirt floor. Only Mateo ever cared enough to pick a fight with Abuela about it, though.

"Oh, my!" Abuela waved when she saw Emma, poking her forehead with the grass cross she held. "God graced me with this surprise."

Emma smiled. "I just finished playing soccer with the kids."

"You know I can't see that far from here." Abuela pulled another grass cross from her basket. "But I would've found out."

Emma stepped over a ditch that wrapped around the church. A cockroach floated upside down in the muddy water, beating its legs. The ditch was supposed to be drainage during the rainy season, but Abuela kept its exit plugged with ferns.

Abuela caught Emma staring at it. "Water that touches the church is holy water."

Emma nodded, finishing the sentence in her head before Abuela got the words out. *And thus, water that touches the church has to remain there.* She wondered how Abuela would feel if she ever learned that each night after she was asleep, the villagers took turns draining the mosquito breeding ground.

Abuela grabbed Emma's elbow with the strength of someone half her age, placing a freshly made grass cross into her hand. "For you."

The pollen caught between Abuela's wrinkles rearranged in new patterns as she smiled; Emma knew she had been picking river grass to make crosses. Abuela spent her days stuffing the church's walls with them—she stuffed for her late husband, for a future female mayor, and for her beloved stool. There was plenty of stuffing to be done, since the church was built from small branches.

Emma smiled, reaching as high as she could to slide the cross between a gap of branches in the wall. With the exception of the priest, who was from Panama City, Emma was the tallest person in Almagro. She knew better than to place the cross in *the* gap—the one that wrapped around the church, branches intentionally omitted at eye level for Abuela to peer out of.

Abuela pushed another cross into Emma's hand. "Did you hear the news?"

"That Hugo caught the biggest tilapia of the week?"

"How behind you are." She handed Emma another cross but grabbed her finger to keep her from turning away. Then she paused, shifting her eyes between Emma's. Finally, she whispered, "The AIDS is coming."

When it came to Abuela's gossip, Emma was used to composing herself like a parent would when hearing their young child swear. But this one drew a flinch.

"What do you mean?"

"The AIDS. It's *coming*."

Emma studied a newborn chick that jumped onto her foot. She wiggled her toes to get it off, watching it peck at ants marching on the grass around Abuela's bare feet. Emma had helped Professor Sonya give an HIV lesson to the ninth graders a few months back. She figured Abuela had to be thinking of that.

A voice came from behind the church. "God is punishing us."

Emma knew such potent words paired with an unemotional voice could only be coming from one person. She poked her head around the corner of the church. "Hello, Father."

"Hallelujah," he said.

A pitter-patter of footsteps sounded behind them. By the time Emma looked over, the bottoms of Maya's purple flip flops flashed towards her as she ascended the *tienda's* dirt steps.

Abuela studied Maya's back, her lips smacking together at an even rhythm, warding off fruit flies wanting their share of the dried mango juice trailing from the corner of her mouth. When Maya reached the top, Abuela put a cross up to her mouth and whispered, "Maya slept with Antonio."

Emma took a deep breath. She didn't care about Maya's affairs. But, without fail, she'd learn about them from the villagers—along with every variation of the real story.

"Did you hear them?"

Emma laughed. "Gosh, no."

"God has given you many good qualities, Emma. But knowing what your neighbors are up to isn't one of them."

Such conversations used to make Emma squirm, especially knowing the priest was nearby. She squeezed Abuela's shoulder. "I need to go."

"Just a few more crosses. I swear on the Virgin Mary."

Emma's efforts to get to the *tienda* had already taken longer than usual. And given that Mateo picked up supplies in Chepo that morning, passing time mattered.

"Next time."

"Just you watch." Abuela's voice squeaked. "'Next times' will be a thing of the past when the AIDS comes."

Emma followed the dirt path behind the church, leading her past the priest who had nodded off in his plastic chair. White rings adorned the chair's orange legs and armrests from bearing his weight over the years.

By the time she arrived at the top of the *tienda's* dirt staircase, Martha greeted her, biting her lip and shaking her head. "One of these days."

Emma smiled, clutching her falling *paruma*. "But I tie it just like you taught me!"

Martha was an Emberá woman in her late twenties with straight black hair that reached the top or bottom of her kneecaps, depending on how far back she tilted her head to show it off. Her hips were so wide they had men and women alike doing a double-take. But she said her hips weren't always that way; her children had pushed them out with each birth less than a year apart.

Martha pulled at Emma's *paruma*, opening the fabric to Emma's back, protecting her from the view of villagers on the *tienda's* patio. Hiding didn't matter though, since Emma wore shorts beneath her *paruma*—cheating, according to Martha, since real Emberá women went commando.

Chuleta jumped, trying to grab at the fabric.

"She's hungry." Mateo winked at Emma as he leaned over the *tienda* counter, handing change to a child.

"A dog can't live off mango pits alone," Maya said, her arms crossed.

Emma sucked in her stomach as Martha tightened her *paruma*. She looked at Maya and shrugged. "You caught me."

The villagers erupted in laughter.

On days when Emma questioned her work in Almagro, she knew that, at a minimum, her presence gave the villagers something to laugh about. And she was right there laughing along with them.

Her eyes adjusted to the shade beneath the patio's thatched roof. The *tienda's* large patio was a necessity; it was where the villagers gathered to gossip, hold meetings, await the rare visitor, and wait out bad storms. Since the inside of the *tienda* was for storage, only Mateo stood there; the villagers would line up on the patio to give him their orders from across a small wooden counter.

It was no secret that Mateo was the most financially well-off villager in Almagro. The villagers received quarterly stipends from the government. Having rare opportunities to spend their money elsewhere, almost all of it went into Mateo's pockets. Most felt he was deserving of it. But those who didn't found it a nuisance that the *tienda* wasn't a true one-stop shop for all things gossip. After all, they couldn't gossip about the *tienda* at the *tienda*.

Emma went up to the counter, her smile teetering between hope and doubt. "Tell me there's ice?"

Mateo began shaking his head before she finished, rubbing a hand over his greying fifty-four-year-old hair. "You spent too long talking with the priest."

Emma narrowed her eyes, fighting to keep the corners of her lips from curling into a smile. She was well versed in the conflict between the church and *tienda*—God deserved the highest spot in the village, but the *tienda* was there first.

"Hey, now. No need to scare the girl," Eduardo said, standing up from his seat on a wooden bench. It was one of many benches on the patio, all of which resembled pews, although Eduardo and Emma were the only ones who seemed to notice. To Emma, Eduardo was a fatherly figure in a grandfather's body. He practiced patience in everything he did, whether it was steadying the limp in his right leg or explaining to the villagers that not all snakes needed to be killed.

Emma put her hands on her hips and looked at Mateo. "So, there *is* ice."

"I may have saved you a piece." Chuckling, he reached into his cooler, pulling out a clear plastic bag. A chunk of ice bobbed in twice as much water, condensation streaming down its side.

Emma grinned and reached for it.

"Hey, now." Mateo pulled it away. "It was a lot of work getting this." He dangled the bag out of Emma's reach, exuding laughter from the villagers.

"And you know I appreciate it."

It was true that getting ice was hard work—eight hours on a good day. It involved mornings before the sun was up, long canoe rides, and even longer walks. Only a few villagers had ever been to Chepo, a town on the outskirts of Panama City. Mateo, on the other hand, went every other Wednesday to stock up on store supplies. Carla's son, Federico, accompanied him on days when the supplies were too heavy for Mateo to manage on his own. Aside from them, most villagers were either too elderly to take the trip or too happy in Almagro to care to leave.

Emma placed a quarter in Mateo's hand, taking the bag he set on the counter. "You know me well."

"Well enough to tell you to leave your house earlier next time?"

~ * ~

A piece of ice the size of a penny floated in Emma's lemonade. Knowing such a treat was coming powered her through challenging days, for cold drinks were a reminder of home. She thought about home often; not in a homesick kind of way but in a before and after kind of way. Even then, it was becoming harder to picture her life before—and without—Almagro.

She squeezed more lemon into her glass, her fingers gliding across its lumpy peel. Back home, lemons with bumpy exteriors would have been tossed. In Almagro, they were cherished.

Chuleta lay beside her, devouring a fish head that she found halfway up their notched staircase when they arrived home. It was an odd place for a gift and an even odder part of the fish to leave. But Emma was always touched by any gift the villagers brought her.

She sunk her toe into Chuleta's side. "Maybe there's something to be said about fish brains."

She took another sip of lemonade and her mind slipped back to home. She wondered how her family and friends were doing. She wondered if her relationships with them would pick up where she left them when she returned. She wondered if she had changed to the point where her old life would feel too unfamiliar to return to. She missed talking with her family and friends. But on more occasions than she wished to admit, she missed reading messages to Jake.

CHAPTER 3

Emma ~ Present

Ten digits. One stranger. Countless messages totaling thousands of words. And yet she couldn't figure out anything about the man who used to own her phone number. Emma shuddered as she peeled *guandú* peas, thinking about how self-conscious she was of social statuses back in college. Her South Carolina area code made locals assume she lived in the hills. She didn't, but not by much. Nevertheless, she changed her number during her first semester at the University of Charleston.

She remembered the excitement of hearing a text message arrive upon driving back to campus after changing her phone number. It could have only been from Matt, her boyfriend at the time. Instead, it was a message from an unknown number.

Dude, you wanna watch the game tonight?

She was amused and unalarmed, but deleted the message upon Matt's insistence.

Chuleta reached across Emma's foot to catch a fallen *guandú* pod. Emma bent down and dislodged the fibers caught between her teeth. "Don't spoil your appetite before lunch, missy."

Emma tilted her bowl; shiny peas rolled together in a green and purple wave. There was no way she'd get through shucking all the pods Eduardo had gifted her before her afternoon class. It would have driven her old self crazy. But the Panamanian version of Emma had, albeit slowly, picked up on Almagro's 'It can get done tomorrow' mindset.

Perhaps Jake had Panamanian blood. Maybe he racked up tomorrows, telling himself he'd inform his friends about his new number soon. Or, perhaps, he had too many friends and acquaintances to care to tell. But even then, it didn't make sense; the people writing him cared. They shared things with him. Personal things. Among the 'dudes' and 'mans' and 'yos', Emma remembered she had her new phone number for a week before she learned his name.

Jake, we're engaged!

The message came on an evening when she and Matt were having dinner in a friend's dorm. Knowing Matt's temper, Emma swiped the message off her screen. It was a reaction she had adjusted to; messages—and photos— of promiscuous women looking for partners and words too raunchy to write were a multi-day occurrence from her new phone number.

Emma wasn't a fan of Jake. Nonetheless, he intrigued her. And so, she felt compelled to answer the person who shared their good news. That same evening, before she took a shower, she responded.

Hi there, it seems Jake changed his number. Congratulations on your engagement!

She had kept her phone in the bathroom while showering, not wanting Matt to see it. By the time she reached for a towel, her screen flashed a response.

Thanks so much.

Disappointment overshadowed her excitement of receiving a reply. She wanted to know about Jake. In hindsight, it was foolish of her to believe the message would spark a conversation. She had considered prodding—telling the person how she had been receiving messages and calls from countless others, all of whom believed they were contacting Jake. But she stopped herself. At its most basic level, her goal had been achieved—the person knew Jake hadn't received the message. Her guilt was gone.

"Chuleta!" Emma grimaced as she watched Chuleta dash across the balcony, the fate of a cockroach—and Chuleta herself—dependent on her stopping before the six-foot drop.

"It's an odd time of day for a cockroach to be out."

The dispassionate voice made Emma shudder, and she became aware of sweat running down her spine. She walked to the edge of her balcony. Maya looked topless from Emma's viewpoint, with the exception of stray leaves poking out of a bra two sizes too big for her chest.

"What can I say? Bugs love me."

Maya rolled her eyes. "Mom wants to know if you're having class today."

"Of course." Emma picked a *guandú* pod off her *paruma*.

The villagers told Emma they loved her unconditionally, with some exceptions—like when she bathed in the cold creek after physical activity and her unwavering attendance as an English teacher. A drop of rain in the air, catching more fish than expected, and God wanting them to take a break were all reasonable excuses for the villagers to skip her class. But with time, Emma realized she misjudged their rationale; the drop of rain turned into a storm that sank an unattended canoe, extra fish needed to be shared with neighbors before spoiling, and who was she to disagree with their interpretation of God's desire?

Maya stared at Emma's staircase. In the silence, Emma remembered how her stomach had clenched when she discovered the villagers had placed her ten-foot notched tree trunk facing Maya's house instead of the river. It was rare for Maya to climb up, but Emma sensed she wanted to.

"Is there something else?"

Maya jumped as if remembering Emma's presence. She pursed her lips in the direction of the cockroach before spinning around to head home. "Squeeze some lemon juice on your floor. It'll get rid of 'em."

Emma rubbed her toe over a groove in her palm bark floor—the place that still had a reddish hue from when Hugo scrubbed it with hot peppers two weeks ago, the surefire cockroach cure.

~ * ~

Abuela squinted. "I can't see."

Rosa lifted her head from the table. "Why come to class if you can't see?"

"Why come to class when you're sick?"

Rosa straightened up. She drew a breath to respond but Abuela beat her to it. "Because God wants us to read and write, that's why." Rosa went to speak again, but Abuela interrupted. "And because women have the right to be educated."

Eduardo cleared his throat and leaned against a post of the outdoor classroom beside the soccer field. "This is all true. And because of it, shouldn't we get back to learning?"

Emma smiled, knowing how much Abuela valued education; the younger generations could read because she helped build a school when she was mayor, giving them the opportunity she never had. Emma turned back to the chalkboard. "Rosa, how do you say this word?" Humidity tugged at the letters written on the board, the 'o' of '*Hola*' clumping at the bottom.

As Rosa sounded out the letters, Emma heard someone run up behind her.

"Yes!" a voice said.

"Andre*yes*!" Emma's tone was firm and, upon realizing it, she winced and looked at Rosa. Weeks had passed since Rosa left her house due to a mysterious illness, so Emma and the villagers had become accustomed to disciplining Andrés themselves. Rosa was far from recovered, but it didn't stop her from shaking her finger at Andrés and threatening a dinner of yucca without fish.

"On that note," Emma set down the chalk. "Your homework is to practice these words." She passed around the papers she had handwritten that morning.

Abuela smacked the paper. A green smear hovered in the upper right corner, just above her index finger. "Is that *guandú*?"

Rosa shook her head. "Says the person who can't see."

Emma nodded, flashing a smile at Eduardo. She had yet to learn the art of balancing gratitude for gifts without making the other villagers feel bad—or competitive.

Eduardo smiled back, every other tooth missing in near-perfect symmetry. A grass cross from Abuela hung on his chest. It wasn't more than a couple of days old, given that its ends were just beginning to brown. Emma knew she was the only person in Almagro with whom Eduardo voiced his views on faith. She wondered if anyone else in the village shared Eduardo's doubts but, like him, were too afraid of jading the believers.

Abuela blessed the *guandú* stain. "Dinner at Emma's!"

Emma knew she wasn't serious; it was a phrase the villagers used when it came to food, similar to how they'd shout, 'You're lonely!' when they spotted her alone. Their words weren't true most of the time.

Only sometimes.

CHAPTER 4

Emma ~ Present

Three . . . Four . . . Five . . .

Emma considered turning around. Crowds at the *tienda* were common; it either meant a visitor was arriving or new gossip was underway. She didn't like being around for the latter, but gossip was undeniably happening given that Professor Sonya wasn't due to return to Almagro for a couple more weeks.

Six . . .

Emma's guilty conscience kept her going, coupled with the villagers having already seen her walk across the soccer field. She and Sonya had surely caused this gossip; Emma needed to rectify it, despite its tardy emergence.

"AIDS."

Seven . . .

"AIDSSSS."

Eight . . .

"Emma." Martha grabbed Emma's hand, yanking her up the last dirt step. Emma tripped, a line of mud marking her ankle. She reached for her *paruma* with her free hand to hold the loose fabric in place as Martha continued to tug her towards the crowd. Given that the clouds were grey, it wouldn't have been odd for the villagers to be gathered beneath the thatched roof in preparation for rain. What was odd, however, was that they were all huddled to the right of the *tienda's* counter, staring at a single place on the wall.

With Martha's maneuvering, Emma stood at the front of the crowd, staring at a piece of paper pinned to the *tienda* with thorns from a spiny palm tree. Children sounded out words to the adults.

A voice came from near the counter. "I told you."

Emma turned and saw Abuela sitting on her stool. She could picture the ordeal that would have ensued to get her there—two men carrying her and a few teenagers rolling the tree trunk up the hill. Abuela rarely agreed to sit elsewhere; the contortion of her buttocks needed her custom-made stool, she'd say. Because of the effort it took to get her there, only special occasions brought her to the *tienda*.

Abuela pointed at the wall. "You see? The AIDS is coming."

A fly landed on Emma's lip. Rain dripped silently from thatched palm leaves, pattering only once it touched the ground. Meanwhile, the villagers stared at Emma in hopeful silence, as if she held the answer to the piece of paper. The word 'AIDS' dominated the top of it in bold letters. She began reading the Spanish words aloud.

"The Ministry of Health (MINSA) will arrive in the community of Almagro next Thursday to test for HIV. Testing is free and required for all people ages thirteen and older. This is part of a health initiative launched by our Sir President. Lunch will be provided to all participants. Five volunteers are needed to cook."

Gasps of excitement drowned out the rain that began pummeling the jungle around them.

"This is good." Mateo leaned over the counter.

Emma couldn't tell if it was a comment or question. "Yes. It's good," she said, giving him a smile and wishing Sonya was there. When she and Emma had given the ninth graders an HIV lesson, they never dreamed that testing would ever arrive in a place as remote as Almagro.

"But AIDS is bad." Federico stepped forward. "You told us so."

Federico had sat through three HIV lessons over the years. Ninth grade was the highest grade level offered in Almagro and, because he loved school, he repeated it as many times as allowed, which would soon be ending on his eighteenth birthday.

Emma nodded. "HIV is a virus, so it's not something you want to have." She patted the air with her hands when fearful looks ensued. "But there's medicine to manage it."

Abuela tapped her legs against her stool. "I heard you can get AIDS from," she cupped her hands around her mouth, "*relations.*"

Emma knew that Abuela intended to whisper the word, but it came out as a high-pitched shout instead. Kids broke out in laughter; adults shooed them into the rain.

"I'm sure MINSA will be happy to address your questions on Friday," Emma said. To herself, she thought about how she was just as curious as the villagers to see what the health officials would be saying.

Rosa leaned against Abuela's shoulder. "Why didn't you put up the paper yesterday?" She directed the question at Mateo, who drummed his fingers on the wooden counter. There was only one way for the outside world to communicate with the villagers—via notes to Mateo when he picked up *tienda* supplies in Chepo.

"It must have fallen on the floor when I was unloading supplies yesterday. Slipped my mind that—"

"It didn't slip my mind." Abuela folded her arms, a grass cross sticking out from either elbow where her hands laid. "You told me about it. Remember? How'd you forget that quickly?"

Mateo leaned over the counter. "I didn't forget. I thought about it when I was out this morning. By the time I got back, Federico had already found the paper behind a bottle of cooking oil."

"You were out this morning?" Eduardo asked.

Emma admired Eduardo's kind tone and trusting eyes. But his head was tilted, which cued to her that something seemed off to him.

"To dig up some yucca, that's all." Mateo shrugged, but it didn't offset how quickly he had rushed through the explanation.

"In the *rain*?" Abuela tightened her folded arms.

Carla pushed through the crowd, a few of her youngest children hanging from her limbs. She whispered in Emma's ear. "This is nonsense, wouldn't you say?"

Emma smiled. "Who am I to judge a person for a yucca craving?"

It was meant as a joke—something that she and Carla exchanged often. But Emma felt unsettled when Carla's only reaction was to pull in her lips.

Meanwhile, Abuela had launched into a monologue about yucca and the rain. While the villagers' attention was on her, Emma turned and whispered to Mateo. "Can I have a bag of rice?"

"For your *guandú*?"

Emma shook her head and glanced away. Mateo had the advantage of watching the villagers interact with each other from the *tienda* counter. He knew what—and who—made them tick.

Carla nudged Emma. "She's wife material, cooking like that. Wouldn't you say, Mateo?"

Emma chuckled. That was the Carla she knew.

"She's always been wife material," Hugo said, stepping towards them. He bumped into Maya, who was staring silently at the paper. Emma knew she could read it, but wondered if Maya knew what AIDS was; she graduated before HIV education was part of the curriculum.

"She'll make a good wife if she wants to, but never for you." Abuela shifted in her stool. "Besides, Emma needs a man with good fertility."

"Who's to say he doesn't have good fertility?" Carla wrapped her arm around Emma's shoulder and winked.

"That's right." Mateo pushed a bag of rice across the counter. "They say a deceased wife returns fertility to her widower."

Emma narrowed her eyes at Mateo as giggles erupted from rain-soaked kids running around the outskirts of the *tienda*. She knew Mateo didn't want to see her and Hugo together, but she also knew he couldn't pass up an opportunity to ruffle up Abuela.

Hugo, on the other hand, was beaming. Openly discussing private affairs was part of daily life in Almagro. And when those private affairs involved Emma, it was all the better for him.

CHAPTER 5

Emma ~ Present

A jagged piece of intestine dangled from Chuleta's nose. She licked the balcony, lapping up fish juice that pooled between grooves of the floor. Fish guts weren't the plan for Chuleta's dinner, but Emma found them draped down two steps of her notched tree trunk when she arrived home. Once again, it was an odd place for a gift, not to mention its questionable contents. Regardless, fish guts were Chuleta's favorite. Whoever left them had to know that.

Water poured over her spoon as Emma stirred a pot of already cooked rice with *guandú*. No matter how many times she tried, her rice, without fail, turned out raw or soggy. Tipping the pot over her balcony, she watched water splatter up grass that was high enough to summon unwanted critters. She glanced at her machete. It hung above the wall of her outdoor kitchen, the same wall her bed shared. Cutting grass would be a job for the next day, she decided.

Her thoughts turned to Jake, as they so often did when she fell into a phase of remembering him. Sometimes, the phases lasted a couple of days. Other times, they lingered for weeks. Regardless, they'd sneak up on her at unexpected times, from unexpected triggers. Maybe disease was the reason Jake stopped communicating with those he knew. It wasn't the first time she considered he could be ill.

She remembered a message that arrived one morning when Matt was in class.

Hey Jake, just wanted to let you know that I heard about it. So sorry, man.

By then, Emma had become accustomed to receiving messages intended for Jake. They arrived a few times per week, sometimes more. She had also taken care of his spam messages. It turned out to be a bittersweet solution; the photos and messages from girls looking to be paid for their services appalled her, but by blocking those X-rated contacts, she forgot about that side of who Jake seemingly was. And as such, she found herself liking what she learned about him from his real contacts.

Emma wasn't blind to the absurdity of her feelings. Liking someone she had never seen or met—not to mention someone who could be dead—was crazy. But at the very least, she found comfort in knowing that Jake was her age. She had received countless messages indicating so on the fourth of November.

Dude. A quarter of a century. That's freakin' old. I'll buy ya a bday beer the next time I see you.

She thought back to when she started responding to Jake's messages. It took a while to get to that point and, even so, she didn't reply to all of the messages. Her approach was simple; if the message was personal, she responded. Guilt drove her decision. She didn't want

LAURA ANN NEULEO

people thinking Jake was ignoring them. Her response to Jake's contacts was a version of the same each time.

Hello, it seems Jake changed his number. Hope you're able to get in touch with him.

Sometimes, she'd throw in a congratulation if the person had written with good news. Every time, she hoped her message would spark a conversation. But for his many faults that she later saw, Matt was right about one thing—the people were strangers. They seemed nice, but what if they weren't? What if Jake was escaping them? 'Delete the messages. They're up to no good,' Matt would drill into her head. And so, Emma's strategy was to keep her messages to Jake's contacts neutral and a secret from Matt.

She would never forget the day someone replied with a real response—not the usual 'thanks for letting me know.' The message wouldn't have seemed grand to an outsider. But to Emma, it offered insight into the possibility of Jake's status.

Yikes. Hope he's okay.

For the first time, Emma sent a second message. She remembered wanting to say—and ask—so much. When was the last time you talked to him? Could you check on him at his house? Do you even know where he lives? After writing and erasing a dozen messages, she settled on four words.

I hope so too.

A bat dove in front of Emma, catching its first mosquito of the evening. The sky—and her room—would soon be full of them, so she shut her bedroom door as more questions invaded her thoughts.

How could people who appeared to care so much not know how to reach Jake? Was he in danger? Sick? Dead? Almost two years later and these questions still kept her

44

up at night. It both impressed and puzzled her that Jake knew so many people. So many people that didn't know what happened to him.

Sighing, she dished up more *guandú* in her open-air kitchen. From the corner of her eye, she saw Eduardo approaching her house. He waved and squinted up at her out of habit, even though the sun had already sunk behind the river.

"It's late, I know."

Emma smiled. "You know I'm always happy to see you." She pointed to the pot. "Would you like some?"

Eduardo placed a hand over his heart. "Oh, that's not why I'm here."

"I figured. But have some anyway, I insist." She motioned for him to climb up to her balcony while she went inside and grabbed a bowl. Through the cracks in her wall, she tried to survey Maya's porch. Dusk was an odd time for any guest, let alone a male visitor. And given that her living alone was already unthinkable, the villagers would be appalled if they knew a man had visited her house at night.

As if sensing her thoughts, Eduardo said, "Forgive my evening visit." He tilted his head towards Maya's house. "I don't think she saw me."

"We'll find out soon enough." She forced a relaxed smile and ushered him towards her two wooden benches. The villagers had placed the benches on either side of her bedroom door. Maya routinely asked Emma why she didn't sit elsewhere on her wraparound balcony. They both knew it was so Maya couldn't watch her, even though Emma's explanation of wanting a view of the river should have sufficed.

A small bulge formed in Eduardo's right cheek, and he trailed his spoon through the rice.

Emma winced. "I forgot to warn you it's soggy."

"It's one of the best rice dishes of yours that I've tried." He smiled down at the bowl but didn't venture another scoop.

"Is everything okay?"

"Oh, yes. Yes, of course. Yes, yes."

"Good."

Eduardo lifted the spoon from his bowl, waving it as he spoke. "It's just . . . it's just I was wondering." Chuleta stood and chased the grains of rice falling on the floor. "Have you noticed anyone passing through here at night?"

Emma paused, debating how to proceed. "No, I haven't." She stopped herself from glancing at the grass path.

"Good, *mi hija*, that's good."

Emma loved when Eduardo referred to her as 'my daughter', but she couldn't shake the hesitation she heard in his voice.

"Bats are incredible creatures," Eduardo said, studying the sky.

Emma pulled her knees to her chest and followed his gaze. She knew he wanted to change subjects—possibly for her sake more than his own. Silence wasn't uncomfortable with Eduardo, so she didn't fill the air with a halfhearted response. He picked a bat to watch, although it was impossible to know which one he chose among the dozens flying around.

Finally, she looked at him, the need to ask her question outweighing the fear of its answer. "Is there someone passing through here at night?"

Eduardo took a deep breath, keeping his eyes on the bat. "I think so, *mi hija*."

CHAPTER 6

Emma ~ Present

The MINSA officials were due to arrive at any moment, but the villagers still hadn't decided who would prepare lunch.

"It can't just be Latinas." Martha wrung a *paruma* in her hand, stepping towards the latest arrangement of five women standing on the school patio.

Carla pushed her way through the crowd. "And I have twelve children to feed." It was a fair point, given that leftovers would be divided among the cooks.

Hugo paced along the increasingly smaller gap between the women and crowd. He massaged his chin, the few strands making up his six-inch beard yielding to the movement.

"If Carla and Martha are chosen," Abuela shifted in her stool, "then I should be, too, as representation of the elderly population."

The villagers murmured to each other; Abuela's morning debacle was still fresh on their minds. She had put Federico in charge of making sure her stool was placed in a prime viewing spot to watch the day's events. It took more tries than seeds in a guava to find a place that satisfied her.

Rosa swung her arms in the air with surprising force for being ill, bumping Andrés' face in the process. "The point is to cook. You won't do anything but sit on your stool and taste test your way through the food."

Hugo twisted a single strand of his beard and looked at Emma. "What do you think?"

Emma stood near the front of the patio, rubbing Chuleta's ears. She gave the same answer as always, with the same smile as always. "It's not for me to decide."

"That's right." Eduardo's voice came from the back of the crowd, his tone balancing disappointment and understanding. "It's our problem. No need to put her on the spot like that."

Emma knew Eduardo was protecting her, just like she knew Hugo wasn't trying to put her on the spot; moments like these were Hugo's opportunity to show Emma his diplomatic ways. It was how he would be if she accepted him as her husband.

"Well, if we're talking fair . . ." Carla paused to shoo off three of her youngest children hanging from her arms. "Then a man should cook too."

The villagers didn't have time to react to Carla's comment; a thump echoed through the village followed by the faint sound of a canoe motor. Emma pictured Mateo at the *tienda*, banging tagua against the wall. Tagua seeds were as wide as the palm of Emma's hand with a hard, brown shell. Tied together in a bundle, they served as Almagro's bell to alert the villagers of a guest's arrival.

Thump. Thump thump thump. Thump.

"They're here!" The adults cheered as kids and dogs jumped with excitement.

Emma recognized the rhythm, knowing it meant the canoe would park at the port on Almagro's backside. Emma's port. A port that wasn't even a port. She expected to hear the thumping rhythm for the *tienda* port, which was at the front of the village. The *tienda* port offered a more attractive presentation to Almagro with logs forming a path, versus the free-for-all grass entryway by her house.

She turned her attention back to the villagers who were creating a thumping noise of their own. Women ran towards the school's outdoor kitchen, their dressy flip flops, used only on special occasions for guests, strewn across the grass. Emma pressed herself against the concrete blocks of the school, a swoosh of air cooling her sweating body as women dove for the pot hovering above fresh firewood. The women shouted as they arrived, smacking the pot before thrusting their ash-covered hands in the air.

"One . . . two . . . three . . . four . . . five!"

And so, the cooks were chosen.

~ * ~

Emma was exhausted before the HIV testing even started. The villagers wanted everything arranged to perfection as a sign of respect for their three guests who traveled from the city. Panama City. A place that by distance was close to Almagro, but was difficult to visit because of the buses, hiking, and canoe ride it took to get there. Even Mateo had only ever gone as far as Chepo on his *tienda* supply runs.

The villagers had arranged one room at the school for testing. However, when Rebecca, the woman overseeing the testing, arrived, she requested that both rooms of the two-room schoolhouse be used. Emma knew Rebecca's request was innocent. She also knew that using both rooms would be counterproductive since her goal had been to save time.

It started with sweeping.

Martha was first to grab a broom, but Carla chastised her for working slowly. Taking their mom's lead, a handful of Carla's kids rushed into the classroom to help the sweeping process with their hands, feet, and clothes. Other villagers looked in, scolding their sweeping technique. They used voices that, in their minds, were hushed. But instead, their comments danced down the plateau into the ears of their guests. Rebecca and the nurses didn't care, though, for they were engrossed in taking selfies by the river.

Outside the classroom, Eduardo shook his head. "This paint won't do." He rubbed his finger along a peeled spot where specks of blue clung to an otherwise grey surface.

Emma remembered helping the villagers paint the classroom six months ago. Professor Sonya had watched them, half amused and half frustrated. 'You should've used a primer first,' she said. Ever since then, the villagers blamed the school's peeling paint on the primer.

"I still have some paint in my house, *mi hija*." Eduardo patted the wall. "I'll go fetch it."

Emma went to discourage him, but instead heard herself saying, "Okay."

Meanwhile, Mateo arrived at the school, having closed the *tienda* early. Mere seconds passed before he began getting wrath from Hugo.

"What do you mean you lost them?"

"I already told you, I didn't lose them." Mateo paced back and forth in front of the school's latrine. "I dropped them."

Hugo slapped his forehead. "Dropping them *is* losing them. How long have they been lost?"

"They've been *dropped* for probably a day or two. Maybe a week . . . a month at most."

"*Dios.*" Hugo looked up at the sky as if to summon God himself.

Emma stepped into the conversation, erring on the side of ignorance. "What's this about?"

"Mateo lost the keys to the latrine." Hugo stood up straighter. "Necessity will call and where will our guests do it?" He darted his eyes at Mateo. "In a hole?"

Emma knew this day would come; the school's latrine was the only one in the village with a toilet seat. It never used to be locked, but Sonya brought a padlock to Almagro upon realizing the latrine was filling up quickly. Too quickly. As it turned out, the villagers preferred the comfort of the school's latrine to their rimless ones at home. Sonya put Mateo in charge of holding on to the spare key. All was fine until a few months ago when Mateo parked his canoe by Emma's house. 'The keys fell into the river,' he had said. 'As if the devil himself grabbed them off my lap and threw them into the water.' Emma reminded Mateo that Sonya had a spare set and recommend he tell her about it, leaving the devil out of his story. But she knew he never told Sonya. Because if he had, Sonya would have mentioned it to her during their after-school chats.

From beneath the plateau by the river, Emma heard her name called. Happy for the distraction, Emma found Rebecca and the two nurses waving to her from the river's edge, mud speckling their skinny jeans.

"Come join us!" they shouted.

Chuleta ran down the slope towards the women, who squealed with excitement and turned their backs for a selfie with her. Rebecca swung in a circle as Emma expertly navigated the last part of the muddy slope. "You live here?" she asked.

"I do." Emma's heart swelled with pride, just like it did when she watched any visitor experience Almagro for the first time.

"It's stunning." Rebecca snapped a photo of a yellow flower she'd never seen before. "Do you know if there's a lot for sale here?"

"Oh, I don't believe so *Señora* Rebe—"

"Rebecca. Just Rebecca."

"Rebecca." Emma smiled. "You see, the villagers are careful about clearing land. Almagro isn't in a national park, but they treat it like it is."

"Mm-hmm, I see. Well, I'll look into it."

Rebecca pulled out her phone. "Would you talk to my mom? She'd love to meet you!"

"Oh yes, mine too!"

"And mine!"

Emma stared at Rebecca and the two nurses. "There's reception here?"

"Yes, silly," the shortest of the nurses said, squeezing Emma's arm.

"There never used to be." Realizing her doubtful tone sounded harsh, she added, "But it would be great if there is."

"See?" Rebecca held out her phone. A woman on the other end waved at them.

Emma went through the motions of the video call. It was hard, given the internal conversation she was having with herself. Should she turn on her own phone? At ten dollars a day, she couldn't justify paying the roaming fee to use it all the time—not to mention the formerly absent signal in Almagro. But she thought about how wonderful it would be to surprise her family with a call. And she was in a Jake phase. Maybe it wouldn't hurt to keep her phone on for a day, just to see if any important text messages came through for him. After all, she hadn't turned it on since leaving home. A lot could be revealed in a year's worth of messages. Or, perhaps worse, nothing at all.

~ * ~

With guilt that never faded, Emma tossed a garbage bag into the firepit. Rebecca and the nurses had left Almagro an hour ago, leaving the villagers with waste they weren't accustomed to dealing with. Behind her, Andrés and his thirteen-year-old cousin, Celia, poked their fingers into each other's faces.

"Mine's bigger!" Andrés spun in a circle.

"That's not fair. You didn't get tested."

The sincerity of Celia's competitive tone would have been ironic, if they were anyplace aside from Almagro.

"So?" Andrés stood on his tippy-toes, smearing his bloody finger onto Celia's cheek. "I'm bleeding more, so I have AIDS."

"No." Celia lunged towards Andrés. "I'm bleeding less so *I'm* the one with AIDS."

Such conversations had been going on all afternoon and, unsurprising to Emma, were started by the adults. The villagers knew HIV was a virus. But somewhere between knowing it was bad to have and something that couldn't possibly exist in Almagro, they had turned getting tested into a game. Leaving the test rooms, they would rip off their Band-Aids and show off how much they bled from the prick. The more bleeding that occurred, the more a person did or didn't have HIV; the verdict was still out on whether more or less blood meant a person had it. As the day wore on, so did the villagers' efforts to win. They would sneak a sharp object into the testing room—a thorn or twig from the jungle's edge— and jab it into their pricked finger before exiting.

Emma looked down at the patio of the schoolhouse. Dried blood clung to the concrete floor. Only a strong storm—one with wind coming in from the west—would be able to wash it away.

"They should've tested me." Andrés sat down on the grass and sighed, wiping his bloody finger on a nearby weed.

"Andre*yes*, I know it may seem unfair," Emma said. "But someday you'll see how wonderful it is that there are things you can't do when you're young."

He laid back on the bloody grass. Upon seeing Emma flinch, he squirmed on the ground and giggled.

Emma crouched by him. "What do you think's going through his mind, Celia?"

Celia poked Andrés' forehead, leaving a spot of blood above his right eye. "Cards."

"Shall we?"

"Yessssss!" Andrés jumped up and ran towards the soccer field, Celia on his heels.

Emma started to follow them but heard someone clearing their voice. She turned around and saw Eduardo running his fingers over the paint on the outside of the schoolhouse, his knobby knuckles blending in with dips in the wall.

He smiled. "How are things?"

Sounding like small talk to anyone else, Emma knew Eduardo's words carried the weight of their conversation from the night before. "They're good." She stepped towards the schoolhouse and pulled the skeleton of a molted cicada off the wall, using gentle movements so its legs wouldn't detach.

"Did you hear anything?"

"Just the sounds of nature."

It wasn't entirely true. Or, at least, Emma couldn't be sure that it wasn't. But it didn't matter; she loved her house and felt safe there. That was the most important part, wasn't it? She didn't want to worry Eduardo, much less the other villagers. If they had an inkling that someone was roaming by her house at night, they'd want her to move in with a family. For as much as Emma loved the villagers, she wasn't ready to give up the little bit of privacy she currently had.

"Very good." Eduardo nodded at the wall.

Sensing he was satisfied, Emma smiled and headed for the soccer field, but she was stopped by Abuela's voice floating across the schoolyard.

"Leaving so soon?"

Emma swallowed back exasperation. It had been a long afternoon and she knew her students were already at the outdoor classroom. Playing UNO with them was the last activity of the day before she'd get to climb into bed beneath the blissful security of her mosquito net.

"I promised the kids I'd play cards with them." She could feel herself saying the words carefully; a positive but nonchalant tone was the only way to avoid prompting more questions.

Eduardo glanced at Emma and then looked at Abuela. "I'll keep you company and take you home when you're ready. Besides," he patted the wall, "the back of the schoolhouse could use some paint, too."

CHAPTER 7

Emma ~ Present

Children two to twelve banged their hands against the table. "You forgot to say, 'Uno!'"

María tilted her head back, faking a cry. Maya shoved more cards into her hands.

"Careful! You're going to give her a papercut." Andrés narrowed his eyes at Maya, then whispered into María's ear, "You'll tell me if my sister bothers you, won't you?"

Emma loved how Andrés was so protective of María. At only six years old, they waffled between delighting and dismaying in gossip about them being a couple. When they weren't happy with the comments, they would keep their distance from playing together. The longest time, Andrés had told Emma, was the eternity of two and a half days.

It puzzled Emma that Maya was at her UNO class. She had never attended before and, given that Emma held the English-geared game weekly, she'd had plenty of chances to do so.

María pouted at Andrés. "Your turn."

Emma nodded at María, approving of how she pronounced the English phrase.

"Yes!" Andrés tossed his last card on the table and threw his hands in the air. "I won," he exclaimed in Spanish.

The rest of the kids sighed, chorusing the same word in English. As happy as she was to see their progress, it troubled Emma that Andrés' English was limited to 'Yes.'

Maya scooped up the cards and shuffled the deck, her chipped hot pink fingernails flashing back and forth. "How was your evening last night?"

Her voice was casual and she didn't take her eyes off the cards, but Emma knew the question was meant for her.

"Fine, thanks."

"Nothing new happening?"

"Just Chuleta being Chuleta."

For as much as Emma didn't like Maya's watchful eye over her house, a part of her now felt comforted by it. If there was something new happening—and that new thing wasn't Eduardo's evening visit—Emma was certain that Maya would have seen it. It was why Emma wasn't scared the night before when she heard rustling in the grass. If a person had truly been near her house, Maya would have made sure word spread around Almagro before the parrots descended on the mango trees for breakfast.

"Okay," Maya said, as she distributed cards to the kids. Maya's skin had the kind of smoothness that never knew acne. When she smiled, trench-like dimples appeared on either cheek—deep enough to attract attention and proportionally perfect. Maya didn't smile, though. Not this time. And that was a relief to Emma since her smiles almost always translated to 'I caught you.'

Emma figured she wouldn't have to worry about Maya tonight; Eduardo wouldn't stop by her house after such a long day. In fact, she figured—and hoped—that he wouldn't come around that late at night ever again. But in either case, when it came to tonight, Emma already had plans. Plans she didn't want interrupted.

María's elbow pushed into a mosquito bite on Emma's arm. "Your turn!"

Emma gave her a thumbs up. Her students had become so proficient at knowing how to say numbers, colors, and phrases in English from playing UNO that Emma often found herself letting her guard down. That was, except when it came to Andrés.

Andrés put a card down. "Yes!"

"Andre*yes.*" Emma looked at him sternly but felt a ping in her heart at the sight of his ripped, hand-me-down shirt falling off his shoulder. "You're supposed to say, 'Your turn'."

The kids pounded their hands against the wooden table as they chanted in English, "Your turn, your turn, your turn!"

Emma remembered Professor Sonya's warning when she first arrived in Almagro. 'Andrés is behind in school. He's smart, in his own way, but not when it comes to his studies.' Given that Sonya had to teach all nine grades together, 'behind' carried an even greater weight in Almagro. Emma couldn't deny Sonya's evaluation compared to the other students, but she also knew that Andrés' parents didn't see the point of education when he and Maya were destined to the traditional roles of fishing and raising a family.

Emma rolled a piece of soggy chalk in her hand. The area by the soccer field where she held her English games was basic, but between having a chalkboard, picnic table, and thatched roof, it served as a fine open-air classroom.

"Yes means *'sí'* and 'your turn' means *'te toca a tí'*," she said, writing the words for him.

"Mm-hmm." Andrés grinned, rocking side to side beside María. He rubbed a hand across his forehead, the bloodstain from Celia becoming indiscernible as it mixed with sweat.

María stood and smiled at Emma. "Is it true that AIDS is coming back?" She spun in her dress but mud caked to its edges muffled its twirl.

"MINSA," Emma said, emphasizing the correction. "Yes, they'll be returning with the results of the tests."

"I heard they'll bring pork next time," she exclaimed, running barefoot into the soccer field. Andrés stood up and followed steps behind her.

$\sim * \sim$

Emma mused at how unfamiliar it felt. It was wider than she remembered. And heavier. So much heavier. It had groves on the side for grip, even though she remembered it being smooth. One thing was certain—it looked different. So different, in fact, that she wasn't sure it would work.

She sighed, setting the phone on her bamboo nightstand. Its screen shifted from the movement; humidity had crept its way in over the past year. Her parents would be thrilled if she called them from Almagro. Before now, her only option was using a payphone in Chepo. And trips to Chepo were rare. Mateo grumbled about her presence whenever she accompanied him since it meant less space in his canoe to stack *tienda* supplies.

Emma watched the sunset between gaps in her wall. Under normal circumstances, it would have been too early for Emma to settle in for the night. But tonight felt different. She walked outside and found Chuleta laying on the edge of the balcony, her front paws hanging over the top of the staircase. 'Leave her outside at night,' Eduardo had told her. 'She'll alert you if anyone's around.' But Emma couldn't—Chuleta belonged in her dog bed beneath Emma's bed. Always.

Emma looked over at her machete. It hung from a bamboo shoot wedged between the palm bark walls outside her bedroom. She smiled, remembering Abuela's advice the day she learned Emma had brought it back from Chepo. 'Make your machete a gift from God. Machetes that destroy more than they need are gifts from the devil.' Abuela accompanied her words with two grass crosses—one for God and the other to spite the devil.

When Emma first arrived in Almagro, she felt uneasy leaving a knife the length of her arm hanging outside her bedroom; anyone could climb up her tree trunk staircase and take it. Or worse, use it against her. Now, such fear was a go-to laughing point for the villagers on days when gossip was sparse. And for good reason—it became an absurd notion to Emma, too, after she got to know the villagers. But now, even though she knew no one in Almagro would physically harm her, there was something about sleeping beside her machete that felt comforting. Emma walked over to grab it. Chuleta jumped up, pounding her tail against the floor.

"We're not going anywhere, sweet pea." Emma tapped her thigh. "Come on, come inside."

Closing the bamboo door, Emma set her machete beside her phone while she got ready for bed. Both looked odd sitting there; neither looked like they belonged inside her house. Slipping into an oversized t-shirt, she made a mental note to bring her machete back outside in the morning to avoid alarming the villagers.

She gave Chuleta a final pat and ducked underneath the mosquito net, kicking off her flip flops and waiting for the familiar thump as they fell four feet to the floor below. Despite her house's height, the villagers insisted that Emma's bed be raised as an additional snake deterrent.

Her phone settled into her lap. She wanted to turn it on, but she was nervous. Nervous about the kinds of messages she would find—not only messages meant for Jake but those from her own contacts who had forgotten that they couldn't write to her while she was in Panama. So much good—and bad—could happen in a year. Jake aside, the positive outcomes from it were inevitable, she told herself. Assuming her phone still worked, she would be able to communicate with her family and friends. Right from Almagro. It was the kind of luxury she had laid in bed dreaming about when she first arrived.

She pressed the power button and her phone responded with a vibration—a good sign. But then a flickering screen greeted her. *Perhaps the humidity will win after all.* She waited a minute. And then a few more.

The flickering subsided—not entirely, but enough so she could make out the apps on her screen. Seeing them felt like looking at a photo from childhood; they prompted memories of things she had forgotten. Already forgotten. It had been a mere year since she couldn't picture living without her phone.

Emma stared at the blank space in the upper left corner of her screen. Rebecca had assured her there would be a signal, but she would need to take her phone off airplane mode to find out. Ten dollars a day for cell service was a lot. But now, sitting in her beloved house a year into her Peace Corps service, she was ready to treat her curiosity. Just this one time, just for twenty-four hours.

She disabled airplane mode. A bar appeared. And then another. She stared at the screen, watching it flicker, willing messages to come through with answers about Jake.

CHAPTER 8

Jake ~ Past

Jake picked up two more buckets, their narrow metal handles pressing into his palms. Numbness never felt so familiar. How was it possible that he had spent six months away from Charleston? How could he have thought Arizona would be good for him?

A new life was what he wanted, he had told his family as they stared at him, a torn backpack draped over his left shoulder. They were teary-eyed and worried but not shocked by his newest rash decision. He had wanted to start over. He *needed* to start over. It wasn't supposed to be Arizona. But when his trusty blue Toyota Camry, Sheba, broke down there it seemed the Grand Canyon state was his ticket to a fresh start.

A plop on the dock pulled Jake away from his thoughts. He watched a shrimp race away from him, mere feet from the freedom of the harbor. Instinctively, he bent down to pick it up. But then he glanced up at his family's shrimp house. His father tinkered with a motor by the door, his back to the harbor. "Enjoy your second chance," Jake whispered as he walked towards the shore.

Jake wished his parents would invest in new shrimping equipment. It would help them bring in larger catches in a shorter amount of time, he'd tell them. But they wouldn't have it. 'Your grandparents didn't come all the way to America for us to bury ourselves in debt,' his mom would say. Jake's younger sister, Tina, saw both sides. But she would end the day agreeing with their parents. She didn't want to make him look bad but, when it came to the Morales family, Tina was the grounded child and Jake was the adventurer.

He hated that word.

'Adventurer' was how Jake's parents explained his choices when talking with their friends and neighbors. It held the kind of positive connotation that shielded anyone outside their tight-knit family circle from seeing his parents' disapproval. Jake had watched them do it countless times during his childhood, feeling—fearing— the wrath of his deceased immigrant grandparents if their son became anything less than a poster child of the American Dream. Now, in his mid-twenties, his parents said he was adventuring more than ever. But they failed to see that he was trying to live the modern version of the American Dream. One that valued experiences over possessions, happiness over other people's expectations.

Slabs of wood and shrimping equipment engulfed the boat's floor as Jake picked through them to locate stray shrimp. It had only been two days since he returned home from Arizona. And as much as he wanted to voice his opinion on his family's business, he vowed not to cause rifts.

Not this time.

Jake's thoughts wandered back to when Pedro found him on the side of a deserted highway in Arizona. Pedro's timing was extraordinary; the afternoon sun had just forced Jake to finish his last sip of water. But it was more than timing. Pedro didn't do a double take when he laid eyes on Jake. He didn't start by asking Jake where he was from, and he didn't ask him where he was *really* from when his answer was Charleston. He didn't speak slowly or shout. And he didn't comment how hard it must have been for him to learn English, despite his flawless American accent.

Jake picked a scab off his arm, revealing jagged pink edges that sprawled out from his brown skin. Charleston was primarily a place of two colors; Black and white, white and Black. American blood fueled Jake's body, but so many people overlooked that during his childhood because of the color of his skin.

Arizona was different, though. Old Sheba's fate looked grim but it hadn't discouraged Pedro. 'I know the perfect person who can fix her up,' he'd said. And just like that, Jake found a new group of friends in Pedro, his mechanic, Oscar, and Pedro and Oscar's friends.

And there were a lot of them.

Jake had gained more friends in one night at Catch 'Em Bar than he had in his entire life. The conversations with his new friends were different; they commented on his southern accent instead of questioning how long it took him to lose the Spanish one he never had. They talked about sports and cars and workouts and relationships without anyone ever asking for a comparison to 'his' country. Deeper conversations led to bonds with third-generation Americans and insight into the lives of first and second-generation Americans. And for those who weren't Latino, the byproduct of having diverse friendships was them recognizing the joys and struggles of it all.

His friends were good people, albeit some of them were lost themselves. And he found himself drawn to those with a rough-around-the-edges attitude—the kind that Jake had envisioned for himself growing up. The one he had tried and failed to achieve in Charleston. As it turned out, he'd gotten the hang of it in Arizona just as he realized he no longer wanted to.

"Daydreaming?" Tina stood on the dock, staring at Jake in the boat. She held a knife in her left hand and a bouquet of wildflowers in her right.

Jake mustered a smile.

Tina took a seat on the dock, dangling her legs over the edge. "How ya feeling?"

"I've got a headache from someone asking too many questions." He threw a rope soaked in shrimp juice towards her—hard enough to make her flinch but keeping the line short enough so it wouldn't hit her.

She gave him a knowing look. "Jake."

"I'm fine."

"You best be revising your answer." She pulled brown petals off the flowers, watching them float down to the water. "The last time you said that you took off to Arizona."

"Consider me wonderful then." He pulled himself up onto the dock beside her, his forearms shaking from the movement. While in Arizona, fat crept into areas that were previously ripped with muscle. He hadn't expected his fitness to change so much, though.

"Just don't run off again." Tina bumped her shoulder against his arm. "We need you here."

~ * ~

"I don't think that's a good idea, honey." Isabella stole a glance at Tina before turning her attention back to the sizzling pot. 'Isabella perfection' was the standard that okra—and any southern or Central American food in her kitchen—needed to live up to.

"Don't get me wrong, Mom, I love your cooking. But I think it would be good for me to get out." Jake ran his hand over the shrimp he had carved into his family's wooden dinner table when he was seven years old. With family roots in Panama and Costa Rica, living in towns that shared the Caribbean Sea a border apart, his grandparents used to say it was destiny that the Moraleses became shrimpers.

"It would be," Tina said. "But perhaps having breakfast there would be better? After all, Mom's nearly got supper ready."

"Breakfast. Why yes, that's an excellent idea." Oil poured through the slotted spoon Isabella held, revealing lumps of deep-fried okra.

"Y'all know I don't believe in paying for the simplest meal of the day."

Tina shooed his hand away with a plate as she set the table. "Don't you have money to spend with everything you made in Arizona?"

"Yup." Jake folded the edge of his napkin, forming the wing of a swan. "And I'd like to spend it on supper at the diner."

It was true—Jake's bank account looked the best it ever had. He arrived in Arizona without skill. It was a landlocked state, after all. But Oscar needed the help and Jake was willing to learn. 'You're the best mechanic I've got,' Oscar had said to him shortly before Jake left. Jake's stomach churned. How long would it take for the guilt to wear off? It wasn't the first time he left without saying goodbye. But the first time he did it was different.

He looked up and caught Tina and his mom exchanging glances.

Tina leaned against a chair. "In that case, bring me along."

"Alright." Jake shrugged. "It's a date then."

"A date for *tomorrow*," Isabella said. "This meal is intended for four people, not just your father and me."

The sunset pushed its way through the screen door. Despite its brightness, Jake saw his phone illuminate. He had set it to silent shortly after driving Sheba out of Arizona. Out of the place where people would wake to find him gone. Putting his phone on silent had worked, but only briefly; his senses adjusted to the flash of light from messages and calls. He glanced down at his phone, regretting it immediately.

A note? Seriously? Where are you, man?

Jake gave Pedro credit; he could have been harsher. Much harsher, and Jake wouldn't have blamed him for it. He hadn't even taken the time to write separate notes to his closest friends in Arizona, much less explained why he left. Not even to Oscar. He could only imagine the look on Oscar's face when he learned that Jake hadn't shown up for work because he'd left the state.

Jake's dad, Jacobo, pushed the screen door open. "There's nothing like the start of shrimp season." Beaming, he tossed his baseball cap on the counter.

"Boots *outside*." Isabella's firm tone didn't match the glint in her eyes—the same look she had whenever seeing her husband.

He winked at Jake and Tina. "Just gotta get back in the habit."

"The kids are going to the diner tomorrow night, sweetie." Isabella set the okra on the table.

"Oh, really?"

"I don't get what the big deal is," Jake said, noting the skepticism in his dad's voice. "I like their fish fry. It's not an escape plan."

Isabella sighed and studied a crack in their ceiling. "I should hope not."

CHAPTER 9

Jake ~ Past

J ake couldn't sleep even though his childhood bed was the best he'd ever slept in. And he would know; he tried out plenty on his journey to—and in—Arizona, each night with a new woman at his side. Not among his finest choices in life, he admitted to no one but himself.

His thoughts shifted to Lizzie before he had the chance to stop them. Things never would have worked between them. It was a truth that was both painful and undeniable. Even so, he knew it was wrong of him to travel to Arizona without explaining himself to her.

Without breaking up with her.

A breeze wove through Spanish moss hanging from an oak tree outside his bedroom window. Crickets chirped, challenging the strength of their tune with birds that would take their place at dawn. Jake knew it was pointless trying to fall back to sleep. He got out of bed and snuck through the screen door of the kitchen to the porch, hoping the creaking wood floors wouldn't wake his family.

His family's hound dog, Tulip, stirred at the far end of the bench swing. Tulip looked at him with groggy eyes, wriggling as much of her body as possible onto his lap when he sat down.

Jake reminisced about the day their family brought the swing home. Their problem wasn't where to place the swing to get the best view of the harbor, but where among all the prime viewing areas was the *very* best. Eventually, his parents decided it would be determined by the person who pulled the longest fishbone. And so, Tina got to choose her favorite place—the one where she had a view of fireflies dancing on the dock. Ten years passed before Tina's spot on the porch became Jake's favorite, too.

He took a deep breath and looked across the harbor. The water was calm, as it so oftentimes was at dawn. The reflection of lights from houses lining the shore was easier to decipher that way. But to him, it didn't matter if he was away from home for six months or sixty years—he would always know which lights came from Lizzie's house; he had spent countless hours as a teen and in his early twenties staring at them and thinking about her.

Dating Lizzie wasn't easy. In tenth grade she scrawled the word 'edgy' on the inside of her forearm with a permanent marker, determined to be defined by it. She would leave her house dressed for a night club and used language she learned from watching reality TV at her friends' houses—friends who weren't brought up in the strict Baptist church like she was. She was the person who all the guys wanted and girls either envied or despised. And she was the person who inspired Jake to be bad. Or, at least, sparked his attempts at being bad, which always fell short in her eyes. For as much as Jake wanted to be with Lizzie, they didn't start dating until after high school. Sometimes, he wondered if she agreed to date him simply to defy expectations. And somewhere between then and when she ran late for yet another Saturday night date, Jake found his truest version of bad.

He left her.

Jake hoped his friends in Arizona would recognize that he had grown, if only a little. At least he left them a note. It didn't say much, but it was there. And they knew Jake's history with Lizzie. How he met them because he left her. Even so, with only days being back in Charleston, he felt the familiar tug of knowing that he shouldn't have left without saying goodbye.

"Up so early?"

Jake looked at the door, seeing the shadow of his mom behind the screen.

"I could say the same to you." He smiled, running his hand along Tulip's back. In her attempt to get as close to him as possible, she had wriggled the front part of her body past him so that her belly was now sprawled across his lap.

"Honey." Isabella walked over to the swing, sitting down as she lifted the front part of Tulip onto her lap. She stared in the direction of Lizzie's house. "You didn't return to Charleston to get back together with her, did you?"

He shook his head. "No, I really didn't."

~ * ~

Shrimping was like riding a bike, but the trick was being away long enough to realize it.

Jacobo ran his fingers through his long grey hair and sighed. "I missed these days." His fingers became stuck mid-way from the salty air.

Jake leaned against the worn stern. "It hasn't been *that* long."

"Tell it to the dolphins."

It was his dad's signature phrase and one that worked with just about any point he wanted to make. Isabella was the only person who gushed over it, despite its predictability. And yet this time Jake didn't mind. Perhaps he had been gone a long time.

Their boat approached Lizzie's house, twenty feet from shore. Jake remembered how he used to hate passing by her house as a teenager. It was no secret that Jake's family had the smallest shrimping boat in the harbor. It also could've used two new coats of paint since the last time a brush was laid on it. But now, Jake loved that adulthood meant he no longer cared about what other people thought—even if he had taken it too far at times.

He looked over at Tina who was helping their dad with an anchor. "Is she still in school?" Jake knew he didn't need to clarify who 'she' was; it would have been like explaining the difference between 'me' and 'I'.

"Oh." Tina glanced at their dad.

"Yep, she is." Jacobo unknotted the rope of the anchor. "And doing a great job."

Jake narrowed his eyes at Tina. "So, art school?"

"You know Lizzie," she shrugged. "She has an eclectic way about her."

Eclectic. That was one way to put it. Jake remembered the time Lizzie's parents told her she couldn't pierce her ears until she was a teenager. Two days before her thirteenth birthday, she hired a man she found on the dark web to tattoo her right hip—an image of a black rose shedding its petals, a drawing she created herself.

"Does she like Atlanta?"

Tina picked seaweed off the anchor. "Mm-hmm."

"Son, why don't you tell us more about Arizona?"

"There's not much to tell. It's pretty, in its own way." He paused. "Different from here."

"I'd love to see the cacti." Tina tossed a snail overboard. "They must be beautiful."

They were. Jake remembered the time when he, Pedro, Oscar, and fifty others had a party out in the desert. The Cactus Hoedown, they called it. It was a great idea in theory, and all started well. But as the night wore on and the empty beer cans piled up, so did the cacti thorns on people's skin. To top it all off, Pedro had the grand idea to dance with a cactus. Jake looked down at his feet. The dots were fading, but still there; a reminder of his stumble over a cactus after he left the party with a girl. He couldn't remember her name. Perhaps he never knew.

Jacobo nodded towards a piece of wood nailed to the boat, serving as a shelf. "Well, one thing's for certain. You made a lot of friends there."

"Uh . . . yeah, I guess I did."

"Your phone, silly." Tina laughed. "For someone as popular as you seem to have been, you sure don't care about checking your messages."

Jake shook his head and walked over to the shelf. It was true; he didn't care about checking his messages. He wasn't ready to confront them. But against all logic, he felt the need to have his phone nearby. A habit that needed breaking.

He brushed fish scales off the screen, and his phone flashed on from the movement. There had to be a way to prevent messages from popping up like that; over one-hundred had already come in since he left Arizona. He made a mental note to look into it. As much as he didn't want to read them, he already processed the words on the screen. The most recent messages were from Oscar.

Just in case you thought you still had a job, you're fired.

Jake. Dude. This isn't funny, man. Tell us where you are. Any message will do, just let us know you're okay.

Did we do something to upset you? I didn't mean what I said earlier, you can still have your job.

Dude. If this is a joke, it's a sick one. We don't even know how to get ahold of your family.

Now there was a silver lining—they didn't know how to get in touch with his family. Jake had kept his friends in Arizona off his family's radar on purpose; he knew they wouldn't have approved of their carefree ways. He also loved the idea of starting fresh when he arrived in Arizona—new friends, new job, new scenery, without the potential for his old and new worlds to seep together. His plan had worked even though he never expected to leave so soon, much less leave the way he did.

He would reconnect with his friends in Arizona, he decided. But not yet. Wounds needed healing. His, perhaps, most of all.

~ * ~

No matter how many years passed, Jake would always know his way to the diner. It was the first place he drove to when he got his license—the only place, for the most part, that his parents would let him drive to on his own. Friday nights used to be hopping there. The profit made from Jake's high school alone was enough to sustain the diner's livelihood.

Tina pulled at her fingers. "It should be quiet today."

"Is that all you're thinking about?" Jake glanced at her hands. Tina's finger massaging was a nervous habit she had picked up as a kid. Their parents said it was harmless, so they never made her break it. Jake, on the other hand, used to get a spanking for stuffing dirt beneath his fingernails, a habit he didn't see as any different from Tina's.

"Well." Tina clasped her hands. "It's Tuesday, so there should be plenty of fish." She reached over to punch his arm. "Wouldn't want you throwing a fit if it's sold out."

"Hey now, have a little faith in me." He looked at her, swerving as he pulled into his favorite parking spot. "Sheba's home," he said with a sigh.

Tina shook her head, getting out of the car. "That's the happiest you've looked since coming home."

He pointed at her window. "Don't forget to push it up."

And by 'push', he wasn't kidding. It was the part of his car that Oscar never managed to fix. Then again, Oscar stopped putting time into trying once Jake and his friends had gotten used to pushing the glass up and down with their hands. It worked great, except for times when someone would push the glass too far down, making it a nightmare to get back up. It usually happened when Jake had a new girl in his car. Because of how frequently that occurred, he taped a note about it on the passenger door.

Jake turned his attention to the diner. It had been painted recently, judging by the brightness of the color. He knew the owner, Kate, hated seeing the blue paint fade from the sun and salty air. Jake loved everything about the diner, even though it looked out of place with its Greek style. Making a fuss about its white and blue colors and rounded top was just about the only complaint customers could come up with. 'What a nice compliment,' Kate would say when they confronted her with their concerns.

Jake reached for the diner door, but Tina cut in front of him.

"Let me do the honor."

"Okay," he said, drawing out the word. He watched Tina cup her hands around the glass, peering into the dining area. "It's open, you know. Says so on the sign right here."

"Right. Of course." She pulled away, leaving three oily forehead prints dotting the glass.

A cheerful hostess met them at the door. Jake figured she was a tenth grader, eleventh at most. Kate believed in giving high schoolers the opportunity to get work experience—even though it meant her spending extra time to hire new employees when they graduated or did 'youthful' things. The hostess led them towards the middle of the room.

"This won't do." Jake stopped. "We'd like to sit there." He pointed to the booth where he and his friends used to sit. It was by a window at the furthest end of the diner— the prime place for people watching. He and his friends used to take their booth spot seriously, with a rotating schedule of who would arrive early on Fridays to secure it.

"Don't make a fuss," Tina whispered.

Jake raised his eyebrows. "There's no one sitting in it. What's with you?"

"Nothing." She glanced towards the kitchen as they approached the booth and the hostess handed them menus.

"No need." Jake held up a hand as he slid into his spot. The worn-out fabric felt even more worn than he remembered. "We'll have fish fries."

"Coming right up," the waitress said, pouring water into their glasses.

Tina watched, shifting her body from side to side.

"Seriously. What's with you?" Jake asked.

"Nothing." She flashed him a smile and continued to move in the seat across from him, no more than a couple inches at a time. "I'm just happy we've got some time together without Mom and Dad around, that's all."

Jake sighed, raising his glass to hers. "Ditto."

"So, tell me. Are you happy to be back?"

"I'm not unhappy." A new message flashed on his phone. Not wanting Tina to catch a glimpse of whatever it said, Jake slipped it off the table and onto the booth seat.

"That's a start." Tina popped a hush puppy into her mouth. They were the diner's complimentary appetizer and the reason the diner was so popular.

"I love Charleston," Jake said, softening his voice. "It'll always feel like home, but I don't think it'll be my home. Not in the future, at least."

"Where do you want your home to be?"

"I don't know. Maybe somewhere where I blend in, even more than Arizona. You know?"

Tina gave him a knowing nod. "So, once you decide on this new home of yours," she wiped ketchup from her face, "you won't disappear on us again. Not without telling us where you're going first. Right?"

Jake smiled. "Right."

"Promise?"

"Promise.

CHAPTER 10

Lizzie ~ Past

Lizzie flicked a cloth onto the industrial size, flat-top stove. Droplets of oil fell from the fryer, sizzling beneath the fabric. It seemed like a thankless task to do mid-shift, but Kate was a stickler for cleanliness.

"I don't care that you're older than your colleagues," Kate tapped a pen on the counter across from the stove. "It's this job or the door. Your choice."

"Fine." Still looking down, Lizzie put exaggerated strength into scrubbing, the tattoos on her fingers vibrating from the motion, as Kate walked away to tend to her other employees.

How did her life come to this? It was a question Lizzie asked herself often, but above all when she was at work. Friday nights at the diner used to be the highlight of her week, her escape from uptight parents and the place where so many adventures started—and sometimes ended. Nonetheless, she was lucky to have her job. She had burned so many bridges in her previous employment gigs that it became pointless applying for jobs that required references. Since Kate advocated for the underdog, she had an easy in.

Lizzie shifted her nose ring. She would have done better as a professor than a student at her Atlanta art school. To her parents' dismay when she dropped out, she used her free time to adorn her body with more piercings and tattoos. It took a moment for Kate to recognize her when she came looking for a job. It was impressive, really, given how even some of Lizzie's old high school friends no longer did. She sometimes caught herself wondering if Jake would recognize her. It was an absurd thought, she concluded every time.

Of course he would.

"Lizzie." Kate snapped her fingers. "The fish."

Without acknowledging Kate, Lizzie lifted two fish from the fryer. "Extra crispy," she murmured, plopping them on plates. Oil pooled beneath them. She considered sending the fish out as they were, but flashes of her parents' disappointment if she returned home jobless again changed her mind. Sighing, she moved the fish to new plates and pushed them towards the small space in the counter that opened to the dining room.

And then she saw him.

Or did she?

He was in their booth, in his favorite spot. Black hair poked out to the sides, framing the hair of the woman sitting in front of him. Lizzie couldn't make out his face; the backside of the woman's head obstructed it. But the guy seemed short—too short, perhaps, when sizing him to the height of the window latch. Then again, Jake was notorious for slouching.

"Lizzie."

"Hey." Lizzie clenched her jaw and turned around to face Kate. "I wanted to make sure I got the order right, that's all."

"It was two fish fries, not complicated."

Lizzie mustered a nod and walked back to the fryer. Ever since she started working at the diner, she kept an eye on her high school booth. She knew better than to think Jake would have returned to Charleston. But then again, he was impulsive. And she had him wrapped around her finger—or so she thought, before he up and left her.

"Is this enough?" A teenage boy, who was pre-plating fish fries with salad, looked at her.

"Mm-hmm."

The boy's hesitance irked her. She didn't know what it was like to lack confidence—that was what her parents told her growing up when they'd scold her for being hard on Jake. But somewhere between Jake's efforts to be confident and his mortifying failures, she had grown keen on him.

They were keen on each other, until he changed his mind.

Lizzie's escape was art school. She wanted to show Jake she was moving on with her life. That she, too, could leave Charleston. Even if they never spoke again, both their families were in the shrimping business, so she knew word would get back to him. If only it didn't work the other way around; Jake would learn she flunked out of school.

She carried four fish fries to the counter and studied the booth again. The man's face was still covered by the woman's head, but Lizzie was becoming convinced it was Jake. That, coupled with the woman sitting across from him being able to pass for Jake's sister, judging by her back profile. Just as long as she wasn't a new girlfriend. Her stomach churned at the thought.

She turned back to the fryer before Kate caught her dawdling. The high schoolers chatted away as they worked in the kitchen, catching up on the latest school gossip.

Kate walked down the narrow kitchen aisle, touching a pot here and there. "Well done. You guys are all caught up."

It was their cue to clean and prep before another rush of customers came through the door. The chances of that happening were slim, though, given that the Tuesday night work crowd had already passed through.

Lizzie claimed the counter to clean before anyone else had the chance. She looked at the booth constantly; anyone watching would have assumed she was glancing at the counter rather than the other way around. If only she could find a better angle, she'd be able to see the man.

Or if the woman moved her head.

Lizzie ran her tongue ring along her lip. "Come on . . . a little more."

The woman at the booth leaned down to take a bite of food. But the man had already bent over his own plate. He looked out the window, she looked out the window. He shifted, she shifted. Eventually, the woman reached for a napkin in the canister beside the wall. He didn't.

Jake.

Lizzie drew in a breath and stepped to the left, out of sight. The wall's coldness seeped through her clothes to her skin. Disappointment gripped her. It wasn't the reaction she pictured having if she saw Jake again. In her mind, she'd cut him deep with her words, using his insecurities against him. Insecurities that only she knew about. She'd throw an object or many—anything within reach. But she wouldn't hide. Not a chance.

And yet there she was.

She didn't get a good look at him, but she could tell he had gained weight. Not much, but enough to lessen the distinction of his overly protruding cheekbones. It suited him, like she knew it would. 'You'd be more attractive if you got some meat on your bones,' she used to tell him. He would get quiet on those days. But for a reason she never understood, he wouldn't change his eating habits. It was out of character, given that he'd do just about anything to make her want him more. Could it be he thought of her while putting on pounds in Arizona?

"Other areas of the kitchen could use that kind of scrubbing too." Kate ran her hand over the counter.

Lizzie jumped. She'd only just hidden behind the wall . . . hadn't she? Or had her thoughts about Jake consumed time she hadn't intended to give him? Based on Kate's reaction, Lizzie went with the former and walked to the far end of the kitchen. For one of the first times in her life, she was thankful to be told what to do.

~ * ~

The evening dragged by even though the diner closed at the early hour of eight o'clock on Tuesdays. Lizzie figured Jake and Tina would stay until closing. It was something she vacillated between wanting and dreading. Two things had become clear from her glances through the counter window—Tina knew she was working in the kitchen and Jake didn't.

Lizzie couldn't decide how to handle the situation. She had considered marching up to their table and putting Jake on the spot. A grand scene was how she ended any relationship, after all—and always on her terms. She also contemplated passing in view of him, pretending she didn't know he was there. Catch him off guard, followed by scene-making. And then, of course, she could do nothing.

But that wasn't her style.

She took the final fish of the night out of the fryer, let the oil drip off it for a few seconds longer than usual, and put it in a to-go box. Then she stuck the spoon back into the boiling oil, running it along the pot's edges to scoop up stray crispy pieces. She let the oil run off those, too, before carefully tipping them into the section of the box meant for salad. *The perfect dinner for afterwards.*

It was just minutes before closing. Go time.

During high school, Jake would make their group wait until closing to leave. 'Leaving even seconds early is wasted time apart,' he would say. It was the Latino in him, Lizzie would tell him.

Lizzie studied the kitchen, making sure Kate wasn't around. No doubt, she would question her if she saw Lizzie enter the dining room. Lizzie's diner cap scraped against her forehead. She tossed it by the stove, fluffing up her bangs to hide the red mark where it sat. She still hadn't decided how she was going to handle Jake. But he would be handled.

She pushed her shoulder against the metal door leading into the dining room. It banged against the wall. People stared at her, but she didn't see them. Not a single one. All she saw was the booth where Jake had been sitting just minutes earlier. She knew because she had checked.

It was empty.

She ran out to the parking lot and fixated on his parking spot. Empty. She looked down the road. To the right, then to the left. Not a Morales' car in sight. Pivoting on her heel, she strode back inside.

"What's with you?" a waitress cleaning the tables asked.

"Nothing." Lizzie glared at her, making the girl look down and continue her work. Not the person she intended to intimidate, but it gave her a rush all the same.

If there was a saving grace to the evening, it was that the diner didn't need much cleaning post-shift. And that she knew Jake was in town. She may have not gotten the chance to call him out for leaving her tonight, but now that he was back, chance was a matter of time.

A waiter's voice rang through the diner. "Putting a phone in lost and found."

"Aye, aye," the employees chimed.

Except Lizzie. It was ridiculous to her that Kate created the saying—they weren't on a boat, after all. 'It creates a fun environment while notifying everyone that a customer left something behind,' Kate explained during Lizzie's first day on the job.

Lizzie turned and put the last pot on a rack as Kate approached her. "All set," she said.

"Excellent." Kate squeezed her shoulder. "See you tomorrow."

Lizzie nodded. It was a noble effort, given Jake just escaped her wrath. She walked to the back room to grab her backpack. Its size didn't match its contents; she only ever carried a sketchbook, pencils, and enough cash to get her by if she stopped for a drink. Nonetheless, a purse wasn't conducive to bike riding and she hated shopping. Snatching it off the coatrack, she stared down at the cardboard lost and found box. Normally, she didn't register—or care to register—its contents.

But something caught her eye.

She bent down to get a closer look at the black phone lying face up. Even though a green sweater draped over its topmost part, Lizzie sensed she recognized it. Glancing around to make sure no one was watching, she grabbed it out of the box, turning her back to the kitchen door.

Sony. The same brand as Jake's phone. She ran a finger over the screen. It had a crack in the bottom left corner trailing up towards the center. Just like Jake's phone. Unlike his phone, it was marked with other cracks and scratches. But time had passed since she had seen it.

Could it be?

She snapped off the cover, thinking back to the time when they went crabbing on the banks of a marsh inlet, a mile from Jake's house. Her line had wrapped around a branch in the marsh grass and he waded in the water to get it. He managed to untangle the snag, but he got stuck in the muddy bottom in the process, relying on Lizzie to help him out. She did, but not before carving their initials on the inside of his phone cover. She chuckled to herself, remembering the look on people's faces when they walked home, covered chest to toe in mud. It was one of her favorite memories of them as a couple.

Looking down at the inside of the phone cover, she was certain it was Jake's phone. But their initials weren't there. Instead, scratch marks took their place. Lots of them. Angry slashes. Only the topmost part of Jake's 'J' and Lizzie's 'L' had escaped the horizontal lines. Lizzie nearly dropped the phone from the jolt of emotion that would have gone into his—or someone's—strokes as they ripped through her and Jake's past.

She snapped the cover back on, slamming her fist down when it stuck. The narrow path leading to the kitchen door was still clear. *Better that way*, she thought, as she slipped the phone into her pocket.

CHAPTER 11

Lizzie ~ Past

Lizzie sat cross-legged on her bed staring at the phone. She had been watching it illuminate at a near-constant rhythm over the past hour—two calls, some direct messages, and many other messages that were part of a group text. The people writing were making predictions—and crude jokes—about the presidential nominees during what she assumed was a debate. She wouldn't have known since she didn't follow politics. Jake never used to either.

She pulled up the pin screen. He wouldn't have changed his pin code. He couldn't have; technology wasn't his forte. She hovered her finger over the number seven for the fourth time in a minute. But what if he had changed it? Or, more probable, someone changed it for him? She was already able to get glimpses of his life by reading the messages inundating his locked screen. She knew herself too well, though. That would never be enough. She wanted to see the contents of his phone. All of it.

Her thoughts drifted to the day Jake revealed his pin to her. 'I don't forget anything', she warned. 'Besides, we're not even dating.'

It was true. Over a year would pass before they had their first kiss—and many months passed after that before Lizzie considered him her boyfriend.

'I just want to show you that I'm not talking with other girls, that's all.'

'What a desperate thought,' she had told him. 'Not fitting for a person trying to live on the edge.'

At the time of the pin debacle, Lizzie was on a break between boyfriends, with eyes on a third guy. She didn't care for Jake back then but loved stringing him along. Somehow, his shortcomings grew charming and, before she realized, she was in the best relationship she had ever been in.

Until he left without telling her.

She picked up the phone, a fresh wave of anger blanketing her doubts. She pounded the four-digit pin into his phone.

It responded instantly and apps she remembered greeted her—they were all there, all in the same spots. But they sat on a backdrop that wasn't of her. Instead, desert hills dotted the screen with a single-lane road running down the middle, sand edging into its territory.

Another message came through for Jake. She flicked it away. Nearly two-hundred unread text messages waited for him. She would get to them, but not yet. His pictures were her first priority.

She clicked the photo icon and scrolled to the top as fast as she could. He had to have kept their photos. It wasn't like Jake to erase anything, let alone pictures of someone he loved. She held herself back from looking at the other photos until she got to where she was going, but noted how they seemed to be darker in tone. Brown, tan, black, grey, some green, and sparse, but occasional, yellow and orange.

And then the screen stopped moving.

"No," she whispered.

There had to be more. She pulled her finger down hard on the phone. Then again. And again. Each time, the result was the same—she had already arrived to the first picture. It was a family photo of Jake with his sister and parents. It was followed by a photo of Tulip, the harbor, and the spot where she and Jake would go fishing for blue crabs. Jake was in the photo, smiling as he held up a group of crabs hanging from chicken bait. Lizzie remembered that photo; she had taken it. But there were so many other photos they took that day, along with hundreds of others from their time together. Gone.

She scrolled up and down, hope unwilling to meet reason. She wasn't there. Instead, she'd been replaced with parties, beer can piles exceeding those they had made with their high school friends, and empty roads. *So many* empty roads. There were occasional sunset photos, the only ones that made it seem like Jake's phone.

And then there were the girls.

Jake's text messages were set to sync with his camera roll—any photos people sent him went straight to it. Lizzie knew as much because she arranged it that way. She scrolled down, shocked by the pornographic images dominating the screen. They had to be sent to him via text messages from other people. Jake wouldn't take photos of girls like that. At least, despite time and new experiences, she wanted to believe he wouldn't.

Why did it take him leaving to change? He had tried so hard to win her over. Despite those efforts, she barely saw an improvement. In her eyes, at least. To the Morales family, Jake slipped through their fingers quicker than shrimp in a damaged net.

When all the pictures began looking the same, she exited them. Her next mission was to read Jake's text messages. She surveyed his contacts first. She scrolled down, scanning for female names. Scanning for her name.

It wasn't there.

She then scrolled back to the top, irritated by the group political chat. She thought about contributing to the conversation, pretending to be Jake. Or she could be herself, saying something that would embarrass him. Then again, from the looks of his photos, she no longer knew what it would take to achieve that.

She muted the group chat.

Writing to his friends as if it were coming from Jake was still on the table. She was ready to get revenge. She just needed to prepare, to equip herself with knowledge.

~ * ~

A thump woke Lizzie. It was daylight, she could tell without opening her eyes. She reached down to grab her phone off the floor. It wasn't until her hand grasped its thick girth that the events of last night came flooding back to her. Her phone hadn't fallen—Jake's had.

Still not fully awake, she typed the pin into Jake's phone, noting a new crack in the upper right corner from the fall. *Fitting*, she thought. New texts and a few missed calls had arrived in the early hours of the morning. She read the messages with muted intrigue compared to the night before.

Sorry man, got too wasted last night. Still mean what I said though. You gotta tell us where you are. We're worried sick about you.

That one was from Pedro. He and a man named Oscar corresponded with Jake the most, from what Lizzie gathered—assuming Jake's hook-up girls counted as individuals. To her, they were one and the same. And together, they dominated Jake's messages.

The text messages taught Lizzie a lot about Jake's life in Arizona. And just as important, she learned how he left there—without saying goodbye, just like he left her. On one hand, the messages comforted her; she wasn't the only person he abandoned. But they didn't reveal the why behind his silent departures.

One thing was clear—Jake never spoke about her to any of his friends or lovers. In text messages, at least. There was something else that became clear—a decision she hadn't expected the messages to lead her to. She wouldn't write to Jake's friends, impersonating him. They were victims of his silent departure, just like her. By pretending to be Jake, they would suffer the consequences instead of him.

An incoming call flashed on the screen. Firefly. It triggered memories from childhood; it was Jake's nickname for Tina. She snickered to herself. "So, you finally figured it out." She watched the pulsing green button, too tempting to resist. She pushed it.

"Hello! Hello? Yes, hello?"

It was Jake.

"Um. Hello? Is anyone there? I believe you have my phone. In fact, it is my phone." He let out a nervous chuckle.

Lizzie remained silent. It wasn't her plan to do so. But then again, she hadn't expected him to call.

"Well, um, if you can hear me, I just...I just would really like my phone back. You know how phones are these days, they've got . . . they've got a lot of stuff on them. And they're pretty expensive. Then again, I suppose that's why you wanted—"

Seriously? It was classic Jake to ramble on like that. Lizzie hung up on him, equipped with revenge. Reaching for her own cell, she looked up the number of Jake's phone company. She'd delete everything on his phone and cancel his plan—she had all his information to do it. Then, on her way to work in the afternoon, she'd stop by the battered women's shelter and donate it.

But first, she pulled a piece of paper from her bedside table and jotted down Pedro's number, just in case.

CHAPTER 12

Emma ~ Present

The villagers would notice Emma's absence at any moment, but she couldn't pull herself away. One more, then she'd get up.

Yo! Back in town because Tess wound up pregos. They say you went MIA. The pranks they come up with, eh?

She hoped Jake knew about Tess by now. She figured he had touched base with his contacts, given there weren't any new messages that had come through to her phone. Then again, messages from her own friends and family hadn't arrived either. She spent nearly two hours re-reading messages sent to Jake last night. There was something comforting about them. Something that made her feel at home. Like smells could bring back the past, so could text messages.

There was the time in chemistry class when she had forgotten to set her phone on silence, the day she broke up with Matt, and the day, many months later, when she broke up with him for good. She developed a soft spot for the people texting Jake, sharing their joys and pain as if they were her own friends, while she experienced the ups and downs of her own life.

She got out of bed and peered through a crack in her wall. Although the villagers had varying opinions on many topics, waking up early wasn't one of them. 'The early fish catches the mosquito, and the early fisherman catches the fish,' was the motto, accompanied with a shaking finger, to anyone who opened their door after six in the morning.

The river didn't appear to be carrying debris, much less a canoe. A good sign. Shuffling along the wall, Emma double-checked from different angles. Abuela would have been distraught to see her going through such trouble. 'Just remove a strip of bark,' she had said when the villagers built Emma's walls. 'And make it eye level for Emma. God made Emma tall so people can't look in on her.'

Convinced the coast was clear, Emma pushed the bamboo door open. Chuleta bolted out and ran down the notched tree trunk. Emma went back inside and picked a bright green *paruma* off the shelf that Hugo had built. It was a housewarming gift that would become theirs when they married, he had told her. She wondered, when Hugo was alone with his thoughts, if he ever doubted their future together. Tucking the *paruma* around her shorts, she grabbed the machete from her table and stepped onto the balcony, checking for, but not expecting, a new message on her phone.

"Whatcha doing?"

Emma jumped, recognizing Maya's voice too late, her body already tingling from fight-or-flight mode. "Just tidying up," Emma said, sliding the machete onto its hook before grabbing the broom beside it with a swift movement. Abuela was right about removing a strip of palm bark at eye level, but it was at the back of Emma's house, not the front, where she needed it most.

Maya spit a piece of sugarcane into the grass. "Oh, really?"

"Mm-hmm."

Emma's patience didn't match the leeriness she felt. It was too early in the morning for a visit from Maya—she should have been helping Rosa prepare breakfast.

Maya bit into another piece of sugarcane, her rotted teeth seemingly immune to pain. Flies buzzed around her chest, diving towards sugarcane pieces clinging to the leaves in her stuffed bra. She looked out at the river, and Emma fixated on Maya's arms. It was the first time she'd ever seen them in such a passive state—they weren't crossed, placed on her hips, or leaning against anything.

"I saw a light . . . a faint one . . . at your house last night." She spit sugarcane into the river, and minnows pulled it underwater. "What were you doing?"

"It was my cell phone. The nurses had signal yesterday so I wanted to see if I could get it too." Emma had wondered if her cellphone light would be detectable at night to anyone looking at her house. Now she knew.

Maya pulled sugarcane from between her teeth. "Did it work?"

"Seems so." Emma sensed this wasn't what she had come for; there was a softness in Maya's voice. "Is there something else?"

Maya stayed silent, looking out at the river with her back to Emma. Then she whispered, "Do you think my mom has AIDS?"

"Oh." Emma climbed down the staircase and walked under her house to get to the river's edge. She tried to put an arm around Maya but retreated when she pulled away.

"I don't know," Emma said softly. "There's no denying your mom's sick." She paused. "But it could be many things."

Maya remained quiet. Her eyes fixated on a shrimp cleaning its antennae in the river grass.

"Did your mom tell the nurses about her health issues?"

Maya shrugged. "I guess. She didn't want to talk about it though. Probably doesn't even remember the conversation."

Emma knew that wasn't true—Rosa was ill, but it hadn't affected her memory. Nitpicking details would scare off Maya, though, so Emma let it slide.

"They'll be meeting with her during the one-on-one sessions next week. You should ask your mom if you can join."

"That's not allowed."

"Yes, it is. Your mom needs to give permission for you to be in the room with her, that's all." Emma watched Maya shake her head back and forth—so slow that she wasn't sure if Maya knew she was doing it. "How about this," Emma said. "If the nurses give you trouble, find me and I'll see if I can help."

Maya tugged at her bottom lip. Even so, Emma noticed a smile form at the corners of her mouth.

~ * ~

Emma blinked. And then again.

Nearly every villager stood near the *tienda*. Even though they could all fit on the *tienda's* patio, many of them had formed a line that overflowed downhill towards the church, to the priest's dismay. In their hands, they held a cell phone. Some had their phones open and were pressing buttons, others waved chargers in the air, and a few banged their flip phone on themselves, trying to get them open.

"We'll make a sign-up sheet." Emma recognized Hugo's voice but, given the number of people crowded around, she was too far down the hill to see him. "I can assure you, as the mayor of Almagro, that everyone will have their turn."

Not wanting to push through the crowd, Emma backtracked to the priest. He sat in his plastic chair in his usual spot. However, the chair faced the *tienda*, a move she had rarely seen.

"Good afternoon, Father." Emma pointed towards the line. "Do you know where all those phones came from?"

The priest looked at her, the left armrest of his chair cracking under his weight as he reached his right hand into his pocket. A flip phone appeared in his hand, the same kind that the villagers had. He massaged it with his fingers. "This," he said, "was a gift from a man running for president some years ago. Hallelujah."

"Oh?"

"The man thought he could send us messages, reminding us to vote."

"Ah." Emma knew where that was going. Shortly after she arrived in Almagro, countless presidential candidates sent gifts to the villagers; the most common were food, bags of cement, and pamphlets about why they were best suited for the job. The villagers used the pamphlets as firewood to cook the gifted food. The cement still sat in a corner of the schoolhouse, destroyed by rodents and humidity.

The candidates failed to recognize the effort it would take for the villagers to get to the voting booth in Chepo.

And even if they managed to arrive there, they didn't understand the shame that would have ensued for those who were illiterate. Nonetheless, the villagers gave each candidate unwavering support from the comfort of their home—until a new gift arrived from a different candidate.

The priest cleared his throat. "The issues, of course, were the lack of signal and that there was no way to charge the phones."

Emma nodded.

"Now, both have changed."

"But how—"

The priest raised his hand. "They say you found reception."

Emma managed a single, slow nod. The priest wasn't keen on corrections, if even a clarification.

"So that takes care of the first issue." The phone slipped from the priest's hand, falling into a crease between his stomach rolls. "And Mateo fixed the second issue. He brought a battery back from the city today."

Emma went to speak but Abuela's voice coming from inside the church stopped her. "Anyone who doesn't believe in Saint Anthony is a fool." She shuffled out of the church towards them. "Isn't it great?" Abuela asked.

"Oh!" Emma forced down a giggle when Abuela rounded the corner. She balanced a flip phone in the palm of her right hand, a green cross shoved between its hinges. Liquid from the fresh cross dampened pieces of crumbling brown grass which splayed out at its base—the place where an old cross had once stood.

"A holy phone." Abuela placed it in Emma's hand.

"Thank—"

"Teacher Emma?" Federico shouted as he ran towards her. "Mateo's asking for you."

Emma smiled at Federico. "Coming," she said, placing the phone back in Abuela's outreached hands. She squeezed Abuela's arm as a goodbye and followed Federico up the hill, the villagers parting for them per Hugo's instructions. Emma smiled when Hugo insisted they part for Chuleta, too, although she knew they would have done so on their own.

When Emma arrived at the *tienda* counter, she found Mateo staring at a black plastic box the size of her head. Wires of various colors protruded from it. It had rusted nails, deep scratches, and mud handprints from whoever carried it.

"This is . . . well it's . . ." she chuckled, "What is it?"

"It's a car battery!" Mateo rubbed the box. "So we can charge our phones."

"Is that so?" Emma became aware of her own phone pressed against her chest—advice Carla had given her when she first arrived in Almagro. 'Don't be like Maya, she wastes her bra space on leaves,' she had said. Emma smiled at Mateo. "How'd you get it?"

Mateo flashed a glance at Carla. "I went to Chepo this morning. Thought it'd be worth the extra trip. Plus, the *tienda* was getting low on salt."

Emma found it odd that Mateo had willingly gone to Chepo on a Friday. Or, for that matter, any day that wasn't every other Wednesday. Under normal circumstances, the villagers would have called him out on it. But the arrival of the car battery stole their attention.

"How does it work?"

Mateo lifted his head. "I thought you would know."

"Well," Emma said, taking a charger from Carla's hand, "This is the kind of charger I'm familiar with, it goes in an outlet." She knew Mateo understood how outlets worked, along with a few other villagers who had been to Chepo.

"But this battery works. They showed me. You just have to hook up the phone to these wires here." He pinched the wires between his fingers and bent down for a closer look.

Emma didn't doubt the car battery could power their phones; she had heard about communities without electricity getting inventive with their efforts to keep pace with the modern world. But she had never seen it done before, let alone attempted it herself.

"Try it with mine." Carla set her phone on the *tienda* counter.

Mateo lunged for the phone. Emma raised her eyebrows at Carla, who shrugged.

Protests from the villagers erupted, defending their position on why their phones should be tested first. Hugo waved a piece of paper in the air. "Silence. Please. We'll follow the order of the sign-up sheet. The first person on this list will give their phone to Mateo for battery testing."

Emma was close enough to see the sheet; Abuela's fish drawing was in the first spot. When Hugo became mayor, he designed a system for illiterate adults where they were assigned a symbol to represent their signature. Shortly after receiving hers, Abuela changed her fish symbol to include a cross on its body. The other villagers followed suit with their own designs, but upon realizing symbol changing would be too hard to keep track of, Hugo banned it. Nonetheless, Abuela was allowed to keep her symbol change—she had a knack at being the first for things. And so, it was unsurprising to Emma that she was the first to sign up for battery charging, long before she found her phone.

"I have a better idea." Maya's voice floated up from the middle of the crowd. It was sweet—the kind she used when she was up to something. "Use Emma's phone. It still has battery." She glanced at Emma and smiled. "It'll be a better gauge if Mateo's efforts are working."

The villagers chattered amongst themselves, all in agreement.

"Excellent idea," Hugo said.

Emma felt the villagers fixate their eyes on her chest. She thought about backing out of the offer. After all, it was risky for both Mateo and her phone to have wires hooked up to the car battery. Plus, her data would run out that evening. What if a text message arrived? If Mateo had her phone, it would give her less time to communicate. But then she realized there was no point in holding onto her phone when it would soon be useless without battery.

"Okay." Emma reached into her bra. The villagers oohed and aahed, not because of where she pulled her phone from, which was perfectly acceptable in Almagro, but because her smartphone didn't look anything like their flip phones. She set it on the counter, patting its humidity damaged screen. "Give it a go." She paused, remembering the photo she had taken of herself with Chuleta that morning. "But first, let me try sending something to my family."

"I want to see!" María said, running up to her.

Andrés ran to Emma's other side. "Yes!" He dragged her hands down so they could watch.

Before long, every villager in Almagro crowded around Emma, learning how to send a photo from their *tienda* to the United States.

CHAPTER 13

Emma ~ Present

E mma didn't want to hunt for iguanas, but 'Maybe next time' no longer appeased the villagers. It would take her mind off her phone while Mateo worked on it, she told herself as she approached the river.

"You're one of us now," Rosa said, stabilizing the canoe as Emma stepped in.

Rosa was having a better day, health-wise, and wanted to join the iguana hunt. Nonetheless, Emma sensed the canoe was Rosa's way of stabilizing herself, rather than the other way around.

"Don't worry, *mi hija*." Eduardo held out his hand as she walked over the wooden benches towards him. "There are plenty of them here."

Eduardo's beliefs rarely conflicted with Emma's. And even now, although she didn't fully agree with his rationale, she understood where he was coming from. It wasn't uncommon to see an iguana lounging in the mango tree by her house or for one to shuffle through the grass at the river's edge. But the Peace Corps training she received prior to arriving in Almagro made it clear—iguanas were a protected species in Panama. She therefore cringed whenever the villagers brought one back for dinner.

But not as much as she used to.

She thought back to her first full day in Almagro. Carla had invited her over, proudly introducing her twelve kids and husband. Some of her eldest children had caught an iguana; they were cooking it over an open fire in their outdoor kitchen. In hindsight, the iguana they caught was small. So small that it wouldn't have provided more than a single bite of meat per family member. Carla had offered Emma the thigh, which Emma refused, explaining how iguanas were a protected species. Even now, she felt sick knowing the shame she put on Carla's family.

Emma wished Carla had come along to see her partaking in the iguana hunt. Emma had invited her but was met with a long—and rather odd—account of the chores she needed to get done; chores that Carla would normally be happy to put off.

"It's impossible. We'd sink." Martha smacked her toes against the mud along the river's edge, pointing at the canoe. "We set up your favorite bench instead."

"My favorite bench is my stool." Abuela put her hands on her hips. "I'll wait while you fetch a canoe without a hole in it."

Emma knew that wouldn't be happening; they had already agreed to borrow Hugo's canoe in exchange for a portion of whatever they managed to catch. The hole in Hugo's canoe was located high enough so water only flowed in when the river was choppy or Abuela brought her stool. Emma's job was to scoop water off the floor with a dried gourd when that happened.

"Don't forget, the children are coming, too," Eduardo said.

Abuela pushed her bag of grass into Martha's arms. "Such disrespect for the elderly. And," she said, stepping into the canoe with the steadiness of someone half her age, "an elderly *woman* at that."

The kids jumped into the canoe as it pulled away. Water dripped from their clothes and pooled around Emma's feet. There were twice as many kids as benches, but even if that weren't the case, they still would have chosen to sit around the one-inch edge of the dugout canoe. Emma knew how to sit on the edge, too, from when Mateo needed to use the benches to keep his rice elevated.

"That AIDS is scary, isn't it?" Abuela asked.

Martha sighed. "But surely no one in the village has it."

"One would assume so." Eduardo pushed his *palanca* stick into the water. "But the wind blows from the city sometimes."

The adults agreed.

Rosa steadied herself on the bench as the canoe tilted from restless kids. "I'm sure it'll be fine."

Emma wondered if anyone else had picked up on the hurry in Rosa's voice. She couldn't see Rosa's face but could picture her cheeks tightening.

"There's one!" Federico pointed to a branch hanging high over the water.

Kids hushed the adults with whispers before slipping into the river. Emma squinted up at the tree, trying to see what they saw. A part of her wanted to scream to warn the iguana. But then she caught sight of the kids arriving at the river's edge, the definition in their ribs visible from afar. It was a strange feeling, tucking away one value to make room for another.

"Do you see it?" Martha tilted her head back to look at Emma, speaking as loudly as possible without breaking a whisper.

"N . . . oh yes, now I do."

The kids had already identified the tree the iguana was in. That alone was admirable, given how the tree trunks along the river's edge twisted and turned together.

Rosa spoke louder. "They've got him."

"They do?" Emma stared at the closest kid to the iguana, who was only halfway up the tree.

"Yes, *mi hija*." Eduardo pointed. "The iguana has crawled to the end of the branch. It's not thick enough for it to push off, it can't jump to another tree." He sighed as if regretting reality. "Its only option is the river."

On cue, the iguana let go of the branch, its body wiggling back and forth through the air before landing on all fours into the water.

"We've got him!" shouted Martha as clapping and hollering echoed from the kids onshore.

"We do?" Emma said, studying the ripples where the iguana had fallen. But her voice was muffled by the villagers' boisterous cheers.

Emma didn't know iguanas could swim, let alone hold their breath for over twenty minutes—a fact that, twenty-two minutes later, she wouldn't soon forget. Sneaking in a few blinks, she refocused her view on the slice of river she was instructed to watch. What she was looking for, they said, was an iguana head. With each passing minute, the villagers' confidence about catching the iguana faded.

Federico sighed. "Maybe it swam around the bend."

"Impossible, I haven't even blinked," Abuela said, who insisted on being given the most difficult section of the river to monitor. Two children were secretly assigned the same spot.

Then, Martha pointed. "There it is!"

Emma looked and saw a brown dot floating in the river—something that could have been mistaken as a branch to her untrained eye. The villagers grabbed four *palancas* and thrust the canoe towards the iguana. Emma grasped her bench as it tipped side to side with each push, speeding along quicker than she knew a motorless canoe was capable of. Seeing them coming, the iguana disappeared under the water.

"We've really got him now, *mi hija*." Eduardo patted Emma's shoulder with one hand as he laid the *palanca* on the canoe floor with the other.

Eduardo was right, but it took time. Four times, in fact, of the iguana coming up for air, chasing it down with the canoe, and waiting for it to resurface. The iguana came up for air at shorter intervals each time as it tired out. On the fifth emergence, Eduardo pulled the canoe close enough so one of the girls could jump into the water, right on top of it. She emerged, holding the iguana by its neck as it tried wriggling out of her grip.

"Well done," Eduardo said, swinging it into the canoe.

Emma sat sideways on her seat, torn between watching and turning away as Eduardo moved the front legs of the iguana behind its head, using the iguana's long nails to hold its own legs in place. He then did the same with its back legs.

Eduardo stroked the iguana's bulging belly, smiling at Emma. "She has eggs."

Everyone erupted in cheers. Emma joined, too, as she pushed down the sickening feeling that clutched her throat.

~ * ~

A grain of rice fell on the full battery bar of Emma's phone. "I can't believe it worked."

"You should have more faith in me." Mateo patted the *tienda* counter.

"You know I do, it's just . . ." she gave him a perplexed look and started laughing, "Well, it's just I'm impressed."

He looked at her from the corner of his eye. "I'll let that one pass." Bending down, he rummaged through a box, emerging with cans of beans to restock the shelf with. "Ah, you should know, though. It lit up when you were gone. I tried to make it go away but didn't know how." He shrugged. "Guess I should've kept up with your English classes."

She smiled at him and tried to suppress hope that the light could have meant a message. "Don't worry about it."

He pursed his lips towards her gourd filled with iguana eggs. "Is that for me?"

Emma had other plans for the eggs. But given the circumstances, it was an Almagro imperative that she shared some with him. "Of course," she said. "Hand me a gourd."

She didn't have the stomach to grab the eggs with her hand like Martha did earlier when she was divvying up the four iguanas they caught, so Emma poured the eggs instead. The villagers had given Emma iguana eggs to eat in the past. But they had been dug up from the ground after they'd already been laid and had a powdery coat. In contrast, these eggs were straight from the iguana's body, veins scribbling stories on undeveloped shells of lives cut short. The liquid sacs made a smacking sound as they fell into the gourd, bumping against each other until they settled into place.

"I'll be eating like a puma tonight!"

Emma scrunched her face. "Enjoy it."

Mateo laughed, pointing at the gourd. "You best be eating the rest of those."

Chuleta ran in circles around the *tienda* patio, chasing a beetle with an injured wing—quite possibly, Emma thought, caused by Chuleta herself. Emma tapped her thigh. "Let's go," she said to Chuleta, smiling at Mateo in response.

She walked down the first dirt step leading to the village. Her foot hovered over the next step but she felt her phone pressing against her chest. *Why wait?* She pulled it out and saw a red eight hovering above the message icon. Her stomach tightened. Knowing the suspense would be with her the rest of the afternoon, she tapped it, simultaneously walking down the dirt steps, her feet knowing how to manage the rocks and tree roots along the way.

Mom. Brother. Aunt. Mom. Friend. Mom. Mom.

And then the final message, from an unknown sender.

Hey. Figure this won't get to you. But it's been so long since we've tried contacting you and, well, Lizzie wrote. Thinking about responding. Thoughts? Probably should let this weed run through me first. P.S.- Sorry to the person who texted me last time if this is still your number.

A thigh-high person ran up to Emma, but she was so engrossed in the message that she looked up too late. "Oh, Andre*yes!*" she said, nearly tumbling over him as he grinned at her. She smiled back, forced the message out of her mind, and quizzed him in English. "How are you?"

"Yes!" he said, taking her hand and pulling her towards the soccer field.

Her phone felt heavy in her hand with the weight of the words she had just read. She looked at him and frowned. "I can't play today, buddy."

He mimicked her frown and jumped up to see the contents of her gourd. "Is that for me?"

"Nope." She pinched his chin. "It's for Carla."

"Then I'll come with you." He grabbed her hand and led her the short distance to Carla's house. Even from Emma's viewpoint in the soccer field, she could see Carla straddling a rock beside the creek, washing clothes.

Carla startled when they approached. "I wasn't expecting you!" She rinsed her hands in the creek and hurried over to Emma, kissing her cheek. "So busy. I've been so busy today, I tell you."

Emma chuckled, alarmed by Carla's jumpiness. She handed her the gourd. "These are for you."

Carla rubbed Emma's arm, giving her a knowing smile. And just like that, a year's worth of guilt faded from when Emma had declined Carla's iguana meal.

"So," Carla turned towards her house, "I wanted you to take a look at my phone." She glanced over her shoulder. "You have a minute, don't you?"

"Of course." Emma followed Carla into her house, setting her own phone on the porch table.

"It's broken," she said, pulling her phone from a woven basket.

Emma flipped it open. "The number eight is missing."

"Can you fix it?"

Emma tilted her head, still looking at the phone. "Do you have the missing key?"

"No," she said, drawing out the word as hope faded from her voice.

Emma mustered the courage to ask what she had been wondering about all day. It was Carla, after all. She wouldn't mind.

"So out of curiosity . . . if your phone was working, who would you call?"

Carla laughed. "Why, the other villagers, of course!" She pulled the cloth door aside and they walked back onto the porch.

Andrés spun around when he heard them, his mouth open and eyes wide as he spread himself in front of the table.

Emma put her hands on her hips. "What were you doing?" She was sure she saw—and heard—her phone thump to the table.

"Nothing." He shook his head, the initial shock of her and Carla returning already wearing off. He ran across the porch, climbing up a post with bare feet.

Emma picked up her phone off the table. The quick movement caused the screen to flash on. There, sitting before her, was the photo of her and Chuleta that she had taken that morning. Beneath it, a single word appeared.

YES

"Andrés!" Her voice came out as a whisper despite the fury in her mind. "Did you do this?" She stared at the photo and message, both of which had already sent through to the person who had written Jake.

Andrés jumped down from the post and giggled, exclaiming in English, "Yes! Your turn!"

CHAPTER 14

Emma ~ Present

It was already time for the MINSA nurses to return, and the villagers were in a frenzy with preparations, guessing the kind of meat they would bring, and arguing about the best way to prepare it. Of the many choices involved with receiving guests in Almagro, deciding who would cook lunch was easier this time; in a village so small, one-quarter of the families already had a family member representing them in the kitchen during MINSA's first visit, so they weren't allowed to be selected this time around.

Emma noticed the taut strings of Rosa's hammock from her balcony, so she decided to pay her a visit before heading to the school. There hadn't been much activity coming from her house the past week, most notably from Maya. While Emma enjoyed the break, it concerned her.

Rosa spotted Emma through a hole in the hammock as she approached. "Perfect timing."

"Is that so?" Emma kissed her on the cheek, handing her a loaf wrapped in cloth. "I made you some banana bread."

Rosa smiled the kind of smile that would seem insincere to an outsider. But Emma knew that on her bad health days, such smiles radiated appreciation. Rosa wiped drops of sweat from her face; sweat that could have been mistaken for tears if it wasn't for the heat, given her pale complexion.

Maya appeared from the side of the house, a gourd filled with coffee beans and dried corn kernels in her hand. She raised her eyebrows at Emma in greeting and poured the contents of the gourd into a rusty manual grinder.

Rosa shifted in her hammock. "Won't you stay for coffee?"

Emma smiled. She never liked coffee—and still didn't. But the corn in Almagro's 'poor man's coffee' mix added a sweet flavor that made drinking it tolerable.

"Of course, thank you."

She helped herself to a seat on a tattered hammock across from Rosa, Chuleta lying on the dirt floor beneath her feet. In moments like these, she was caught off guard by her life; it amazed her how comfortable she had become with making herself at home in the villagers' houses.

Maya ground the mixture, pausing every few strokes to stare at the river. "Did you hear the floating *tienda's* coming?" she asked.

The floating *tienda* was on the brink of its twenty-fifth birthday. Although there were those who were still leery of it, most villagers welcomed its presence—including Mateo, despite it distributing a portion of the villagers' stipend to his competition. Until Mateo built his *tienda*, there wasn't anything within reasonable distance to purchase with the government's quarterly offering, which was distributed per household. So once Natalie, the floating *tienda* owner, found out about the stipend, she started taking her canoe to Almagro in tandem with its arrival.

"I did." Emma watched a piece of Maya's chipped nail polish dangle over the coffee mixture, threatening to fall in.

Rosa sighed, looking at Emma but directing her words at Maya. "I don't know where you get the money to buy all that stuff unless you're hoarding the cash we give you to buy food." She looked at Emma. "The things she buys are expensive."

A thin smile crossed Maya's lips and her eyes fixated on Emma's house. "I have my ways."

Rosa rubbed her stomach. "I wish she'd get married. We have a plot of land right beside us where she could build a house."

"Is that what you want, Maya?"

As much as Emma didn't care to get involved with the topic, she didn't like talking about Maya as if she weren't there.

Maya stared at the river, giving no indication she had heard the question.

~ * ~

The schoolhouse had been attacked by mosquitos, according to the children who Emma encountered along the way. Emma took a deep breath, assessing the wall when she arrived. Light blue paint spotted the original darker blue paint where touchups had been made. "It's not so bad," she said.

Eduardo ran a hand over his face, brushing off sweat. "I can't believe I used the wrong paint."

It was an innocent mistake. A couple of years ago, the Ministry of Education promised a second teacher in exchange for Almagro hosting students from a village an hour upstream. And not just any teacher—a professor, like Sonya, who had the credentials to teach secondary school. The villagers in Almagro worked together to build a second classroom, using cement blocks sent from the ministry. They also sent paint, but it was a lighter shade of blue. So, the villagers decided to use the new paint inside the classroom and their extra cans of original, darker paint for the outside.

"Maybe you started a trend." Emma smiled at him. "It's undeniably Almagro's school."

Carla walked up to them, holding a box that nearly covered her face. "I agree," she said, the two words separated by heavy breathing. She set the box down.

Abuela clapped her hands and pointed at the cardboard. "Not there!" She had been managing the villagers carrying supplies from the river for the past half hour, honing her skills from when she used to be mayor. But this time, she did so from the comfort of her stool beneath a tree. She stared down at the sun encroaching on her feet and called to the nearest teenager. "Help me. The shade is moving."

Meanwhile, Hugo redirected those carrying lunch supplies and medical equipment so they'd be taken to the correct locations. There were more boxes than last time. Many more. And many were bigger. The villagers had their own hunches about what they were, ranging from snacks to spearguns.

Rebecca and the nurses emerged into the schoolyard. Despite the long canoe journey, they looked shower fresh with their hair gelled and pulled back in tight buns. They boasted more bling than last time—a fashion trend in Panama City—with shiny, plastic diamonds protruding from their hair ties and jean pockets. It was a stark contrast to their solid blue-collared MINSA shirts. But Emma knew this was acceptable, to the point of being expected, from professionals in Panama.

Rebecca rushed over to Emma. "It feels like forever since the last time we saw each other," she said, giving her a kiss on the cheek.

Red lipstick ran from the corners of Rebecca's lips and Emma wished she had a mirror to check if any had rubbed off on her face. "It does," Emma said, thoughts of the cell phone incident with Andrés coming back to her. She pushed it from her mind; now wasn't the time to dwell on what happened.

Rebecca's smile faded. She took Emma's hand, leading her near the latrine where they were out of hearing range of the villagers. The smell of stale feces permeated the air from the door being open ajar; Hugo managed to break the lock that morning.

"We're bringing bad news today." Rebecca took Emma's hands, checking again to make sure no one was nearby. "Some of the villagers have HIV. It's not many, but given how small the community is, it makes for a high percentage."

Emma felt her body go still.

Rebecca let go of her hands. "We're trying to figure out how it got here. Are there many people from *afuera* that visit? I can't imagine the villagers have the means to leave very often."

Emma shook her head slowly, knowing that *afuera* meant any place outside of Almagro. "Not that I can think of." She paused. "Not really. I mean, people from the government occasionally visit; political candidates and those who give the villagers their stipends. But their visits are short." She looked across the schoolyard where the villagers continued their duties while keeping a watchful eye on her and Rebecca. "And monitored, if you know what I mean."

"Right." Rebecca took a deep breath. "So, let's do this. We'll give them time to get the rice and pork going, then I'll start the meeting. I'll explain the situation followed by the one-on-one consultations they were already promised. It'll be impossible for them to guess who tested positive that way." She put her hand on Emma's shoulder. "I imagine there'll be *bochinche* that comes from this, but things have to remain confidential."

Rebecca was right. Emma could only imagine the gossip that would ensue. She felt a pang for those who would be receiving bad news—whoever they were—and knew that gossip was the last thing they needed while coping with their diagnosis.

~ * ~

"I've failed as mayor." Hugo stood at the back of the classroom, staring at Rebecca and the nurses with sadness so deep that Emma wondered if he—or any of the villagers—would find happiness in the schoolroom again.

Rebecca shook her head, her voice firm. "No, you haven't."

They were nearly two hours into the meeting and Emma knew Rebecca's patience was on the verge of clashing with her empathy. Even so, she commended her for taking so much time to address the villagers' questions and theories. There was still more to be done, though; she and the nurses had to start—and finish—the one-on-one sessions before mid-afternoon so they could get back to Chepo before dark.

"I'm telling you, it's Rosa. She's been ill for ages." Abuela's steady voice didn't match her nervous fingers. They worked away weaving crosses from the newest batch of grass she had sent Federico to collect mid-meeting.

"Haven't you been listening?" Maya glared at Abuela. "She said people can have it without showing symptoms."

Emma wished she could scoop up Rosa and take her out of the room; she had been the villagers' main target during the meeting. Rosa seemed to vacillate between frustration and sadness, a tear from both emotions occasionally escaping. As much as Emma didn't appreciate the villagers trying to identify those who tested positive, she, too, was curious. It was human nature to want to know, she reasoned.

"This is the work of the devil." Abuela flung her hand behind her head. Eduardo took the cross she held and passed it to a villager behind him. Two-thirds of the villagers now had a cross from her, and Abuela was determined to make one for everyone.

Rebecca cleared her throat. "The important thing to remember is that there's medicine. That, and kindness, will make HIV manageable."

"*Si Dios quiere*," the villagers murmured.

"Yes." Rebecca nodded. "If God wants."

Hugo pointed at the chalkboard, trying to re-establish his leadership role. "And we must follow the recommendations of Rebecca," he added.

Emma wondered how Sonya would feel if she saw her chalkboard. The visuals she and Emma drew for their ninth grade HIV class were far less explicit than those drawn that day. It wasn't Rebecca's intention to elaborate on such details. But when the villagers asked for repeated clarification on which body parts HIV most commonly entered through, she gave them a visual. Multiple visuals. It was worth it, Emma decided, for the laughter that ensued in an otherwise sorrowful room.

The sound of footsteps running down the hall outside of the classroom interrupted Emma's thoughts. Instead of using the door, which children under thirteen were instructed to stay away from, Andrés pulled himself up to the window. He wrapped his arms around the window's open-air, decorative cement pieces, peering in at the adults. "The rice is burning!"

The room filled with gasps as people jumped up from their seats. Pushing each other, they tried to defy the bottleneck effect created by a single door. Outside, smoke rose from the pot which hovered above firewood that even Emma, with her lack of kitchen knowledge, knew was burning too strongly.

Rebecca wiped sweat from her brow. "Looks like we'll be eating crispy rice today."

"Indeed," Emma said, staring at the pot. The villagers dashed around the kitchen, determined to find a person to blame. The issue, she knew, was that there wasn't a single villager they could identify, for the task of finding and managing the firewood was never assigned to one person.

It was always two.

CHAPTER 15

Emma ~ Present

Life in Almagro revolved around consistency. It didn't mean that the villagers' emotions never varied, as a day was deemed good or bad depending on how many fish they caught. Or whether or not it rained, which was good or bad depending on the season. But the day of MINSA's visit turned out to be a day when the villagers went through an extreme range of emotions.

"It's here?" Maya rounded the corner of the school, where she had been hovering all day.

Emma noted the unusual behavior, given that Maya typically avoided village gatherings. "Seems so." She dragged a burned plantain leaf to the compost pile, left over from the pot of rice. Chuleta bit and stepped on it, black ashes streaking her coat.

"Good."

Emma stopped upon hearing Maya's lackluster tone. Mere hours had passed since she ground coffee on her porch, excited for the floating *tienda's* arrival. Emma understood why that would've changed, given the nature of Rebecca's meeting. But the strangest part was how Maya's stature didn't match the lifelessness in her voice. Her head was held high, her back curved. Since there wasn't anyone within hearing range of them, Emma brought up Rosa.

"Did you talk to your mom about joining her one-on-one?"

Maya nodded.

"And?"

"She said I could go." Maya stared back at the classroom door. "But she changed her mind after the meeting."

"Ah." Emma tossed the plantain leaf into the compost pile. She gave Maya a reassuring smile. "Well, at least she went."

"Yeah. She went home."

"Oh." Emma's heart sunk, both for Maya and Rosa. She walked back to Maya, attempting to brush the soot off her hands. But instead of ridding herself of the powdery pieces of plantain leaf, they smeared across her palms. "Do you want me to talk to her?"

"There's no point." Maya's words were sharp. She lifted her torso higher so that her head was level with Emma's shoulder.

Emma knew meddling could do more harm than good. "Very well."

"Emma, look!" Carla ran towards them with clamped hands.

"What's that?" Emma's heart filled upon seeing Carla's enthusiasm since Rebecca's meeting had drained the villagers' happiness like rain stripped away topsoil during a storm.

"They call it a card." She opened her hands and held them up to Emma's chin. Can you put it in my phone?" Carla pulled the card back and examined it. "I know I can't call everyone, but not all the villagers have an eight in their number."

Emma smiled. "Of course."

"I want to learn too!" Abuela waved at them from her stool.

Carla raised her eyebrows at Emma as they walked together towards Abuela, whose stool sat between the doors of the two classrooms, fifteen feet back. Abuela had wanted to watch—and listen—to everyone meeting with the nurses, but Rebecca wouldn't have it.

"So, as I was saying," Emma held up the card for Carla and Abuela to see, "you have to scratch off this area here—"

"I'll do it." Abuela pulled a cross from her basket and used the long end to scratch off the film. "The end where Jesus' blood rolled down," she said. Her arthritic knuckles hid her progress, but even so, Emma could tell she was almost finished.

"Careful not to scratch too much, you could damage the numbers."

Abuela brushed the card with her cross to get rid of the debris. Bits of dried grass took its place. "All set. And," she looked at Emma, "not a scratch too much."

Emma smiled and showed them how to add data using the code. "And just like that, it's ready to be used."

"Oh, I can't wait!" Abuela wiggled her feet back and forth on her stool, trying to grab the phone from Carla. "I'll be able to call the villagers to ask if they have the AIDS!"

"Carla!"

Emma looked up at the nurse standing in the classroom doorway. She had a big smile on her face, the same kind Emma used to hide her exhaustion at the end of a long day.

"What would I do without you?" Carla asked. She hugged Emma before hurrying towards the nurse, smiling at Emma one last time over her shoulder.

~ * ~

The floating *tienda* was impressive. Its store operated from a canoe longer than any canoe in Almagro. But its width was most stunning of all. It was packed to the brim and divided into sections—food, beauty, clothes, toys, and tools. The full load made it impossible for the villagers to walk through, so shopping was done from the outside, in the river.

Emma took another step. Mud from the river's bottom oozed between her toes. She was almost to the backside of the canoe, the deepest part she would have to stand in and the area that took the most time to get around, for the villagers stopped to admire, touch, and pray by the canoe's motor. Meanwhile, Chuleta swam around her, fascinated by the human chain circling the canoe.

"I'm all out." The voice came from somewhere inside the canoe.

"Already? What a shame." Emma recognized Martha's voice and moved her head around the boxes piled high in the canoe, trying to get a view of her standing in the water on the opposite side.

Martha caught a glimpse of her. "Just the person I was looking for. Emma, is there anything else I can put in my phone to make calls?"

"No," said the voice from inside the canoe.

"That's right. Unfortunately, there isn't." Emma shrugged, but Martha didn't see it since she already moved forward in line.

A thick wedge shoe flashed by between a gap in the boxes. Natalie's shoe. It looked high enough to throw her off on even ground, let alone a canoe. Diamond studs lined the straps and her bare ankle showed, although Emma knew more skin showed than that, based on the account of villagers who had visited the floating *tienda* earlier in the day between their one-on-one meetings.

"So, as I was saying, I think he'd be perfect for you." Rebecca moved forward through the water in her skinny jeans and flicked a floating leaf away from her waist. While the other two nurses finished up the last one-on-one sessions, Rebecca had decided to accompany Emma to the floating *tienda*.

Emma shook her head. "It'd be too hard. Almagro's so remote, it would basically be a long-distance relationship."

"But you've got cell phone signal now. That's something."

"Right, but my phone isn't set up to use Panamanian phone cards. I'd have to pull data from my plan in the U.S. which would cost more than my living expenses."

Emma walked around the back of the canoe, running her hand around the motor. She knew better than to ignore it—Mateo had received backlash from the villagers when he failed to do so earlier in the day. She understood where he was coming from; motors weren't as big of a deal for him. He'd sometimes see them on the river near the port that led to Chepo when he picked up *tienda* supplies.

"So," Rebecca said, pulling a *paruma* from the canoe and holding it in front of her, "there are two fixes to your dilemma. First, we'll get you a flip phone. Then," she set the *paruma* back in the canoe, "I'll let you connect to my data so you can check your U.S. phone. You can tell your friends and family about your new number."

Emma didn't know what to say. One of the many things she loved about Almagro was her distance from technology. But sometimes she missed having it.

Her thoughts turned to Andrés' cryptic photo and 'Yes' message. She hadn't turned her phone back on since that day. A part of her wanted to respond as soon as she realized what happened. The other part of her wondered if the message even mattered, if it was too late. After all, reception in Almagro was far from good, so it seemed likely that the text she received was from a long time ago. She decided to meet her feelings in the middle—wait and see if the sender responded before her data ran out. The person never replied, so she shut off her phone before being charged for another day of international use. She then fell back to the familiar place of pondering scenarios about what could have happened to Jake.

A high-pitched voice came from behind the boxes. "Did I hear you're looking for a phone?" Natalie emerged with her forty-three-year-old body tucked into a twenty-year old's clothes. A thick layer of makeup clumped around her eyes and cheeks from a day's worth of sun and humidity. She leaned down, her breasts flapping back and forth as the canoe tipped towards Emma. "Pick your favorite," she said, holding up five flip phones.

Emma hesitated, trying not to stare at Natalie's shaved eyebrows painted over by a black streak of makeup.

"Go on." She moved the phones closer to Emma's face.

"Do you have a preference?" Rebecca asked.

Emma took a step back, the phones too close for her to see them well. "Oh, well, I don't really think I ne—"

"We'll take this one." Rebecca pointed to a grey flip phone, careful not to let water drip off her finger and onto it since she pulled her hand out of the river.

"But—"

"No buts." She winked. "It's my brother, my treat."

Emma couldn't tell who else came down to the floating *tienda* while she was behind the canoe, but she was thankful that Maya had already visited and Abuela wasn't feeling up to walking down the muddy slope to the shore. That eliminated two sources of gossip. It didn't mean she was in the clear, though. She reluctantly watched Rebecca pay for her new phone.

"Would you like some lemonade?" It was the least she could do, Emma decided.

"Oh, yes! There's something about Almagro's produce that I love."

Emma chuckled. "It's fresh, for starters."

Water ran down their hips and streaked through the mud on their feet when they walked out of the river. Emma led Rebecca to her house, following the river's shoreline. It was the long way, distance-wise, but would save them time compared to cutting through the soccer field where they'd be stopped by others.

"Oh, my!" Rebecca exclaimed as they approached Emma's house.

Emma found Rebecca's reaction excessive since Hugo had already shown the nurses the outside of her house. But then she followed Rebecca's finger to a spot halfway up her staircase where a chunk of fish lay. This time, it was the middlemost part, including a fin and part of its belly. Black spots speckled its flesh—not from the color of the fish's skin, but from flies. Blood dripped onto the step beneath it. It pooled there, the outermost edges beginning to dry. Chuleta barked and dashed up the stairs, picking up the fish and dropping it on the balcony beside Emma's outdoor kitchen.

"Looks like someone left a gift for Chuleta," Emma said.

"Oh, how nice! Does that happen often?"

Emma paused, then softly said, "Lately, it seems so." Subconsciously, she glanced at her machete. If her gut was right, she'd be hearing rustling in the grass by the river that night.

"So, about this American phone of yours." Rebecca followed Emma up the notched tree trunk, leaning forward and clutching its round sides as she made her way to the top. "Let's get you connected to my data."

Emma went into her room to get her phone and then sat with Rebecca, who already had her legs hanging over the six-foot balcony. She admired how easily Rebecca adapted to life in Almagro. Perhaps her moving there wasn't such an impulsive idea after all.

Rebecca grinned and handed the phone back. "All set."

The phone vibrated just as it landed in Emma's hand. She looked down, instinctively swiping it open before taking the time to process her action. There, sitting in front of her, was a message from Jake's friend.

Dude, glad you found someone and you're alright but what kind of response was that? Where are you?

CHAPTER 16

Jake ~ Present

Jake was thankful his callouses had rehardened, though it wasn't part of the plan. More than a year had passed since he returned to Charleston. With each day, he felt a stronger urge to leave again. But not to Arizona.

He lugged another bucket of water onto the dock. "It doesn't make sense."

"You know how they are." Tina scrubbed the shrimping boat's stern. "It would cost money for a system that already works."

"Easy for you to say." Jake tossed water in her direction. Tulip barked, running back and forth on the dock, watching its spray fall into the harbor. Jake headed back to the hose to fill up another bucket. It was a new hose, by the Morales' family standards. His parents bought it when he was a teenager after they grew tired of patching up the old one. The hose was long enough to rinse off the first half of the dock but not the far end where their shrimp boat sat—and thus, where most of the debris accumulated.

Tina jumped off the boat and walked towards him. "Know where your phone's at?" She attempted a sly grin.

Jake watched a cloud cast its shadow over the dock. He had become the joke of his family after losing two phones in less than two years. The most recent incident happened last week when he forgot he'd put his phone on the dock. 'No, son!' his dad had shouted as Jake blasted his phone with the hose, realizing his mistake only after it hit the water. The worst part was diving to retrieve it on the muddy harbor bottom. Not ideal, but manageable. Losing his first phone, though, was rougher than he expected. If he'd been smart, he would have backed up his contacts. In hindsight, he also would've purchased a new phone sooner.

"Looking forward to tomorrow night?"

Jake stayed silent and kicked a shrimp tail off the dock.

"C'mon, it'll be fun. It's been too long since you've gone shaggin'." Tina winked. "You might even meet a girl."

Jake looked away from her. Tina knew how much summers at Shaggin' on the Cooper meant to him. As much as a person could know who wasn't Lizzie, that was. Lizzie was the reason he had learned to shag; he even won *Most Likely to be a Famous Shagger* his senior year of high school. It wasn't until June of that same year when she agreed to dance with him for the first time. 'You're not so bad,' she'd said. It meant more to him than any award. Shaggin' with Lizzie was hit and miss after that, until they started dating. They soon grew a reputation at Shaggin' on the Cooper. Attendees would circle around them, cheering them on to perform together.

"Your father said you wanted some sweet tea." Isabella approached them with two glasses.

"Thanks, Mom." Jake walked over and downed half a glass before Tina took a sip of hers.

"You know how I feel about drinking tea so soon before lunch."

Jake set his empty glass back on the tray. "We're plenty hungry."

"Agreed." Tina lifted her glass. "But I'll keep mine here a little longer."

Isabella smiled and turned towards the house. "Very well."

"You know," Tina said as she and Jake walked back to the shrimp boat, "we should go to the diner sometime."

"Yeah." Jake's voice trailed off. He had gone to the diner a few times since returning home, but it didn't feel the same anymore. He would have only gone a couple of times, if it weren't for realizing that he lost his phone the day after having supper there. He and Tina returned to the diner—and gas station and store—the next morning, retracing their steps trying to find it. The answer was the same every time. 'I'm sorry, we don't have your phone.'

Except at the diner.

The cheery hostess they spoke to said, 'Why, there was a phone left here yesterday. Just give me a moment, and I'll see if it's yours.' It turned out the phone had already been claimed, although Jake sometimes wondered if it was his that had been taken.

He grabbed at his pocket, feeling for the lump of his newest cell. He didn't have many people to talk to these days, but the issues he went through with his first phone didn't make buyer procrastination worth it.

Tina chattered on about Shaggin' on the Cooper. "I've heard quite a few of our high school friends have been there lately. Back in town for the summer, I'm sure. It'd be great to see them again."

"They wouldn't want to see me."

She shook her head. "Time has passed. They're older now. We're all older."

"Even so, I didn't treat them well . . . .at the end and all."

"Right. And I'm sure they'd love to hear that from you." She shrugged. "Could be a new start."

It wasn't a bad idea. For as much as Jake longed to leave Charleston, he felt an equal pull to make things right with the people he hurt, including Lizzie, though without her he wouldn't have made rifts with his high school friends in the first place.

Guilt nudged him as he thought back to Arizona. He didn't mean to cut ties with his friends there. Not permanently. An easy escape was all he wanted. Once he realized that Arizona wasn't fulfilling him, he had the urge to leave. Fast. Without anyone trying to convince him otherwise. Even then he knew it wasn't fair to leave his friends the way he did.

But leaving was familiar.

He would see Lizzie again someday, he figured. After all, they had almost crossed paths at the diner, just after he returned from Arizona. A neighbor told him so the next morning when their shrimp boats passed each other. Jake's dad tried to stop the man, but it was too late.

Jake sighed and ran his hand through his hair as he and Tina walked back to the house. "Do you think she'll stay in Kentucky long?"

Tina hesitated. "I don't know."

"Just thinking. If I'm going to make amends with the past, it might as well include her."

Jake watched Tina tense up. He knew his family was relieved when Lizzie got let go from the diner for taking home fish fillets. She built a side business selling them on a street corner, figuring she wouldn't get caught doing so one town over. Exasperated, Lizzie's parents sent her to Kentucky to help her aunt on the farm.

"That's . . . thoughtful of you." Tina spoke the words carefully.

"She's not the hardest one to track down, though." Jake stopped in the yard before they got close enough to the screen door where their parents could hear. "I don't have the means to get in touch with the people I knew in Arizona. All my contacts were lost with my phone."

He remembered the day he went to the cell phone store, nearly four months after he had lost his first phone. 'We're sorry. We gave your number to someone else,' the man in customer service had told him. 'You canceled your plan.' At the time, Jake didn't care, aside from the nuisance of putting his family's contacts in his new phone. It was just as much the phone company's mistake as it was his; his account was set to automatic billing, so he never checked to see if money was—or wasn't—being paid to them. But he never would have guessed that they reassigned old phone numbers so quickly.

Stress-free months ensued during the time he spent without a phone. It was almost enough to negate the impact of being disconnected from the people he met in Arizona. But before long, the guilt for how he left Arizona gripped him. A small nick on his heart at first. Then more, until the nicks became scratches that piled up in depth, a wound he knew could only heal by making amends.

He turned his attention back to Tina, who hadn't stopped talking. ". . . or you could drive out there."

"To Arizona?"

"Yeah. I mean, I don't want you to, of course. Just trying to cover all the bases."

"No." Jake shook his head. "Besides, old Sheba would never make it."

Tina bent down and threw a tennis ball for Tulip. "Good. We can't risk losing you to impulse again."

~ * ~

Jake never pictured being in his twenties and driving to Shaggin' on the Cooper with his sister. He also never imagined there would be so much traffic in Charleston, the Lowcountry lifestyle turning unsuspecting tourists into residents. He wished change weren't so constant. But since it was, he'd rather be the one making it.

"There's nothing like the smell of saltwater on shaggin' night," Tina said, stepping out of her truck.

Jake took a deep breath. "Agreed."

Shaggin' on the Cooper didn't feel the same as it used to. Jake leaned against the railing and stared at the river. The tide was low. Despite the darkness, enough light shone from the boardwalk to showcase shadows of crabs racing to and from their mud homes. He took a sip of beer. How did people find strangers to dance with? He never needed to know the trick before tonight. And now he knew that whatever the trick was, it didn't come to him naturally. Tina was long gone, dancing with a guy in overalls. 'He's so cute!' she'd said. 'But I don't want to leave you alone.' 'Nonsense,' he told her.

And then there were his high school friends. Tina was convinced they would be there. He hadn't seen any yet, but he wasn't proactive about looking for them, either.

"Shrimp for your thoughts?"

Jake's skin prickled. Lizzie hated overused sayings, so she switched 'penny' to 'shrimp' one day when they were peeling a bowl of shrimp by the harbor. Even if it weren't for that saying though, he would recognize her voice with a single word. Any word.

He turned around and looked at her.

"I took a bus back." She leaned against the boardwalk railing, facing the river, mimicking his pose. There was a five-foot gap between them—far from a conversational distance. "Couldn't stand that place." She pulled a blade of grass from her mouth, twirled it, then put it back in on the opposite side.

Jake turned back to the river. He wasn't sure what he would feel if—when—he saw Lizzie again. But he expected to feel *something*. Realizing he looked shocked, he unclenched his jaw and softened his gaze.

"Running away got you far, huh?" She pressed her hip into the railing. "All the way here."

Jake continued looking at the water. This was an opportunity to make amends with his past. He knew so, even as he pushed down the anger that began stirring within him. Growing up, Lizzie knew how to tug and pull at his emotions. She knew what she was doing, and he knew it too. He let her do it. He left for Arizona angry with her and now, with her standing there, he could only be angry at himself for not walking away sooner.

But he also missed her. Her voice, her perfume, her confidence.

"You're lucky I'm even talking to you."

"You're right." His voice cracked, but it was a start.

She scraped her tooth with a pinky. "You used to tell me I was right all the time."

"I shouldn't have." He looked at her from the corner of his eye, his head still facing the river.

"Hey." Her voice was sharp. "You're the one who left."

He turned towards her. "I left," he said slowly, "because nothing I did was ever good enough for you." He found his strength and continued. "And anything I did that was good in your eyes was the wron—"

"Not fair. You left without telling me. Without even calling me. Don't act like you're better than me."

"I'm not trying to—"

Lizzie held up her hand. "If you're not going to apologize, I'm gone."

"I *am* sorry." Jake took a step towards her. "Truly." He took another step. "It was wrong of me to leave the way I did." He paused, then sighed. "But leaving itself wasn't wrong."

She swung her body around so her stomach pressed against the railing. He studied her arms and hands. She had added more tattoos—far more—since he left. He knew she wouldn't have done so unless they meant something to her. It led him to wonder what kind of experiences she'd had since they last saw each other. And how long it took her to be with another man. He shook his head; it wasn't a thought that was good for him.

Lizzie remained quiet.

"Time has a way of showing the same situation in a different light, don't you think?" he asked.

She pulled the blade of grass from her mouth, which slumped in uneven segments. Releasing its hold, she watched it fall to the mud. "You were always too philosophical."

"Lizzie."

"Fine. Agreed. Happy?"

"No." He leaned towards her. "Relieved, perhaps." He sighed. "Funny, I was just talking with Tina about wanting to reconcile the past."

"So just like that everything's better?" She stepped away from him. "I was angry with you. So—" her voice choked—for less than a second—and what came after sounded twice as strong to make up for it. "Livid. So livid."

"I know."

"No." She squeezed the railing. Tight at first, then tighter. "You don't. I wasn't the nicest to you, I get that. But I still loved you."

He nodded "I—"

Lizzie flung up her hand. "And then you *left*." She paused, long enough for the silence to feel awkward if it were between two people other than them.

"If it's any consolation," he said, "I left other people, too."

She held his eyes in her stare, staying silent. Then, when she was on the verge of blinking, she spoke. "Oh?"

"Yeah." He noted the shift in her tone. "I made friends in Arizona. Lots of them. In hindsight . . . well, Arizona wasn't good for me. And . . ." He glanced over to make sure she was listening. She met him with a steady stare. Oddly steady, he thought, considering he was rambling.

"And?"

He glanced down at the railing. "And, well, I left."

"Have you spoken with them since?"

"No." He looked down and shook his head. "I lost my phone and didn't have their contact information anywhere else. And you know how I feel about social media." He chuckled. Lizzie joined. Hers was with half the enthusiasm as his and as such, it was classic Jake and Lizzie. He closed his eyes to savor the moment.

"Hey."

They spun around and saw Tina making her way towards them through the crowd. To her side was a now inebriated man in overalls, repeating Jake's name. 'I didn't know she came back,' Tina lipped to Jake.

"Listen." Lizzie grabbed Jake's forearm before he could respond. "Come to my house tonight."

"What?" His eyes raced between Lizzie and Tina, who only needed to maneuver through a few more dancers before she'd be beside them.

"Just do it," Lizzie hissed, the words barely leaving her lips before she sprinted off the pier.

CHAPTER 17

Jake ~ Present

J ake ran his thumb over the crumpled strip of paper. Five letters and ten digits. That was all that had been standing in his way of an apology.

"So, you . . . you took my phone," he said, still staring at the paper.

"That's right." Lizzie's tone was matter-of-fact. She sat on the windowsill, one leg dangling inside her bedroom, where Jake stood, and the other dangling outside, where he had climbed in.

He nodded slowly, unable to take his eyes off the word scribbled on the paper. *Pedro.*

"Okay." He paused, trying to process it all. "And you're sure you didn't talk to him?"

"What kind of question is that? I told you I didn't talk to him."

"Right." He pulled his eyes from the paper to look at her. The only light in her room came from her bedside lamp, the soft yellow glow offering glimpses of even more tattoos that she had gotten after he left. "You didn't even try?"

"No." She shifted her weight on the windowsill. "Seriously, Jake. Do you really think I'd bring you all the way here to lie to you?"

Flashes of arguments they used to have when he'd catch her in a lie—oftentimes involving another guy—came rushing back to him.

"Don't answer that."

Jake smiled gently. He held up the paper. "Thank you for this."

"I know what it feels like, you know. The way you left them and all." She reached down, broke the stem of a coneflower, and stuck it in her mouth.

"You're more sensitive than people give you credit for." He walked towards the windowsill, amazed there were plants still living outside her bedroom window. "I best be getting home."

"No." She pushed his stomach with her foot as he approached her. "You'll call him here."

Jake shook his head. "Not a chance."

"Then I want it back." She spun the stem of the coneflower in her mouth. "If you change your mind, it'll be here."

"No." He slipped a hand into his pocket, squeezing the piece of paper. Then, he opened her bedroom door.

"You wouldn't," she whispered, jumping off the windowsill towards him.

Jake knew it wasn't likely that Lizzie's parents would catch him sneaking out the front door; they should have already been a couple of hours deep into sleep. But if they did see him, Lizzie would get kicked out of the house. And Jake doubted she'd risk that again.

"It's settled then. The window it is." He kissed her on the cheek. "Bye, Lizzie."

~ * ~

Jake waited for the monthly shrimp vendor meeting since it was the only guarantee that his parents would be out of the house long enough for his phone call. Not that he knew how much time he would need, but he wanted to cover his bases. Tina already knew about the call and promised to make herself absent.

As Jake sat on the porch with Tulip leaning against his leg, he was unsure what would end up being worse—the conversation itself or waiting to have it. He had run through how it could go multiple times a day for the past week and a half.

It was time.

"Hey ya."

Jake recognized the voice. He expected him to pick up—Pedro always did. And, given how long it took, he figured he already had some marijuana in him.

"Pedro, it's Jake." He paused, waiting for his words to sink in before jumping into an apology.

"What? No. No way! Who is this really?"

"It's me. I'm so sorry, man, the way—"

"Jake? Dude. Really?" Then Pedro shouted. He meant to do so away from the phone, but it landed in Jake's ear instead. Even so, Jake knew Pedro was in the garage based on how his voice echoed. "Hey, Oscar, get over here! You're not gonna believe this." He then lowered his voice, turning his attention back to Jake. "Hang on, man, gonna put you on speaker."

Jake waited, picturing Pedro fumbling with the buttons. Relief began replacing fear, but he knew it could be premature.

Pedro came back on the phone. "Okay. Ready, ready!"

"Dude. What happened?" It was Oscar, and his tone was more somber than Pedro's. For good reason, Jake knew, since his departure had left Oscar's busy car repair business down an employee.

Jake apologized, explained himself, and apologized some more. This pattern repeated itself more than he had planned. In hindsight, he realized how faulty his rehearsals had been; he hadn't included drugs in the mix.

"So, you pulled a Lizzie on us," Oscar said, summing things up before Pedro asked for another round of clarifications.

"Yeah, pretty much." Jake took a deep breath. He wasn't sure how to end the conversation. And, given his track record of leaving, it didn't seem right for him to initiate it.

"You know." Oscar cleared his throat. "A girl messaged us from your number recently."

A wave of relief overcame him; Oscar had dropped his tough-guy tone—the closest, Jake knew, he would ever get to an 'I forgive you.' Jake raised his eyebrows. "A Lizzie girl?"

"No. Well . . . yeah, her too. But that's all good. This was someone—"

"Pretty." Pedro began laughing. "Someone very pretty."

"Dude," Oscar said, a slapping sound ringing through the phone.

Jake laughed. "So, what did this pretty girl say?"

"That your number was hers now. She was a curious thing, started asking about you."

"But why—"

"Said she's never known someone with as many contacts as you have." He chuckled. "Can only imagine the messages she received."

Jake cringed, knowing exactly the types of messages—and photos—she had surely seen. It was his fault; he had let peer pressure get the best of him when he signed up for those raunchy escort sites. Nonetheless, he joined Pedro and Oscar in on the laugh. For a split second, he felt he was back in Arizona with them. A good kind of back.

"And get this," Pedro said. "She was writing from Panama."

"Is that so?" Jake rubbed Tulip's stomach. "What was she doing there?"

"Peace Corps." Oscar took over since Pedro began another laughing fit. "Lives somewhere in the jungle, a place called Al . . . Almagro, or something like that."

"Almagro." Jake felt his mind racing. A familiar kind of racing, the kind that happened when he was excited about the prospect of a new adventure. And this time, it'd be in a place that he belonged to by blood. "Hey, could you write her?"

"Uh yeah, I guess. What'd you want us to say?"

"Ask if she'd be okay with me contacting her."

"You betcha." Oscar paused. "Don't do anything stupid."

~ * ~

Pedro was right. The girl was pretty.

Jake touched his screen again to keep it from turning off. He mused at how much information one could gather from a photo. There were the obvious details—her curly brown hair, sunburnt cheeks, green t-shirt, and the sunny day framing it all. And then there were the subtle ones. The details that could be inferred if enough time was given to study them. Like how she either had good vision or wore contacts, since she didn't wear glasses. Or how she didn't mind a little mud, based on the trail of slobber on her face. And how kind she was to the dog who left that slobber, for it willingly had its face pressed against hers.

Oscar was right, too. The girl was curious.

Pedro had forwarded his correspondence with the girl, who based on the photo, was clearly a woman. Jake read through the messages quickly the first time, eager to know what the woman had said as much as what Pedro had said to her. Whether it was the marijuana, a change of heart, or, most likely, direction from Oscar, Pedro managed to avoid commenting on her photo.

This is so embarrassing.

I'm not Jake. He must have changed numbers.

I know this will be hard to believe, but I'm going to tell you anyway.

Jake laughed, thinking about how ecstatic Pedro would have been to become so popular with a lady. The woman must have sent him fifty messages—all one-liners, all sent within a minute of the message before it. She was right; it was hard to believe that a child accidentally messaged him from Panama. Hard to believe, that was, if it weren't for how concerned she seemed to be over it.

And if it weren't for how much she asked about him.

How could such a popular man not tell anyone where he went?

The messages I've been sent, I tell you. Is it true that tomatoes are his favorite fruit?

Have you called the police? I've thought about it a time or two.

Pedro didn't correspond with the woman after that day. Jake was confident, though, that she would respond to him, giving Jake the okay to contact her.

CHAPTER 18

Emma ~ Present

Emma stood at the shore, surrounded by the villagers, waiting for the canoe to arrive. They hadn't seen Professor Sonya in over a month, due to a family-related leave of absence. It was Federico's idea to make a welcome back sign; a kind gesture that Emma helped with, though she doubted it would hold up for Sonya's arrival.

"I want to help!"

Emma looked over at Andrés, who tugged at the bottom of the banner. The humidity-soaked paper yielded to his pull. He rolled the portion that pulled off between his index finger and thumb, then dropped it to accompany the others laying in the mud around his bare feet. María giggled, mimicking him.

Federico looked at Emma from across the banner. "I wanted it to look nice for her."

Emma smiled. She was thrilled that Sonya was coming back but was just as happy for Federico, whose favorite day was Mondays since it was the start of the school week. "She'll love the gesture, regardless of what state it's in."

"Agreed." Hugo stood over his canoe, puttering with its hole. He stopped to look up when he heard Emma's voice.

Abuela chimed in from a nearby canoe. "God knows Professor Sonya needs to get here soon if He doesn't want me dying a stiff woman."

Eduardo stood up from a bench at the back of the canoe and walked towards her. "God rewards patience." He held out his arm. "Go on, lift yourself up. I'll fluff your seat."

She puffed her lips out twice in contemplation. "I don't need a man to help." She grasped both sides of the canoe and lifted herself up, swaying both of them in the process. "Ready."

Emma flashed a knowing smile at Eduardo as he tried to fluff up the flattened grass on Abuela's canoe bench. Most days brought showers now that the rainy season was upon them, so getting her stool down the muddy slope wasn't feasible.

Eduardo touched Abuela's shoulder. "That'll have to do. But it would help if you didn't pull from the grass to make your crosses."

"The issue isn't the crosses." She shook her head. "It's that no one's replenishing the grass."

It was still a strange feeling to Emma, preparing for Sonya's arrival when the villagers didn't know if she would show up. Before Sonya left, she had given them her tentative return date. In the meantime, the children wouldn't have class. However, there wasn't a way for Sonya to communicate changes to her schedule until

Mateo made his trip to get *tienda* supplies where he'd receive any note she may have left. His last trip to Chepo was nearly two weeks ago. The villagers were accustomed to such uncertainty; they lived it all of their lives. But how much easier it would be, Emma thought, once Sonya learned the villagers had working cell phones.

Emma jumped upon feeling something touch her hips.

"*Tranquila*, it's just me." Martha whipped off Emma's falling *paruma* and retied it.

Emma chuckled. "We'll see how long it lasts." She tilted her head towards Chuleta who stood posed with her face in the mud, butt in the air—ready to tug her *paruma* the moment Emma wasn't paying attention.

Meanwhile, Carla sat on a nearby log at the river's edge doing laundry. With twelve kids, it was an endless task, she'd say. She smacked a pair of pants against a rock with three flicks of her wrist. The noise echoed across the river, traveling to the forest on the other side. For as normal as the task was, Emma sensed something was on Carla's mind; her children had to repeat her name to get her attention, and she didn't show excitement about Professor Sonya's arrival.

Andrés squealed, grabbed María's arm, and dashed under the banner. "I wonder what Professor Sonya will bring us!"

The villagers began making guesses. Children jumped with excitement, to the banner's further demise. Cereal, barrettes, and candy were among the ideas. The latter was the most probable, Emma knew.

"I wonder if she'll bring anyone." Emma turned around to see Mateo walking towards them, his arms full of food from the *tienda* to sell to the villagers. "Like that time she brought her aunt," he said, looking around for the cleanest place to set up his makeshift shop.

More excitement ensued. Emma wished she could bottle up moments like these. During her first year in Almagro, despite the villagers' frequent questions and concerns about when she would be leaving them, her departure felt distant. But time changed when the three-hundred-sixty-four-day mark arrived. She would no longer be in Almagro one year from then, nor one year from any day after that.

Federico lifted the tattered banner higher. "She's here!"

The villagers hushed each other as they listened for the motor, whose hum gradually became louder. It was the same reaction they had any time a motorized canoe arrived in Almagro. Emma wondered if the villagers ever had access to motors themselves, how long it would take for them to become indifferent to their sound and who they carried.

~ * ~

Professor Sonya arrived alone, aside from her canoe driver who headed back to Chepo. Emma decided to visit her in the evening, once the villagers had time to individually welcome her—driven, in part, by wanting their share of the candy she brought them.

Flip phone in hand, Emma settled into the hammock beneath her mango tree for a rare mid-afternoon break. Chuleta nudged her arm, trying to climb in with her; it was her ideal scenario, being pressed so close to a human.

Emma opened her messages. Data had come with her new cell, a curse the villagers considered a blessing, given that the floating *tienda* had run out of phone cards.

I'm great!!! How are you?!?! What are you up to??

"Ugh." Emma looked at Chuleta. "Do I have to answer him?"

She would, of course. But perhaps she'd wait just a bit longer. Emma wasn't keen on Rebecca sharing her new number with her brother, Diego. Since backtracking was no longer an option, Emma made it a point to pace herself between answering Diego's enthusiastic—and oftentimes repetitive—messages. How different they were from the messages she had exchanged with Jake's friend. Those were messages she would have liked to continue.

She looked up at her house. It would have been crazy, not to mention financially impossible, to keep data on her U.S. phone. So, she had buried it beneath a pile of *parumas*. There was no point in looking at something she couldn't use.

Jake's friend had handled the photo of her and the 'Yes' message that Andrés sent with grace. She knew it was an odd claim—that she was in Panama and one of her students had gotten ahold of her phone. But he didn't doubt her story. Or, at least, he hadn't let on to his doubts. On the contrary, he didn't balk at her questions about Jake, ones that even she admitted were intrusive. And most importantly, she finally learned why Jake's contacts had been messaging his old number.

He left. No warning signs, just a note saying he wasn't coming back. And above all, no phone contact.

Those three sentences answered the question that had been on her mind for over a year. The answer was far simpler than the murders, kidnappings, and identity changes she had conjured up. Leaving seemed so simple.

And a copout.

In some ways, the whys of Jake's silent departure were as mysterious as when she didn't know why people kept contacting his old number. But it was over now. Jake's friend promised to inform those who Jake was closest with about Emma having his number. He told her anyone writing her from there on out were people who wouldn't have mattered to Jake. *No need to respond*, he wrote. *Jake knew people who cared a heck of a lot more about his wallet than they did for him.* Girls, Emma assumed. The same ones who had been sending the raunchy photos.

"Where's your machete?"

Startled, Emma snapped her flip phone shut, along with her thoughts. She tilted in the hammock towards Maya, who made a final turn around Emma's house, from the opposite side she usually came from. Emma's heart sunk. She knew Maya must have been looking for the machete elsewhere on her wraparound balcony.

"Oh . . . I was cutting a mango in the house."

"You couldn't have done that outside?"

"Yes," Emma said, wishing she was quicker at thinking of believable lies, "but it was in the evening and you know how I am with spiders."

"But what about washing your hands? Weren't they sticky?"

Yet again, another catch on Maya's part. There wasn't running water in Almagro, so the villagers cleaned up for the night in the river or creek, whichever was closer to their house. They then waited until sunrise to do activities that would soil their hands.

"They were, but I was hungry." She knew she needed to change the subject and contemplated bringing up the question weighing on her mind. It was a risk; Maya could pick up on the correlation. But since no time was a good time when it came to Maya, she decided to go for it.

"Hey, have you seen anyone leave anything for me lately?"

"Like fish?"

"Yeah."

Maya twirled a piece of her hair. "Mm-hmm."

"Who's leaving them?"

"Kids."

"Oh yeah? Which ones?" She tried to sound casual; Maya would stop talking if she sensed Emma was eager for the information she held.

Maya leaned against the trunk of the mango tree and shrugged. Her gaze fell to the river.

Emma decided to change subjects, hoping to loop back around to the kids later. "How's your mom feeling?"

"Not well."

Knowing Maya would see through the insincerity of a comment about anything other than the reality of Rosa's condition, Emma responded with a nod. She felt vulnerable since her back faced Maya, so she sat up in the hammock to look at her.

Maya stared at the grass near the river's edge. "Do you think a person will live longer if they don't know when they're going to die?"

Emma followed her gaze, noting the grass seemed more matted than the night before. She hoped Maya didn't notice. It could be missed with a glance but not for long, if things kept up. "It's imposs—"

"Oh, Maya, I didn't know you'd be here." Hugo walked under Emma's house towards them.

Maya shook her head and headed uphill towards her own home. "If it's worth anything," she shouted back to Emma, "I think it's better not to know."

Hugo handed Emma a bouquet of three wildflowers— two pink and one white. "I didn't mean to interrupt."

Emma reached for the flowers with a smile. "I know. Thank you for these," she said, holding up the flowers. She glanced towards the pile of decaying plants to the right of her house. All of them were gifts from Hugo. Eduardo had helped her disperse the pile in the jungle a few months ago to keep the snakes from congregating. She figured she'd have to do it again soon.

"Carla asked if you could stop by her house at some point. She seemed off, although they say I'm bad at judging emotions." He chuckled and shrugged. "Also," he nodded towards her house, "I was thinking I could check your floor."

"That would be great, thanks."

Emma's floor didn't need checking. In fact, Eduardo told her it would need minimal maintenance during her two-year service, since the villagers had built her house brand new upon her arrival. But Hugo was proud of being one of only a few Emberá men in the village. And given that Emma had an Emberá house, he insisted on being the person to monitor it. 'You could fall through the floor,' he would say on days when she didn't feel up to having him poke around.

"Take as many mangos as you'd like while you're at it," Emma said, getting out of her hammock. "I'm going to Carla's."

"Good." Hugo poked her floor above his head with a branch. "She was crying. I think she'd really like some company."

Emma's eyes widened. "I'd say so."

CHAPTER 19

Emma ~ Present

A tissue would have come in handy but Carla wouldn't have known, since she'd never seen one before. Emma sat across from her, their knees touching, and offered her *paruma* instead.

"I couldn't possibly," she said between sobs.

"Please." Emma pushed the cloth into her hands.

Carla rubbed the fabric, her fingers pruned from tears. "It's my fault."

"No, it's not."

"Maybe not all of it, but some of it."

Emma stayed quiet. She knew it was true, and denying it wasn't helping. Carla and Emma were close, so Emma never imagined that she had been living a secret life; what came out during their conversation would have given Abuela enough to gossip about for a lifetime. It was Emma's duty to make sure that didn't happen. Carla hadn't even told her husband about it.

"It's not just that I cheated." Carla looked up from her lap. "Maybe you should check to make sure they haven't come back yet?"

"Of course." Emma walked across the room and peeked through the curtain door's hole. Carla's husband had taken the kids to their plot of land across the river to dig up some yucca. She worried they'd come back early. "All clear," Emma said, trying to process the news. She wasn't sure how Carla would hide her distress when her family returned; it was the kind of cry that, even after a full night's sleep, wouldn't be able to eliminate the puffiness from her face.

"Promise you won't judge me." She said each word with effort, trying to steady her shaking voice. "I need to know this before I tell you the rest."

Emma leaned in, feeling their sweaty legs slide against each other. "I won't."

Carla paused, then whispered, "I'm pregnant with his baby." She sobbed. "With Mateo's baby."

Emma rubbed Carla's left hand, the one that wasn't holding her *paruma*. "It's going to be okay." She then let minutes pass, comforting her while she cried.

The question Emma wanted to ask was intrusive. But depending on the answer, it could lessen the impact of a bad situation. When she felt enough time had passed, she gently asked, "Are you sure it's his baby?"

"Mm-hmm." Carla looked around the single room where they sat. Nine beds for her family of fourteen dipped down in uneven waves between bamboo box frames. "We haven't had the time or privacy lately." She fiddled with the *paruma*. "And, well, Mateo had been bringing me injections from the city. The woman who sold it to him said it was guaranteed to make a woman infertile." Carla looked back at the door. "Maybe you should check again."

Emma obeyed, glancing through the hole in the curtain and shaking her head upon seeing the empty soccer field. "Have you talked with Mateo?"

"No. And you can't either."

"I won't." Emma paused, thinking about how the weight of carrying Carla's secret was incomparable to the guilt that Carla would feel the rest of her life.

"I've thought about telling my husband it's his baby. He's never been the best judge of time. He might not know the difference. Plus," she snorted, "we all look the same."

Emma winced. Carla was referring to Emma's arrival in Almagro, when many of the villagers had looked the same to her. She was especially notorious for mixing up Carla and Rosa. But the villagers had long stopped looking similar to Emma. Features such as a subtle bend in the nose or extra definition in the cheekbone were oftentimes enough for Emma to recognize entire groups of family members—and knowing the names of each person within them. Her mind drifted to the faces of Carla's kids, but she pushed them away as soon as they came, ashamed of looking for Mateo's features.

"There's one more thing but . . . but I'm not sure I should say." Carla looked down at her lap. "It's shameful. More shameful than anything I've shared with you so far."

Emma brushed away a strand of hair stuck to the tears on Carla's face. "I won't judge you for it. But you've already shared so much, perhaps you'd rather wait and think about it?" Emma already felt gutted from the news, as if she herself were carrying the pain that Carla was going through. She couldn't imagine what else there could be.

"I . . . well, I don't think there's a point in holding it back now."

Emma watched Carla stare at the curtain again, so she got up to look through the hole before Carla even had to ask. Carla's cheeks crinkled ever so slightly, sorrow muting what would have otherwise been a smile.

"It's clear." Emma sat back down.

"Okay." Carla took a deep breath, her tears on hiatus as if they knew they'd be needed for what came next. "They told me I have HIV."

"Oh, Carla." Emma slid her bench beside Carla's and wrapped her arms around her. The hug served as both comfort and to keep Carla from falling to the floor. All the while, Emma tried to process the news. It was hard enough to learn that HIV was in Almagro. But she'd gotten used to the idea of not knowing who had it, and that somehow made it easier. Not much, but a little. Now, she felt like she got stung by a wasp that was already dead. Emma loosened her grip. "Do they know you're pregnant?"

Carla nodded. "They were the ones who told me. They . . . they . . ."

"Take your time."

"They made me take a pregnancy test after I tested positive." She shook her head. "It's such a strange thing to know you're pregnant before you're showing." Then she straightened up, pushing the *paruma* back into Emma's lap. "I should get water boiling for the yucca."

"I'll do it. We don't need anyone starting rumors if they see you like this."

Carla nodded, silent tears and softer breathing replacing her sobs. Emma grabbed a bucket off the hook, the same one she'd seen Carla fill countless times. She walked straight to the creek, her eyes only looking at what was needed to get the job done, for the villagers would question if they saw her there. She then walked behind the house to Carla's outdoor kitchen. It was simple and typical of kitchens in Almagro—four bamboo posts held up a thatched roof, a pot in the middle sitting on rocks. When Emma returned, Carla had moved into bed, facing the wall. She turned towards Emma when she heard her.

"Not even death could erase your kindness from my memory. I'll lay here until tomorrow. My family will know I'm not feeling well. Nothing more."

"Okay. I'm here for you if you need anything." Emma went to walk away.

"There's one thing."

Emma looked at Carla's side, since she had already turned back towards the wall. "Yes?"

"Just in case." She paused long enough for Emma to wonder if she had drifted off to sleep. Then she whispered, "Do you know how to get rid of babies?"

~ * ~

The schoolhouse had a glow about it since Professor Sonya's return. And so did Almagro, which was abuzz with talk about her arrival and the candy she brought. Emma stepped onto the school patio, walking towards Sonya's single-room house attached to the school. Blood from the villagers' game during MINSA's first visit had sunbaked into the cement floor. Emma could only imagine the stories the villagers would have told Sonya to explain it away.

Sonya stepped out of her room. "Finally!"

She and Emma embraced in a long hug. "It's a wonder you're alone," Emma said. "I was starting to think I'd have to battle it out with the villagers to get some time with you."

"It was a close call. Hugo just left." Sonya winked and gestured towards her room. "Come in. The candy is long gone, but I brought something better for us."

Emma's eyes widened as Sonya walked to the far side of her cement block room and pulled a bottle of red wine from her bag. "My kind of candy," Emma said, going over to the shelf to get two glasses.

Emma loved being in Sonya's room. It felt like a bridge between Almagro and the outside world. Sonya would leave for holidays and summer vacation, bringing back a few items from the city with her each time; the rest of the space on the canoe was reserved for school supplies. Three years later and the result was a mini stockpile of luxuries, including two wine glasses.

Sonya and Emma each grabbed a bench and dragged them outside.

"So, tell me. What's the real version of how my patio got bloody?"

They laughed and drank as Emma filled Sonya in on everything that had happened with MINSA's visits. But on the inside, she felt sickened by Carla's news. She also felt guilty. Sonya asked if she knew which villagers had tested positive, and Emma said she didn't know. Sonya was a confidant, but Emma didn't feel right revealing Carla's secret. And if it got out, the consequences that would come of it—not only for Carla and her family, but Almagro as a whole—were unbearable to think about.

"It's strange," Sonya said when Emma finished the details, right down to the latrine debacle. "Almagro is so isolated. How did HIV get here?"

Emma shook her head. "I don't know." It was the truth. She didn't know. But with Carla's news, an ever so rough sketch began to form.

"I assume they're going to try tracing it."

"It seems like they'd want to. But then again, there's the issue of confidentiality, so I'm not sure how far they'd get."

Sonya chuckled. "If every secret revealed in Almagro had a grave, there'd be no room left for the villagers to plant."

It was true. Emma hadn't known a secret that didn't make its way to the villagers' ears, if even a version that only somewhat resembled what had actually happened. Then again, well-kept secrets would never be put in a position to spread. What if there were secrets in Almagro? Perhaps secrets that had been held for many years? Emma was sure about one thing—Carla's secret would remain a secret, as long as she was the only one who ever knew about it.

Emma studied the piece of paper taped to the outside of Sonya's room. A list of names ran down the left side and their corresponding phone numbers on the right.

"I see they told you about our cell reception."

"Oh my, they did indeed! Only time will tell if it's a good thing." Sonya threw her hands in the air. "Going back to the city used to be an escape from my job. Now they all have my number."

"I wouldn't lose sleep over it." Emma chuckled. "Mateo's old car battery holds out long enough to charge 2.4 phones, according to his calculations. One of those charges he saves for me since he says I'm the only one with a need for it." She looked at Sonya over her glass of wine. "I've asked him not to. It's embarrassing, not to mention unfair."

Sonya raised her eyebrow. "Is that right? This wouldn't have anything to do with Jake, would it?"

Emma laughed. "Actually, it kind of does."

She filled Sonya in on Andrés sending the photo and 'Yes' message, talking with Jake's friend, and how she tucked her phone away now that the mystery had been solved.

"Fascinating." Sonya shook her head. "Who would've thought Andrés would be the one to save you from wondering about Jake the rest of your life." She paused and chuckled. "Using the only English word he knows, no less."

Emma lifted her glass. "Cheers to that."

They chatted until the bottle was empty, Emma catching up on Sonya's time in Panama City and about her grandmother who passed away the week before her return. When they finished, Sonya wanted to check on the school.

Emma followed her to the classroom, since she needed to pass it anyway to go home. As they entered, she had flashbacks to the last time the nurses were in Almagro and the multi-hour meeting that ensued. It was too late to warn Sonya; they were already standing at the front of the room.

Sonya tilted her head. "Is that what I think it is?"

"Yes." Emma nodded slowly, staring at the chalkboard full of male and female anatomy. "The things you missed while you were away from Almagro."

CHAPTER 20

Emma ~ Present

The villagers believed they were going to be rich. Emma stood at the *tienda*, condensation from her bag of ice dripping onto Chuleta's fur. She didn't mind it for a change—she was intrigued by the news Mateo brought them from his *tienda* supply run.

"Sixty dollars. Imagine it." Mateo stood on the *tienda* patio, in front of the counter, his arms spread out. "All it takes is an ounce. And they say there could be thousands of them here."

Martha stepped forward. "We'll start digging today."

"No." Hugo shook his finger, standing to the side of Mateo. "We won't set a shovel to Almagro that isn't for a seed." He puffed out his chest. "We'll dig upstream."

"He's right." Mateo nodded. "Besides, gold mining involves more than digging. They showed me some pieces." He pointed his thumb at the crowd. "Most of them are as thin as your nail, some even thinner. And they can be as small as the size of a newborn flea."

"It's for young eyes then." Abuela's voice drifted up from the church, where she sat outside on her stool.

"That's true." Mateo swatted at a bee. "But that's not what I was getting at. There's a special kind of pan you need." He walked to a nearby fern and snapped off a branch. "It looks like this," he said, drawing in the dirt by his feet. "It has a narrow bottom that drops down. That's where the gold gets caught."

"And then we'll get rich," Maya said, who leaned against a bamboo post at the back of the patio. Emma wasn't sure if it was a comment or question, but it was accompanied with a mocking tone.

"I don't know about this." Eduardo shook his head. "Can these people be trusted?"

"Of course they can." Mateo ran his hand over the fern. "They're my friends, the ones who told me about it."

"Okay." Eduardo's voice was kind, one that would make people doubt themselves if they flirted with the idea of him acting judgmental. "So, we get the gold. What would we do with the money?"

Hugo pulled the fern out of Mateo's hand. "That's simple. We'd buy more food from the *tienda*." He paused, waving the fern through the air as he thought. "We could get more car batteries to charge our phones. Oh! And shovels, we could get more of them. And then there's the floating *tienda* . . . the possibilities are endless."

Emma heard movement behind her and turned, smiling at Carla who just arrived. "They're talking about gold mining," she whispered.

Carla raised her eyebrows. Emma was glad to see Carla looking more relaxed since their conversation five days ago. They hadn't spoken of it since, except once when

Emma reminded Carla that she was there for her if she needed anything.

Mateo scanned the patio. "You should leave before your ice melts." He motioned for Federico to step towards him. "So, to summarize, Federico will be in charge of organizing the men who will carve the wooden pans. They shouldn't take long to make. Once that's done, we'll set a date to mine."

The villagers chorused in agreement, followed by a rush to return home with their ice. Emma looked at Carla, who pointed at her bag. "I've still got to get mine. Go home and enjoy yours."

~ * ~

The mining pans were ready three days later, but the villagers decided to wait until the following day to take their trip upstream, for Rebecca was returning. Emma had gotten the call two days prior, which turned into a village event.

It started with Rosa, who had heard the phone ring from Emma's house; she sent Maya to fetch her. Since Emma was in the middle of teaching English at the school, she said she would call the person back when she returned home. The next half hour carried on as normal. But then, as news of Emma's missed phone call spread, the villagers began piling around the schoolroom door.

Hugo had been the first to speak. 'Maya said you received a phone call.'

Then it was Martha, who rushed into the classroom to tighten Emma's *paruma*. 'You have to call them back. It must be important.'

Emma eventually gave in and brought her phone to the school. The villagers passed the phone around to listen to Rebecca in groups, asking her to repeat the same information about her arrival that she had told the others. Emma was glad that Rebecca recognized the momentous occasion; it was the first time in Almagro's history that the villagers learned about a guest's upcoming visit without a note brought by Mateo during his *tienda* supply runs.

What the villagers didn't know, however, was that Rebecca would be bringing her brother, Diego. It was news Diego himself told Emma later that same day in a text message with exclamation points that outnumbered any she had received from him before.

Now, on the day of their arrival, Emma was grateful to be stopped by a snake sighting, for she didn't want Diego to interpret her waiting by the port with the others as eagerness to see him.

"It's not poisonous." Eduardo tilted his back as he stared at a thin snake coiled in a branch hanging over the soccer field. "I wish it would move."

"It blends in with the leaves. Maybe they won't notice."

Eduardo laughed. "Oh, they will."

Emma knelt down and held Chuleta away from the branch, fearing the breeze would knock the snake to the ground. It was odd for a breeze to arrive in Almagro so early in the morning; she figured rain would fall earlier in the day than usual. "Could you move it?"

Eduardo's eyes widened. "Why no, *mi hija*. Even though it's not poisonous, it can still bite." He sighed. "Staring at it won't help its cause. Let's ignore it. Maybe it'll move on its own."

"Are you headed to the port?"

"Yes. I think it's wonderful that Rebecca's visiting us again. And so soon. We need all the support we can get, given her news last time." He paused. "I've been meaning to ask you. Have you heard any more noises by your house?"

Chuleta wriggled out of Emma's arms to pounce on a trail of ants. "I have." Her tone was upbeat; she knew if she showed fear, he'd insist she move in with a family. And for much as she loved the villagers, she wasn't ready to give up the one place that gave her privacy. She shrugged. "It's only on occasion. Probably just an animal."

Eduardo rubbed his chin. "I'm not convinced. That's an old path, the one by the river leading to your house. People in the village haven't used it for years, yet it's getting matted down."

"I appreciate your concern, but there's no need to worry. I feel safe at my house." It wasn't quite the truth or a lie. Whoever or whatever was making the noise didn't appear to come *that* close to her house. "Besides," she said with a wink, "I've got Maya watching over me."

He smiled. "I can't argue with that."

They heard the hum of a motor approaching Almagro. Parrots flew out of the trees, disrupted by noise that wasn't nature.

Eduardo squeezed her shoulder. "She's here."

CHAPTER 21

Emma ~ Present

"Emma has a boyfriend."

Emma looked out the schoolroom door, taking a deep breath of the increasingly stronger breeze and willing it to fill her with patience. The adults could have been mistaken for children from afar, squeezed into the seats of student desks and whispering secrets among their peers. Emma glanced at Martha, who winked at her from her chair. Emma mouthed the word 'No', shaking a finger down by her hip. The information Rebecca was presenting about HIV was important for the villagers to hear; Emma was mortified that they were focused on her.

Diego wasn't helping.

He stood at the other end of the classroom. The back of his ironed, collared shirt was speckled with paint from him leaning against the wall. On a normal day, the villagers would have made quick work of pointing it out.

Instead, they were captivated by his presence. And even more so by his claims that he and Emma had been talking. He flashed another smile at a group who leaned over their desks to whisper about him and Emma.

"Any questions?" Rebecca asked as she finished her presentation.

Abuela raised her hand, the grass cross she held extended above her head. "Why didn't Emma tell us she was talking with a boy?"

The room erupted in agreement. They were met by Rebecca and Diego's beaming faces while Emma leaned into the wall, humiliated. Hugo sat in the front row looking out of place with his eyes to the floor.

"Excellent question," Diego said. "I'm sure Emma had her reasons."

Everyone in the room, Hugo included, looked at Emma. She felt like an outcast in a community that loved her so dearly only an hour earlier. Even so, she knew it was temporary. It was a feeling she had become accustomed to, although never on such a personal level. The villagers treated her similarly the day she forgot to remove the stringy veins from yucca before putting it into a pot of communal soup. And the day she swam in a cold stream while still hot from working in the school's garden.

Emma took a deep breath. "Well—"

"Relax." Sonya walked over to Emma, putting an arm around her and scanning the classroom. "Who Emma talks to in her personal time is her business."

Abuela shook a cross in front of her chest. "I respectfully disagree, Professor."

With the exception of Abuela, who didn't mind challenging her, the villagers had a special kind of respect for Sonya. But Emma knew the Sonya effect would wear off the moment she wasn't around.

"On that note," Rebecca said, "the meeting is over. I'll be in the other classroom to hand out bags of food that MINSA has gifted Almagro, along with any follow up medicine we spoke about last time." She paused, then spoke the next sentence firmly. "Remember, you must visit me individually and maintain distance from the door."

Emma glanced towards the window, relieved to see Carla there. She arrived late, so Emma feared she wouldn't receive her HIV medication—medicine that MINSA vowed to offer free for life.

As the villagers piled out of the room and formed a line in front of the classroom next door, Emma approached Rebecca. "Can I talk to you for a minute?"

Rebecca beamed. "Of course!" She spun towards the door, the plastic diamonds on the tassels of her belt clinking as they hit one another. "Just give me fifteen minutes to start the one-on-one meetings, then I'll come out for a break."

Emma hesitated but knew she wouldn't have gotten far by insisting otherwise.

"In the meantime," Rebecca grabbed her brother's arm and pulled him towards them. "Talk with Diego!"

~ * ~

Andrés stood between Emma and Diego, holding a dead green snake by its tail. It had been over two hours since Rebecca started the one-on-ones and, given how short the line now was, Emma knew she wouldn't get to talk with her until everyone had their meeting. Nonetheless, Emma was thankful for two things—clouds to ward off the heat and the snake, which saved her twice in one day.

"Oh, God!" shouted a villager mid-congratulations before running off. It saved Emma from yet another conversation about how happy the villagers were that she finally found a man.

Andrés laughed. "Yes!" he said in English before switching to Spanish. "It can't hurt us now that it's dead."

Such a statement was unquestionably true when it came to snakes in Almagro; the villagers decapitated them for good measure. Andrés swung the snake in a circle but miscalculated its length. The headless creature smacked into Diego's chest. Diego yelped, stumbling backward.

"Snake blood!" Andrés shouted between laughs, pointing at the red spot on Diego's increasingly wrinkled shirt.

Emma gasped. "Andreyes! Go fetch soap and water." She turned to Diego. "I'm so sorry about this."

A few women saw what happened and circled around Diego. They grabbed the nearest leaves within reach and on tiptoes attempted to scrub the blood out. Earlier, they had picked his shirt clean of paint pieces while congratulating him and Emma. No doubt, they loved having another reason to swoon over him.

Diego tilted his head at Emma and gave his best go of a smile. "Don't worry about it."

Emma stood back, watching the women work on his shirt. Diego was Panama City tall. She used to think the villagers were exaggerating when they used such words to describe people from the city. But after spending twelve months in Almagro with people shorter than her, those from Panama City truly did look like giants.

Although she would never admit it to the villagers, she didn't mind talking with Diego that afternoon. As it turned out, he was a better conversationalist in person than over text messages. That was, during the rare moments when they were alone to talk one-on-one. Just like with Sonya and Rebecca, Emma partook in a different kind of conversation with Diego. A modern conversation. The kind of conversation she didn't know she missed until she was having it. The kind of conversation that also made her realize how much she missed being in a relationship.

Andrés came back with a gourd of water and bar of soap. "I'm sorry, Mr. Diego," he said. The water was still needed, but judging by the thunder rumbling from seemingly all sides as it approached Almagro, it wouldn't be that way for long.

Diego smiled, his dimples returning. "That was quite the catch you found."

The women shooed Andrés away, continuing to scrub at Diego's shirt. Meanwhile, Abuela rounded up children to shower him with grass crosses. She shouted to Diego from across the schoolyard as the kids approached him, their hands overflowing. "It'll rid you of the snake, Almagro's worst devil."

Emma noticed how Diego seemed to enjoy the attention. He joked with the women, making them laugh so hard that they didn't even flinch with each new clash of approaching thunder. Emma couldn't tell if he was genuinely flirting with all of them or if he wanted to show her his charming ways. In either case, the men kept a firm eye on him. They had a rotating schedule, passing by at one-minute intervals.

"That took longer than expected." Emma turned around to see Rebecca walking towards them. "But I see you had good company." She winked.

Emma gave Rebecca a knowing look. "Good company is never in short supply in Almagro." She left the group of women who continued fussing over Diego's shirt, even though the blood smear had long since disappeared.

Before Emma and Rebecca had the chance to exchange more words, Hugo stood on the school patio and called everyone over. "I'd like to make an announcement, if I may." Hand over his chest he turned to Rebecca and waited for her nod before proceeding. "A storm is coming. We shall put our mining trip on hold."

The villagers paced the schoolyard as the air filled with murmurs of their agreement. It was a good call. A potentially lifesaving one, Emma knew. She arrived in Almagro during the rainy season last year. It was common to see strong currents and a fallen tree or two floating in its entirety down the river. Even when the weather was sunny in Almagro, if it was raining in the mountains, the river could still be hazardous. Silent currents were dangerous. But the most dangerous kind of river was a flooding one.

Emma had heard more stories about Almagro flooding—and variations of those stories—than the number of days she'd been in Panama. There ended up being more truth to them than she thought, upon fact-checking with Sonya.

Hugo paused, waiting for the villagers to settle. "It's best to hold off on fishing until the storm passes, unless you absolutely must. There's no point in being wasteful."

"This will be bad." Abuela's voice trembled. She reached in her basket sitting on the ground beside her stool, grabbed a hand full of grass crosses, and spread them across her lap. "God help us."

"It might not be so bad." Hugo pulsed his hands, palms facing the ground, to calm the chatter. "In fact, it may not be bad at all. It's just preparation."

When Hugo finished talking, and long before the villagers settled down, Rebecca turned to Emma. "What did you want to talk about? We should do it soon before we have to leave."

"Yes." Emma motioned for Rebecca to follow her. She took her to an area in the schoolyard out of hearing range of the villagers and away from trees that children could hide behind.

Rebecca skipped beside her, unphased by Hugo's announcement. "Isn't Diego wonderful? Oh, Emma!" She grabbed Emma's hand. "We could be sisters-in-law!"

"He seems like he'd be a great broth—"

"And a great boyfriend!"

"I'm sure he'd be that too." Emma smiled. Despite Rebecca's persistence and the unsolicited public date that had happened in the schoolyard, she wasn't wrong in thinking that Diego and Emma could be a good fit. And as loving as the villagers were with her, Emma did get lonely at times. Nonetheless, she wasn't interested in a relationship with someone who lived as far away as Panama City. Emma lowered her voice. "Now, before anyone comes, I just wanted to ask you something."

"Yes, go on." Rebecca flicked her palm to the sky. "It's starting to rain."

"This will be quick. I was . . . I was wondering if MINSA has plans to test everyone in the village."

"By everyone you mean the younger children?"

"Yes." Emma wiped a drop of rain from her cheek.

Rebecca narrowed her eyes. "Do you know something? Did word get out about who has HIV?"

Emma shook her head, suppressing thoughts of Carla to look convincing. "No, it's nothing like that. I was just thinking about it." She glanced across the schoolyard.

"Since we know there are people here who have it, it seems that the younger kids should be tested, too."

"Agreed." Rebecca nodded. "And that's already in the works, so don't worry about it. Now," she looked at the sky, "shall we find a roof and your man?"

Emma grabbed her arm to stop her from turning back towards the school. "There's one more thing." She checked to make sure the villagers remained out of hearing range. "Of those tested, is there anyone who doesn't know they have HIV?"

"No. We were able to meet with all of them."

"Good," Emma said, jumping at a clash of thunder. Chuleta rubbed her damp fur along Emma's leg. "In that case, would you come with me?"

"Um, sure. Let me just ask Dieg—"

"No." Emma walked past her, away from the school. "Just you and me."

~ * ~

Emma looked at Rosa, trying to ignore the pain from Rebecca's hip digging into hers as they sat side by side in a hammock on Rosa's porch.

Rosa stared at them. "I don't know whether to be happy or disappointed."

"It's always a good thing when a disease is eliminated." Rebecca shifted in the hammock.

"I suppose so." Rosa reached down to pet Chuleta who had rested her head on her knee. "But now we don't know what I have or if there's medicine to treat it."

Emma turned to look out at the river. It was hard to judge the intensity of rain from roofs alone in Almagro since the palm leaves softened its sound. She could still see her house from Rosa's balcony, but she wished she had brought her umbrella since the rain showed no signs of letting up.

Rebecca rubbed her arm, smearing droplets of windswept rain. "I think it could be Dengue. Your symptoms—and that rash you showed me—are consistent with the disease."

"My God." Rosa lifted her left hand to her mouth and blessed herself with the other.

Emma knew Rosa didn't need an explanation of what Dengue was; she had heard the stories of people bit by mosquitos becoming infected with the disease. Some recovered and others weren't so lucky. There wasn't medicine to cure Dengue—or, at least, no modern medicine—but the villagers had plenty of holistic treatments they used.

"I've got some medication with me which will help with your pain." Rebecca glanced at the rain. "It's at the school."

"Perhaps Maya or Andrés could fetch it," Emma said.

Rosa nodded, her eyes filling with hope from learning recovery may be possible. "I'd gladly send them, but I'm not sure where they are."

Emma smiled. "Probably still up at the scho—"

Federico ran onto the porch. Water dripped from his shirt and mixed with Rosa's dirt floor, turning it to mud. "I'm sorry," he said between gasps of air, "to interrupt like this. I've been looking all over for you two. It's just," he set his eyes on Rebecca, "everyone at the school is worried about you and Diego. They say it's too dangerous to take the canoe back."

"They're right." Rosa nodded. "It's too late. The storm's moving closer and the current's already strong."

Rebecca sat still for a moment, as if imagining what spending the night in Almagro would be like. She sighed. "Very well. But where will we sleep?"

"Professor Sonya says you can stay at the school," Federico said. "You and Diego can each have a room. But it's just that…" He shifted his eyes away from her. "You'll have to sleep on the ground. She has two small mattresses but nothing to put them on."

Rosa grasped her hammock. Upon seeing Rebecca startle at her reaction, she clasped her hands together. "Well, at least it's a cement floor." She paused in contemplation. "You'll be okay."

Emma pulled herself out of the hammock, then lent a hand to Rebecca. "It's been quite the day. We should get back to the school."

"Wait." Rosa stood and studied the river—an increasingly more difficult task, given the rain.

Federico pointed. "Who's out on the water?"

Emma and Rebecca turned. A canoe rushed down the river, away from Almagro's shore. Two people sat in its center, the current whipping them downstream without the aid of a *palanca*. To Emma, it appeared to be one adult and one child, though even on a clear day, she had trouble identifying villagers from so far away. Rosa walked to the edge of the balcony, leaning against a post for support.

Rebecca reached for her arm. "Take it easy."

"How can I take it easy," she said with a trembling voice, "when that's my Andrés and Maya in the canoe."

CHAPTER 22

Jake ~ Present

J ake saw the pothole coming. He grabbed the bar in front of his knees to brace himself as the wheels approached it, the driver noticing at the last second and swerving mid-bump, making an already bad experience worse. The driver's assistant, *El Pavo*, they called him, was standing on the steps of the bus. He lost his balance and slammed into Jake's fingers.

El Pavo turned to Jake grinning, giving him a thumbs up. "Good!"

It seemed to be the only word in English the man knew, and fifty minutes into what Jake was told would be a twenty-five-minute journey, he learned that 'good' carried more meanings in Panama than its American definition.

The road looked clear of major potholes, so he pulled up the translator on his phone and spoke into it. "*El Pavo*, how much longer?" He showed the written translation to the man, noting that *'el pavo'* translated to 'the turkey'. It made sense. The *pavo* seemed to be in charge of gaining new clients, poking out his head from the bus and shouting its destination.

The *pavo* read the translation, flashed a two and five with his hand followed by a thumbs up. "Good!" he said before chatting with the driver between bursts of laughs. The driver stole a glance at Jake, grinning as he shook his head.

Arriving in Panama didn't conjure up the emotion of feeling at home like Jake had expected; his reliance on his phone for translation was met with weary looks and snickers. Embarrassed, he spent his first days in Panama City communicating only when necessary. In those moments, before speaking, he fit in. But acceptance on such terms felt lonely.

Jake sighed and leaned back on the grey school bus seat. He was glad he got an early start to the day. The *diablos rojos*—red devil buses—were something he had read up on before leaving Charleston. Panama City and its surrounding areas had converted former United States school buses into flashy, public buses. And everything he read about them proved to be true. But nothing, absolutely nothing, could prepare him for experiencing a *diablo rojo* ride in real life.

He leaned forward on the bench, freeing his skin from the arms of two stocky women on either side of him, as he tried to catch a breeze that failed to come through the half-open window. The bus returned to standstill traffic, making him long for bouncing over potholes at a high rate of speed again. Every fiber on his shirt turned damp. It unsettled him to think about how much sweat had soaked into the ripped foam fabric over the years from other strangers sitting where he sat.

The driver beeped his horn, the noise barely audible over reggaeton music blaring from expensive speakers hanging inside the four corners of the bus. Red and orange lights flashed around the mirror in front of him, a decal of a voluptuous, near-naked woman beside it. A phrase written beneath her involved Jesus, accompanied by a diamond stud cross.

The driver shouted at a car cutting in front of him and threw his hands in the air before pounding his fist against the horn. Jake grabbed the bar in front of him. The bus sped towards the car, which was only a few feet away, before the driver hit the brakes, throwing Jake forward. He turned around and looked at Jake with a grin. "Good," the driver said, giving him a thumbs up.

Jake reciprocated the smile and thumbs-up, figuring it was the best reaction to have. He had contemplated changing buses shortly into the journey but changed his mind upon observing other *diablos rojos* driving more recklessly than his.

He looked out the window at the bus beside his sporting flashy colors and graffiti—intentional graffiti, it seemed. It was in competition with Jake's bus to see which speaker could claim more of the communal air to fill its reggaeton with.

Even if he didn't end up finding Almagro, the experiences Jake already had impacted him. He traveled to Panama in part because he wanted to connect with his Panamanian roots on his dad's side of the family. He was now determined to learn Spanish to do his Latino blood justice. His thoughts drifted back to Charleston. Ever since his conversation with Oscar and Pedro, his plans—and quick ones, at that—revolved around arranging to meet his relatives in Panama. But an underlying motive, when he was being honest with himself, was to meet the woman who had asked so much about him.

He checked the messages on his phone. Still no word from Oscar or Pedro. Last he heard, Pedro's message to the woman about Jake wanting to contact her still hadn't been marked as delivered.

In hindsight, Jake assumed her receptiveness to the question was a given; he hadn't considered the possibility of her saying no based on the interest she took in his wellbeing, much less the message not arriving to her at all. The irony wasn't lost on him—he had wanted the woman's permission before messaging her but was headed to Almagro without letting her know. Anyone could visit any place in Panama, he rationalized. And he'd leave if she wanted him to, assuming he managed to find her. He didn't even know her name.

"Good!"

Jake snapped out of his thoughts. The bus had stopped and both the *pavo* and driver were giving him a thumbs up. It still looked like they were in the heart of Panama City, given the traffic. But a faded sign resembling the word 'Chepo' gave him confidence that he was in the right place.

The *pavo* pushed his thumb closer to Jake's face. "Good!" He and the driver laughed some more, pointing at Jake's phone.

Jake placed a quarter in the *pavo's* hand for the bus fare. Stepping off the bus, he tossed his small backpack over his shoulder and stood on the cracked concrete sidewalk. People rushed by him as they went about their shopping in what seemed to be an outdoor market. They bumped into him but didn't stare. When he caught someone's eye they smiled back. He relished in the feeling that these were strangers who believed he belonged, as long as they didn't try to talk to him.

A strong breeze tousled Jake's hair. He wasn't sure if he would be able to travel all the way to Almagro in one day. Now that he was in Chepo, he didn't even know the next step in getting there. He looked up and down the street. No hotels. He opened the GPS on his phone. Almagro was still far, but it was early in the day. Surely now that he was in Chepo, someone would be able to tell him how to get there.

His phone flashed a battery warning. Twenty percent remaining. Looking around, Jake zeroed in on an older woman who chatted with a client as she weighed plantains. He took a deep breath and walked over to her, hoping she'd know how to get to Almagro.

~ * ~

Hiding seemed unnecessary but it was hard to kick a habit, Jake thought, as he changed into shorts behind a tree. He hadn't encountered anyone on the trail yet. Nonetheless, mosquitos and other critters rustling in the jungle reminded him that he wasn't alone. As he shoved his pants into his backpack, he wondered how Panamanians did it in the city, moving around in jeans. Tight jeans. In the case of women, flashy jeans with silver-colored thread and shiny, plastic gems poking about.

He felt a sting on his toe and shook his foot, but it wasn't enough to dislodge the pinchers of an ant that had latched on. He grabbed the nearest twig and flicked it off. "Ouch," he said, his voice echoing through the forest. Sneakers would have come in handy, but flip flops were the only footwear he brought. Stomping, he made his way out of the brush to the relative safety of the path.

A raindrop dripped from his hair. He looked up at the canopy hundreds of feet above him as another rumble of thunder rattled the decaying jungle floor. He sensed the rain pick up, but even so, the canopy helped shield him. In hindsight, it was a bad decision to dawdle at the entrance of the trail. He had decided to hold off entering right away, first wanting to fact check directions to Almagro, which varied—but only a little—among those he asked, and then deciding to eat lunch at the market. His worst enemy, however, was procrastination in deciding whether to hike that day or the next.

'It's far.' That, accompanied with enlarged eyes and a shaking head, came from a man selling herbs.

Then there was the teenage girl. 'You need a canoe, which doesn't come around very often. And if it does, it doesn't mean it's going to Almagro.' She had been batting her eyelashes at Jake. 'It's best to stay here and wait for Mateo to arrive.'

'When will that be?' he had asked.

'It could be a while. But you can stay with me.' The girl leaned so far over a table of tomatoes that Jake had watched one, already soft from the sun, squish into her shirt.

Mateo seemed to be the ticket for Jake's arrival to Almagro; he heard the name mentioned from others at the market, too. But between his love for adventure and the only accommodation in sight being with a teenage girl, he decided to take the risk and travel to Almagro on his own.

Now, he regretted it.

A lizard ran in front of him. *Should I check my phone now?* Just a bit longer, he decided. His battery was nearly dead and GPS signal gone, but the clock on his phone still worked.

It felt strange relying on time as the only way to orient him. The people Jake spoke with agreed that the walk through the forest would take under two hours. Mateo could do it in much less, they said. Jake figured he was nearing the two-hour mark and hoped he hadn't made a wrong turn.

'You can't get lost,' the woman selling plantains had told him, after placing a hand on her heart when he used his phone to translate. 'Walk straight. Just follow the rut from Mateo's wheelbarrow.'

The path wasn't straight, and the wheelbarrow tracks had disappeared, but the main path seemed evident— wide enough where he would only brush the low-lying ferns and other foliage with his fingertips if he held out both arms. Nonetheless, partially cleared paths branched off in a few areas. Narrower paths. Older paths. Or, perhaps, newer paths that needed more foot traffic before being labeled a main trail.

"Yikes!"

Jake's foot hovered over a toad larger than any he'd ever seen. It was buried in the mud, its camouflaged stomach sprawled flat across the ground, making it hard to distinguish where the toad ended and where the soil started. He pulled his foot back and knelt to get a closer look. It opened its eyes; its gold cornea stood out against its body the size of a dinner plate. "Hey, big guy. Wish you could tell me if we're close to the port."

Jake stood back up and stepped over the toad. Danger had been miscalculated, but his heartbeat hadn't settled.

Breeze turned into wind, although he couldn't feel it from the shelter of the forest floor. Instead, leaves rushed down from the canopy. The leaves that didn't dislodge whipped around, dumping water onto him that had gotten caught in their crevices.

He shook his head. "This was a bad idea."

He doubted he'd make it to Almagro before nightfall. But where would he sleep? And would it be warm? He never would have dreamed that Panama could feel cold. Dampness seeped into his pores, attacking his body's attempt to stay warm. Pushing on, he vowed to check the time after he counted to sixty—if his phone still worked. Holding onto the hope of it not being water damaged was becoming an increasingly stronger sensation than him wanting to know the time.

A noise interrupted his thoughts. It was different than that of the wind, rain, and thunder surrounding him. It was a sound that grew louder as he walked. The sound of water flowing.

The river.

A rush of hope overcame him, powering his steps as he ran down the path. His feet slid along the muddy ground, mixing newly fallen leaves with the rotting ones beneath them.

The river came into view. And with it, disappointment. The port didn't resemble the kind of public ports Jake was used to; there were no shops, restaurants, or accommodations. Or people, for that matter. Instead, the port was a place where the dirt path met a river of the same color.

He stopped a couple of feet away from the river. Water surrounded the base of trees that normally would have lined the edge of the port. Hundreds—if not thousands— of branches rushed downstream. To his left, a full-size tree fought against water, its branches caught between living trees in a place that used to be the shoreline. The current pushed water over its trunk, shoving the fallen tree inches at a time. One of the smaller trees it was caught in gave way, falling against it. The river swept them both away.

Jake heard yelling and looked upstream. Through gaps between tree trunks, he saw two people rushing down the river. At first, it appeared they were on a log. But as the current moved them closer, he realized they were in a canoe.

A sinking canoe.

One person held a long stick and was trying to push the two of them towards the shore. The canoe yielded to the movement, but barely. There was also a small child. The boy tossed water out of the canoe so quickly that one scoop of water didn't have a chance to hit the river before he threw another scoop.

Jake hurled his backpack as far down the path as he could. He ran into the forest, grabbing the first long stick he encountered. Ants stung his fingers. He ground his hand into the branch to kill them before running back to the shore.

When he returned, the canoe was about to pass, barely out of arm's reach of his makeshift pole. He inched into the water—cautiously, to not get swept away; ankle-deep was all he needed to get to them.

"Grab on!" he shouted, lunging the stick between the boy and girl.

They did, the force dragging Jake another couple of inches into the river—dangerously so. He leaned back, adrenaline kicking in as the canoe made progress towards shore. The girl shouted something to the boy and the boy let go of the stick, returning to his job of scooping water out of the canoe. Jake held tight as the stick jolted in his hand; the canoe teetered on its side from his hold, threatening to flip the people into the river.

Still holding onto the stick, Jake watched a floating branch twice as long as his body and as wide as his torso barreling towards them. "Move over, move over," he muttered, knowing there was no way he'd be able to hold on if the branch hit the canoe from behind.

As if on cue, the current whipped the branch around to the far side of the canoe, jolting it closer to shore. But not enough. The impact nearly tossed the boy into the river, saved by the girl who let go of the stick with her left hand to grab him.

The current had already yanked Jake past the path. He wrapped an arm around a tree for support, hoping it wouldn't dislodge. The girl lost her grip; the canoe jerked away at the opportunity. He knew if she let go, there would be no way to rescue them. His adrenaline pumping, Jake reached the farthest he had and made a one-handed grab at the wooden gunnel of the canoe. The tree supporting him creaked from the added weight, but he clutched it and the canoe, refusing to let the river win.

When Jake pulled the canoe close enough, the girl jumped into the river to help him drag it to the path. But she was shorter than he was. Much shorter. The river whipped her off her feet and pulled her under. She flailed her hand in the air, landing it on the edge of the canoe where she pulled herself up.

"Stay in the canoe!" Jake shouted over the thunder and pounding rain.

The girl shouted something back as she climbed in, but he couldn't understand.

A sharp object punctured Jake's flip flop. Yelping, he shook his foot in the water. The flip flop pulled off and resurfaced out of reach.

One flip flop it'll be.

Jake didn't let it stop him. He grabbed the canoe's side and pulled it against the current towards the path. Debris littered the riverbed; flip flop or no flip flop, he moved with caution.

The girl dug her stick into the river on the opposite side to help him. The boy continued to scoop out water. Jake noticed a hole in the upper front corner of the canoe where water continued to flow in.

Using their last bit of strength, they pushed the canoe onto the path. Jake waited for the boy and girl to get out on land, steadying the boat before joining them. Breathing heavily, the three of them looked at each other. The boy trembled and fought back tears. The girl put her arm around him. The boy's torn shirt exposed bleeding cuts. The girl's clothes were also tattered, though not as bad. Rain dripped off long black strands of hair that had escaped her ponytail. Lean muscles protruded from both of their thin limbs.

The boy looked at Jake. Slowly, with a thick accent, he spoke in English. "I am Andrés and she is sister Maya."

CHAPTER 23

Emma ~ Present

Emma wouldn't sleep in her bed that night. And, according to the villagers, it could be many moon cycles before she would sleep in it again. With a stack of *parumas* already piled high in her left arm, she grabbed one more off the shelf with her pinky. Emma mused at how *Parumas* proved to be useful in more ways than a skirt as of late. Tonight, they'd serve as a wall and blankets.

A shiver ran through her. How could Almagro get so cold? It wasn't the kind of cold she was used to, growing up near the mountains. It was a cold that was relative. Seventy-degree weather used to be comfortable before she arrived in Panama. Now, her body was accustomed to temperatures twenty degrees higher.

Fried anchovies and rice caked to the sides of a pot from breakfast. "Chuleta, eat this," Emma said, scraping the contents into her dog bowl. If the villagers were right about the storm, she wasn't sure when she'd be cooking for Chuleta again.

Parumas still balanced on her arm, Emma reached her right hand under the bed and flung her backpack onto her mattress, pushing the bag into other items already there. Her bed was the highest place inside her room, and the villagers instructed her to do so. They said if the river flooded, the water wouldn't likely reach her floor, let alone the four extra feet to her mattress. Big floods were rare, they said. But they could happen.

"How's it going?"

Emma closed her eyes. The voice came from Diego who shouted to her from the balcony. Her wall gave into his weight, creating an indentation she could see from inside.

Hugo chimed in. "Yes. How is everything?"

Hugo knew better than to lean against the wall, but through its cracks, she could see him pacing back and forth beside Diego. A mere afternoon had passed, but she was already getting worn down from the two of them competing for her attention. She looked up at her ceiling. A few pieces of a palm leaf drifted onto her face. "I'm almost ready," she said.

She picked up her phone—the one from the U.S. that she hadn't opened in weeks. It was the last item needing a spot in the stay or go pile. "You'll stay," she whispered, slipping it into her pillowcase along with faith that the villagers had, in fact, built her house to withstand flooding. She tucked the mosquito net tight around her bed. It wouldn't do much if the river rose to her mattress. But it might, at the very least, contain her belongings so they would be there for her, soaked and all, after the storm.

With her free hand, Emma grabbed the small basket of belongings she'd chosen to take with her. She looked around her room one last time, engraining its features in her mind. A familiarity that was only hers. The knots in her bamboo door. The vines tied around her thatched roof. The height of her table. The streaks on her floor. Together, they made up her independence. Her space. Her alone time. She took a deep breath, put on a smile, and stepped out the door, Chuleta by her side. "All set."

Hugo and Diego lunged to grab her basket, then let go and went for her *parumas* when they realized the other was seemingly claimed. "Here," she said, giving the basket to Diego and the *parumas* to Hugo. "I won't say no to help."

Hugo and Diego beamed. "We're at your service," they said.

Emma walked around the balcony to her notched tree trunk, taking one last look at her mango tree along the way, the base of which was already engulfed by the river. She searched for Maya's house, but it was impossible to see through the rain. Chuleta bolted past her down the steps.

"Chuleta," Emma warned, looking out at the river as she climbed down the tree trunk. Rain pooled on the steps and her hands slipped along the trunk as she attempted to steady herself. "Stop playing with those branches!"

Emma waded ankle-deep into the water, which had already reached under her house and was approaching the base of her staircase. Small pieces of debris swirled around her feet as she pulled a branch out of Chuleta's mouth. She tossed it towards Maya's house to get her away from the river.

"Keep a close eye on her," Hugo said as he and Diego reached Emma. "The river won't be kind to anything in it tonight."

~ * ~

188

Word was out about Maya and Andrés by the time Emma arrived at the *tienda*. Most of the villagers were already there, building a makeshift wall out of *parumas* to shield them from the wind and rain.

"But why did they leave?" Martha asked, shouting over a clash of thunder.

Rosa leaned her pale face against the *tienda*, the bench she sat on teetering from its uneven legs. "I don't know. They didn't say they were going to. They . . . they've never done anything like this before."

"No." Eduardo held a *paruma* in his hand, helping Diego piece together the highest part of their makeshift cloth wall. "They wouldn't have gone without a good reason. Not Maya, at least. She knows better."

Mateo leaned over the counter from inside the *tienda*. "There's never a good reason to leave during a storm. Never."

"Hallelujah," the priest said, who sat in his plastic chair beside Rosa. Abuela insisted he sit there to pray for her, as the mother of two children who were lost to the river. It was a rare sighting; storms were the only time the priest ever set foot on *tienda* soil.

Rebecca stood by Diego, handing him *parumas*. She turned to Emma, who was on the far side of them. "Do they really gather like this? All the villagers, for every storm?"

"Not every storm . . . not even most storms." Emma scanned the room, noting who hadn't arrived yet. "But they've told me stories about the biggest ones and how everyone gathers here at the *tienda*. Almagro has never entirely flooded—"

Diego snorted. "Seems impossible."

"Yes." Emma nodded. "But they're not willing to take the risk, so they gather here during the worst storms. The *tienda* is the highest place in the village."

Hugo tapped Emma's shoulder. "They say Abuela's asking for you. She's down at the church."

"I've been worried about her. She should be up here by now."

"They've been trying. But you know how she is, with her stool and all." He paused. "I'll go with you, it's safer that way."

Emma waved her hand. She intended it to be a casual swing. Instead, it turned into a firm stop, palm forward. "I've got it, thanks Hugo."

"She's right," Diego said, turning towards them. "I'm young and steady. I can help you down the slippery slope."

"No." She turned to Rebecca who, catching on to the tension between the two men, shooed Diego back to work. "Chuleta and I will manage," Emma said, walking away from them.

And manage they did, though it wasn't as graceful as Emma had planned. She slipped on the mud steps twice. The first time, she landed on her bottom. The second time, she caught herself with one calf, which slid down the next three steps, pulling muscles that wouldn't soon let her forget about the experience.

A doorless entryway greeted her at the church. It was a wise decision to remove it, given that even with a gentle breeze the wooden door threatened to yank away. Abuela sat hunched over her stool in the narrow aisle, looking no taller than the stool itself.

Emma cleared her throat to get her attention. The wind and thunder made it a futile effort, so she resorted to shouting. "They said you wanted to see me?"

"Emma." Still facing the altar, Abuela held out a grass cross in her hand. "Thank God you're here. Take this. Sit with me."

Emma kicked off her flip flops—one of Abuela's rules before entering the church—and walked along the dirt floor, turning it into a trail of mud as water dripped from her clothes. She took the cross from Abuela's hand, squeezed past her stool, and sat in a pew just inches away. Normally, cataracts clouded Abuela's eyes. But that night, lightning changed them. It reflected off raindrops clinging to grass crosses shoved between branches in the church's wall, casting an eerie light in her eye.

Abuela rubbed a wilted cross between her fingers. "I came here to pray."

She talked facing the altar, her focus fixed on the Virgin Mary statue. The Catholic diocese in Panama City had gifted it to Almagro many years ago. It arrived painted in a rich blue and white color, the villagers had told Emma. Now, moldy green crevices took its place, accenting the Virgin Mary's stands of hair and crease in her lips.

Emma nodded. "It's a good time to say a prayer."

"Yes." Abuela sighed. "But now I want to stay."

"In the church?"

"They don't want me to, but I'm eighty-three years old. If the river takes the church, then I'll be taken too." She paused and reached for Emma's hand. "You don't think the river will take me, do you?"

While Emma agreed with Diego's reaction to the river flooding all of Almagro, this was different. "Abuela." Emma stopped, trying to find the right words. "I don't believe the river will rise as far as here. But you've lived through many storms in Almagro. You know more about that possibility than I do."

Abuela stroked her skirt in contemplation. Finally, she pulled her eyes away from the Virgin Mary and looked at Emma. "Would the villagers come get me if it floods here?" She twisted a grass cross around her finger. "Would they rescue me? Do you think?"

Emma's thoughts flashed to hours earlier when she watched Maya and Andrés float down the river. She didn't try to help them—not that there was anything she could have done. She was too far from the river. And they were already passing Almagro. She didn't even fully understand the gravity of what the storm—and the river's current—entailed. She knew all that. Even so, she could have tried to do something, if only for her own conscience.

"Emma?"

"I think," Emma said slowly, "if it were safe for them, the villagers would do whatever they could to rescue you."

"Then it's settled." Abuela shifted in her stool. "I'll think about it."

"So, you'll stay here?" It wasn't the solution Emma wanted, but she couldn't bring Abuela to the *tienda* against her will.

"Yes." Abuela returned her gaze to the Virgin Mary. "Would you send Federico down? It's best I have company while I do my thinking."

"How about I send him down in a little bit?"

Emma had been studying the gaps in the church's wall. It was hard to see through the rain—and impossible to hear—but she was sure no one else had gone to the *tienda* since she arrived at the church.

"Why not now?"

"I just need to run a little errand."

"An errand? Don't be foolish, Emma. Nothing and no one are worth going out for in this weather."

CHAPTER 24

Emma ~ Present

"What are you doing here?" The curtain door brushed against Emma's face. She peeked through its hole. "I wanted to check in on you."

Carla smiled from her bed. "That's sweet of you. I'm fine, really. You shouldn't have gone out in the storm for me." She leaned her single, flat pillow against the wall and propped herself up. "Come in."

Emma pushed the curtain aside, a gust of wind helping it along. "I was already out. Plus," she said, wringing her shirt before stepping inside, "there's no staying dry until the storm passes."

Carla chuckled, touching her damp sheets from rain that had swept through the cracks in her wall. "Are they looking for me?"

"Not yet. It's only a matter of time, though. Your husband told me you wanted to get your yucca off the floor before heading over."

Emma pulled a bench up to the bed. Her fingers fell into a triangular chip in its corner; it was the same bench she had sat on the day Carla revealed her secrets. Chuleta laid at her feet lapping water droplets as they fell from Emma's *paruma*.

Carla pointed to the far corner of the room. A lopsided bamboo table buckled at its center, weighed down by a pile of yucca still caked in mud. A lit candle teetered haphazardly on top. "He wanted to do it, but I told him to take the kids to the *tienda*." She smiled. "He knows better than to argue with me."

Emma didn't doubt it. Carla was known for being outspoken with her husband—too outspoken, many villagers would say, since she'd do so publicly.

"Well, when the time comes," Carla smoothed the sheet, "you can tell them that I'm not going to the *tienda*."

"But Car—"

"Please, Emma. My decision is made."

Emma forced down the words inundating her mind. Words pleading Carla to go to the *tienda*. It was just one night. But knowing a confrontation with Carla wouldn't end in her favor, she took a deep breath. "I can't guarantee they won't come looking for you."

"It's never flooded here before." Carla looked at her dirt floor. "It gets muddy, of course. A bit of standing water from the creek sometimes. But not the river."

It made sense to Emma. Carla's house was by the soccer field, on the opposite side of the church. It was in the centermost part of Almagro's plateau and the highest area of the village, aside from the *tienda*.

"It's hard living with what I know, with what I've done."

Relief enveloped Emma's body. They hadn't talked alone since the day she revealed her secrets eight days ago.

Whenever Emma would try to approach the subject, Carla would suddenly have to go somewhere.

"I'm sure it is." She set her hand on the bed. "They've given you medicine, is that right?"

Carla leaned over and lifted the corner of her mattress. It was only a couple of inches thick and had holes where solid foam used to be. She pulled out a bottle. "They have."

Emma smiled. "How's it settling with you?"

"I don't know." Carla rolled the bottle in her hand.

"Well, I'm sure it'll take time to see how your body adjusts."

"No. It's not that." A gust of wind pushed rain through cracks in the mud wall. Carla brushed a fresh layer of mist from her face.

"What is it then?"

"I'm not taking it."

Emma opened her mouth, but no words came out.

Carla held up her hand. "I know what you're thinking. Don't say it. I don't want a lecture."

Emma tried gathering her thoughts. "May I ask why you're not taking it?"

Carla moved her pillow to the mattress and laid back down. "I'm worried about how it could affect the baby."

"But it could help—"

Carla sucked in her lips until they disappeared, leaving nothing but a seam connecting brown skin to brown skin.

Emma lowered her head.

"That's the issue." Carla paused. "Sometimes, at least. Depending on the day." She rolled her head in her pillow. "It could help the baby."

Once the silence between them became uncomfortable, Emma spoke. "Rebecca's here. She couldn't go home because of the storm. I could ask her to talk with you tomorrow, if you'd like."

Carla mustered up her motherly smile. "If it'll make you feel better."

"It's a plan then."

Carla peeked through a hole in her wall. "The rain's letting up, so you should get back. It might not stay that way for long."

"You're sure you don't need anything?"

"There's one thing." She rolled on her side. "Tell my husband and children I love them when you see them at the *tienda*."

~ * ~

Emma walked to the *tienda* at a more relaxed pace than when she left Abuela at the church. The rain had slowed, the lightning now serving as a soft lamp over the soccer field rather than a deadly spotlight. Thunder still rumbled, but in a lulling kind of way, announcing its departure. Beside her, Chuleta jumped in puddles, footprints from a recent soccer game drowned beneath them.

"It's time, but don't let it trick you!"

Emma recognized Hugo's voice echoing from the *tienda*. She squinted at the stairs and saw him moving towards her, a line of villagers behind him. They handled the muddy steps with grace that only those raised in Almagro seemed capable of. Upon seeing Federico, Emma remembered her promise to Abuela. She rushed to the bottom of the steps, trying to catch him before Abuela did.

"Emma!" Hugo said with open arms. "You must come with us."

"I will." She ran past him, not stopping to ask where they were going. "I just need to do one thing first."

Emma eyed Federico as he made his way down the last few steps. She greeted the other villagers as she waited for him, curiosity growing about what was making them so happy. "Federico," she said before his foot touched the last step. "Abuela asked for you."

"Let me guess. Her stool?"

"No." Emma paused. "Although that could be it too. I think she's looking for company, more than anything."

"They say I should be thankful I'm so wanted, but I have my doubts." It was a rare moment of exasperation from Federico as a result of him being the go-to teenager in the village. He sighed. "First the canoes and now her."

Martha flung her *paruma* at him from behind. "Canoe. The *canoe*."

Federico glanced at Emma as he walked away. "I'll check on her."

"Emma." Martha grabbed Emma's *paruma* to retie it while pulling her back towards the soccer field. "Hugo's canoe is gone."

"Oh?"

"Rosa said you were with her, that you saw Maya and Andrés in the river."

"That's right."

"Did you see which canoe they were in?"

"The canoe?" Emma shook her head. "No, it was so far away. You know how I am. I can't even tell who is who from my house on a clear day."

"Right, of course. It's just . . . it's just that Federico went to pull the villagers' canoes back to shore when the river first started rising. Hugo's wasn't there. It seems odd the river would've swept it away like that, so early on."

197

"It's possible they took it," Emma said, thinking about how Maya would have been smart to target Hugo's canoe, given that he often parked it on the backside of the village near Emma's house.

Sonya and Diego ran up behind them. Diego rested a hand on Emma's shoulder. "Have you ever been shrimping?" he asked.

"Ah," she said, realizing where they were going. "Yes, but not like the kind we'll be doing."

"I filled him in." Sonya smiled at Emma.

It wasn't Sonya's first shrimping experience after—and sometimes during a lull in—a storm. When Emma arrived in Almagro, the villagers had shared countless stories about storm shrimping. Curiosity gripped her as she straddled a makeshift stream in the footpath.

"Chuleta's going to love this." Emma reached down and squeezed Chuleta's muzzle. She wagged her wet tail against Emma's leg and licked her hand.

Diego shook his head. "You're braver than I am."

"Bravery is relative to what you're used to," Emma whispered as they arrived at the river.

Emma, Sonya, Rebecca, and Diego stopped ten feet back from the raging water. The villagers, on the other hand, ran up to the shoreline—a new shoreline that would soon be drowned and replaced by an even newer one. Thousands of branches rushed down the river, lightning in the distance casting shadows on them. They ranged in size from twigs to branches four times as long as an adult; branches that just a short time ago had been hanging hundreds of feet high over the river. And those were just the branches. Whole trees raced down the river. Emma could see two from her viewpoint alone. She figured more were out there, if it were daylight.

And then there was the fish.

Silver tilapia bellies spun around in dozens of mini whirlpools created by the current. It was impossible to know if they were alive or if the rushing water made their already dead bodies appear to have life.

"They're gasping for air, *mi hija*." Eduardo walked over and stood beside her. "It's a sad sight. Every time."

Emma looked at him. "But why are they gasping for air when that will kill them?"

"It's their reaction from panic." He sighed. "When the river rises this much, this strongly, the mud makes it difficult for them to filter oxygen from the water."

A tree passed close to shore—a whole tree, its girth wide from hundreds of years of growth. Emma watched a section of its leaves move against the wind. An animal, she figured, although it was too hidden beneath the branches to make out what it was. She wondered how any critter living in and around the river would make it out alive tonight. "It's hard to watch," she whispered.

Sonya, Rebecca, and Diego all murmured in agreement. And then it struck her; she hadn't felt like such an outsider since her first days in Almagro. But there she was, standing with three others who also hadn't been raised there, watching a scene unfold in front of them with people who instinctively knew what was happening and how to handle it.

"Mother Nature wouldn't want it any other way." Eduardo squeezed her shoulder and pointed at the shoreline. "Do you want to catch some shrimp?"

Storm shrimping was easier than Emma expected, and Chuleta became the villagers' prize shrimp hunter. Unlike fish, a shrimp's reaction to the river saturated with debris was to exit the river and die on dry land. Emma mused on how the word 'shrimp' didn't do the creatures justice with their massive bodies resembling lobsters.

"It's hard . . . impossible, really, to catch these big ones in the wild," Eduardo said, grunting as he leaned down to grab a shrimp running up the grass. "They live too deep. They hide too well."

Chuleta ran over to them with her own shrimp, dropping it at Emma's feet. "Good girl," Emma said, picking it up and setting it in Eduardo's basket. The shrimp swung its pinchers, which the villagers had warned her could break a finger if she weren't careful. Tail to antennae, the shrimp was as long as Emma's forearm—big, but not the biggest one they caught that night.

Emma's eyes fell on the silver flashes in the river. "What about the fish?"

"We'll collect them tomorrow. Just focus on the shrimp for now." He looked up at the sky. "You see? Hugo was right. The storm really did trick us into thinking it was leaving. We don't have much time, let's hurry."

At that moment, an extra loud sound of rushing water caused Emma, and all the villagers along the shore, to whip around towards the river. The current pushed water over a lodged branch in the riverbed, creating a makeshift waterfall.

Chuleta ran towards it, her front paws smacking into the water.

"No!" Emma shouted, running towards her.

Chuleta barked at the branch, moving forward and backward as she did it. She put her front paws in the water. Then pulled them out. Then put them back in. And pulled them out.

"Come on girl, come over here." Emma tried to steady her voice as she slowly moved towards her; she didn't want to startle Chuleta.

Chuleta wagged her tail and looked at Emma, smiling wide through her panting—the way Emma always loved, under normal circumstances. Then she turned back to the branch and barked twice, stepping deeper into the water.

The current whipped the front of Chuleta's body to the side, dislodging the grip her blacklegs had on firm soil. Emma screamed, running towards her, as the river pulled Chuleta in. Emma tried to jump into the water but Hugo caught her by the waist. He yelled to others for help. Despite the approaching thunder and new round of rain, Emma heard the villagers shout that it was too dangerous, that there was nothing they could do.

It was too late.

Emma felt the villagers pull at her, trying to get her to turn away from the river. They wanted to protect her from watching Chuleta thrash and fight to keep her head above water. But she wouldn't let them.

The current turned Chuleta to the side and held her there, facing Emma. With their eyes locked on each other, she watched as the river carried her Chuleta away.

CHAPTER 25

Jake ~ Present

Jake and Andrés sat on a log after they finished scooping water out of the canoe. Jake had suggested sleeping in the canoe so they'd be off the forest floor. 'Dangerous' was Andrés' response. As it turned out, he was right. Jake and Andrés had to keep an eye on the canoe, moving it further up the path in increments as the river rose. With it, went Jake's hopes of getting sleep.

"Maya has been gone a long time," Jake said, pulling a soaked but clean shirt out of his backpack.

Andrés beamed when he handed it to him. "Yes! Thank you!"

"Where did she go?"

Jake said the words slowly to help Andrés understand. He sometimes had to repeat his questions and use hand signals to get his point across. Even so, Jake was impressed by Andrés' English level.

Andrés looked at his hands. "I do not know."

"There's nothing here." Jake opened his arms and twisted his body. "But I'm sure she's okay," he added, upon seeing Andrés' worried look.

It was true, though. There wasn't anything there. Jake hadn't seen a soul on the path earlier, and the middle of the night was upon them. Could it be that Maya walked all the way to Chepo? She must have known what she was doing when she set off, he kept telling himself. In the meantime, he tried focusing on how to get out of the port.

"Andrés, do you know where Almagro is?"

"Yes!" Andrés nodded. "Almagro I am from."

"You are?" Jake grinned, rain pouring from his upper lip to his lower one, the spray falling into his open mouth. "Is there . . . is there an American woman living there?"

Andrés began giggling and flashes of Panama City came back to Jake; he longed for the day when he'd be able to communicate in Spanish. Jake reworded his question. He reworded it again. And again. Andrés reacted the same each time. Giggling. Jake's phone battery had either died or the phone itself did from the rain, so he couldn't show Andrés the photo of the woman.

Andrés poked his chest. "Emma."

"Emma? No, no, my name is Jake." He moved his leg so that he straddled the log, facing Andrés. "Can you tell me how to get to Almagro?"

"Emma yes!" Andrés giggled.

"Andrés, no. I'm Jake. Please, this is important. How far is Almagro?"

Andrés mimicked Jake, straddling the log, smacking his hands in front of him to find his balance. "Yes! Emma yes! Yes Emma!"

For the first time since they met, Andrés seemed happy. He was only six years old, he had told Jake, and

Jake didn't want to strip away his moment of silliness. He playfully bumped Andrés' shoulder. "Emma no," he said.

They went back and forth with this game for Jake didn't know how long. It was a mindless one, the kind that let him get lost in his own thoughts while still participating. He would get his answer about Almagro. He had to. If Andrés was from Almagro, had he come from Almagro just now? Was he still living there? Would he and Maya be going back?

Jake heard footsteps approach them, squishing down the path.

"Maya!" Andrés stood up and ran towards her, embracing her thighs in a hug.

Maya patted him twice with one hand, her fingers spread apart. They spoke in Spanish; Jake stayed on the log observing them. Maya's pink nail polish stood out unnaturally against the backdrop of the forest. In her right hand, she held a package. A colorful cloth wrapped around it and fit in her palm. When her eyes met Jake's, she swung the package behind her back and whispered something to Andrés.

Andrés turned to Jake, pulling Maya towards him. "Maya asks do you have food."

"Yes," he said, reaching into the plastic bag beside his backpack. He and Andrés had already eaten a few bananas that he had bought in Chepo that morning. They left some for Maya and for the next day, although Jake knew they'd do little to appease three hungry stomachs.

Andrés went to sit down beside Jake, but Maya pulled him away, sitting between them. She crossed her legs. "Thank you," she said in English.

Jake nodded, conscious of her eyelashes batting. But then he became conscious of his own eyelashes, how the weight from raindrops dripping from leaves forced them down.

"Andrés, can you ask Maya why she left?"

Andrés obeyed, but based on Maya's shortness and firm tone, Jake already knew the answer.

"No said she." Andrés shrugged.

Maya's arm brushed against Jake's as she lifted the package in her hand and attempted to stuff it into her bra. She looked away as she grabbed handfuls of leaves from her chest, throwing them onto the path. A leaf fell on Jake's knee, and he didn't brush it away. Water from the rising river began teasing their feet. Maya checked that all the leaves were gone, then dropped the package down her shirt.

Andrés stood. "We move canoe."

"Yes," Jake said, unzipping his backpack. He handed a shirt to Maya. "Take this."

She took it before he released his grasp, tugging it over her shirt. Then she ran her hands up and down its drenched fabric.

Andrés already stood beside the canoe, water halfway up his shins. Since the river had risen so far into the forest, the trees protected them from the current, allowing them to go deeper into the water without it being so dangerous. A cracking noise sounded; its echo was muted by a clash of thunder.

"Tree again!" Andrés said.

Jake didn't flinch from the sound. Instead, he focused on helping Maya pull the front of the canoe back onto the path—the brand new, but short-lived, shore of the river. The sound of falling trees was near-constant; he had learned to judge if one was close enough to kill.

"You strong said she." Andrés pointed at Jake, translating what Maya said.

He laughed and winked. "I move wooden canoes all the time."

Andrés spoke to Maya. Jake couldn't tell if her reactionless expression was from a poor translation on Andrés' part or from the sadness she seemed to carry.

They decided to push a new log onto the shore, now that there were three of them needing a seat. "You go," Andrés said, tapping Jake on his knee. "You tall."

Jake waded in the water towards the log they agreed upon. He turned it parallel to the path, admiring how easy it was to control such a heavy object when it was in water. The wind continued to blow across the canopy but the rain had let up, so when it wasn't suffocated by a cloud, pockets of moonlight shone down through the treetops.

Suddenly, something brushed against Jake's leg. He yelped, even though earlier in the day plenty of things in the river had touched him. But this didn't feel right. It wasn't the hard poke of a branch. Nor was it the soft tickle of a clump of leaves. This was something different.

Something like skin.

Andrés and Maya made noise. It was in Spanish at first and then, remembering, Andrés switched to English. "What happen?"

Stunned, Jake stared behind him. "It's . . . it's . . ." his breathing was heavy. He heard Andrés and Maya run into the water to get a different angle, to see what he was seeing.

They gasped together, Andrés clutching Maya's arm. "It's a dead person."

CHAPTER 26

Jake ~ Present

Jake's thighs and right arm felt heavy. He could tell it was daylight without opening his eyes. A bird chirped above him and then he focused, realizing that many more were singing in the canopy. He wiggled his toes. No standing water, a good sign. The river was near, based on the sound of water funneling around the trees. But it was in a slower way. A peaceful way.

He opened his eyes. Andrés was laying on the log, his head in Jake's lap. Maya was to the right of him, her head leaning halfway up his forearm, her hand on Andrés' chest. Jake's stomach growled. He wondered which had a better chance of waking them—the noise itself or his stomach moving from it.

Andrés stirred first. "It is gone," he said, sitting up.

Maya muttered something in Spanish, pressing her head deeper into Jake's arm.

Jake looked at the canoe. The river had risen more after they'd fallen asleep, enough to press its back side into a nearby tree. But a portion of the front of the canoe still teetered on land. They would need to scoop rainwater out of it before going anywhere—if they were going anywhere.

He reached for his bag. The movement caused Maya to move and, although it was necessary, he was reluctant to give up the feeling of her warmth. During the night, the package had fallen down her shirt and onto her lap. He glanced at it, noticing plastic poking through the fabric it was wrapped in. Maya snatched it upon realizing and stuck it back where it came from.

"Banana?" Jake asked, handing them to Andrés and Maya.

Maya said something to Andrés, who translated. "Today we go to Almagro."

Jake opened his mouth, both laughing and smiling. "That's wonderful."

"Yes!" Andrés said, giggling at Jake's reaction.

"Are we leaving now?"

Andrés turned to Maya, then translated what she said back to Jake. "Yes. River dangerous. We take dead person."

Jake looked past the canoe into the flooded forest where he and Maya had dragged the body last night. They lodged the woman between a few short, close standing trees to keep her in place. It never crossed his mind that they'd be taking her with them.

"Do you know who the dead person is?" Jake repeated the question a few times, in a few different ways, before Andrés understood.

Andrés nodded, looking solemn. "Yes."

"Okay." Jake paused, trying to flesh out Andrés' cryptic translation from earlier. "If the river is dangerous, maybe it's better we wait a while before leaving?"

Andrés translated to Maya and based on Maya's confused look, Jake wasn't sure if Andrés had understood the question.

"Almagro far. We be careful."

Jake followed Maya and Andrés' lead and stood. "To the canoe it is, then."

~ * ~

It was a surreal feeling, standing in a dugout canoe in an unfamiliar country with two strangers and a dead woman. Jake and Maya took turns pushing the canoe with a stick—a *palanca*, they called it. From land, the river looked calm. But out on the water, the undercurrent prevented them from making much progress. Whoever didn't have the *palanca* sat at the front of the canoe, moving debris out of the way and directing the *palanca* holder around large branches and full-size trees they needed to yield to. Andrés was in charge of keeping water out of the canoe. It was an easier task than the day before since wind wasn't pushing waves through the canoe's hole.

"*Rama*," Maya said, lifting her arm so Jake knew which way to steer around the branch.

Jake was amazed by the Spanish words he had already picked up on. He no longer cared that his phone was dead or damaged—or, most likely, both. Digging the *palanca* into the riverbed, he leaned back, using his body weight to move the canoe forward.

After a while, Jake and Maya took advantage of the branches and trunks of flooded—but still standing—trees to pull the canoe along with their hands. It didn't make the trip easier but gave certain muscles a break. His arms burned from the strength it took to push against the current. But not wanting to look weak, he waited for Maya's cue to switch positions.

"Your turn," Andrés said, poking at a spider floating on a thin layer of water inside the canoe.

"Great." Jake handed the *palanca* to Maya, who ran a hand across his stomach as she passed him. He felt her fingers tickle him as she did it. He glanced over at Andrés. Andrés smiled at him, pushing the spider in and out of the water with his toe.

Jake walked to his backpack, holding his breath to avoid the smell of the corpse that he and Maya had placed at the back of the canoe that morning. The woman's location helped some, but they couldn't avoid the body's stench when a breeze hit them right. And now, the sun was only making it worse.

Even when the corpse's scent didn't waft towards them, the river itself was like a deceased organism. Dead fish swirled around the canoe, their silver bodies speckling the otherwise brown river. At first, Jake avoided hitting them when pushing the *palanca* into the riverbed. But he stopped when he realized it slowed his rhythm, allowing the current to take advantage and undo his work.

Andrés pointed to the woman, scrunching his face. "Fly."

"Yes," Jake said, trying not to look at the body. "Lots of flies."

Maya shouted something to Andrés, who leaned over the canoe. The movement threw Jake off balance and he landed on his knees, just missing the river.

"Leaf," Andrés said, reaching for a whole fern floating in the water. Its roots were still intact, wiped clean of dirt.

Realizing Andrés' motive, Jake pulled Andrés away. "Let me get it."

Jake knelt in the canoe, balancing his body weight in the center. He then reached into the water for the fern, shaking off a dead fish as he pulled it in.

Andrés squealed. "Big arm!"

"Yes," Jake said, grunting as he dragged the fern into the canoe. He glanced at Maya who had stopped pushing the canoe to watch him. She looked at the corpse and flinched before shoving the *palanca* back into the water.

Andrés jumped over a bench in the canoe, tugging at the fern when it snagged. He threw it over the woman's face, plugging his nose with one hand.

Jake stole a glance before turning away. Based on Maya and Andrés' stoic attitude towards the body, Jake figured they couldn't have known the woman well. And they had plenty of time to get emotional, given what a venture it had been getting the woman into the canoe that morning. They had made Andrés wait on the path since, even as an adult, the water came up to Maya's chest. Jake did the brunt of the work—the hardest part was dislodging the woman from the trees, one of which had spines. At the time, putting the woman there seemed like a good idea to keep her from floating away. In hindsight, that made it a nightmare to dislodge her.

Jake was thankful, at least, for Maya's foresightedness in telling him to fetch the corpse in his bare feet. 'Leave your flip flop onshore,' she had told him via Andrés. Jake thought she was crazy for suggesting it and following the advice herself. But after hitting his feet against debris hiding beneath the water, for as painful as it was at the time, a flip flop wouldn't have offered protection and his sole piece of footwear would have been destroyed.

Once they dislodged the woman from the cluster of trees, getting her to the canoe felt easy. Jake and Maya had waded slowly through the water, one on each side of her.

They pushed branches out of the way to keep the woman's hair from getting tangled in them.

Lifting her into the canoe had been far from pleasant, and again, fell mostly on Jake. Her body was bloated, both from death and the river. Jake remembered squeezing his eyes closed as he dragged her into the canoe. The force from doing so didn't scrape her up much compared to the gaping wounds she already had. Nonetheless, Andrés and Maya washed blood off the canoe while Jake washed the corpse's bodily fluids off himself.

Jake shook the thoughts from his mind, wanting to clear his head from the smell of the woman's rotting body. He grabbed a tube of toothpaste from his backpack and walked a few steps to the middle of the canoe by Andrés. "Would you like some?" he asked, squeezing some into his mouth.

Andrés giggled. "Green!" he said, pointing to the fern. He pointed to the sunscreen. "White!" In a grand finale, he lifted both arms in the air. "Emma!"

"Andrés," Maya scolded.

Sitting back down, Andrés continued to giggle.

Jake winked at him and whispered, "Emma no."

"Secret," Andrés whispered back, cupping the spider in his hands and tossing it overboard.

CHAPTER 27

Jake ~ Present

The sight of flooded forest and the river saturated with fallen debris lost its thrill quicker than Jake expected. There was a time when he thought they were arriving in Almagro—an area where trees became sparser and a couple of thatched roofs stuck up between foliage. But Andrés had said, 'No Almagro.'

Now, his hope laid in bends in the river. He stuck the *palanca* in the water, farther in front of him than usual to manage the curve. The bend was gentle but unforgiving in length; he figured it would take a dozen such moves to get around. He hit a sunken log—perhaps a whole tree trunk—and let the *palanca* maneuver its way to the riverbed before pushing. Even after it latched onto the river floor, the current relentlessly tugged at it. Jake noticed it was the strongest undercurrent they had encountered so far, requiring him to engage muscles he didn't know he had.

Andrés translated Maya's words. "Push hard."

"I'm trying."

Sweat poured down Jake's body. He knew he couldn't last much longer unless he drank water, followed by food and rest. They had stopped awhile back to take the canoe inside a flooded portion of the forest where a creek flowed. It ended up being as brown as the river, so they didn't drink from it. But nearby passionfruit had helped quench the worst of their thirst.

"Almagro!" Andrés ran past Jake, who nearly hit him with the *palanca*, and hung his legs over the front of the canoe.

Relief gave way to newfound strength. "That's Almagro?"

Andrés squealed. "Yes!"

"*Rama*," Maya shouted, swinging out her left arm.

Jake pushed the canoe around the branch, wondering why Maya didn't seem excited, relieved, or *anything*. How could she not be thrilled that they were arriving to safety? But he pushed those thoughts aside, consumed with studying Almagro.

The river straddled a partially forested mass of land, branching off evenly around it. Jake knew Almagro was an island based on the maps he'd seen. As he pushed the canoe up the river, closer to the area where the river branched out into a 'U' shape around the island, a small hill with a hut at the top and a long thatched roof protruding from it caught his attention. He saw a few other roofs at lower elevations, but only partially so since trees surrounded them.

A clunking noise echoed from the hill. *Thump thump. Thump. Thump thump.* Another noise sounded from the same area. The sound of people.

"Andrés, what are they saying?"

"Too far. But they happy."

Jake smiled. "Me too."

Maya bent over the front of the canoe to push a branch out of the way. She pointed and said something to Andrés.

"Maya say move canoe to hand."

Jake looked to where Maya was pointing. It was towards the forest, across from the island. His heart sunk—could it be they weren't in Almagro? But then he realized that Almagro sat in the middle of the river. Since the river split to form around the island, the undercurrent from the two sides uniting pushed against them, keeping their canoe at a near standstill. He dug his *palanca* into the riverbed again, willing his muscles to work just a little bit longer.

Andrés pulled Maya back, leaning over the canoe to check for branches. "Maya help, I watch."

Maya walked back to Jake and picked up a shorter *palanca* stick. She could have grabbed it closer to the front of the canoe. But instead, she picked it up beside him, brushing her body against his in the process. Her dark brown eyes studied his face, her lips expressionless.

Andrés bent over the side of the canoe to push a branch away, rocking it in the process from his quick movement. Maya rested her hand on Jake's stomach to steady herself. He wanted to hug her. A hug of joy. A hug of celebration. A hug to show her that whatever was troubling her would be okay. But before he had time to react, she turned back to the front of the canoe, touching the package in her chest.

Together, Jake and Maya pushed the canoe towards the forest. Maya's strength amazed Jake. If only they had pushed the canoe together from the start, they could have arrived sooner. But it was too late to think about such things. And he figured Maya had her reasons, if they could communicate.

Once they arrived at the edge of the flooded forest, they dropped their *palancas* and grabbed onto tree trunks and low-lying branches. Jake didn't need a translator to see what they were doing; the *palancas* would never hold up against such a strong current. Their only hope was to grab at the forest, pulling the canoe around the bend, away from the epicenter of the two merging currents.

Little by little they pulled. Branches cracked. Others broke. Spiny tree trunks punctured their hands. Insects bit and wasps attacked. But they made progress despite it and, eventually, made a ninety-degree turn, picking up their *palancas* and directing the canoe towards Almagro.

As they drew closer, Jake saw canoes parked by a path that led from the river up to the top of the hill. The sun reflected off the back of one of the canoes. A motor, it seemed. Jake watched people pour down the path from the hut. Children played at the edge of the river. Adults stepped in to drag back the youngest ones when they went out too far. Andrés shouted to them once they got within hearing distance. The people gasped and murmured, presumably at the stories he told.

Once the canoe was within feet of land, people ran into the water, surrounding them and pulling them ashore. Getting out of the canoe was a blur. Jake wasn't sure if he himself got out of the canoe or if the people, all much shorter than he was, had carried him. Nonetheless, he found himself sitting on a rock with Andrés and Maya on either side of him. The people passed cup after cup of water to them in dried gourds. It was a better welcome than any Jake had imagined, and he had time to think of plenty during the journey.

Andrés turned to him, grinning above his gourd. "Good!"

"Yes," Jake said, nudging him. "The very best kind of good." He looked behind them and saw that the people had formed a human chain down the path, passing along gourds of water. And then leaves.

"Food!" Andrés pointed to the rice, meat, and fried plantains sitting on large banana leaves that were handed to each of them.

Jake watched Andrés rip the end of the leaf and bend it so it could be used as a spoon. He followed suit. The food was room temperature and seemed to be a combination of different meals piled into one, based on the different textures of grains of rice and the mishmash of fish and sauces used. Jake pictured the people scrambling to put leftovers together when they saw them arriving. Even if he wasn't starving, the quality of fish and the natural flavor of rice and plantains made it the best meal he'd ever had.

While Jake ate, women tenderly touched his wounds and men carried buckets of water from the river. When Andrés finished talking, they began speaking to Jake.

"I'm sorry, I don't understand," he said.

Jake felt hands release their touch on his body. The men paused mid-stride. All took a step back and looked at him, some even turning their heads and peering at him from the corners of their eyes.

Jake felt Maya slide closer to him, their hips brushing. A woman shook her finger. Many others surrounded them, all directing stern tones at Maya and stealing glances at Jake. Suddenly feeling bad for Maya, Jake set his leaf spoon down and put an arm around her shoulder.

The people drew a sharp breath.

"Husband! Wife!" Andrés said.

Jake knew it wasn't a direct translation, for they spoke more words than that. Many more, from many people, all at the same time. And while he was accustomed to going against the grain, he pulled his arm away, knowing he was in a culture that was his by blood but not by upbringing.

Maya stood, placed her hand on his shoulder to steady herself, and jumped off the rock, looking at him with her same deep stare and blank expression. He watched her hold her chest in the process and wondered if any of the people noticed she was carrying something in it. Talking to no one, she pushed her way up the hill through the crowd.

"Carla."

Jake heard a thump and turned around, unwanted familiarity greeting him. The smell was familiar. The sound of skin slapping together was familiar. The sight of a fern leaf covering her face was familiar.

"Carla."

More people said the name as they pulled the body off the canoe. They laid the woman on land considered dry, even though it was still saturated from the storm. Jake assumed everyone already knew the story; Andrés hadn't had time to finish his food from all the questions they asked.

A child came up to Jake and handed him a grass cross. She gave one to Andrés, too, who blessed himself with it before setting it on his banana leaf. It slid into the rice, sauce splattering up its side. Jake watched Andrés and decided to do the same. It went over well with the people, who nodded.

Before long, a mound of grass crosses covered Carla's body. Jake watched the human chain pass down the crosses, one by one. They originated from over the hill, as far as he could tell. At least fifty people were participating in the process. Children of varying ages and one man knelt around the body, placing the crosses around it, the browner ones serving as a sponge to soak up their tears.

Jake felt a prick in his hair. And then another. He reached for his head; fingers pulled away, just missing his grasp. Turning around, children ran away from him, waving an invisible something in the air that had the adults swooning. He felt another prick. It was Andrés, beaming as he stared at his prize.

"Hair!"

Jake laughed. "Yes." He rubbed his head. "*My* hair." Another child approached him, and he decided to use the best defense he had.

He stood.

The children ran around him, hands in the air, playing a game to see how far up his body they could touch when they jumped. Jake played along, holding a hand against his chest where the highest child had reached, wincing when they hit a wound. It felt strange to him to be the tallest in the crowd; in the U.S. he passed as average height for a man.

Jake scanned his surroundings. He hadn't expected it to be difficult to find the woman Oscar and Pedro had told him about. Then again, he had been so concerned about how to get to Almagro that it rarely crossed his mind about the process of finding her once he was there—especially since he thought he could show people her photo on his phone.

Andrés tossed his now empty banana leaf onto the dirt and jumped up on the rock. He wobbled, teetering backward. Jake grabbed him by the arms and pulled him up, holding on until he steadied.

"Emma!"

Jake laughed and shook his head. "Emma no."

"Emma yes!" Andrés pointed.

Jake turned and squinted as he looked up the hill, trying to see what Andrés saw.

Andrés continued to jump, reaching for Jake's arms when he lost his balance. "Yes Emma, Emma yes!"

CHAPTER 28

Emma ~ Present

The cross sunk into Emma's hand, its grass splinters digging into her wounds. Wounds she had gotten from trying to rescue Chuleta. Punctures and scrapes. Injuries that were numb until she knew Chuleta was too far to rescue, her body only then allowing pain to take its place.

Abuela squeezed Emma's hand, pressing the cross deeper into her cuts. "It's Carla."

Emma already knew. She had heard it from Eduardo, who heard it from Hugo who had been consolidating the villagers' canoes above the now flooded *tienda* port. Sonya rubbed Emma's back. They were in line to pay their respects to Carla, a line that ran from the soccer field, up over the *tienda*, and down to the river.

Abuela pressed another cross into Emma's hand. "This one's for Chuleta."

Emma offered Abuela the best smile she could manage. It took effort; the swelling around her eyes weighed down her cheeks. Smiling felt foreign to her even though twenty-four hours hadn't passed since she was last happy. Since the last time she spoke with Carla. Since the last time she petted Chuleta.

"It'll be okay." Diego's voice came from behind Sonya.

Emma's nod was barely noticeable as she took another step forward. The villagers talked to God but she didn't process their words; her mind was on Mateo.

She crossed through the *tienda*, which Mateo had closed in mourning, and questions invaded her thoughts. When was the last time he talked with Carla? Did he know Emma knew about them? 'No' would have likely been Carla's response, had Emma brought up the subject before she died.

Emma was certain about one thing—the pain Mateo would feel with Carla gone would linger longer than that of most of the villagers. Forever, even. She wondered if he would want to know about Carla's pregnancy—it was his baby, too. Not yet, of course. It was too soon. But maybe someday, maybe after Emma had time to weigh the consequences of telling him.

She crossed through the *tienda* patio and took her first step downhill towards the river when she heard her name being called.

"Emma!" Then, a pause. "Emma yes!"

Andrés. She would recognize his voice anywhere, although she couldn't see him through the crowd of villagers who had formed a circle around where Carla presumably laid.

"Yes Emma, Emma yes!"

Emma turned to Sonya. "As happy as I am that he's okay, I wish he'd stop. It's not the time."

Sonya sighed. "To be a kid."

Through the crowd, Emma spotted a man. She blinked a few times, trying to clear the coating of tears that blurred her vision. He was taller than the others, and his shirt was ripped at the shoulder, revealing a streak of lighter brown skin against the deeper, sun-soaked brown on his legs and arms. He stood still as children jumped around him.

The line felt like it was moving quicker now, though Emma knew it was a trick of the mind. The farther she moved down the hill, the more the other villagers surrounding the man meshed together into a single, shorter crowd, making him poke out even more above them.

The man grinned and waved, seemingly fixing his gaze on Emma. Everyone in front of Emma returned the gesture; Abuela's grass crosses swung through the air in rhythm with their movement. Meanwhile, women and girls squealed, gushing about the handsome stranger on Almagro's soil. Emma moved both crosses to her left hand and waved twice with her right.

Diego leaned around Sonya. "Is he here to see you?"

Everyone within hearing range turned to Emma.

"No." She shook her head, looking at Diego and the villagers, then back to the man who continued to stare in her direction. "I don't know who he is."

A woman a few people ahead of Emma spoke. "They say he came with Maya."

It seemed likely—the only option, really, given that no other canoe had arrived in Almagro after the storm. Plus, it explained the baggy shirt Maya had on when Emma had passed her earlier. It was a man's shirt and looked new, despite being strewn with dried mud. Emma squinted. Andrés jumped beside the man, tripping on a similar collared shirt that draped past his feet onto the rock.

Rebecca stood in line behind Diego, responded to the woman. "But that's impossible. Eduardo didn't tell us about the man. He wouldn't have left that part out."

"He could have," Sonya said. "With everything going on. He's a sensible man."

Emma knew Sonya was right. It was just like Eduardo, knowing when to exclude information.

"Emma! Yes, Emma!"

The line brought Emma at a conversational distance between her, Andrés, and the man. The man looked out of place to her, like all visitors to Almagro did. But this man looked even more so; he didn't bring boxes of supplies or paperwork. Even if it weren't for the storm, his collarless shirt and shorts weren't as formal as she would expect from someone coming from a Panamanian agency. What were they doing sending him there, and so soon after a big storm?

The man shrugged with both arms in the air and smiled. "I take it you're Emma?"

He spoke in English. Perfect English. And yet it took time for Emma to process his words, to recognize they were in her native tongue, to decipher what they meant.

"I am," she finally said. She offered the best smile she could, both recognizing and not caring that he'd be able to tell she had been crying.

The man continued to smile but softened his enthusiasm. "I'm Jake."

"Nice to meet you." Emma moved in line which took her past Jake, and close enough to Carla where she caught the first glimpse of her corpse through the crowd. She took another step forward in line. A step closer to Carla; the first of her last steps towards her. Sensing Jake wanted to talk, she said, "Can you give me a minute?"

"Oh yes, of course." He wavered between a nod and a bow. "Take your time." He paused. And then, with the most genuine voice a stranger could use about the death of another stranger, he said, "I'm sorry for your loss."

Emma heard him but didn't respond; she had already knelt down beside Carla's shoulder, swallowing against the urge to vomit from her smell. A fly landed on Carla's cheek. She brushed it away and removed a piece of fern dried onto the crevice of her eye. She looked at Carla's stomach. It was bloated, along with the rest of her body. Emma hoped that if the fetus was large enough to be noticed, the river had the decency to carry Carla's secret away.

Federico sat next to her, and Emma rubbed his back. "Your mom was a wonderful person," she whispered.

"Yes, she was," Sonya said, who stood behind Emma.

Emma nodded. "Don't feel like you have to wait for me." She meant those words for Rebecca and Diego more than Sonya, since they had barely known Carla.

"We came together, we'll leave together." Diego squeezed Emma's shoulder.

Emma placed a grass cross on Carla's stomach. Holding Chuleta's cross, she reflected on the last time she saw Carla. Did Carla know where she was going when Emma left her? She knew it shouldn't matter, but Emma sensed it would be haunting her. She brushed away more flies. *I'll tell your husband and children you love them, just like I promised.*

She pushed back the instinct to squeeze Carla's hand and tried focusing on the loss of life alone. And she did, but she still felt conflicted. Could she really be the only person who knew about Carla's pregnancy? And did the promise of keeping a secret become negated after death? Mateo would be devastated to know two lives were lost, but it was his child too. Emma wouldn't want anyone else finding out aside from him, of course.

I miss you and I'll be missing you. Take care of Chuleta for me, if you see her.

Emma didn't know how long she spent with Carla, but it was long enough for her legs to have fallen asleep. Diego held her waist as she stood; she didn't push him away. She took one last look at Carla's body. Only hints of yellows, pinks, and purples from the *parumas* that the villagers had used to cover her skin were visible beneath the grass crosses piled on top of her.

Then Emma remembered the man. She looked over to see Jake standing in the same place as before, with the same children still jumping around him. *Who is this man that came with you, Carla?* She walked over to him, Diego on her heels.

Andrés ran across the rock and tripped into Emma's arms. He smelled of Carla. Emma wondered what they went through out on the river. What they must have seen with Carla. Still embracing Andrés in a hug, she looked at Jake. "I see you found good company."

Andrés looked at Emma pensively. "Yes, Emma!"

"Very good company," Jake said, giving Andrés a fist bump when he ran back to him. "This guy can do a lot for his age."

Emma mustered a smile. Still feeling the weight of losing Carla and Chuleta, Emma tried to focus her thoughts on the moment. The first reaction that came to her was the flawlessness of Jake's English. She assumed he must have spent time in an English-speaking country or attended a private school in Panama City.

"I can't imagine what you all went through," Emma said. "Which leads me to ask," she paused, not sure how to ask it. "Did you . . . did you mean to come to Almagro?"

"I did." Jake leaned against the rock, patting it so she'd join him. Diego shuffled to the side of Emma. Jake glanced at him but didn't say anything. "I believe you spoke with my friend, Pedro."

Emma closed her eyes in contemplation, which made her even more aware of the pressure she felt from her swollen face. Pedro. Jake.

"Oh my gosh," she whispered.

"That was my reaction, too, when I learned that my phone number had been given away."

Emma leaned deeper into the rock. She always imagined telling and asking Jake so many things if they ever met. She had practiced them, too—in the shower, when she should have been studying, and sometimes sitting on the couch beside Matt. Now, they all vanished except one thought. She waited for something better to come to her, but it didn't.

"You're a popular guy."

Jake's soft laugh didn't match his deep voice. "With a certain type of crowd, you could say."

Emma smiled but didn't feel as collected as he seemed to be. He was an attractive man, mud matted hair and all. But given his popularity with the ladies, she had him pictured twice as buff. Then again, there was that deep voice of his. And his kindness, judging by how he treated Andrés.

Eduardo walked up to them, extended his hand to Jake, and looked at Emma. "Who's your friend?"

"Um . . . well, this is Jake." Emma looked at Jake. "Do you speak Spanish?"

Jake shook his head.

"Welcome to Almagro, my friend!" Eduardo held Jake's hand in a handshake as he patted him on his back.

Andrés jumped off the rock, flying through the air towards them. "Mr. Eduardo say welcome," he said in English.

Jake let go of Eduardo's grip, catching Andrés before he hit the ground.

"Andre*yes*," Emma said. "That was excellent. Where . . . how . . ."

Andrés giggled. "Yes!" He stuck his tongue out at her but retracted it upon meeting her firm stare.

"He knows a lot more English than that," Jake said, raising his hand up and down as Andrés tried to jump up and catch it. "He translated for me the whole way here."

Andrés winked at Emma. One eye after the other, back and forth, as fast as he could.

"And here I was thinking that 'Yes' was the only word he could say."

Jake smiled. "He must've had a good teacher."

"Good teacher," Andrés said. He had already spun around to play hide and seek with María behind a log, his face falling as he caught a glimpse of Carla's body.

By then, the villagers had finished paying their respects to Carla and congregated around Emma and Jake. Emma was taken aback by how relaxed Jake was. Not even she, after two months of Peace Corps training, felt as comfortable as he seemed to be when she first arrived in Almagro. The villagers were also taken aback; Jake looked like a Panamanian from the city but didn't speak Spanish.

Hugo pushed through the crowd. "How long will he be here?"

Emma translated, noticing that Hugo had the same expression as Diego—a forced kind of friendly that didn't succeed in masking skepticism.

"They want to know how long you'll be staying here."

"I'm not sure. I just came on a whim, I didn't know what to expect." Jake paused, then lifted his shoulders. "Could I stay awhile?"

CHAPTER 29

Emma ~ Present

The villagers busied themselves with preparing for Carla's funeral and finding a flip flop for Jake.

"Mine. He must take mine." Martha shoved her flip flop onto Jake's foot. It was too narrow to pass his toes, so she tugged at the *paruma* looped through it to force it on.

"Don't be silly. Mine's bigger," a teenage girl said. She tossed her hair over her shoulder and batted her eyelashes at him.

Emma leaned against the schoolhouse, feeling Jake's pain as he drew in sharp breaths while women and girls shoved flip flop after flip flop onto his wounded foot. They were each convinced that theirs would fit him best as they vied for Jake's attention; they would hear nothing from the men, who wanted to lay the flip flops side by side to see which pair was the biggest.

Abuela blessed her flip flop in a basket of grass crosses for the third time. "Now it will fit." She looked at Martha. "Go on, try it."

Martha rolled her eyes. "It's the same flip flop. God didn't change it between now and five minutes ago."

Abuela banged her flip flop against Jake's big toe, a location she had insisted her stool be within reach of. "*Try it.*"

Watching the fuss, Jake reached for the flip flop himself and put it on his foot. "See?" he said in English. He turned his foot so Abuela could see its bleak fate; the portion of his foot hanging out was longer than the flip flop itself.

Abuela grabbed Federico's arm. "Get me fresh grass from higher up in the village."

Then Abuela said something to Jake, which Emma translated from afar. "She said her crosses aren't working because the grass grew by the river, the part that's now flooded."

Jake twisted around to look at her. Although he was squinting from the sun, she was pretty sure he threw in a wink. "I'm sure that's it." He then scanned the schoolyard, a habit Emma noticed he had picked up since sitting there.

Carla and Chuleta consumed Emma's thoughts, but she still found herself intrigued by Jake. She appreciated how at ease he was interacting with the villagers—how he enjoyed playing with the kids, how patient he was with what she knew seemed like unusual tendencies to him, given his American upbringing. Likewise, the villagers were patient when Jake behaved strangely in their eyes, just like they showed patience when Emma did questionable things, too.

Sonya leaned against the school patio beside Emma. "Something's on your mind. Shall I fancy a guess?"

"Nope." Emma paused. "Unless it's about that other bottle of wine I saw in your bag. We should have a drink sometime in Carla and Chuleta's honor."

"And here I was thinking I'd be able to surprise you. But I think—"

"Emma!" Rebecca hurried over, looking down at her hands. "I found this." She looked up and realized Sonya was talking. "So sorry!"

Sonya smiled and shook her head in response.

"It's just that I found another injection, it was stuck in the crevice of a box."

Sonya's eyes widened. "That's great news."

Emma nodded. "But let me talk with Jake about it first."

Diego had tagged along with Rebecca, stopping so close to Emma that his arm hair rubbed against hers. The perfect time to move. She walked over to Jake, who had gotten caught in a disagreement between Eduardo and Abuela.

"I'm sure God has been taking note of your generosity, Abuela. But Jake is a man. So naturally, a man's flip flop will fit him better." Eduardo studied the group of females surrounding him with their flip flops in hand and sighed.

"How chauvinistic of you." Abuela shifted in her stool, and the grass crosses in her lap fell to the ground. "God created us equal. My flip flop will fit him." She smacked her lips together. "It just needs more time to be blessed."

Jake smiled as he watched the situation unfold. He looked at Emma. "How long do you think they'll fight over me for?"

"As long as you let them."

"I wish I could understand what they're saying."

"You'll pick up on it if you stick around long enough." Emma didn't know what Jake's version of staying for awhile was but, so far, she didn't think she'd mind if it were for a long while.

"I can imagine." Jake looked around the schoolyard again. "Do you know where Maya is?"

"Oh." Emma shook her head. "No, but if I had to guess she's probably at her house."

"She lives here?"

Emma hesitated, feeling like it was a trick question. "Yeah." Then she chuckled, unsure if it was from the question itself or the irony that the man she had thought about for over a year was asking about Maya. "There's nothing else around here but jungle."

"Should I stick it in him?" Rebecca walked up to them, pressing droplets out of a syringe. Diego followed her, his eyes shifting between Emma and Jake.

"Listen," Emma said, turning back to Jake. "Rebecca's a nurse. She wants to give you an antibiotic."

Jake tilted his head. "An antibiotic with a needle?"

"Yes. I forgot I used to find it strange until now."

"Happy to remind you of your American upbringing. And sure." Jake looked at the scratches on his body. *"Gracias,"* he said, turning towards Rebecca.

"Hey, does she have anything for athlete's foot?"

"I doubt it, but I do. How about you settle for Eduardo's flip flop and come with me."

~ * ~

Branches floated halfway up the wooden stilts of Emma's house. With one foot onshore, she reached out her other foot and set it on a log in the water. She twirled it around, pushing a dead fish away from her and Jake. Flies flew up in protest around her leg.

Jake stood beside her. "It doesn't look safe."

"No." Emma sighed.

The river forced them to stand ten feet away from Emma's house. Almagro's new shore. A shore that didn't include her house, her mango tree, her Chuleta. If only it were Chuleta that was still there, she would have gladly given up her home and the mango tree—both of which would recover once the water receded.

She walked along the water's edge to assess the damage from a different angle. The river had dragged her tree trunk staircase almost off her balcony, Mother Nature teasing her with a missed opportunity to have an excuse to place a new one on the other side, away from Maya's view. She squinted to see if a fish part was in any of its notches above the waterline. There wouldn't be; everyone knew the river took Chuleta, not to mention how difficult it was to access her house. But looking for fish parts on her staircase had become a habit.

Emma pushed another fish away from shore. "Chuleta would have loved chasing these guys."

"What's that?"

"Oh." She had walked further along the shore with her thoughts than she realized, forgetting that Jake was hobbling behind her in his new flip flop. "My dog." Emma's voice broke. "The river . . . it carried her away during the storm."

"I'm sorry." He reached for Emma's hand and squeezed it.

Pain shot up her arm, causing her to wince. She pulled away, lifting her palm so he could see her wounds. He nodded in understanding.

"This would have been paradise for her, with so many fish and branches floating in the water."

"Tulip would love it, too."

"Tulip?"

"My dog back home," he said with a gentle smile. "Sounds like she and Chuleta would've gotten along well. We've got shrimp in Charleston. Those are her favorite to chase."

A dog. Home. We. *Accompanied by a wife, child, and white picket fence.* Emma shook the image from her mind. She would get to those conversations, finding out who Jake was. But now wasn't the time. They were still in the same clothes from before the storm and needed to get ready for Carla's remembrance ceremony.

"I know it seems pointless," she said, "but I think I'll walk the shore for a little while longer, just in case the river somehow circled Chuleta back here."

"I'll help t—"

"Jake!"

Emma grimaced. But she knew Jake didn't notice since he'd already turned towards the voice.

Maya waved. "Hi!"

She spoke the word in English, one of only a few she knew how to say. Because the river was so high, Emma and Jake were already a good way up the hill, close to Maya's house. Emma looked at Jake, expecting to see him happy and hoping that, somehow, he wouldn't be.

Jake waved both arms in the air. "Hi!"

Maya motioned for him to come over to her porch.

Jake turned to Emma. "Do you mind? Just for a minute. I want to make sure she's okay. We . . . we went through so much together."

Emma forced a tightlipped smile. "Of course."

Maya was more than fine. Rosa was known for storing more fresh water than any of the other villagers, so Maya had already taken a bucket shower. A fresh coat of pink nail polish laid over the bumps of her old polish. She wore the tightest clothes she owned and a bra stuffed with fresh leaves, which Emma knew she had taken extra care to layer smoothly.

Emma translated Maya and Jake's small talk. She did so verbatim, but it lacked their enthusiastic tone—and gushing, in Maya's case. She was sure Maya wanted to say more to Jake, things that she didn't want Emma hearing. And then there was Jake, who looked at Maya with an intensity that Emma hadn't yet seen from him. She didn't mind that he was flirting with a girl. What troubled her was that the girl he was flirting with was Maya.

"Jake yes! Emma yes!" Andrés ran towards them, swinging around his favorite porch post that leaned over the hill.

"Careful, buddy," Jake said, reaching out to grab him.

Emma tried, unsuccessfully, to retighten her *paruma* while Jake was distracted, wishing Martha was there to help her. "It scared me, too, when I first came here," Emma said, nodding towards Andrés as she spoke to Jake. "But I'm used to it now, for the most part."

Seeing Jake's reaction, Maya ran over to Andrés, brushing her hand against Jake's as she grabbed her brother. Not being able to rely on language, Jake exaggerated a smile and gave her a thumbs up. He glanced at Emma. "I found out on the bus they do thumbs up here."

Emma smiled. "Quick learner." Then she turned to Maya. "Your mom seems to be doing well today, despite the circumstances." She figured Rosa would have told Maya about her Dengue diagnosis.

Maya shrugged. "She'll be in bed before long." She then looked at the entrance of the porch where María rounded the corner. Jake had moved so close to Maya that their skin was touching.

"Girlfriend," Maya said in English, gazing up at Jake as she pointed towards Andrés and María.

The vocabulary they choose to remember, Emma thought.

"Is that right?" Jake said, giving a thumbs up to Andrés and María.

As María got closer, they could see her lip trembling. Earlier, María had been convinced that Carla was sleeping by the shore, ignoring anyone who tried explaining otherwise. Andrés gave her a long hug.

"That's one of Carla's children," Emma whispered to Jake. "One of twelve."

His eyes widened.

Emma looked at Maya, not bothering to translate what they had said. "We should get going," she said first in Spanish then in English. "The remembrance ceremony will be starting soon."

~ * ~

Carla's ceremony was held in a flooded ditch in front of the church. It was Abuela's idea, given that an inch of mud covered the church floor and Carla had died in the river.

The villagers had draped Carla's body across two pews pushed together in front of the church's door, three feet away from a canoe in the ditch. The priest sat at the back of the canoe, giving his sermon. Abuela sat at the front on her custom canoe bench, just feet away from the priest. She rocked them both as she reached down to pick up grass crosses floating in the ditch that had dislodged from the church's walls during the storm. Every villager in Almagro was in attendance, standing around the ditch, staring at the canoe in the foreground and Carla in the backdrop.

Jake bent down to whisper in Emma's ear. "How'd they get the canoe there?"

"Some men carried it up from the river." Emma leaned forward in anticipation of Diego and Hugo huddling closer to her from behind, which they had been doing every time she and Jake talked during the ceremony. Jake, on the other hand, was collected. He maintained his personal space beside her, looking down frequently at Maya who stood to his right, and Andrés who leaned against his leg.

"But it must have been heavy."

Emma nodded. "They chose the smallest one, though."

Even then, with the narrowest and shortest canoe, it barely fit in the ditch. Muddy water had sprayed the closest attendees when they first set it there. At various times during the ceremony, Abuela's hand became wedged between the canoe and side of the ditch as she fished for grass crosses beneath the water. The villagers took turns dislodging it, careful not to interrupt whatever memory someone was sharing about Carla. Emma's own thoughts were interrupted when she heard Mateo's voice.

"She was a great friend. From a generation that has given Almagro so much life." He stopped and smiled at Carla's husband and children, who lined the front of the ditch, closest to the canoe. "May she rest in peace. And may her family and all those in Almagro who loved her find peace."

Emma glanced across the soccer field, which was bloated with mud from the storm. It never flooded, though. Not even close. She spotted Carla's house. The more Emma tried to avoid thinking about how Carla died, the more it gnawed at her. At times, she chalked it up to human nature. In other moments, she knew it was because she had been the last person Carla saw. For as much as Emma didn't want to wonder about the 'hows' of Carla's death, she did. Was it an accident? Perhaps. But in her heart, she sensed it was her worst fear but best guess. A choice.

"I just want to say one thing." The ceremony had ended and Abuela attempted to stand up in the canoe. It wobbled back and forth, rocking between the now chaffed sides of the ditch. The movement made the priest lose his grip on the bible. It landed face down, pages open into the mud.

"Hallelujah!" The priest drew out the word as the bible fell to the ground.

"Yes, Hallelujah," Abuela said, smiling at Federico as he picked it up, wiping it with one of the cloths his family had been using to dry their tears. "Now, listen here." Abuela waited for the villagers to quiet down. "God has shown us, with this storm, why the church must take the *tienda's* spot. It's what Carla would want." She swung out her arm towards a pile of mud looming at the base of the hill. "Just look at this mess."

The villagers reacted—many agreeing, a few groaning.

"This is not the time." Hugo pushed his way to the front of the ditch. "On the day of Carla's death."

Jake leaned into Emma. "What's going on?"

"Just an argument that's been around since Almagro was founded—that the church should have the highest place in the village."

Emma closed her eyes, pushing back a new wave of tears as she thought about how Carla would have loved Jake's presence in the village and how good he was with Andrés. She tried occupying her thoughts with savoring the feeling of Jake beside her, how he chuckled at the things she told him, his breath brushing her skin.

238

"Emma." Jake paused. "I'm worried about being an inconvenience."

"Don't be." She nudged him. "You're giving the villagers something to fuss about. They love that. Especially now, with everything going on." In her head, she continued. *I like having you here. I want to know more about you.*

He nodded slowly. "I just . . . I just know that sleeping space is limited and all."

"I'm not about to tell you it'll be comfortable. But I'll be sleeping there too. We'll make do."

Emma turned back to Abuela, who continued giving her speech, accusing the *tienda* of dumping its rainwater on the church. The villagers at the back of the crowd had already begun heading home. Meanwhile, Mateo challenged Abuela, his voice trembling from emotion, given the day's events. The hill was dumping the rainwater, not his store, he said.

Diego hovered behind Emma and yawned. Emma shifted her shoulders to avoid him. And with that movement, it cleared the way for her to watch from the corner of her eye as Maya scooched closer to Jake, stretching out her pinky, reaching for his.

CHAPTER 30

Jake ~ Present

J ake woke up to a scorpion sharing the wall by his arm. He pulled away, pain searing through his body as the mattress and floor rubbed against his wounds. He had moved halfway off the foam mattress during the night, preferring the concrete to Diego's feet on his chest. The scorpion raised its tail higher, its pinchers poised for an attack.

Snoring came from the schoolroom next door. *At least the girls are getting some sleep*, he thought. Then a soft something brushed against his finger; he pulled away, daring to look too late. The critter had already scurried away. Shifting his eyes from the scorpion to his flip flops, he sat up. Eduardo's flip flop looked like a hardier match for the scorpion, but Jake felt guilty using his gift in that way.

Diego stirred.

"Shh," Jake said, pointing at the scorpion.

Diego gasped and said something in Spanish. Jake wished he understood, especially after his and Diego's conversation the evening before. Now more than ever Jake desired to learn the language his grandparents spoke. To speak the language people expected of him. To belong in both body and tongue.

"Whatcha find?"

Jake jolted, already on edge. He looked up to see Emma peering at him through the open-air classroom window. The work of her pillow and humidity had bent her brown hair at angles that even her curls weren't accustomed to. He could tell her eyes were still glazed from tears, but they weren't as swollen as the day before. Her skin was makeup-free, something he assumed had been the case since she arrived in Almagro, if not before. It suited her. What Diego had told him last night, however, didn't suit him. His English was far from good, but Jake had gotten the gist.

Snapping out of his thoughts, he said, "It's a scorpion."

"Ah." Emma let herself into the classroom—the 'boys' room' as Sonya called it last night when she had helped him, Diego, Rebecca, and Emma set up their sleeping arrangements.

Jake waited for Emma to exchange words and smiles with Diego. When they finished, he pointed to the scorpion. "It seems small, but . . . well, look at him."

Emma nodded, assessing it from different angles. "The smallest ones can be the most dangerous." She slipped off her flip flop and flicked it against the wall. "But I can't tell the difference and, in both cases, they sting." She smacked the side of her flip flop against the wall. Scorpion parts fell into a crack between the mattress.

"Wow. Thanks for that."

"That's a bad second day impression of me." She smiled, putting her flip flop back on. "I don't like killing things, even insects." She shrugged. "Well, besides mosquitos. So, I guess you could say scorpions are an extension of mosquitos to me. Both can send you to the hospital if the right one gets you."

Jake chuckled. "Have you had a run-in with something poisonous here?"

"Thankfully, no. But it happens. And, given how far away Almagro is from civilization, it can be deadly when it does."

"I can imagine." Jake realized he was still sitting on the floor next to Diego and the mattress that they had shared during the night. Embarrassed, he stood as gracefully as possible, sore muscles working against him.

"That's the beauty of mosquito nets." She winked. "They keep a lot more away than just mosquitos."

With Emma and Diego pressing on in Spanish, Jake took the time to walk around the inside of the classroom, studying a half-solved arithmetic equation on a student's desk and peering through another window. Although the sun was out, little light penetrated through the decorative concrete holes. He couldn't imagine how dark the classroom would get on a cloudy day.

The sound of female voices came from the door. Jake turned and was greeted by Rebecca and Sonya.

"Do you drink coffee?" Emma asked.

"Most definitely."

"Great," she said, pointing him towards the cup Sonya was holding, "because you never know what a day in Almagro will bring."

~ * ~

"Is this okay?" Jake felt a tap on the back of his thigh; he raised his hand higher. "How about now?"

242

Abuela smacked her lips together. "*Sí.*"

"Good." He took another grass cross from her hand.

Jake had spent an hour adorning cracks in the church's walls with crosses, and he couldn't picture forgetting the Spanish word for 'yes'. He placed the newest cross in a visible area, just below where the lowest palm leaves of the thatched roof hung over the branches of the church's walls. Abuela tapped his thigh again and said many more words than *sí*.

Emma looked up from the ditch, shovel in hand. "She said to put them under the roof, where the wall meets the palm leaves."

"Not sure how I feel about that." He bent down and tilted his head up. "For starters, there's a bat."

Maya stepped out of the ditch and onto the few feet of dry land where Jake stood, following his gaze. She pressed her head into his lower stomach. He became self-conscious of its bulge—it was a small one, but he hadn't been able to lose it since leaving Arizona. He chuckled at Maya with politeness, hoping she wouldn't interpret it as flirtation. Knowing they couldn't exchange words, he made an exaggerated expression, pointing towards the bat.

He tried to catch Emma's eye, but she had already turned back to the ditch. Or rather, a moat. Emma had explained to him that the villagers wanted to build a deeper, wider trench around the church, complete with its own log bridge for crossing. The purpose was to safeguard the church from future storms and runoff from the *tienda*. Abuela had gotten the idea from photos of castles she'd seen during Emma's English class on Europe. They looked sophisticated, she'd said, and Almagro deserved the same. It made Jake curious to watch Emma teach. Based on seeing her interactions with the kids so far, he sensed she'd be good at it.

Everyone worked on the moat, ankle-deep in water, except Abuela and Carla's family. Abuela had requested that a bench be set on either side of her, holding six children each, plus a stool for Carla's widowed husband. She sang to their broken hearts and stroked the youngest ones while they watched the others work.

"I've never seen this side of her before," Emma said, wiping either sweat or a tear from her eye—Jake couldn't be sure, since the villagers had been alternating between the two throughout the morning. Emma smiled, watching Abuela rock María in her arms. "She never had children herself and," she glanced at her shovel, "I have to admit I had my doubts about how she'd be as a mother if she did."

Jake smiled. "I suppose I should be glad I wasn't assigned to the moat." He watched Emma toss another shovelful of half dirt, half water into a bucket. Maya stood beside her doing minimal work, from what he could tell.

"So, this is what Peace Corps Volunteers do?" he asked.

Emma rubbed sweat from her forehead and unknowingly replaced it with a clump of half-dried mud from her forearm. "We do *everything*."

"Even when it comes to religion? Isn't it a bit . . . well, a conflict of interest?"

"Not in this case." Emma glanced over at Eduardo who stood behind them, hands on his hips, his head tilted as he studied the ditch being expanded into a moat. "All the villagers are Catholic. Plus," she shook her head, "if there isn't peace between the church and *tienda*, I'd never be able to keep the villagers' attention long enough to teach English."

"Fair enough." Jake smiled, wondering if he should tell her about the mud on her forehead. He decided against it, given that a new round of sweat was already washing it away. "How did Catholicism arrive here? Almagro's so remote."

"A Panamanian priest, funded by a Catholic congregation in Panama City, came here years ago. I guess they sent priests to quite a few communities. I'm not sure about the details in between, but you're looking at the final product."

"Sounds like . . . hey now!" Jake felt a splatter on the back of his legs, which ran down to his ankles. He turned around to face Maya and looked down, wondering which would leave him dirtier—the mud on his legs or cleaning them with moat water. He faked a lunge towards her. She giggled, splattering him with water as she ran away.

He turned back to Emma. "She's something isn't she?"

"Mm-hmm."

The priest and Mateo exited the church; Jake watched Emma watch them. She narrowed her eyes so slightly that he wondered if it would've been discernable if he wasn't already studying her face.

Something tapping his muddy calf pulled him away from his thoughts. They were quicker taps than usual, followed by jabs. "Sorry, Abuela," he said, taking her fistful of crosses.

Jake heard a voice from behind him. The villagers went silent and turned towards Eduardo, so Jake followed suit. Even though he couldn't understand what he was saying, based on the tone of his voice, Jake sensed Eduardo was a kind man.

"He's saying we should stop now so we can get cleaned up for Carla's funeral." Emma swooshed her hands through the moat water.

Knowing Abuela wasn't looking, Jake shoved the remainder of the crosses into a single crevice in the church's wall. "It'll be held here, I take it?"

"No, on the other side."

He lifted his eyebrows. "Sounds like we'll be joining Carla."

Emma chuckled. "That was Almagro lingo. I'm not used to translating it to English." She stuck the shovel into dry land and pulled herself out. "The river. We'll be crossing to the other side of the river."

CHAPTER 31

Jake ~ Present

Jake wasn't thrilled about crossing to the other side. It felt like déjà vu, except with Carla's body at the front of the canoe instead of the back. That, and he had a clean shirt and pair of shorts on—something that would be a luxury in a few days' time if he wasn't able to wash his clothes.

The villagers packed into canoes, most of them sitting around its narrow edges. Kids laughed when the canoes tilted from shifting weight. No one startled when the canoe rocked except Jake and, to a lesser degree, Emma, who would reach out to steady themselves. Jake could feel the current had returned to what was likely normal for Almagro. It was the kind of gentle pull that would carry a canoe downstream if one let it but that required identifying a fixed object to notice the change.

"Jake yes! Emma yes!"

Jake waved at Andrés, whose legs hung over a canoe, his feet dangling in the river, just feet away from the one that he and Emma were in.

Emma looked behind her shoulder at Jake, while waving at Andrés. "I still can't believe he knows so much English. 'Yes' was all he ever gave me and," she sighed, "it seems he's reverted back to it."

Jake smiled and made faces at Andrés. "I can relate to him. I was a lost cause in school. My parents saw through it but my teachers never did." He shrugged. "I didn't let them. It was part of the fun."

Rebecca and Diego approached him and Emma in a different canoe. It was the canoe with a motor, which, Jake had learned, belonged to the Ministry of Health. Jake waved to those in it. Over half the canoe sank beneath the water from it being so tightly packed. "And here I was thinking that our canoe was full," he said through a smile.

Diego shouted above the noise. "We leave soon," he said in English.

Although Diego was far from fluent, his English impressed Jake. It was enough for them to have a conversation about Emma last night, although Jake was still unclear about the details. Now, he watched Diego look at Emma, frowning and pointing to his eye as if making a tear fall. Jake felt awkward being a part of it, so he looked the other way, focusing his attention on one of the many branches still floating in the river from the storm.

An arm waving over the water caught his eye. Jake was sure he would recognize it anywhere, given what they went through. And if not, there was the scrape between her thumb and index finger from when they had pulled Carla's body out of the river. Jake tilted his head around the people sitting on the edge of the canoe and flashed a smile at Maya.

"Hi," she said in English, wiggling her fingers above the water.

Jake responded with a smile. He wished he didn't have to rely on body signals to communicate with her. Andrés translated well when they were on their way to Almagro, but even so, he didn't have the skill to handle an in-depth conversation. And then there was Emma. She was the obvious go-to person for translation help. But there was something about it that made Jake uncomfortable asking her for such a favor.

The canoe hit the earth, thrusting forward everyone in it. "Welcome to the other side," Emma said.

Jake scanned his new surroundings. "Looks like more jungle." He went to stand; the villagers gasped as the canoe rocked from his movement. Maya's giggle rose up from the noise.

"Just follow my lead," Emma said. "They'll take Carla from the canoe first and then—" she stopped, watching Carla being carried away. Carla's husband, a couple of her older boys, and Mateo carried the bamboo posts that her body laid on.

Jake knew he should have been more fixated on Carla, but Emma's face stole his attention. It was as if he could read the villagers' stories and the relationships they had with each other through the subtle movement of Emma's lips and the crease in her eyes. Even so, pages were missing.

It was a slow walk through the jungle; Abuela wanted to be at the front of the line to accompany Carla's children. The relaxed pace was important, she said, since it gave everyone more time to think about Carla.

Jake stepped around a grass cross that Abuela had thrown from her basket. The villagers in front of him hadn't noticed it, given that mud oozed through its fibers from it being pressed into the ground. He looked at

Emma, who walked beside him when the path was wide enough.

"Did you know Carla well?"

"Yes." Emma teared up. "She was like a mom to me."

He put his arm around her shoulder. "I can't imagine what you must be going through."

She nodded, but he sensed it was fueled with hesitation. Knowing Diego was behind them, he pulled his arm away.

"We're here," Emma said as they emerged to the center of a narrow strip of land cleared of trees. "It's in the shape of a cross."

Jake followed Emma's finger, which pointed to the three shorter ends of Almagro's cemetery as they walked around the center of the cross.

"Wow."

"And," she pointed behind them to the longest part of the cross where they had just walked in from, "they can extend the cemetery as much as they need to, by taking down trees from the ends of it."

"Amaz—" Jake stopped upon seeing Rebecca walk up to them.

Emma translated. "She and Diego are leaving now."

"So soon?"

"They just wanted to pay their respects, to see that Carla made it here okay. But they have to get to Chepo before dark, otherwise they'll be spending another night in Almagro."

"We wouldn't want that." Jake kissed Rebecca on the cheek and shook Diego's hand. "I've been dreaming all day about having the mattress to myself."

Emma nodded. "Ditto."

Jake smiled at Rebecca and Diego, then walked away. He felt uncomfortable being near Emma when Diego was around so he stayed busy by studying the graves, most of which were marked with sticks in varying phases of deterioration. In some cases, a smaller stick laid at the base, a mere memory of the cross it used to form. The men busied themselves with digging a grave for Carla, dirt already piled high on two sides. Behind them, women stood by a line of trees that formed one arm of the cross, somberly eating sugarcane they had picked by the river. They were talking about Carla, given how many times he heard her name mentioned. Meanwhile, children ran through the cemetery, oblivious to the bodies beneath their feet.

Something tickled Jake's hips. He jumped and heard Maya's giggle before he turned around and saw her. "Hey, now."

He laughed gently, not wanting to make her feel bad, but stepped back. Without looking, he knew the eyes of the villagers were on them. And since he didn't have the courage to face them given the circumstances, he continued to face Maya.

She was undeniably his type. Dark features, flirtatious, and with a mischievous side to her—he could tell without even exchanging words. His old self would have gotten to know her far more intimately by now. But he didn't want to, and that relieved him. Nonetheless, he wished he could talk with her to reminisce about their experience on the river. An innocent conversation, nothing more.

With her back facing the villagers, Maya stood on her tippy toes, feet apart from Jake, and puckered her lips. Jake glanced over at Emma. It was an odd reaction, he knew, even as he was doing it.

Diego and Rebecca had left, and he saw Emma speaking with Eduardo. Even from a distance, her face looked pale. Jake knew Carla's funeral was enough to explain it, but there was something about Emma's expression that once again made him sense that it wasn't the only reason.

He looked back at Maya. She had only been holding the pose for a matter of seconds but was now rocking from heel to toe, her lips still puckered. "Excuse me," he said with a nod, passing Carla's grave as he walked back to Emma.

Emma startled when he arrived. "Hey," she said, looking at him hesitantly. As if sensing his concern, she put on a smile. "Are they making progress over there?"

"Gosh, yes. At an astonishing rate, though I can't tell if it's thanks to or in spite of Abuela's directing."

"I wouldn't expect anything less."

Eduardo started speaking to Jake, with Emma translating. "He said he's happy you're here. That your presence is welcomed by the villagers. And," she paused, glancing at Eduardo as he said it, "to make wise choices with the welcome."

Jake exaggerated a nod, which felt both strange and necessary since he couldn't exchange words with Eduardo. "He seems like a wise man."

"He is. Now, how about we check on their progress?" Emma motioned them all towards Carla's grave.

Jake rushed to keep up as she headed towards the villagers. "Hey, is everything okay?"

"What's that?" Emma paused. "Oh, yeah." She looked behind her. "As okay as possible, that is, given the circumstances."

"Right." Jake followed Emma's gaze. Instead of looking at him, she looked at a place past him. There, he saw a faintly matted path cutting through the knee-high grass in the cemetery, forming an almost perfect line. The path ended at the jungle's edge, which seemed to give way to a trail—an old, mostly overgrown one.

"Seems like some animals came through here." His eyes widened. "Could it be a puma of some sort?" They had already arrived at the grave, Carla's husband and Mateo barely visible from the hole, scoops of dirt flying out, adding to the now four piles around them.

Emma shrugged. "Could be."

Abuela clapped her hands to get Jake's attention. He smiled and walked over to her, kissing her cheek as he took a cross from her hand.

"She'd like you to tell everyone about how you arrived in Almagro," Emma said. "While we wait for them to finish digging."

Jake glanced at the shaded area where Carla's body was covered in *parumas* and Abuela's crosses. It didn't feel like the right time for storytelling, let alone a long one. He assumed Maya and Andrés had already filled in the villagers on their experience with him. Between that and wanting to impress the villagers with his Spanish, he decided to sum up his arrival in two words. Grinning, he said, "*Diablo rojo.*"

Jake managed to hear Emma's "Oh, no" above the sound of the other villagers gasping, fanning themselves, and searching the ground for Abuela's crosses strewn about Carla's grave. He looked at Emma. "I take it that was the wrong thing to say?"

"Mm-hmm," she said, flashing him a hesitant smile through clenched teeth. "It means red devil."

"Right, but that's what the buses are called. Ah . . . they don't know that, do they?" he said, remembering how far away they were from the city.

She shook her head. "They do. But since it has the word 'devil' in it, they believe the entire bus system is a sin."

"Oh, man." He covered his face. "I feel bad."

"Don't. I did the same thing when I arrived. But—" she looked at Abuela who was already rummaging through her bag of crosses, divvying them up between Carla and Jake. Jake's pile was so high that it teetered into Carla's. "You're going to have to go along with what they're about to do."

Abuela shouted to Emma, who translated to Jake. "She said that they'll begin taking the devil out of you as soon as Carla's buried. Also," she paused, waiting for Abuela to finish. "You'll need to remove the clump of crosses you shoved into the church wall when we get back."

~ * ~

Jake watched Sonya walk out of the classroom, willing her to walk faster. As it was, she had been chatting with them for too long that evening. It would have been fine—wonderful, even—on a normal night. But not that night. Once she was out of sight, he looked at Emma, not wasting time on small talk.

"So. I've got a rather . . . personal . . . question."

"Sure," Emma said, folding her hands on the student desk she sat at.

"Well, I'm not sure how to say this." He looked down, then back up at her. "Have the crosses . . . have they ever made you . . . itch?"

Emma looked up at the thatched roof in contemplation. "Not per se, but my legs sometimes get a small rash when I walk through fresh grass."

"Mm-hmm. Uh . . . well you see, it's not my legs." He glanced down at the crotch of his pants, still feeling the aftermath of the crosses. The villagers had covered him head to toe in order to rid him of the red devil. The men even pushed some crosses down where his shorts sat on his waist.

Emma chuckled. "Oh, that kind of itch. I get where you're going now."

Jake smiled, trying his best to look cheerful but unable to see the humor in it.

"I'm sorry," she said, no longer holding back her laughter. "It's just that it's a running joke us volunteers have here, talking about the first time we had *coloradillas*." She got up. "Hang on a sec."

Jake wasn't sure where she was going, but he hoped it wasn't to fetch the villagers. He glanced at his mattress propped against the back wall. Emma had told him that Sonya set it outside earlier in the day to burn off sweat and Diego's germs. He suddenly felt bad for wanting Sonya to leave, despite his discomfort.

Emma returned with a bottle of clear liquid. She handed it to him. "This will take care of it."

He unscrewed the cap and took a whiff. "Rubbing alcohol?"

"Yup. If it were your own bottle, I'd tell you to tip the top right over your itchy spots. But since it's Sonya's, it's best to pour it on your finger first."

"Right." He gave her a wary glance.

"Turning around, don't worry." She paused. "Or, on second thought, I'll just go to bed."

"Don't bother. Something tells me this isn't your first run-in with it."

Emma turned her back to him. "Definitely not."

"So, why don't you fill me in on what this thing is I'm treating."

"Do you have a weak stomach?"

"After what I've seen in the past few days? No way."

"Right. So, *coloradillas* are tiny red insects that sit on blades of grass and other low-lying foliage. They wait for any creature with blood to brush against it."

"Woah."

"I know."

"Not that . . . well, that too . . . but this rubbing alcohol."

Emma laughed and this time, Jake joined.

"You'll never look at rubbing alcohol the same way again."

"No way. Can I just dump the whole bottle over these spots?"

"I know it's tempting, but you'll need to use it again over the next few hours to kick the itch for good."

"Gotcha. Okay then, tell me more about these critters on my body."

"*In* your body," Emma corrected. "*Coloradilla* search for the warmest, most protected spots. So, in humans, they target the groin, panty line, armpits, and rolls of fat." She paused. "And well, in women they love to congregate under bra straps."

"I'm getting itchy again just thinking about it."

"Yeah, well, the itchy part doesn't begin until they bite through your skin and burrow inside. It's possible to pick them out, but they're minuscule so most people need someone else to do it for them and . . . well, you can see where that could get complicated."

"Right." Jake moved from treating his groin to his waistline where his shorts sat, relishing in the rubbing alcohol's euphoric relief. "Wait . . . are these chiggers you're describing?"

"Exactly. You've heard of them?"

"A little. They say they're in South Carolina but since I grew up surrounded by water and city I never had a run-in with them." He shrugged. "I guess it took me coming to Panama."

Emma smiled. "I hadn't ever experienced them either. I don't know how they treat them in the U.S., but here we use rubbing alcohol—it kills the chiggers and the itch. But the best way to avoid getting them in the first place is to put Vaseline around your ankles, that way they get stuck and can't climb up your body."

"Fascinating."

"I've got some Vaseline at my house, so I'll give you some, once we're able to access it."

"Sounds good. Oh, and you can turn around now. I feel like a new man."

"You'll really be a new man once your scabs peel from all those scratches."

Jake eased onto the desk of the student chair he was sitting in and exchanged a knowing look with her. He couldn't believe his life, sitting in a Panamanian schoolroom, in a jungle, talking about insects burrowing into his skin. And all because of a phone number. He softened his voice. "I'm really glad we connected, Emma. Who would've thought?"

"I know," she said, following his lead by sitting on top of a student desk next to him. "I had conjured up countless scenarios about you, about why so many people you knew didn't know where you were." She paused. "Oftentimes, I didn't think you were alive, let alone that we'd meet."

"I suppose it was hard not to wonder about me with my friends . . . and, well, others writing you as much as they did."

She flashed him a smile. "Yeah."

"Hey." Jake scooted closer towards her, the desk wobbling from his movement. "You still have your phone, don't you?"

"Yes. I mean, I'm not sure if it works since I haven't turned it on in a while. I left it at my house during the storm."

"Right. But maybe if it does, I could use it to translate with Maya?"

CHAPTER 32

Emma ~ Present

Ever since the storm, time in Almagro was measured by branches on the shore. Hugo stood in front of the villagers, his legs teetering between two branches with girths wide enough to be trees themselves. They were the driest set of branches, the first ones the river had pulled away from after it began receding. Six layers of increasingly wetter branches lay behind him. Seven days since the storm.

Hugo scanned the crowd. "The time is right."

"Finally," Martha whispered.

Emma looked at her, feeling her *paruma* push against her stomach from how tight Martha had tied it. "Do you think they'll find any gold?"

"We." Martha patted Emma's arm. "Do you think *we'll* find any."

"How many canoes are you taking?" Mateo asked. He had closed the *tienda* to participate in the meeting.

Hugo held up his fingers. "Two. Just for now, just until we know how it goes."

"And how will you decide?" Rosa's voice came from behind, halfway down the hill from the *tienda*. Her health was improving, likely from a combination of Rebecca's medicine and the Dengue running its course out of her body. Even so, Emma knew she was taking it easy; it would have been difficult for her to walk back up the hill if she went all the way down to the shoreline.

"We'll do it by family. One person per household." Hugo paused. "Plus Emma and Jake, of course."

Jake leaned over. "I heard my name."

The air was so still that Emma swore she felt his breath rustle strands of her hair. "They want you to go along."

"Wow, that's great."

"That's one way to look at it." She bumped his arm with her elbow. *I need to stop doing that*, she thought as she watched him flinch from a bruise he'd gotten during the storm. "You may feel differently after they put you to work."

Hugo cleared his throat. "We need to get going soon if we're to take advantage of the day. Let's meet back here in an hour." He stepped onto another branch. It wobbled from his weight since it straddled smaller branches beneath it. Emma caught a whiff of decaying fish. Once the villagers had taken their pick of fish to eat after the storm, they pushed the beached ones back into the river for the current to carry away. But even so, it was impossible to find them all.

Emma looked up at Jake. "We'll need to pack an overnight bag."

"Sounds great."

They walked together to Emma's house after picking up Jake's bag at the school. The villagers insisted that her house wasn't in a livable state yet. They warned her that an array of creatures living in the branches would climb up her house at night and attack her in her sleep. Emma knew it was a notion rooted in truth; snakes, spiders, and other critters had already made the branches their home. But she found comfort in having a mosquito net. The villagers disagreed, saying her independence clouded her judgment.

Emma watched Jake stare at Maya's house as they walked by. She knew he was hoping that Maya would be on her porch; it was the place where he had been spending much of his time since arriving in Almagro. Emma never noticed him stopping by uninvited, but she also hadn't seen him decline an invitation from Maya, which involved animated hand waving. It was no use—and more importantly, it wasn't her place—to stop him.

"Would you rather stay here while I run down to my house?"

"And miss the chance to walk up that tree trunk of yours? Never."

"Alright. Hugo said he shifted my staircase so it doesn't fall from our weight, but I can't guarantee what state the house will be in."

Jake smiled, and her heart pattered upon seeing three small ripples form at the corners of his mouth. She swore they weren't always there when he smiled at Maya.

"No judgment here," he said.

Emma hadn't expected her first time going home after the storm to be on such rushed terms, but she didn't want to delay the gold mining trip. From afar, a watermark on the wooden stilts was the only indication there had been a flood. That, and the new location of her staircase. They made it halfway over the floor of branches to her staircase when Jake slipped.

"Yikes!" he shouted, yanking his foot up between the branches. A tarantula stirred, running up the side of a log.

Emma jumped to a branch away from it, sharing Jake's leery stare. "That kind isn't poisonous . . . but still." She shuddered. "Maybe the villagers weren't so wrong when they said my house would be full of critters."

And so it was. Emma heard the scattering of cockroaches and other creatures at the first push of her bamboo door. When she opened it, the breeze stirred debris on her floor—fallen pieces from her palm roof, termite wings, and critter droppings. "It's only been a week," she whispered.

"This is so cool!" Jake ducked under the low-lying door, scanning the space that had only ever been Emma's.

"It's musty." She walked over to her bed, shaking the mosquito net to free it from pieces of dried palm leaves before pulling it open. "Ugh, still damp," she said, squeezing her mattress. "Can you help me carry it onto the balcony?"

"Sure. And I bet Maya can bring it back in if it rains while we're gone."

Emma bit her cheek—a habit she had picked up on since Jake's arrival. "A little rain may do it good to kick the smell."

She removed her backpack and all the loose items she had placed on her mattress before the storm. Hoping her bamboo nightstand would withstand the weight, she piled them on top of it. She grabbed her pillow. It felt heavy, with a weight that slid from the back to the front of the pillowcase as she tossed it onto the nightstand. Then she remembered her phone. She grabbed at the air seconds too late as it thumped to the floor.

"Would you look at that!" Jake grinned, making Emma's stomach churn since she knew what would come next. "You still don't mind if I use it, do you?"

"Of course not." She hoped her smile looked genuine as she bent down, picked up the phone, and handed it to him. "I'm just not sure how much battery it has left."

A creak came from the backside of her house. She knew Jake didn't hear it because he made noise himself as he walked across the floorboards of her home, dissecting her life with his eyes. She didn't mind; it was an unusual feeling, given how much she valued her privacy. She instinctively peered through a large crack in her wall to see where the creak had come from.

As if she knew Emma would be there, Maya looked at the same spot. With a smirk, she shouted from below, "They'll leave without us if we don't get going!"

~ * ~

Afternoon hadn't even come yet and the villagers already realized that gold mining wasn't as easy as Mateo was led to believe. Their disappointment was offset, however, by their discovery of clay. Red clay bearing streaks from the current clung to the edges of the river where the water had receded. It prompted passionate discussions about their ancestors' intuitiveness and theories about why Almagro's clay had disappeared.

Emma stood waist-deep in water in a cove they discovered a half-hour from Almagro. It took them over an hour to clear the cove of branches but, once they had, it was the cleanest water she had seen since the storm. A piece of hair fell across her face. She brushed it away, letting go of her wooden pan. It bobbed in the water, bouncing against her hips.

"Not like that." Mateo waded over to Martha. "It's with the wrists, not the arms."

"Easy, Mateo." Eduardo leaned against his shovel on land where the river met the cove. "Let everyone find their own way."

Mateo shook his head. "But they showed me." He took the pan from Martha. "Everyone watch. It's like this." He swirled the pan in a circle, dipping down one side to pick up a small amount of water. But he tipped it too deep into the river, causing water to splash out on the other side, taking half the mud—and, presumably, gold—with it.

"See?" Martha slapped his hand and pulled the pan back towards her. "It's harder than it looks."

"Maybe we can look for it in the dirt," Maya said.

She strolled out of the river, leaving her pan bobbing alone. Smiling at Jake as she passed him, she thrust out her chest, water dripping down it. Jake smiled at her and hovered a fresh scoop of dirt above the soil as he waited for Mateo's directions on where to take it. Emma chuckled to herself; Maya hadn't realized that the river had rearranged the leaves in her bra, many of which now poked out of her low-cut top.

Mateo walked back and forth through the river, monitoring the villagers' panning jobs. Most were doing better than his example, but not by much. Emma realized she was more comfortable looking at Mateo now. When news first arrived about Carla's death, she worried—albeit unreasonably—that a single stare at him could reveal Carla's secrets. A week wasn't much time, of course, but she hadn't heard any gossip about Carla. Not even from Abuela. It was enough to comfort her, but it didn't alleviate her own thoughts.

Could Mateo have known Carla was pregnant? If he didn't, would he want to know? They were questions that crept into her mind often, ones that made her wonder if

Carla and Mateo's time together was sparked by boredom or by love. Emma would replay interactions she remembered between Carla and Mateo countless times in her mind. Each time, she saw a scene that showed an increasing amount of love between them—how he'd sneak her a piece of candy or fill her bag with a little extra rice. But was it because of what she now knew?

"He's a nice man." Martha waded through the water to Emma. She stopped so close they were practically brushing arms as they circled their pans in the river. "But," she sighed, "even nice men can be misguided."

Emma narrowed her eyes. "What are you getting at?"

"You know very well." Martha winked. "I'm on team Emma."

"Keep it down." She batted her hand at Martha. "The last thing I need is rumors flying around."

"So, it *is* true."

"Ay, you guys are so set on marrying me off. First Hugo, then Dieg—"

"Oh, Hugo. Poor man."

Emma nodded. "It's got to be hard, in a village so small. Choices are limited . . . nonexistent, really."

"Maybe someday it won't be that way." Martha touched Emma's arm. "They say there are lots of people in the city." She tilted her head back and looked up at a sky crisscrossed with treetops. "The opportunities to find a mate must be endless."

Emma smiled at her. "Just about." Flashes of her Peace Corps training in Panama City came to mind. She couldn't imagine not knowing how to picture crowds of people. With the exception of a few, most of the villagers didn't know what it was like.

"Ugh. She makes me sick."

Emma followed Martha's gaze to Maya, who crouched over the ground, poking at dirt as she pretended to look for gold. Her knees were straight, making her bottom stick out and her shorts ride up. It gave Jake—and everyone in the cove—a view of near unobstructed skin.

"Got to give the man credit, though." Martha nodded towards the hammocks where Jake had walked off to. "Team Emma."

If only. Emma knew Jake's departure from Maya wasn't as innocent as it looked. She swirled her pan, knowing Mateo would be looping back to check on their progress soon. But her eyes stayed on Jake. He reached down into his hammock, the one that would be his bed that night. It had been a scene trying to install the hammocks on the trees when they first arrived. Once ready, she had watched Jake place an object in his. Now, he walked back to Maya, swinging it in his hand.

Maya jumped up and down when she saw it, patting her chest as she stared at Emma's phone. She tried to grab it from him, but Jake said something to her. He was talking too low for Emma to make out his words, but he wasn't too far away for her to read his lips.

"Later."

CHAPTER 33

Emma ~ Present

The villagers huddled around Eduardo, staring at the spec of gold.

"It must weigh at least a few ounces," one of the villagers said.

"No." Mateo spun around in the water, creating waves that bumped into the wooden pan the gold sat in. "But it's a start."

"Careful," Martha said, narrowing her eyes at him.

Hugo patted Eduardo's back. "We should've had you panning all along."

Emma stood beside Jake and watched Eduardo nod, looking solemn. She knew it was a conflict of interest for him, finding the item the villagers wanted, the one he sensed could be bad for Almagro. Maya came up from behind and wedged herself between Emma and Jake. Emma waited until they exchanged greetings, keeping her eyes on the wooden pan. Then, she turned to Jake.

"It can't even be an ounce."

He shook his head. "Not even close."

"It's amazing though, how even that tiny piece has value." She looked at the shore where mounds of dirt hovered above the brush. "I'm just not sure it's worth it."

Martha shouted, pointing at Eduardo's pan as Mateo dipped in his finger to pull out the gold. "There's another one! Look, it's even bigger."

Jake leaned in to see what the fuss was about. "It looks like they were on to something when they said to dig around the roots. Maybe the gold does get caught in them." He glanced at Emma. "Poor trees."

She nodded, resisting the urge to wrap her arm around his waist. He had moved closer to her when he leaned in to look at the pan.

Hugo spoke above the excited chatter. "My dear friends, let's take a break to prepare dinner. We'll return at sunset."

Emma listened to Hugo assign dinner tasks before translating to Jake. "C'mon," she said, waving for him to follow her. "He's asked us to collect banana leaves for dinner."

"Seems like an odd time to stop panning, right when they found something."

"It does, but the stomach can't wait."

Emma slashed at grass as they followed the contour of the river. "This is for the spiderwebs, just as much as the brush," she explained, waving the machete in front of her.

Jake raised his hands in the air. "More than happy to walk behind you. Time has clearly served you well here...unless you used to walk around the U.S. with a machete."

"You'd be surprised," she said, turning around to playfully tap his arm. Looking back at the path ahead of her, she felt the question lingering on her tongue. She had been wanting to know the answer to it for days. Now seemed like the right time to ask. "Speaking of time, do you know when you'll be leaving?"

Jake fumbled, paused, and fumbled again. "Do . . . do you want me to leave?"

"Oh, no. Of course not. You're welcome to stay as long as you'd like." *How could you so poorly word the question you repeated countless times in your head?* she thought as she tried to undo her words. "The villagers love having you around. Your height alone makes you valuable." She turned around, realizing how that sounded amongst the rest of her rambling. "Not that they wouldn't want you here if you weren't tall."

"Okay, good." He laughed and let out a sigh. "But what about you? Does it bother you that I'm here?" He paused. "I'd understand. I know it's a lot, the way you have to translate for me and all."

"No, I don't mind." And while that was true, it was watching Jake and Maya together that bothered her. Emma would never say it though. Even if she hadn't developed feelings for Jake, she would mind any decent guy hanging out with Maya. For she knew, without needing to consult her gut, that Maya couldn't be trusted.

"Great," Jake said, smiling at her. "Well, to get back to your question then, I'm not sure when I'll leave."

Emma stopped by a group of bananas, nodding at them in response as she walked around, studying them from different angles. She bent down to make sure wasps or bats wouldn't attack them from beneath the leaves.

Jake stood beside her, following her gaze. "To be honest, I have a bad habit of leaving . . . leaving without warning."

"Well, Almagro will take care of that for you." Emma pulled down the tip of a banana leaf and slashed her machete through its stem. She passed the leaf to Jake.

"There's no way to come or go without the villagers knowing."

"See? Maybe the higher powers knew Almagro was what I needed."

Emma cut another banana leaf, finding courage in facing the foliage. "Did you really come here just to meet me? It seems like a bold move to seek out a stranger in the middle of the rainforest."

"I know." He spotted the next banana leaf she zeroed in on and pulled it down for her. "I've always been curious about my roots, though."

"But aren't your roots on the northern border?"

"Yes." He chuckled and, for the first time, Emma sensed nervousness in his tone. "I'll be making my way there next. But when I found out through Pedro and Oscar that you were in Panama and you—" he paused, and Emma stared at him, holding her machete mid-strike. "Well, he made it seem like you were asking a lot of questions about me. I thought it would be interesting for us to meet before I go up there."

Emma lowered her machete and looked at him. "That's true, I was asking a lot of questions." She squinted as a ray of sun emerged from a cloud. "I got bits and pieces of your life, of who you could be, through the people writing to you. And every time someone wrote, I felt like it raised more questions than answers. Plus," she paused to slash her machete through another stem, "I wanted to know why no one knew your number had changed. I . . . I was starting to worry right along with those writing to you." She smiled at him. "Don't let it go to your head, but you seem to be a better person than the man I had conjured up in my mind."

Jake laughed. "That's a relief. Arizona was . . . well, it was a phase in my life. I made friends there, but I began to see them as temporary ones, company to my adventure." He shook his head. "They cared more than I thought."

"And the ladies?"

Jake snorted and flashed a look at Emma through the corner of his eye. "Above all else, you could say."

Emma laughed and turned back to the banana tree.

"You know, I left Arizona because I didn't see the point in it, the point in that adventure. I was going down the wrong path, a path I thought I wanted until I was on it."

"You recognized it. That's good."

"But the thing is, I didn't see the good that came of it, even after a year went by. My family was distressed." He tilted his head to the side. "I told them I was leaving the same morning that I left home. And then there was the guilt of not having closure with those I knew in Arizona. Of course, staying silent on them indefinitely wasn't part of the plan." He shrugged. "But I already told you about Lizzie."

Emma smiled, remembering the conversation they had a few evenings back about Jake's ex. They had laid on their mattresses pressed against the same concrete wall, a classroom apart, as Jake told her about how his phone was lost and recovered. It was Emma's favorite moment with him, until now.

"Anyhow, I've been rambling too much about me. Why don't you tell me about Diego?"

"Diego?"

"Yeah, your boyfriend."

"My what?" Emma swung around, nearly hitting him with her machete. "Eek, sorry about that." She paused and composed herself. "Who told you he's my boyfriend?"

Jake's mouth hung open and he shifted his eyes back and forth. "He did." He said each word so slowly it was as if each one was its own sentence.

Emma began rambling in Spanish. "I'm sorry," she'd say in English between another round of Spanish. The only thing that made her stop was Jake standing there, a concerned expression on his face.

He lifted his shoulders in a half shrug and attempted a smile. "Sorry I brought it up?"

"No. Thank you." She stuck her machete into the ground. "He told you since he knows you can't communicate with the villagers."

"So—"

Emma heard Jake catch himself, but she already knew where he was going with it. She softened her voice. "No, he's not my boyfriend."

Jake made an okay sign with his hand. "Crystal clear."

"Did he say anything else?" Emma cut a final banana leaf and swore she heard Jake draw a breath to speak before stopping.

"Nope. Just that."

"Good." She glanced at the sky. "We should get back. It's already taken us longer than it should have."

"Of course. But um . . . there's just one thing . . . just so you know."

Emma looked at him, noticing how he pulled at his fingers. "I told Maya I'd do the translating thing with your phone later, I—"

"No problem." The words came out shorter than she would have liked, but it was the best she could manage. She swung the machete towards the trail. "Let's get dinner."

~ * ~

If pruney legs were possible, Emma was sure hers would be by the end of the trip. She dug her heel into the mud, leaning forward in the water to stretch her calf. Even though the moonlight was now stronger than the glow leftover from the sunset, Mateo insisted gold would still be visible. His claim no longer appeased the villagers; they were satisfied with the day, given they had found more gold after dinner.

"My friend, it's time to give the earth a rest." Eduardo pushed his shovel into the dirt and stepped away from it.

"Agreed," Martha said, tugging at Emma's *paruma* so she'd follow her out of the river. "Now that it's dusk, anything could be lurking around."

"Why, that's what the fire is for." Mateo opened his arms and spun in a circle in the water.

Emma squeezed water out of her *paruma*. "There's always tomorrow. Isn't that what you tell me when I invite you to English class?"

"Well done, *mi hija*." Eduardo tipped his head towards her.

Emma smiled warmly at him, then walked over to Jake, who was crouched over a root trying to remove soil around it without damaging the tree.

"You've gotten bold during your week here," Emma said.

"By digging up soil?"

"By digging up soil with your bare hands when it's too dark to see what could bite you."

He laughed. "Tell me we're done?"

"Your service won't be needed until dawn." She smiled at him, then walked to her hammock, kicked off her flip flops, and made the best attempt she could at covering the mosquito net around her. She knew it needed to be tucked all the way under her body or else the mosquitos would bite her through the cloth hammock.

Eduardo followed suit, a couple of hammocks away from her. "Hammocks are a funny thing," he said with a tone that was equally upbeat and bemused. "They feel like a luxury to lay in, a break from a hard day's work, until you have to spend a full night in them."

Emma nodded, reaching up to make sure the mosquito net covered her head. Her legs would fall asleep before long, due to the curvature of the hammock. And, with the jungle as her floor, she'd have little choice but to put up with the discomfort until morning.

She closed her eyes, picking one of the many forest sounds to focus on. It was a game she played each evening, to count how many nights in a row she could identify a new insect or animal.

A crunch on the ground broke her concentration. She opened her eyes just in time to see a shadow passing over her stomach. She followed it, watching another shadow accompanying that one into the jungle. A long one and a short one. She felt her throat tighten. Jake didn't owe her anything. On the contrary, he had warned her that he'd be meeting up with Maya that night. At least, she had interpreted it as a warning.

The crunching noise sounded again, this time quicker. Closer. It wasn't a person, not from the rhythm of its walking. Besides, she was so close to the jungle's edge, a person wouldn't have had room to walk behind her. She leaned over to look around at what it was, her hammock tipping down, right into the panting creature.

Emma screamed and squealed in the same breath. "Chuleta!"

CHAPTER 34

Jake ~ Present

The villagers noticed the empty hammock at dawn. Eyes closed, Jake heard footsteps circling a fire that still crackled, fed with enough firewood to get them through the night. Whispers turned to shouts. He flung his eyes open just as Emma crouched beside his hammock.

"Maya's gone."

Jake sat up in his hammock. "What?"

He fumbled his way out, forgetting the mosquito net was around him. A dog jumped up at him, ripping the fabric. Emma held it back and Jake swore he heard her say the name Chuleta, but his mind raced too fast to make sense of anything going on around him.

"Where'd you go last night?"

Emma's tone was harsh, clearing the way for his first coherent thought. *I was the last person who saw her.*

"We went down to the river, not far from here." Jake stood and scanned the scene of villagers frantically dashing about, calling Maya's name. He looked at Emma. "That's it, I swear."

"Did she come back with you?"

"She started to. And then," he paused, remembering the moment, not sure how much to say. "She . . . she said she didn't want to go back yet."

"And you didn't stay with her?"

Should he tell her? It wasn't the right time; he didn't want to embarrass Emma. And yet, if the villagers were thinking he had done something to Maya, embarrassment didn't seem like such a bad byproduct. Regardless, he decided to omit it—for now. "No, I didn't stay with her."

"You left her in the woods alone?"

"Yes, but it was because she insisted." He looked at Emma, then to the ground, shaking his head. "Please, Emma. I swear I didn't do anything. You have to believe me."

Emma nodded. "I do. She's a tough one, there's no way to change her mind once it's set on something." She turned around and spoke to the other villagers, presumably translating the conversation they just had. Then she turned back to Jake. "They want you to take us to where the two of you went."

Jake instinctively reached down to pick up Emma's phone. "Of course," he said, waving his hand for them to follow.

It wasn't a difficult path to remember, and Jake felt strange leading the way this time instead of Maya. He hoped she hadn't done anything self-destructive after their conversation. Maybe it was the phone's poor translation, he rationalized to himself. The signal was mediocre at best. Then again, no translation was needed for body signals.

And then there was Emma.

He looked back and tried to smile at her, but his lips felt weighted. His stomach twisted at the thought of how last night could impact her. It wasn't intentional; he couldn't have known that Maya would react so poorly. Or how the phone may have translated his words.

Emma interrupted his thoughts. The path forced her and the villagers to walk in a single path behind him, but the tremor in their voices resonated so clearly within him that it was as if they were all shouting their worries in his ear, all at once. "They want to know how much further it is," she said.

"Not ver . . . oh!" A dog came up to him, running in circles around his legs.

"Chuleta!" Emma said.

"Is this *the* Chuleta? Your dog?"

"Yes." Emma smiled as Jake playfully grabbed her face. "She appeared last night. A skinny version of herself, but that'll soon be fixed."

"Good news feels extra good at a time like this." He paused, emerging through the trail to the river's edge. "This is it."

He spotted Maya right away. She was impossible to miss, wrapped in a bright green *paruma*, laying on a washed-up tree trunk to the left of them. It was where she and Jake had sat last night. Where they had shared laughs . . . and where those laughs had ended. The villagers ran past him, shouting. Jake's legs felt heavy, as if remaining in place would protect him from the consequences. But he knew it was too late, that it wouldn't make a difference. For whether Maya was dead or alive, consequences were inevitable.

~ * ~

The villagers agreed they would return to Almagro without mining, given the morning's events. But first, they needed to cut down a vine for Rosa.

Spines pricked Jakes's fingertips. He pulled away, shaking his hand. He wondered if he'd be able to grab the vine before Hugo and Eduardo accidentally thrust him into the thorny tree it clung to. The two men each held one of Jake's legs, hovering him unevenly a few feet above the ground, parallel with the tree.

Emma coaxed him on from below. "You're almost there."

Distracting himself from the threat was his way of coping with the villagers' latest use of his height. "Does it really work?"

"They say it does . . . I feel like it could."

"Here's hoping." He slashed at the vine above his head again.

"They're having a fit that you won't use a machete."

"I know, but I don't trust myself." Sensing that Eduardo and Hugo had steadied his legs, Jake batted two more spines with the edge of his knife and then, with the path clear, hacked the vine three times. He pulled his hand back, feeling Eduardo and Hugo shifting their weight again, making his legs wobble.

Jake flashed Emma a look and held up his small knife. "I've got all I can do not to drop this one on them."

Emma laughed with a sound that seemed sweeter since Chuleta's return. Jake joined her but was conscious of the effort it took. He glanced over at Maya. A quick one—he didn't want to draw more attention to them than her disappearance already had. She was lying on the floor of the canoe, her spine curved up the back of it, picking at the chipped hot pink paint on her fingernails.

"That look of yours." Emma stopped short of rolling her eyes. "She's fine. And no one blames you."

Jake turned back to the vine. "Right. But it's—" he stopped; it wasn't the time for it.

"But it's what?"

"Nothing."

"You can't leave me hanging like this."

"Fine." He smiled at her and when he felt his legs were steady enough, he laid his knife against the vine a few more times. "It's just that you sound like me, the way I see you."

"Sound. See. I'm not following ya here."

"It's the way you are with the villagers. Your face can practically tell a story about who means what to whom and," he grunted, slashing the vine, "your opinion about it all."

She placed a fist on her hip. "Such a peculiar observation from someone who just got here. Go on, give me an example."

"Okay, like the day of Carla's funeral. There was a look on your face when they carried her body, an expression that was different from the other villagers."

"I—"

Jake cut her off, knowing she'd protest. "It was fleeting, but it was there."

"It wasn't. You're just looking for things since you can't communicate with the villagers."

Emma's voice was firm. Jake wished he wasn't looking at the vine so he could see her. The last thing he needed was to make waves with someone else, let alone Emma. "You're right. Forget I even said it."

Upon hearing Martha clap, Hugo and Eduardo attempted to join, jolting Jake's face within an inch of the spiny tree. Once Jake's feet were safely on the ground, he held up the chunk of vine. "Got it."

"Rosa will be thrilled," Emma said. Jake reveled in hearing her voice return to its gentle ways. "Betcha she's already got the pot boiling."

~ * ~

It was discrimination at its finest, according to Abuela. They hadn't even pulled up the canoe to the port before Jake heard her protesting from the *tienda*.

Emma turned around, looking at Jake on the bench behind her. "You know Abuela's upset if she's at the *tienda* when there isn't gossip happening."

"So maybe there is gossip?" Jake wanted to know the answer to that question more for himself than anything. It seemed impossible for word to have already gotten out in the village about his and Maya's evening the night before. But then again, gossip in Almagro seemed to have uncanny ways of spreading.

"Nope, there isn't." Emma stood up once the canoe rammed into the muddy land, Chuleta racing ahead of her. She looked up at the *tienda*, which began filling with people. "But there will be, now that we're here."

Jake let out a long breath. "Just what I was afraid of."

"Lucky for you, you can't understand them." She took the vine from his hand as they stepped over the benches, inching towards the front of the canoe to disembark. "Not that it matters, since it wasn't your fault."

Jake closed his eyes a second too long, stumbling over a bench. The movement rocked the canoe, making those behind him murmur words he couldn't understand. He recognized Maya's voice among them.

He'd managed to stop himself from glancing behind him during the trip. Emma was right; the villagers continued to treat him as usual once Maya had been found. Jake was determined to keep it that way for as long as possible. And he knew that looking at Maya wouldn't help that cause. But just how long would she make him wait before acting? Maya was alive, so it was Emma, not him, who would suffer the consequences.

It wasn't until they arrived at the *tienda* that Jake noticed he was out of breath from walking up the hill. Children and villagers flooded onto the patio, claiming their spot under the shade of the thatched roof. Mateo and Hugo hushed them, leaning their backs against the *tienda's* counter. Federico, who had been running the *tienda* in Mateo's absence, greeted them.

Emma whispered to Jake. "They're going to give a rundown of our trip."

"Okay," he said. His hands were already sweating from the sun, but he was convinced they were now also sweaty from nerves. He listened carefully, waiting for Maya's name and, most importantly, the villagers' reactions that would follow it. They didn't know much yet, he figured, since his side of the story was told through Emma. Maya had been quiet in the canoe, as far as he could tell without watching her. And then it came.

Maya. Jake. Words he couldn't understand. Maya. Maya. Jake. Maya. He latched his hands together; counting wasn't helping.

Emma glanced at him. "Everything alright?"

Jake forced the easiest looking smile he could manage. "Just hearing my name, that's all."

She chuckled. "We need to get you learning more Spanish while you figure out how long you're going to stay."

Staying. It seemed like such a feasible option the day before. Now, he wasn't sure. He scrunched his eyes and nodded at her.

"She's already gone, you know. She never stays around for these kinds of meetings."

Momentary relief washed over Jake. But then again, did he appear that worried? Up until then, Emma hadn't seemed to realize that something bad had happened between him and Maya the night before. And, contrary to what Emma believed, he was sure he could read her facial expressions. Regardless, he took comfort in knowing that for the moment, Maya wouldn't be contributing her version of the story.

Jake was so wrapped up in his thoughts that he hadn't noticed Abuela fussing about the location of her stool, directing the kids to move it in front of Hugo and Mateo. "What's this about?" he whispered to Emma.

"She's upset we didn't take her with us. She thinks we discriminated against her because she's a widow."

"I hope I'm as feisty as her when I'm her age."

Emma chuckled softly. "Me too, but don't ever tell her that."

Jake tilted his head. "Noted." He paused. "Do you think she'll be upset with us since we went on the trip?"

"No. She knows we watch drama take place in Almagro, but that we don't create it."

"That's good." Then Jake finished the sentence in his head. *But what if I do?*

CHAPTER 35

Jake ~ Present

The deck of cards felt familiar in Jake's hands. He had gained impressive card skills during his time in Arizona, helped along on nights when he balanced drinking just enough tequila to take riskier moves. But the cards he now held were different; he hadn't seen those large numbers and colorful displays since he was a kid.

Emma glanced over at him from the chalkboard as she erased the word 'Eight', setting down the eraser beside the vine Jake had cut that morning before they returned to Almagro. "Are you sure you're up for one more?"

"Yes!" Andrés said, reaching out his arms as he ran around the picnic table, pretending to fly. María laughed, stepping in his footprints as she chased after him.

"I was asking Jake, mister." Emma held up curled hands, pretending to be a puma as she shuffled towards him. She turned to Jake. "I swear. Do they get any more stubborn than him?"

"I'd go with clever."

She shook her head. "Either way, gone are the days I talk to him in Spanish."

The rest of the kids huddled around Jake, pointing and gasping as he shuffled the UNO cards. They seemed immune to the heat and humidity; their bodies piled three people deep around him. At least he didn't have to worry about his hair anymore. It took a good deal of convincing on Emma's part, but the children eventually gave in to her insistence that plucking his hair wouldn't bring them luck.

Jake pointed his finger around the picnic table. "Alright now, sit down."

The kids squealed and clapped, rushing to get a seat at the table. They had to rotate spots, given that there weren't enough cards for all of them. Emma said something in Spanish, causing some of the kids to sheepishly get up and give their seat to someone else.

Jake shook his head. "I don't know how you keep track of them all."

"It's easy, after some time. But that," she tilted her head towards Andrés who gave up his place to María, "was not my doing."

"Smart and chivalrous. A good combination."

Andrés stood behind María, his hands on her shoulders, and looked over at Jake. "Girlfriend," he said, sticking out his tongue.

The kids began chanting as they started their new UNO game. "Girlfriend! Boyfriend!"

Jake glanced at Emma. "I see they've got those words memorized."

"As do the rest of the villagers," she said, setting down the chalk and petting Chuleta who fell asleep by her feet.

The kids had played as if speed determined the winner, so the game didn't take long to finish. As he walked beside Emma towards the school, it was hard for Jake to believe that he had awoken that same morning to Maya's disappearance. Being back in Almagro felt familiar. It felt safe.

"Gosh, we still need to get this to Rosa," Emma said, holding up the vine as they crossed the schoolyard.

He smiled. "I'm just following your lead."

Sonya heard them and walked out of her room, exchanging words with Emma. Jake watched Emma talk away, her hands flying, Chuleta's name mentioned too many times to count. It was a happy conversation. But then Maya's name came up and Sonya looked at Jake. It was supposed to be a glance, he assumed, but it was held too long. Their tone became serious and, at one point, Sonya reached out to rub Emma's arm.

Jake felt uncomfortable being there, knowing they were talking about him, knowing they knew he couldn't understand. He distracted himself by throwing a stick for Chuleta.

"So." Emma turned to Jake, smiling when she saw Chuleta running towards him with her catch. "Sonya says a rodent got into your mattress last night."

"Is it bad?"

"Sounds like it." She nodded towards the classroom. "Let's take a look."

Pieces of foam greeted them, strewn around the mattress in uneven chunks. They were accompanied by droppings, though given the varying nature of them, it became clear Jake's mattress had been graced by a number of critters.

"Looks like they wanted to create their own mattress," Jake said, poking some stray pieces with his toe.

"Yeah." Emma chuckled. "Not sure how you feel about sleeping on the recreated one, though."

"That's a negative." He looked at Emma. "But hey, are you planning on sleeping at your house tonight?"

She hesitated. "Well, not really. I'd like to get it back to how it was before the storm came, without critters. Or, at least, with fewer of them."

"Right, of course. In that case, do you think I could stay there?"

"Um, well . . ." Emma turned to Sonya and said something. Sonya's eyes widened, but just for a second before she nodded. Emma looked up at Jake. "Yup, I think that could work."

"I mean, I don't want to stay there if it makes you uncomfortable or if it's going to cause issues. There's always the hammock . . . it was just a thought."

"No. I agree, it'd be more comfortable that way. I'll spread the word on our way there to avoid unwanted gossip." Emma glanced at the wall that divided the two classrooms.

Jake wondered if she was thinking the same thing he was. What could it hurt?

"I'll miss our evening chats," he said.

~ * ~

The ramshackle house Jake had spent so much time in during his first week in Almagro looked the same. But approaching it felt different.

"So, Rosa lives with Maya?"

Emma snorted. "Yeah, silly. That woman who you see sitting on the porch sometimes. That's Rosa, Maya and Andrés' mom."

Jake shook his head as he slowed his steps, wishing he'd had the smarts to put that together so he could have made an excuse to stay back at the school. But it was too late—Maya had already spotted him. She and Emma exchanged words as they stood on Rosa's porch. On Maya's porch. Meanwhile, Jake fixed his eyes on Emma's house, willing their conversation to be short. It was, and he heard Maya walk away from them to go inside.

Emma nudged him. "You okay?"

"Yup." He took a step back from her. A slow step, not wanting Emma to find it odd and not wanting to upset Maya, in case she was watching. "Just tired, that's all."

Rosa came around the backside of the house, chattering away with Emma. He studied Rosa's face. Did she look upset? Would she kick him out? Her arms flung open, taking the vine from Emma's hand and embracing her in a hug, smiling at Jake from over Emma's shoulder. He returned the smile and waved, feeling relieved. Maya couldn't have told her. Not yet.

"C'mon," Emma said, nodding towards the kitchen. "She'll show us what she's going to do with it."

Jake followed them around the porch to the side of the house where a pot of boiling water straddled three rocks. The original grey color of the rocks showed through in just a few spots; the rest of them were covered in black soot. Rosa looked at Jake as she pointed at the pot with enthusiasm, dropping the vine into the water.

"She'll boil it for a few hours." Emma stood beside him, translating what Rosa said. "Once it's cooled, she'll drink the water. Kind of like a tea. In this case, a tea for Dengue."

"Fantastic. She's feeling better already though, isn't she?"

"She's getting there, but this should help with any remaining symptoms." Emma petted Chuleta, who had placed her paws on her stomach. "It's a rare species of vine. The villagers won't forget you helped get it for her."

Jake smiled and went to respond but lost the words when he saw eyes peering at him between mud cracks from inside of Rosa's house. His heart sunk. "You know, we should get going, don't you think? I'd like to get settled in before nightfall."

"Of course." Emma initiated goodbyes to Rosa then led them down the hill to her house.

Meanwhile, Jake's mind raced. Staying at Emma's was a bad idea; he had forgotten Maya would be so close. Should he tell Emma he had changed his mind? Hanging a hammock at the school no longer seemed like such a bad option. But it was already too late, he knew. Emma would find it odd if he had a change of heart now, not to mention the villagers since they had already informed them about his new evening location on their way to see Rosa.

"So, this is my latrine." Emma brought him over to a narrow bamboo structure on the hill between her and Maya's house. "They built it up here so the river wouldn't touch it if it floods." She laughed, staring at the line of branches just a couple of feet away from them, marking the highest point where the water had risen. "I thought they were crazy for building it this high on the hill, but I should've known better than to doubt them."

"Wow. Do you come out here at night?"

"Oh, no. No way." Emma shook her head. "I cut the top off of a two-liter plastic water bottle. I can let you borrow it." She chuckled. "I know it may sound gross, but it works."

Jake laughed. "I'll happily conform and use your water bottle."

"In that case," she looked back at him as she walked across the branches towards her house. "Tomorrow morning, bring it up here and dump it in the latrine. I don't need my house smelling musty *and* like an unflushed toilet."

"Noted. You really . . . oh, wow."

Emma had already stopped, staring at her staircase. The sound of flies could be heard even from where they were standing. And the smell. It was one that Jake would recognize anywhere, ever since the storm.

"Oh, gosh. Chuleta, no!" Emma ran to stop her from going up the steps.

Jake stared at the rotting fish, one on each of the notched steps leading up to Emma's house. "How'd they get there?" he whispered.

Emma shook her head. "I'm not sure."

"Maybe it was an anim—"

"No. It wasn't that."

"And look at that one." Jake took a few steps closer to the staircase, staring at a fish's head which was pressed behind an intact tilapia, its body nowhere to be found.

Emma took a deep breath. "Probably just the kids. They knew Chuleta came back."

"Right."

"Let's get this cleaned up." She picked up two fish and began walking over more branches to get to the river. She shouted over her shoulder. "Make sure to throw them far out in the water. We don't want them coming back to shore."

"No problem." Jake tried to keep his tone casual. But it was difficult, knowing that Maya could have been watching it all from her house.

Removing fish from the tree trunk didn't take as long as they had expected since he and Emma resorted to piling them up in their arms. It was the best of two bad options, given how difficult it was to walk over the branches. They cleaned up Emma's room, enough for it to be livable for one night. Jake decided he would do more for her the next day before she came back.

"Alright, I guess that's it then." Emma made her way to the door.

Jake had been toying with the thought when they were cleaning and, now that she was leaving, he decided to go for it. "Hey, Emma? Since I won't be staying at the school tonight, I thought maybe we could have one of our evening chats here." He paused. "A quick one, I know it's getting late."

Based on her smile, he knew the answer before she replied. "Sounds great."

"Good." He looked around, not having thought much past that point.

"How about we sit on my balcony? I miss hanging my feet over the ledge and looking out at the river in the evenings."

They settled into a spot, and Chuleta sprawled out behind them. "You can really appreciate how high it is from here," Jake said.

"All six feet of it." She smiled at him, then said, "Something tells me there's a particular something you want to talk about."

Jake nodded. "That something is Maya."

"Ah." Emma looked down and circled her finger over a flower print on her *paruma*.

"I wanted you to know that nothing happened between us last night."

"I believe you. But even if it did, it's none of my business."

"And I appreciate that. But," he paused, trying to figure out how to word it. And more importantly, just how much he should say. "She tried to kiss me last night. It . . . it probably could've been more, if I let it."

"Well, she likes you. That's no secret."

"Yeah, I guess I knew that too. She wasn't happy when I declined her advances."

"Makes sense."

"And, well . . . I'm not sure how accurate the translator on your phone is."

"Mm, I haven't used it in a long time. I remember it being pretty good, though."

"I guess that's good then." Jake paused. He had already said a lot. Not all of it, but more than he thought he'd say. Maybe it was best to leave it at that. Losing a relationship with Maya was one thing, but he wasn't willing to lose one with Emma.

"Listen, if she gives you trouble, let me know." Emma held up her arm, flexing her muscle. "I'll take care of it."

Jake chuckled. "I have no doubt." Except he knew that it was Emma who Maya would be giving trouble to, not him.

By the time they said their goodbyes, it was already dusk. Getting ready for bed didn't take much time in Almagro; Jake had already washed off in the river after tossing the fish. He blew out the candles that Emma had lit for him, calculating how many steps it would take to walk to her bed in the dark. Once there, he tossed around, trying to find a comfortable position on the lumpy mattress. Eventually, he settled on a spot facing the wall, his eyes already adjusting to the darkness.

Through a crack, he saw a woman. She stood in the moonlight beside the house, looking in his direction. Her long black hair submitted to the breeze as she twisted what looked like strands of curly brown hair between her fingers.

CHAPTER 36

Emma ~ Present

The branches would have marked fifteen days since the storm if it hadn't been for more rain. Emma dragged a log to the new pile of brush Hugo had started, stepping on bark that Chuleta pulled off from other branches throughout the morning. She stopped to soak in the scenery.

Seven piles of brush lined the river; a river that had retreated, welcoming the sun to reach every inch of her stilt house. The villagers hauled branches through the ever-growing grass, making jokes about how the puma would want the debris to remain there. Her heart swelled knowing they had set aside their own chores to help with hers. Children chased beetles disrupted from their homes, singing the latest song she had taught them in English class. Jake worked at their side, encouraging them along. She appreciated Almagro every day, but especially during moments like these.

"You'll be back in your house soon, *mi hija*." Eduardo walked up beside her, tossing a branch from each hand into the pile.

Emma smiled at him. "Staying at the school has its perks, but I'm ready to be home."

"And Jake will go back to staying at the school?"

"Yes, he'll be fine. Sonya will look after him." Emma knew that Eduardo was well aware of Jake's sleeping arrangements—where Jake would be laying his head at night was the main topic in Almagro ever since they had returned from mining.

"It's just—"

"I know." Emma squeezed his arm. "But I'm not worried about it. It was just kids being kids."

"Normally I'd agree." He stared at the pile of branches. "The villagers do. But it's the fact that no one's seen them leave the fish. No one knows who they are."

"Perhaps generations of gossip have bred smarter children."

Eduardo sighed. "Perhaps." He looked past Emma's house, to the area where a path had been forming before the storm. New blades of grass poked through branches that matted down the old. The river had surpassed the tree line, so it was impossible to tell a trail had been there. "Jake hasn't mentioned anything?"

"No. And he would have, had he seen or heard something. I'm sure of it."

"Okay, *mi hija*." He paused. "I was always hesitant to put you here at the back of the village. It's just . . . so isolated."

Emma flicked a fly away from her face. "Just because my house can't be seen from the *tienda* doesn't make it isolated." She glanced up at Maya's house, her own version of the *tienda*. "You'll be the first to know if I hear or see anything out of place. I promise."

"Check this out!" Jake walked over to them, pointing at his shirt where a brown and black beetle clung, bearing a snout the length of his fingers. "Does it bite?" Not being able to communicate with Eduardo, he pulled his shirt further away from his stomach and exaggerated a fearful look, drawing a chuckle from him.

Emma laughed. "That's a Hercules Beetle, totally harmless. But," she reached for a branch and coaxed the beetle onto it, "its legs can scratch you up pretty good, so let's get him off before he touches your skin."

She set the branch away from the pile of logs. It could be weeks before it was dry enough to burn them, but even so, she didn't want to put the beetle in future harm's way.

"You're amazing," Jake said.

Emma felt a flutter in her stomach. It wasn't so much the words but the way he said them, with a soft whisper. She smiled. "Well, if that's all it takes."

Ever since they got back from gold mining, things with Jake had been perfect. The time he used to spend at Maya's house was now spent with her, Sonya, and the villagers. He'd study Spanish for hours a day, and the villagers commented with pride on how he was picking up on it faster than Emma had. It was a given, they said, since he shared half their blood. Jake hadn't even brought up Maya's name since the night they sat together on Emma's balcony. Nonetheless, he was jumpy. In particular, she noticed, when Maya was nearby.

Emma glanced up the hill and was met by Maya's stare from her porch. Maya didn't react—it wasn't like her to smile or wave. But she didn't turn away, either. Emma could see her toying with something in her hand, staring at her straight in the eye. She turned back to Jake, realizing that he had been watching Maya watch her.

"Don't mind her," Emma said. "She doesn't participate in community activities unless it benefits her . . . or if she gets tired of Rosa insisting."

"She seems to be keeping to herself ever since we got back."

"Yeah. Maya's an observer. The issues arrive when she acts on her observations." Jake's eyes widened and she bumped his arm. "You're fine. Her disappearance on the trip is old news."

He leaned away from her. "Do you ever lock up your stuff?"

"In Almagro?" Emma laughed. "No."

"Don't you ever worry about someone taking something? It's never even crossed your mind?"

She shrugged. "When I first got here, I guess it did. But no one here would steal. Besides, nothing I have is that valuable."

~ * ~

No one in Almagro could have guessed the news that the floating *tienda* would be bringing. The first thump of tagua rang through the trees, everyone knowing which port to go to before the second thump hit; they were overdue for a visit because of the storm.

Emma set down the chalk as students whizzed past her and Sonya without permission. She shrugged, looking at Jake who stood at the back of the room. "So much for that."

Sonya began walking out the door, then looked back at Emma. "You know, I still have that other bottle of wine. It's small so I put it in my underground storage."

She glanced at Jake. "But even so, with this heat, I'm not sure how much longer it'll last."

"In that case, I think we can share." Emma turned to Jake, who had walked up beside them. "We'll head there shortly, but Sonya's got something for us first."

"Please tell me it isn't another mouse to chase out of her room?"

Emma laughed, shaking her head. "This will be—"

"Oh!" Jake eyed Sonya, who had already returned with two wine glasses and a plastic cup. "Where'd you get this from?" He held up his glass, nodding to Sonya in thanks.

"Sonya brought it from the city. I miss her when she's gone, but she makes up for it when she returns."

They clinked their drinks together, Emma savoring her last taste of the outside world she'd get for months.

Jake fished out a fly with his pinky. "Do the villagers drink?"

"Yeah." Emma hovered her lips over the glass. "They make it. Actually, they're due to make some more anytime now."

"Emma." Sonya whispered her name. "How are things going between you two?"

"Sonya!" Emma laughed and looked at her through the corner of her eye. "He's right here."

"Who cares? He can't understand if we talk fast."

Jake shifted his eyes between them and reached up to cover his ears. "I get the feeling I'm not supposed to hear this."

Emma laughed. "Take them down." She batted his arm.

"That was cute." Sonya winked.

"Stop." Emma chuckled. "He may not understand, but he can read body language."

"Fine, don't tell me anything over our last bit of wine." She looked at Jake, who was staring at Emma, his lips resting in a small smile. "Words ruin things anyway."

After they savored their piece of the outside world, they walked towards the port to join the villagers as they relished in Almagro's version of it. But it took longer than expected; Abuela stopped them from her stool at the top of the *tienda*, watching the activity down at the floating *tienda*.

"Have they told you?" she asked.

Emma leaned down to kiss her cheek. "Yes. We're going there now."

"No, no. It's not the floating *tienda*." A low thump sounded from her stool as she tapped her heels against it.

"Well . . ." Emma started.

"Don't bother, I'll just tell you. But first—" She yanked her basket of grass crosses onto her lap and handed one to each. Then she took a deep breath. "The devil's coming to Almagro."

Sonya snorted. Emma nudged her; Sonya knew Abuela, but not to the extent that she did. And Emma knew, like the rest of the villagers, that one shouldn't snort after Abuela spoke.

Abuela glared at Sonya before continuing. "Father is devastated. Who would've thought he'd have to compete for God?"

"Oh?" Emma hoped her concerned expression looked convincing.

"Here. Read it." Abuela leaned forward and handed her a soggy piece of paper.

Emma went to look at it but was distracted by María, who was playing with a shiny square piece of foil down by the river. Beside her, Andrés inflated an elongated balloon.

Jake saw it and pointed. "Is that—"

"Emma." Abuela kicked out her leg, nicking Emma's shin. "Read it. The floating *tienda* didn't bring it here just to be held."

Emma exchanged a glance with Jake then looked down at the paper. The letter was written with a red pen— the first time Emma had seen a letter sent to the villagers that wasn't in black ink. Raindrops smudged its letters and fish guts smeared its edges. Even so, it was legible.

To the Community of Almagro:
This letter arrives to you with love from God, myself, and the Evangelical Church of Kentucky, USA. I hereby inform you that I, Pastor Raúl, will be visiting on Friday. I will come with the word of the Lord and food.
Your warm reception will be rewarded, God willing.
Pastor Raúl

Jake leaned over Emma, staring at the paper. "What does it say?"

"That a pastor will be coming to Almagro." Emma shook her head. "The chaos that'll ensue."

"Isn't it awful?" Abuela snatched the letter from Emma's hand and buried it back into her basket of crosses.

Hugo rushed up the hill when he saw Emma. "I trust you've heard?"

Emma's eyes fell on his hands. He had already shopped at the floating *tienda*; even if he hadn't purchased anything, the water mark around his waist was proof alone. But he had, undeniably, purchased things. In his left hand, he held a bottle of Vaseline and rubbing alcohol. His right hand swung as he spoke, a strip of condoms flapping in the breeze.

"I expect you to take care of this," Abuela said, looking at Hugo. "You're the mayor. It'll be your fault if something goes wrong."

Emma was still trying to decipher Hugo's question, wondering if 'you've heard' referred to the pastor or condoms.

"Of course, of course. God will keep his place here."

The pastor it was.

Jake spoke, looking at all of them even though Emma was the only one who could understand him. "This is quite a sight."

Emma nodded towards the floating *tienda*. "C'mon, let's take a closer look." She led him to the beginning of the line. "So, you walk around the outside of it, in the water. If there's something you want just flag down Natalie, the woman over there."

"She . . . doesn't really look dressed for the part, huh?"

Emma laughed, shielding her eyes from the glitter of Natalie's fake diamonds reflecting off the river. "The woman has been coming to Almagro for years. In her eyes, she's perfectly dressed for the part."

The floating *tienda* was divided into sections like always but this time with an extra one for the rainy season. Umbrellas, tubs of Vaseline, and bottles of rubbing alcohol were piled high in the canoe, sticking out of soggy cardboard boxes.

Jake patted the water that came up just past his knees as he walked around the canoe. "Such an interesting concept."

"She stops at a few other communities, too, so leaving merchandise on the canoe saves her time." Emma shrugged. "She's got a motor, so she can manage it in a day. Speaking of merchandise . . ." She stepped out of line and peered at the back of the canoe. The villagers were blessing the motor as usual, but they also rummaged through plastic bins filled with colorful squares.

Jake leaned around Emma, setting his hands on her shoulders. "Guess we know where the condoms came from."

"Condoms! Oh yes, there are condoms!" The canoe swayed back and forth as Natalie ran towards Jake's voice from behind the boxes. She shoved two aside, poking her head between them.

"Natalie, I didn't realize you spoke English," Emma said.

"I don't. Just know a few words." She winked. "The important ones."

"Got it." Emma paused. "So . . . why—"

"The market. It's all about the market, where the money's at. 'Cause," she lowered her voice, "*you know.*"

"Um . . ." Emma paused, mouth open, aware that all the villagers were listening in on their conversation. Between the narrow gaps on either side of Natalie's head, Emma watched Maya wade along the other side of the canoe, staring down at her handful of condoms.

"Man, it sure is taking you a long time, huh? Considering they say you preach it and all." Natalie paused. "AIDS, Emma. Everyone knows it's arrived in Almagro."

"Ah. I see."

"Here." Natalie strode over to the plastic bin, swishing hands out of the way as people picked through the condoms, contemplating the colors they wanted. "Take these." She poured them into Emma's hands. A few fell into the river. "They want me to do a demonstration." She waved her finger in Emma's face. "Oh, no. No way." She huffed. "My job is to sell, yours is to teach."

"Um," Jake lowered his head so it hovered to the side of Emma's. "Looks like quite the conversation you're having."

Emma chuckled, handing him some condoms. "We'll give these to Rebecca on Thursday." She watched the villagers compare designs and colors, discussing their favorites. "I've gotta say, they're more receptive to them than I expected." She looked up at Jake. "It appears the floating *tienda* brought good news along with the pastor's letter."

"Most definitely." He pointed to the rubbing alcohol and Vaseline, catching Natalie's eye. "I'll take a few of those."

CHAPTER 37

Emma ~ Present

S nake bites didn't happen often in Almagro, and the villagers attributed it to Hugo's snake prevention program. Since becoming mayor, he had widened public footpaths by two feet and ensured the villagers ran a machete over their yards once a week. So, on the rare occasion when there was a snake bite, the villagers blamed Eduardo.

"See what it gets you?" Mateo paced up and down the patio of the *tienda*, flicking drops of sweat from his brow onto the nearest bystanders.

"Settle down." Abuela beat the air with a grass cross. "It's not his fault this time."

Hugo stepped forward. "How can it not be his fault?"

Abuela put her hands on her hips. "Because the devil wrote to us. It was *its* doing."

Jake gripped the edge of the bench he sat on, glancing at his left leg propped up along the top. Emma sat to his right, leaning into him and bracing her foot against the ground to keep from sliding off.

He looked at her. "You're sure it wasn't poisonous, right?"

"Positive. An innocent brown snake." There wasn't space between their arms to give him a nudge so she pressed her side against him. "Anything will bite if you step on it."

Meanwhile, the villagers continued a conversation of their own. "The important thing is that it's dead now." Hugo held up the headless snake.

Eduardo stood up at the back of the patio. "But it was provoked, my friends."

"Poor Eduardo. He loves his critters." Emma sighed and looked at Jake. "How's it feeling?"

"Still hurts, but not too bad." He rubbed his hand near the red spot on his calf. Two narrow punctures sat in the middle of it, dark from drying blood. "Hey." He grabbed his bottles of rubbing alcohol and Vaseline. "Do these work for snake bites?"

Emma tipped her head to the side. "The rubbing alcohol will come in handy, but it won't be pleasant. Let's give them a little more time to fuss over you, then we'll get some cotton balls from my house."

In Almagro fashion, the fussing lasted longer than the pain from Jake's snakebite. The conversations were cyclical, but by the time Emma and Jake left the *tienda*, the villagers were in near-perfect agreement—Jake's snakebite was Eduardo's fault with the help of a devil named Pastor Raúl.

"That poor pastor. He doesn't know what he's in for." Jake hobbled beside Emma as he settled into a chair at the school. The pain had returned once he began walking; Abuela told him it was from the devil's poison circulating in his body.

Emma shook her head. "There's always something. Now, let's get this disinfected." She coaxed a cotton ball out of the bag she had grabbed from her house on her own, not wanting to make Jake walk down the hill.

He drew in a sharp breath from the pain, then forced a laugh. "This is so different from treating chiggers."

"I know." She patted his knee. "Do you want a break?"

"No. Go for it all at once, as quickly as you can."

She did so but selfishly wished she could have treated his leg longer. Anything that involved being near him made her happy. And now that Maya was out of the picture, she wasn't resisting her feelings as much as before.

"One more, then you'll be good to go . . . for tonight, at least." She grabbed another cotton ball off the table, cleaning a large area around the bite for good measure.

Chuleta took advantage of the opportunity and snatched the used cotton ball on the floor. "Ay, no!" Emma said. She and Jake reached down to grab her at the same time, their cheeks brushing. Even with her hand in Chuleta's mouth, pulling out the cotton ball, Emma swore Jake held his face against hers on purpose, helping her hold a Chuleta that didn't need holding.

"Ahem."

Emma and Jake looked up at the door in unison, still bent over Chuleta with their cheeks pressed together. Emma's heart sank; it was just like Maya to ruin a moment.

Emma and Jake had already sat up but, even so, Maya's focus was and had only been on Jake. Maya squeezed her crossed arms and slowly prodded her tongue along her cheek. Before Emma had the chance to say anything else, Maya spun around and walked out the door.

Emma pulled a stray piece of cotton out of Chuleta's mouth, whose head now rested in her lap. "That was weird."

She could barely make out what Jake said as he agreed. "Yeah."

~ * ~

Emma dangled her legs over her balcony, relishing her first night home in almost two weeks. It was her first time being alone—truly alone—without anyone within hearing distance of her every movement. She took comfort in knowing time hadn't changed nature. The sun began its descent, bats started their nightly performance, and cicadas sang.

She loved being alone. And yet, now that she was, she couldn't help but think about how lonely she'd feel if Jake left. He had been in Almagro for a while now. No doubt, he had adjusted well to village life and didn't appear to miss the outside world. But leaving was in his bones—he had shown Emma so with his stories about Lizzie and Arizona. She figured he couldn't have possibly spent so much time in Almagro without toying with the idea of leaving. He hadn't even gone up north yet to trace his roots.

A fish jumped, reminding Emma that her eyes were on the river. It was hard to imagine that the now peaceful body of water was the same one that had destroyed so much. She still loved the river, but in a more conditional way than before; Chuleta made it out alive and Carla didn't. She shook her head. It wasn't until now, when she was truly alone, that she had time to begin processing Carla's death. The death of two people. What drove Carla to visit the river after she had checked in on her the night of the storm?

"*Mi hija.*" Eduardo walked in front of Emma's balcony, standing six feet below her dangling legs. "I know I promised not to worry. But I wanted to make sure you got settled in okay."

Emma took a deep breath and smiled, trusting he had been discrete when walking to her house. "Everything went well, thank you."

"Good." He looked around, zeroing in on the area where the matted grass used to be.

"I was just thinking of you, actually." Emma knew the question could give her away, but she also knew he wouldn't bring it up to anyone. "Do you think it's okay," she paused, wondering if it was too late to stop. "Is it okay to share someone's secret after they've passed away?"

"Oh." Eduardo rubbed his chin and took a step closer to the river. He looked out, watching bats dance across the dusky sky. "Did you know your mango tree might have had fewer mangos if it weren't for bats?"

Emma rested her head on her hands. "No."

"Few people do. It's a bat's secret. Humans have made them out to be dangerous, disease-spreading creatures. There's truth to that, no doubt." He sighed. "But it's not the full truth." He looked up at Emma. "How does it make you feel that bats pollinate your mango tree?"

Emma contemplated, unsure what he was getting at. "Good, I guess."

"So, your answer is in the bat. If your secret will make the receiver of it feel good, then yes, I think it's okay to tell someone's secret after they've died."

Emma smiled. "I'm glad you stopped by."

"Me too." He turned around. "And on that note, I'll hand the evening back to you."

Emma spent a few more minutes on her balcony after Eduardo left. Chuleta had fallen asleep, her head pressed against Emma's back. The familiar blanket of humidity clung to her skin, sheltering her from what would have otherwise been a cool evening. A mosquito landed on her arm and she slapped it with the precision that over a year of practice had taught her; strong enough to kill but gentle enough so it didn't splatter.

She leaned back to wake Chuleta. "Time to go in, sweet pea." She scooched away from the ledge before standing, like she did every time, but stopped when she heard squishing along the still soggy ground. She glanced at the machete hanging on the outside of her wall.

"Hello?" she said.

The noise picked up speed towards her, from underneath her house. Chuleta stood up and barked. Emma stepped backward towards the machete on her wall, the noise giving away the person's location from beneath her house. She watched a figure pop out from underneath, on the side facing the river.

"What's with you?" the person said.

"Maya." Emma exhaled through clenched teeth. "What are you doing here so late?"

"Same could be asked about you and Eduardo."

Emma shook her head, not bothering to hide her irritation since it was too dark for Maya to see. She asked again. "What are you doing here?"

Maya walked back under the house. Emma followed the noise and was already waiting at the top of her staircase by the time Maya emerged at its base. Maya rubbed her hand along the notched tree trunk, studying each step, staying silent. Finally, she spoke.

"You like Jake."

"All the villagers like Jake."

"No." Maya stared at her. "You like Jake how I like him."

Emma went to speak but realized it was better to stay quiet. Observation was Maya's weapon; it was time she followed suit.

"The issue is this." She rubbed her finger along a step, following a stained trail of fish blood. "Jake would have already been mine if it weren't for you."

Emma bit her cheek, focusing her energy on scratching Chuleta's ear. Chuleta sat beside her, eyes half-closed, leaning into Emma's leg.

"And so, you need to stop flirting with him."

"I'm not—" Emma stopped herself and shook her head. "You're talking crazy."

"They do say that, don't they?"

Emma moved on to scratching Chuleta's other ear.

"So. This is my proposal." She paused. "Proposals, actually. You gave me an idea for another one."

Emma curled her toes, feeling them slide against her flip flops from the humidity. Or was it sweat? Maya's pause was long and Emma knew she was waiting for a reaction from her. And Emma could control that. She held her stare until Maya spoke.

"If I see you and Jake dating . . . flirting, even . . . I'll either say the two of you slept together on the gold mining trip when you went to get banana leaves. Or," she said, setting both elbows on a step, resting her face in her hands, and smiling up at Emma, "I'll say Eduardo's been visiting you in the evenings." She sighed, swinging her body around the staircase before letting go. "I was going to let you choose." She looked back at Emma as she walked back up the hill. "But on second thought, I will."

CHAPTER 38

Jake ~ Present

Thursday couldn't come soon enough for the villagers. And now that it had arrived, they congregated around the outside of the church. Jake moved his leg to the side, felt a bump, and moved it back. Hands and shoulders pushed at his lower back. People talked at volumes that would have hurt his ears, if he were as short as them.

For the first time in Almagro's history, the priest put on a meal. But to Jake, it seemed that the villagers prepared a meal with ingredients the priest provided.

Jake made his way through the crowd until he arrived at the pot of fish. The priest had claimed the role of placing fish on the villagers' banana leaf plates; it was the main dish, the item they would be most grateful for. Meanwhile, Abuela sat on her stool beside him, making sure Carla's kids received the thickest pieces of fish with heads attached, for good nutrition. Grass crosses adorned the table; three times as many surrounded the pot of fish.

The priest shouted down to Emma, who was in line a few people behind Jake.

"I bless this food in the name of God," she responded in English.

The priest turned to Jake and repeated a jumbled version of what she had said. Jake went to nod, which turned into more of a bow. "Thank you. That's very kind," he said in Spanish. With the help of the kids, his language skills were progressing.

He left the line and found a spot with just enough room to stand and eat his breakfast. As he ate the fried fish, he watched Martha place fried *hojaldra* bread onto Emma's banana leaf. She then ducked under the table to help her retie her *paruma*. Emma had been smiling all morning, muscles fine-tuned to her life in Almagro. He loved her smile. But he was all too aware it was something she had rarely exchanged with him over the past week.

Once Emma's breakfast was piled high on her banana leaf, she and some of the children running around her walked near Jake. Emma stood close to him but not next to him—a move he had both come to expect and become concerned about.

When he didn't succeed in catching her eye, he approached Emma with an upbeat tone. "So, all this is because the devil's coming?"

Emma glanced at him quickly, her smile gone. She looked around the room, smiling at the villagers as she caught their eyes and said, "Yup. He's trying to win the villagers over before the pastor arrives tomorrow."

"Seems it's working."

"You would think." She glanced at him, still smiling from when she was looking at the villagers.

"Hey." He felt like the opportunity was right. She had, after all, smiled at him, albeit indirectly. "Is everything okay? You seem . . . distant with me lately."

Emma looked away from him. But this time when she spoke her voice was soft, the kind of voice she used to use with him. "I probably have, I'm sorry . . . I've just got a lot going on."

"This wouldn't have anything to do with—" Jake stopped. "Never mind. I get it, no worries."

And Jake was almost positive he did get it. The villagers had been acting normal around him, as far as he could tell. But it didn't change the fact that he couldn't understand them most of the time. They could all be standing there eating their breakfast, talking about the rumor, and he wouldn't even know it. Maya had promised him one thing before she disappeared—that she would tell them. She would spread a fact that never happened.

There was always leaving.

The thought crossed Jake's mind now more than ever before. It felt odd to him; he never spent time contemplating whether or not to leave Charleston and Arizona. Back then, he had the desire to leave so he left. But now, thoughts of leaving a place he didn't want to consumed him. He'd still go north to trace his family, of course, but figured he could come back. Nevertheless, if it meant Emma getting her life back to normal in Almagro, he'd leave for good.

"Jake yes!" Andrés tossed his empty banana leaf in the air and ran to him, hugging his leg.

"Hey, buddy!" He ruffled Andrés' hair.

Andrés giggled and María shouted, "Me too!" Jake reached over to ruffle her hair as she clung to his other leg.

Suddenly, thumping rang throughout the village, coming from the *tienda*. The villagers pushed their way out of the church patio as banana leaves dropped to the ground. They ran fingers through their hair, flattened creases out of their clothes, and checked to make sure they had their dressy flip flops on as they hurried towards the port to greet their guests.

Emma followed them, looking back at Jake. "Let the lunch preparations begin."

~ * ~

Jake stood at the back of the classroom, staring at the table of condoms. He rocked forward, trying to catch a glimpse of Emma past Rebecca and Diego who blocked his view. The three of them talked amongst each other in Spanish, pointing towards a table at the front of the room as well as nearby vacant areas.

Jake offered his opinion when he sensed a break in the conversation. "I think it needs to slide to the right."

Diego nodded. "Smart."

"No." Emma went off speaking in Spanish before switching to English. "We're trying to decide whether or not we should set up a second table so they can see better."

"That's a good idea." Jake smiled widely to show her his support.

"It is, except we'd need someone else to demonstrate. Rebecca and the nurses will be testing the children for HIV in the other room and Diego," she sighed with frustration, "is too embarrassed."

Diego watched them intensely, but Jake knew he couldn't keep up with Emma's fast spoken English.

"I could do it," he said. *Anything to get back on normal terms with you.*

"I figured." Emma studied the window.

Jake followed her gaze, watching the villagers rush around to prepare their second free meal of the day—lunch from the Ministry of Health. Federico walked into the classroom, casting down his eyes as he held up a cluster of thick plantains. He said something to Emma, who responded in English, although Jake wasn't sure if it was for his benefit or simply the way she processed the situation.

"The villagers don't want to pick the bananas because they're too green."

Jake stared at the plantains in Federico's hand, each one the length of the boy's forearm. He had learned the hard way that the villagers prided themselves on fertilizer. The key ingredient, they said, was *gallinaza*. Chaos ensued the day Jake thought he was helping Martha by spreading fresh chicken droppings on her flowers. 'It's only good for the plants if it's been composted,' Emma had explained to him as she helped him scrape the soggy feces off the soil.

Emma turned to Jake. "Looks like we're going to have to work with it." She said some more words to Diego who shook his head and repeated the word 'no', among many others.

Jake offered a reassuring smile. "I'm sure we can manage." He didn't care about the oversized plantains; Emma was starting to acknowledge him again.

She walked to the door and scanned the classroom from her new viewpoint. "Let's set up two tables. Sonya and I will give the demonstration."

And so it was. The villagers—ages thirteen and older only—piled into the classroom. Jake chose a spot by his mattress, which leaned against the wall. It was a strategic place—one that was in line with Emma, who stood at the front of the class, giving the presentation with Sonya. The younger children, when they weren't being tested for HIV, huddled around the windows to watch.

The kids whispered to Jake on occasion, saying a word or two in English and many more in Spanish. But those in the classroom didn't notice, for they were riveted by Emma and Sonya's demonstration. Jake was riveted, too, having an excuse to stare at Emma. Even though he was standing directly in her line of view, he could have sworn she was looking at him intentionally. In fact, he was sure of it.

The villagers piled out of the classroom as quickly as they had entered when the presentation ended. It was lunchtime, and they were ecstatic that they'd be eating another free meal.

Jake walked to the front of the classroom to help Emma and Sonya clean up. A dozen of Natalie's open condoms littered the floor. They ended up opening them all so the villagers could practice with the plantains. Jake bent down and picked up a wrapper off the ground. "They're quick learners."

"Yeah. I can imagine it was entertaining to watch." Emma flashed a smile at him, and then at Sonya.

Jake felt more confident now that Emma was warming back up to him. He decided to try asking her again. "As long as you're—"

"Emma." It was Rebecca's voice; she had spoken the words before she and Diego had even walked into the room.

Jake didn't bother finishing his sentence—Rebecca's presence felt urgent. Picking up the rest of the wrappers, he watched Emma's face slip into contemplation and offer words between what appeared to be Rebecca prompting questions. He watched Diego watch her, too. It was a strange feeling, looking at Diego knowing what he knew now. After Diego had told him that he and Emma were dating, all Jake saw was how close the two of them were. Now, with nothing changing but the truth, Emma's efforts to keep her distance from Diego were palpable.

"What a day." Emma turned back to Jake after Rebecca and Diego stepped out of the room.

He laughed. "It's only lunchtime."

"Don't remind me." Turning to Sonya, she whispered in her ear. Sonya's eyes widened before she offered Emma a cautious nod.

Emma looked back at Jake and gestured towards the far corner of the classroom. "Would you mind picking up that broom over there and sweeping that side? I'll sweep up over here."

"Sure." He forced a collected pace as he grabbed the broom.

Emma began sweeping the floor but brushed the broom's dried grass blades over the same spot. "I'm sorry I've been acting strange."

Jake stopped sweeping and looked at her. "Was it something I did?"

"No . . . not per se." She paused. "Keep sweeping. And talk in a normal voice." She glanced over at Sonya who stood inside the classroom with them, keeping an eye on the windows and door.

"Does this have something to do with Maya?"

She nodded. "But let's not use her name. Let's call her 'M', okay?"

"'M' it is."

"She came to my house the other night."

Jake's chest tightened. "I'm sorry, Emma, I should've warned you."

"Wait . . . you knew?"

The sharpness in her voice made his stomach clench. "Yes. I think so, at least."

Emma looked at him. "What do you know?"

"I didn't want to tell you because I thought maybe she wouldn't do it. I . . . I didn't want to worry you."

"That wasn't the question."

"Right." He rolled the broom in his hand. "Remember when I asked you if the translation on your phone works well?"

"Yes." She swept the floor with quick strokes and exchanged looks with Sonya.

"It's because 'M' used it to tell me she was going to spread a rumor about us . . . you and me . . . the day of the mining trip, when we went looking for banana leaves."

"And what was her condition for spreading it?"

"There wasn't one . . . not that I understood, at least. She was upset for . . . well, you know, me turning her down. She knew," Jake paused and shook his head knowing Emma was upset, not wanting to upset her more, "*thought*, I liked you."

Emma stopped sweeping and Jake followed suit. Even from across the room, he saw her staring into his eyes. And in doing so, he felt her anger dissipate.

"So," he said more softly, leaning against the broom, "since I refused her advances, she said she'd get back at me . . . well, us . . . by making up a story about why you and I were gone so long the day we went mining."

Emma nodded slowly. "I wish you would've told me."

Jake was relieved her voice held forgiveness. "Me too."

"Well," she took a deep breath and went back to sweeping, glancing at Sonya. "That doesn't change anything."

Jake followed suit and continued to sweep. "What did she tell you?"

"What you said, which wouldn't have been an issue if she had stopped there. Unfortunately, she's smarter than that." Emma pushed a strand of hair out of her face. "She knows my reputation with the villagers, that they wouldn't have bought her story about us." She paused, whispering loud enough for Jake to hear from across the room, but no further. "We're going to refer to Eduardo as 'E', okay?"

Jake nodded.

"'E' has been stopping by my house some evenings. It's an innocent visit. A quick one, just to check in on me." Emma looked back at Sonya, who nodded. It was an all-clear signal indicating Maya wasn't around, Jake now realized. Emma turned back to him. "Well, 'M' caught on to his visits. It's hard to say how long she's known or if she realized it for the first time the other night."

"Why is it an issue that 'E' visits you?"

"It's not, except that it's at night. Dusk, really, but close enough." A bug crawled onto her foot and she shook it off. "The thing is, it's hard enough for the villagers to accept that I live alone as an unmarried woman. So, add a man sneaking to my house at night and, well . . . it doesn't look great."

"Mm-hmm." Jake paused, trying to process it all. "But I don't get it. Since the villagers know your reputation so they wouldn't believe a rumor about us, then why would they believe a rumor about you and 'E'?"

"Because 'E's' visits to me happened. The villagers could figure it out, it wouldn't be hard."

"Oh."

Emma continued. "Surely someone would've gone to his house in the evening to find it empty. Or checked his canoe to find it gone from its spot . . . he parks it closer to my side of the island sometimes to avoid the villagers seeing him walk there."

"But why does 'E' visit you at night? He seems too intuitive to ignore social protocol."

Emma stopped sweeping and stared out the window. "There's . . . there's been an odd thing happening around my house." She paused. "He caught onto it before I did. It's a path. It gets more matted down at night." She leaned against the broom. "Not all the time. Not even most of the time, really. And since the storm, well, it's pretty much gone."

"Were you . . . are you scared?"

"Not really. At least, not at first. I was so sure it was an animal. But now, well, I'm not convinced. Then again, I haven't really heard it recently."

"I'm still confused, though. Why can't you just tell the villagers about it? It seems they'd understand why 'E' visits you."

Emma nodded, letting her guard down to sweep closer to the center of the room. "It's true. But 'E' knows that if word gets out, there'd be villagers sleeping on my balcony every night. Heck, a few would probably even build houses on my side of the river just to watch over me, or wear me down with their worries until I moved in with them. Don't get me wrong, I love them but—"

"The price of independence."

"Right. I won't lie . . . I sleep with my machete. I didn't at first, but it's become a habit. Even so, whoever or whatever it is appears to be using the area around my house as a means only."

Jake shook his head. "You're brave, Emma."

"Not brave enough to give up my little piece of privacy. Which leads me to this." She looked at Jake and then at the floor. "We need to act distant with each other in front of the villagers. Even my house isn't a safety net since 'M' has a view of it."

He nodded, matching her downcast look and wishing he could hold her in his arms. It killed him to ask, but he knew it was the selfless thing to do. Taking a deep breath, he put a hand in his pocket.

"Would it be easier on you if I leave Almagro?"

CHAPTER 39

Jake ~ Present

With full stomachs and their guests gone, the villagers changed gears in the afternoon; they were overdue on making palm wine. Jake shielded his eyes from the sun as he watched Hugo prepare to climb the tree, Emma translating from a distance about his technique.

"It's all about the *paruma*. He says to watch closely since you'll go up the next one."

Hugo wrapped a *paruma* around himself and the palm tree, making sure a couple of feet of space remained between his body and the trunk before tying the fabric in a tight knot. He then leaned back into the *paruma* and jumped with both feet onto the tree. Rocking back and forth, he tilted forward, pushing the *paruma* higher. He then sat back into the *paruma* and jumped a couple of more feet up the trunk, repeating the motion until he reached the base of the palm leaves. The villagers crowded around the outskirts of the tree, watching Hugo in silence.

"The strips of *paruma* cloth tied to his feet create traction for climbing," Emma said.

Jake looked down at the cloth wrapped around his own feet. "Are they supposed to be tied so tightly? I feel like I won't be able to feel my toes by the time it's my turn."

"I think so, but . . ." She said something to Eduardo who walked over to Jake. "Eduardo will check it."

Abuela sat in her stool, which was positioned just outside the circumference where debris—or a person—could fall on her. Some of Carla's youngest kids sat around her, playing with the grass in her basket. She wove grass crosses without looking down at her hands, watching Hugo slash fruit kernels at the top of the palm with his machete. Abuela murmured something to Jake. He looked at Emma from a few people over for help, forcing an expressionless gaze.

Emma returned the blank look. "She says he went up too slowly."

Jake nodded, laughing to himself.

He wondered if the villagers found it odd that he and Emma were being so distant with each other. Behind him, he sensed Maya move. He stepped forward to create space between them. She followed his lead, inching even closer.

As the minutes passed, Jake began longing for his turn to climb the palm. He and Emma kept their eyes on Hugo who hung a gourd from the cut fruit kernels to catch its liquid. With their heads stretched up at the palm tree, Jake and Emma stole a glance at each other out of the corner of their eyes.

Hugo's descent down the tree was closer to a slide. A skilled slide, gained from a lifetime of practice. He smiled at Jake when he arrived at the bottom, giving him a thumbs up.

"Your turn!" Andrés said in English, holding up his hands for a double high five.

"Alright buddy, wish me luck."

Jake walked over to Hugo. The villagers cheered him on until the *paruma* was strapped to him and the tree. Then they went quiet, just as they had with Hugo.

Emma positioned herself closer to the palm, a necessary move, given that she'd need to shout instructions to him. He looked over at her, maintaining a blank face with ease from nerves. "So, how many times have people fallen?"

"None since I've been here but they say it's happened." She paused. "You don't have to do this, you know."

Jake ran his eyes up and down the palm. "And turn down an adventure? No way."

The villagers assigned him the shortest palm tree that needed climbing that day. Hands batted the air when they discounted the climb as a mere forty feet. But now that he stood at the base of its trunk, it seemed taller. So much taller. To make a challenging climb more difficult, Jake needed to ascend with a three-foot machete and a basket formed from a gourd.

"Just take it easy," Emma said. "The wine will be there regardless of how long it takes you."

As it turned out, time was a blessing that Abuela had summoned from Jesus himself, she informed anyone who passed her. Jake hadn't looked down since he began the climb. He couldn't; he would have panicked. But judging by how much space remained before reaching the top, he figured he was about halfway there.

Emma's confirmation soon followed. "Halfway. You're doing great. How are you feeling?"

"Tired." Jake paused, waiting for his breathing to slow. "I don't think I can make it."

"They're telling me you should lean back into the *paruma*. Make sure it's positioned around your lower back and lean into it."

Jake did as instructed and was surprised by how the *paruma* became a seat. He carefully hung both arms down to his side, dangling the machete and gourd. He kept a firm pressure on the tree trunk with his legs, his knees bent in a squatting position.

Such breaks became the norm during the remaining ascent; he'd climb five feet and take a break. The villagers remained quiet the entire time. It was out of character for them, and he tried not to wonder if it was because they worried about him falling. As it was, he had been listening for tearing noises from the *paruma*. They had told him it wouldn't rip, but how could they be so sure?

When he finally arrived at the top, finding the fruit kernels proved to be a new challenge. "I'm cutting in more places than I should be," he shouted to Emma.

"They say it's okay, just as long as you're not chopping up the base. You could kill the tree that way."

Jake sat back in the *paruma* to study the palm leaves. He reached up to wipe away sweat from his forehead, his machete smacking into bees buzzing around him. Zeroing in on a new spot, he tapped it once with the blade, shaking his hand when liquid splattered.

"Found it!"

The villagers erupted in applause. He then hung the gourd from a stub and watched the liquid fall into it, taking in its sweet scent. It was a slow drip; no wonder the villagers had to climb so many trees to collect palm wine, he thought.

Descending the tree proved to be both easier than going up and less graceful than Hugo's demonstration. Grass crosses crunched beneath Jake's feet when he touched soil; Abuela winked at him.

Beaming, Jake turned towards Emma and saw that she was smiling, too. It felt natural, until they remembered. They turned away from each other, exchanging their smiles with those around them instead.

After he untied the strips of *paruma* from around his feet, he slipped on his flip flops, noting how normal it felt for his heel to hang out of the one Eduardo had gifted him. He figured it'd feel strange once he wore shoes that fit again. And now, given his conversation with Emma, it was looking like that time would come sooner than he wanted it to.

He glanced at the creek running behind the palm trees. "I'll be back in a minute," he said to her.

He waded into the water with his clothes on and slipped his body beneath it. His head underwater, he felt for grass at the side of the bank and pulled a handful, scrubbing the palms of his hands to rid them of the stickiness from palm sap. It was peaceful there. But when he came up for air, the villagers were standing at the edge of the creek, shaking their fingers, their voices trembling.

Emma pushed her way to the front of the crowd. "They say you need to get out of the creek. The cold water will kill you," she said calmly.

"What?" Jake sat up, laughing.

"It's this belief they have, that going in cold water when a person's body is heated from activity will cause an array of health issues." Her guard was down, and a smile escaped her lips. "The final result is death, regardless of how many years it takes."

"Well then, my dreams of living forever are crushed." He stood and stepped onto dry land, smiling at the villagers, hoping it would help soothe them.

"I did it, too, when I first arrived."

Jake looked at the villagers, touched they cared so much about him. Maya stood to the far left. He swore he saw tears in her eyes and, in looking for them, felt his gaze linger on her face. He turned back to smile at the villagers as he said to Emma, "I think there's a heart somewhere in her." He knew Emma would know who he was referring to.

Emma sighed. "On occasion, in her own way, I do too."

They walked back to the palm trees and the villagers crowded around Jake, rubbing his skin to warm him. But Jake had his eyes set on Abuela, whose tears trickled down her cheeks onto the half-made grass cross in her lap. He wasn't sure how long it would take to show her he wasn't going to die right then but was he willing to do just about anything to convince her. It made him wonder how she and the other villagers would react when he left, whenever that would be. Because somewhere between his first hodgepodge meal and now, he had grown attached to them.

"Hey, Emma?" Jake looked at her from three people over, his voice soft. "How long will it take you to decide if I should leave Almagro?"

CHAPTER 40

Emma ~ Present

Humidity dripped off oil droplets that clung to Emma's outdoor kitchen. She flipped a fish in the pan, stepping back to avoid its splash. The fish had been sitting on her step when she arrived home the day before. This time, it was the backend—a few inches of meat and its tail. And as expected when a fish showed up, noises woke her in the middle of the night. The squishing sound alarmed her; the storm changed the landscape around her house, so the noises were no longer a rustle.

Chuleta stared at Emma, her tail sweeping away a cockroach that ran across her pepper-stained floor.

Emma bopped Chuleta on the nose. "It needs to cool before you eat it, sweet pea."

A splash drew her attention towards the river. She watched Hugo push his canoe to shore with a *palanca*. He waved to her and shouted, "It's not the hole."

Laughing to herself, she climbed down her tree trunk staircase and met him at the shore. A fluorescent blue butterfly landed on Chuleta's nose. Chuleta jumped, chomping at air as she tried to catch it. Drops of water flew through the hole in Hugo's canoe when her paws hit the river.

"This is for you." He handed Emma a banana leaf with a freshly caught tilapia. He had already cleaned and sliced it so salt would seep into its flesh when she cooked it.

She smiled in thanks, folding the leaf so it wouldn't slip out.

"I wanted you to know . . ." He paused, pushing his toe into the soggy ground. "That I'd be okay . . . happy for you, even . . . if you marry Jake."

"Oh." Emma stammered, startled by the unexpected topic. "Well, Hugo . . ."

"Don't worry. No explanation is needed. I've seen how the two of you don't talk like you used to. Jake seems sad. And, well," he took a deep breath, "I know I've been persistent, pursuing you and all."

"It's not that." Emma looked down at the fish and then smiled at him. "Well, you have been persistent. Or perhaps better put, dedicated."

"See? But I understand, and I won't stand in your way."

Emma nodded, knowing she couldn't explain why she and Jake had been acting distant. "You'll find someone. Maybe," she tilted her head towards the river, "someone who can finally fix that canoe of yours."

"We can only hope," he said with a sigh. "Okay then, see you at lunch."

Emma turned back to her house. 'Lunch' was the word the villagers had been using to refer to the pastor's visit, for they didn't want to utter the devil's name. She salted the fish and threw it in the pan. Time was limited, though; she needed to get up to the church before mass started.

Abuela insisted all villagers attend, for the priest had to bless them before lunch arrived.

The fish sizzled in the pan, its eyes turning opaque. Could it have been Hugo who was leaving fish parts on her staircase? The one who was walking near her house at night? It made sense. He had always been vigilant over her, believing that someday she would be his wife.

When the fish was ready, she set it on a slab of wood, pulled her machete off the hook, and chopped it into thirds. Then, plate in hand, she walked into her house, wondering how many empty steps and quiet nights it would take to convince herself that it had been Hugo all along.

~ * ~

Mass got delayed because Jake picked a lemon. The villagers huddled around the tree he had pulled it from, praying, bowing, and touching its leaves. They picked all lemons within reach—both ripe and green—kissing them and placing them gingerly on the ground between the same roots that had given them life.

Emma and Jake stood behind the villagers, watching the situation unfold and making sure Maya kept her back to them. "This is my fault," Emma whispered.

Jake glanced at her. "But I was the one who picked it."

"Yes, but I should've told you after you got bit."

"By the snake?"

"Yeah. You see, they believe that anyone who's lived through a snake bite keeps a portion of the snake's venom inside them."

"But I didn't get bit by a poisonous—"

Emma shook her head. "I know, but it doesn't matter."

"So, you're saying I can never eat a lemon again?"

"No. I'm saying you can never *pick* a lemon in Almagro, or any fruit off of a tree, ever again." She glanced at him. "Not when the villagers are watching you, at least."

Jake chuckled. He did so softly, not wanting to draw the villagers' attention, some of whom dabbed at tears as they paid their respects to the lemon tree.

"It's because . . . oh, gosh." Emma bent down and pulled a lemon out of Chuleta's mouth. "We'll have to put this one back." She wiped the lemon on her *paruma* to rid it of Chuleta's slobber and turned her attention back to Jake. "The villagers say that any person who picks a fruit when they've been bit by a snake, regardless of how long ago it happened, kills the plant they took it from."

Jake's eyes widened. "I killed the lemon tree."

"To them, you did. But . . ." she looked over at Abuela, who was handing grass crosses to the villagers so they could hang them on the tree. "The kicker is that the poison could take a long time to kill the tree. Years, even."

"A lifespan of years?"

Emma winked and nudged him, knowing Maya was focused on the tree. It was hard for her to pull away from Jake because, even with the heat, she wanted to cuddle in his arms. But she did. She had to. How much longer she could put up the façade for, though, she wasn't sure. She could barely admit it to herself, much less to him—asking Jake to leave was inevitable.

"Jake, come here." Rosa pushed through the crowd and grabbed him by both arms, looking at Emma as she shook her head. "It was because of the creek."

The villagers overheard her and chimed in about the impact of overheated skin mixing with cold water. Emma was happy to see Rosa back to herself again; she even had enough leftover vine water to share with every family in Almagro.

Once the villagers paid their respects to the lemon tree, they piled into the church. Lunch would be arriving soon, and the blessing would take time. Abuela and the priest led the way inside. Abuela stopped at the entrance, surrounded by Carla's children, and made sure everyone took off their shoes after they crossed the two-branch bridge of their new moat.

Emma followed the crowd and walked to a back corner, brushing ants away with her bare foot as she claimed her spot along the wall. Jake stood in the back, too, on the opposite end of the same corner, allowing enough distance for people to stand between them.

Emma's eyes began adjusting to the darkness of the church. It seemed impossible what she saw, yet the longer she stared, the surer she became. She glanced at Maya picking at her nail polish. Knowing it was safe, Emma exchanged a silent laugh with Jake, for he, too, had noticed that the statue of the Virgin Mary had been moved into the aisle. It sat on a lopsided bamboo table that, like the statue, had mold growing in its crevices. It would have seemed normal enough if it weren't for the adornments around it. There, surrounding the Virgin Mary's feet, were offerings of Vaseline, rubbing alcohol, and condoms.

Abuela waddled up to the table and set a green lemon in front of the statue's toe. "For you, dear Mary," she whispered.

She turned to the villagers, nudging the priest who had nodded off in his plastic chair. Then, Abuela proclaimed for all to hear, "We must start mass now, before lunch arrives."

CHAPTER 41

Emma ~ Present

L unch didn't deserve to be received at the highest point in Almagro. It was an agreement as unanimous as it was unavoidable—meeting the pastor at the *tienda* made the most sense. While the villagers waited on benches and leaned against the *tienda's* posts, they decided to do some housekeeping.

Mateo tapped his fingers on the counter from inside the *tienda*, waiting for the villagers to settle down as he looked out at them standing on the patio. "Double. We'll go back with double."

Martha pulled Emma's *paruma* tight. "*Digits*. Double digits."

"We can't bring everyone." Mateo sighed and shook his head. "Some people have to stay back in Almar—"

"No." Abuela slapped a grass cross against her thigh. Its dried edges broke off and joined pieces already clinging to her sweaty legs. "I refuse to stay back in the village again."

Martha thrust her hands on her hips and looked at Mateo. "Taking four canoes to go gold mining isn't enough. What's wrong with you? Just a couple of weeks ago you were all for it."

Mateo began tapping the counter with both hands. "And I still am. But even so, not everyone can—"

"Lunch!"

Silence filled the air as the villagers stared in the direction of Andrés' finger, his shout still echoing across Almagro. Even though everyone was already at the *tienda*, out of habit Mateo grabbed his tagua seeds and banged them against the *tienda's* wall, indicating that it was the *tienda* port the canoe was docking at.

Andrés ran over to Emma and tugged at her *paruma*. "Did lunch bring us snow?" He dashed over to Jake and pulled his shirt, in English exclaiming, "Snow!"

Emma smiled at him but couldn't muster a laugh. "No," she said softly. "That's Styrofoam."

Within minutes of the pastor's arrival, the *tienda* sat vacant and word had spread—the pastor's snow was carrying their lunch. Emma and Jake walked down to the port last, wanting the villagers to be the first to give their welcome. Since the pastor was carrying food, Emma knew it would be a friendly one. Just how long their welcome would last, though, she didn't know.

Abuela reached out her hand when she saw Emma approach. "Get one for me." She placed a finger on her chin. "A couple, on second thought." She looked down at the pastor's canoe from the *tienda*, smiling as she zeroed in on Carla's children receiving their meal.

The villagers ended up eating their lunch on the soccer field. The pastor was happy because it was easy for him to be seen as he preached. Abuela was happy because the villagers had a clear view of the church—with the exception of the area where the pastor stood.

Jake leaned around Rosa, who sat between him and Emma. "Where's 'M'?" he asked.

Emma looked behind her and strained to scan the soccer field from her spot on the ground. She lifted her eyebrows. "She was just here a minute ago."

Ironically, Emma found their situation easier to manage when Maya was present; they could keep an eye on her to see when she became distracted. It was in those moments when Emma and Jake interacted more freely.

Rosa set a pork chop bone in front of Chuleta. "A *chuleta* for Chuleta." She turned to Emma with narrowed eyes. "The pastor didn't make us cook. *And*," she shoved a spoonful of potato and beet salad in her mouth, "gave us food we don't have in Almagro."

Emma smiled as murmurs of agreement from the other villagers surrounded her. She shifted her legs to the side so they wouldn't fall asleep; she had long given up trying to keep them clean. A few villagers had dragged benches into the soccer field but, like her, most sat on the ground.

Rosa laughed. "Carla would've loved this. Can you picture it?" She looked up at the sky. "A mother of twelve children, receiving a prepared meal, not just for her family but for everyone in Almagro."

Emma put an arm around her and they rocked together. "Maybe Carla sent the pastor."

Rosa grinned, then put a hand to her ear. When the pastor prompted, she shouted "Amen!", joining the rest of the villagers in throwing their hands up in the air.

With their lunches already finished, Emma was surprised they continued interacting with the pastor's sermon. She squinted towards the front of the church where Abuela sat a short distance from the pastor. Abuela was on her stool sucking on a pork chop bone, her feet wiggling back and forth. The priest sat in his plastic chair beside her, reaching out his tongue to lick a piece of beet stuck on his cheek.

Eduardo scooched up behind Emma. "I don't know about this, *mi hija*."

"Do you think he'll return?" She leaned back so he'd hear her whispering.

"Maybe. If he does, though, I worry how it could change the dynamics in Almagro."

"But I think everyone is already set in their beliefs."

"No." He shook his head. "An empty stomach will always believe in food before anything else." He looked at Emma. "And I trust my gut."

She smiled and thought back to when they picked oranges a few months after she arrived in Almagro. Eduardo had told her that he'd always been leery of the church. It was the first time Emma realized how much he trusted her. If the villagers found out about his doubts with the church, they would give him a hard time until his last breath on earth, the place where his true faith laid.

Rosa squeezed Emma's arm. "They're back."

Emma looked over and watched six men approach the soccer field, holding baskets made from gourds. She looked at Jake. "Ready to try palm wine?"

Jake's eyes widened. "Already?"

She nodded. "If they leave it more than a day it'll start tasting like vinegar."

The gourds passed among the villagers as fast as their 'Amens' died out. Somewhere between the last 'Amen' and Jake on the brink of taking his first taste of palm wine, the pastor caught on.

With his arms in the air and eyes closed, he said, "An evil habit is no match compared to God's message. We'll build an Evangelical church to save Almagro."

But the villagers didn't process his words, for they had already turned their attention away from him, busying themselves with enjoying their freshly harvested wine.

~ * ~

There was an uninvited guest at Emma's house, judging by the Styrofoam box. It lay on the ground, tipped on its side to the right of her staircase. Hundreds of ants had already found it, although she knew they weren't a reliable indication of how long the box had been laying there. Emma had wanted to make a quick trip, merely to give Chuleta her dinner since she didn't want her living off pork chop bones alone.

Emma's eyes fell to a notched step halfway up her tree trunk. There, laid a whole fish. A stalk of grass as thick as her index finger pierced its stomach. From it, blades of green grass splayed a foot above the fish, blowing in the breeze.

A sobbing noise came from Emma's house. Following the sound, she climbed the tree trunk and walked around her balcony to the side facing the river. Emma hesitated when she rounded the corner; a woman sat hunched over against her bedroom door. The woman's long black hair revealed glimpses of her hands which were wrapped around her legs, pulled to her chest.

Chuleta gave up chasing a rabbit on the hill and ran up the staircase to find Emma. She barked upon seeing the stranger on her balcony. Startled, the woman looked up. She lifted her arms to cover her face, but it was already too late.

Emma gasped. "Maya."

Chuleta put a paw on Maya's shoulder and licked her hands, pushing her way to her face. Maya stood. Without looking at Emma, she moved the short distance to the end of the wall and crumpled up on the floor.

Emma slid her back down the end of the other wall. "Do you want to talk?"

Maya continued to cry—a quieter, controlled one now that she had an audience. She didn't respond. But she also didn't motion for Emma to leave.

Minutes passed before Maya broke the silence. Head tucked to her knees, she whispered, "I'm scared."

Emma leaned towards her. "What are you scared of?"

More silence ensued and then, "He died."

"Who died?" Emma asked gently.

"My boyfriend."

Emma's mind raced. How long had it been since she saw Jake? Not long. He was on the soccer field when she left. She was sure of it . . . wasn't she?

As if reading her thoughts, Maya lifted her head. "You didn't know him."

Emma nodded. For once, she was thankful for Maya's ability to tune into people's emotions. She had questions. Many of them. But where to start? Keeping her voice gentle, she began with the obvious. "So, he wasn't from Almagro?"

"No." Maya stuck her hand down her shirt, pulled a leaf from her bra, and began tearing it apart.

"Where was he from?"

"Colombia."

"Oh?"

Emma watched Maya rip apart the last piece of the leaf. Meanwhile, she tried to process the news. How could

Maya know someone from Colombia? He must have been lying to her. It was the only way.

"It's my fault he's dead." Her voice cracked between each word.

Emma got up and sat back down beside her. "Why do you say that?"

"He . . . I . . . gave him medicine."

"What kind of medicine?"

Maya looked towards the spot where the matted path used to be. "For the thing that Rebecca came for."

Emma felt her body go still. "I see."

They sat in silence, Emma trying to process the information, trying to figure out how to move the conversation forward, how to not scare Maya off.

"I have it too."

Emma looked at her. "HIV?"

Maya nodded.

"Have you been following the treatment Rebecca gave you?"

She pulled a bottle of pills from her pocket and rocked it back and forth in her hand. "He went to a clinic after I told him about it. He had it too. But . . . I already knew that." She stopped and took a deep breath. "He gave it to me."

Emma reached out to hold Maya's hand. She didn't pull away. "Did they give him medicine?"

"No," she whispered. "They were going to, but they didn't have any in stock. He was supposed to go back the next day, but he didn't have time."

"Why was that?"

"He had to go on a trip."

Emma squeezed her hand. "Was this trip to see you?"

"You could say so."

"So, you think it's your fault because he left to see you instead of waiting for his treatment?"

Maya shook her head. "He told me there was a special medicine, prepared by a shaman of sorts, and that I could get it in Chepo. He didn't have time to go himself."

Emma nodded slowly. "So that's why you went out in the storm."

Maya shrugged. "I figured it'd be the easiest time to slip away, with everyone preparing for it. Plus, with the current, I'd get there quicker."

"But why did you bring Andrés?"

"Because he saw me getting ready. He said he'd tattle tale unless he came along."

"So." Emma paused, considering how to word her question. Knowing Maya wasn't keen on euphemisms, she decided against them. "You think the medicine you bought killed your boyfriend?"

"Yes." She hesitated. "I mean, anything could have happened, but it makes the most sense."

Chuleta laid down, resting her head on Maya's now stretched out legs. For the first time ever, Maya petted her.

Emma smiled, but Maya didn't notice since her eyes were on Chuleta. "Don't blame yourself, he—"

"I'm not," she pulled her hand away from Emma's. "Just because it's my fault doesn't mean I'm to blame." She shook her head and softened her voice. "He asked for the stuff."

"Right." Emma paused. "How did you find out he passed away?"

"The fish." She gestured towards the front of Emma's house. "It was his symbol . . . our symbol. We had lots of them."

"So, the fish I'd find on my staircase. That was him?"

"Yes." Maya nodded slowly as she talked. "He'd cross over from the other side, leave part of a fish. It meant we could meet that evening. The part of the fish he left indicated the time. And sometimes," she sniffled, "it meant he was upset when I didn't show up."

Emma thought back to the staircase full of fish the day they returned from their overnight gold mining trip. The path on the other side of the river the day of Carla's funeral. The fish parts left on her staircase at random intervals. It was beginning to make sense. Eduardo would never believe it . . . and he may not ever know, depending on how Maya chose to end the conversation.

"And the rustling I'd hear at night . . . that was you?"

"Mostly. But it was him, too. We'd meet by the river around the bend. Out of sight—and hearing range—of everyone."

"But I don't get it. Your boyfriend would've had to cross over to Almagro in broad daylight to leave the fish."

"Yeah." Maya pulled out another leaf and began tearing its edges. "But broad daylight from our side of the village. You're always out in the community during the day. And my family . . . well, mom was sick and impressionable. Andrés is young and impressionable. And dad's always out finding us food."

Maya watched Chuleta, who tried catching the ripped-up leaf falling from her hands. "He didn't take a canoe, of course. Just swam with a log he could hide behind. And I could see the fish from my porch. Your staircase was perfect, it gave me a great angle to view them from."

Emma nodded in response, remaining silent. Finally, she asked, "Who put the fish there?" Her voice softened. "This last one, that is."

"One of his friends."

Emma stared at her until the silence made Maya turn and look. Then, with the firmest voice Emma had used up to that point, she said, "You're telling me there are other people passing by here, just across the river from Almagro?"

"Just sometimes. And they won't come to Almagro anymore." She teared up again.

Emma wanted more details but decided against it. "Can I ask one last question?" She paused, letting Maya gather herself, and proceeded when she didn't protest. "Why were you pursuing Jake if you already had a boyfriend?"

Maya looked down at her lap. "Because I was jealous of you."

"Of me?"

"You live on your own, which is something I'd never be allowed to do. Not as long as I'm single." She shook her head. "You took the only space that had ever been mine."

Emma swallowed, tears pricking her eyes. Nausea swelled in her stomach as she thought about her notched staircase on the backside of her balcony. She would only ever pass by there to get to and from her house, along with an occasional visit to sweep the floor. But for the most part, she saw it as a place that was hers controlled by Maya. How could she have overlooked that she had been the intrusive one?

"Maya, I'm sorry. I—"

"The irony." Maya sighed. "Eduardo was visiting your house because of my boyfriend. And now you have blackmail on my blackmail."

Emma reached over, placed her hands on Maya's shoulders, and pulled them towards her. "Blackmail is no way to live a life."

"And because of that, I know you won't use mine against me."

CHAPTER 42

Emma ~ Present

Emma chose the path through the jungle to get to the school. She was sure the pastor had left. But she knew the villagers would still be in the soccer field gossiping about his visit. And right then, the only people she wanted to see were Sonya and Jake.

She held her machete out in front of her, swinging it to clear spider webs as she walked along. The path reminded her of Carla; it was her favorite place in the village, and increasingly so shortly before she died. Perhaps using it was the key to keeping secrets in Almagro.

Maya's news about a stranger crossing into the village would have rocked Rebecca's theory. The last time she was in Almagro, she had asked Emma if she had any hunches about how HIV could have gotten there. Rebecca tossed confidentiality to the side, saying she believed it came from the *tienda*. It was a logical thought. The one that Emma had arrived to on her own as well. And even now, knowing what she knew, she still felt

Mateo played a part in bringing HIV to Almagro, in giving it to Carla. It was now clear that at least one other person had played a part in it, too.

Emma's flip flop slid across a rotting mango, one of only a few remaining as proof that mango season had come and gone. Its juice oozed through a hole to her foot. It was only a matter of time before insects and rain would consume the mango's flesh, leaving behind a seed with ambitions to grow beneath the shade of its elders.

Emma promised to give Maya her house once her time in Almagro ended. Maya said the villagers wouldn't allow it, that she'd have to find a husband first. Emma knew they would lean into that argument. But Maya taking Emma's house was a fair proposal. And when it came down to it, after their doubts and theories and gossip and meetings, the villagers would choose fairness. Every decision they ever made was rooted in it. A fairness that adapted with time and experiences. If only Emma had listened to the villagers more carefully in the first place, she would have made a fairer decision about where to build her house.

Her thoughts wandered to Eduardo and his bats. Would revealing Carla and Maya's secrets make anyone feel better? Would it change anything? She studied a spider web spanning the path, the final obstacle standing in the way of her and the school. Sighing, she batted it down and vowed to make a habit of using Carla's path.

"I saved you some palm wine."

Emma jumped and looked over at the plantain trees where Sonya tossed pineapple scraps into a compost pile. "What would I do without you?"

"Jake saved you some too." Sonya winked. "It'll be a good night."

Emma smiled and shook her head. Jake. It was time to talk with him, to clear the way for his plans. She stepped onto the patio of the school. Despite the storm, a red hue still clung to the concrete from blood stuck in its narrow crevices. It felt so long since Rebecca and the nurses had first arrived in Almagro.

It was before Jake.

Emma walked over to the classroom window and peered in. Jake sat on his mattress, his knees bent at chin height and sprawled apart so he could read the beginner Spanish book Sonya had lent him. His hair had grown longer since he arrived; growing it out so he could put it in a man bun was his new goal. Her heart pounded. She would watch him a little longer to gather her thoughts, she decided. Just to figure out how she was going to say it.

But then he looked up.

"Woah." He laughed. "You're like the kids now."

She gave him a 'you caught me' look. "I just got here. I swear."

"Yet again, just like the kids." He patted his mattress. "Come over to my humble abode." He paused and looked towards the windows. "As long as you think it's okay."

Emma nodded and hoped he couldn't sense her nerves. She sat down on the far side of his mattress. It sunk so low her tailbone touched the floor. She flashed him a look. "This is worse than I remember it being."

"It's gotten a lot of use. I don't notice it as much anymore." He leaned his elbow down on the mattress towards her, setting a cheek on his fist. "You still haven't told me if I should leave."

"Right." Emma smiled, her eyes roaming the room to find the words. They fell on the chalkboard, which still had faint outlines of human anatomy from Rebecca's

HIV presentation. Despite their many efforts, Emma and Sonya failed to get it completely erased.

"You look relieved."

"I do?" Emma chuckled and looked over at him. His head rested a foot away from her side. "You know," she said, holding his stare. "Maybe you weren't so wrong when you said you can read my facial expressions, the ones I didn't know I was showing."

"Oh yeah?" He gave her an uneasy look. "Does this mean you're relieved because you want me to leave?"

She smiled. A smile that came easily, one that felt natural. "No." She scooted off the mattress, not caring what kind of dirt and insects her legs ran into in the process. She placed her head in her hands, her elbows sinking into the foam just inches away from his. "Although I do want you to visit your family up north. But after you do that, find me again. Please."

He smiled and leaned in closer. "It's settled then." With his thumb, he brushed away a beetle that landed on her cheek. "Do we still need to tiptoe around 'M'?"

"No." She leaned into his hand, which cupped her face. "And we can go back to calling her by her real name."

"I'd ask what changed but . . ."

Emma wasn't sure who kissed who first, and she didn't care. They held each other's faces, their arms crisscrossed, tangled in each other. The mattress buckled under their elbows, pushing them closer together. Emma ran her hand up Jake's arm. Her fingers lingered on scabs from his cuts and scrapes, patterns she had memorized from afar. He breathed softly on her cheeks, the sweet smell of Almagro's corn coffee enveloping them. They explored each other intimately but cautiously, knowing at any moment they could be interrupted.

"Emma yes! Jake yes!"

Emma and Jake pulled away from each other—the least distance they could manage without it being uncomfortable for bystanders.

"Andre*yes*," Emma said, throwing her hand up to smooth her curls.

Andrés hung from the cement window's decorative pieces as he peered in at them. María dangled next to him, struggling to hold herself up. She stretched her neck out, trying to land her puckered lips on Andrés' cheek.

Emma looked at Jake and then back at the kids. Beaming, she asked, "Do you want Jake to come back and visit?"

Andrés tried to clap his hands but lost his grip of the window. A thump rang through the schoolhouse, followed by the pitter-patter of bare feet on cement. He burst into the room, his arms out. "Yesssss!"

Emma laughed and leaned into Jake, taking in his features from her new, up-close view. "We'll have to check with the rest of the villagers."

She was sure Jake's face showed agreement, but Andrés had already wedged himself between them, balancing his knees on each of their thighs as he hugged them, pushing the sides of their faces together.

Through the window, Emma watched Maya pass by. She smiled at Emma, clutching a stalk of grass to her chest, its blades blowing in the breeze. Behind Emma, bats made their first appearance of the evening. To her side, Chuleta pawed at her shoulder. An ant crawled up her leg and sweat dripped down her face.

Emma used to believe that the feeling of being at home was fixed. Once achieved, it didn't change. But sitting there she knew she was wrong, for whether it was the structure itself or a feeling, home was made to evolve.

LAURA ANN NEULEO

A NOTE FROM THE AUTHOR

It takes an average of ninety days for a phone number to be recycled in the United States. Upon moving back to the U.S., I learned firsthand about the issues that such a short turnaround can cause.

My Jake (pseudonym) proved to be as mysterious as Emma's. Unlike Emma, however, I never found out my Jake's story. To this day, I still wonder why he never informed his dozens of contacts that he no longer had his number. Years later, I still receive messages from those he knew, albeit less frequently than in the beginning.

The messages to my Jake came in as many forms as Emma's. And, in one case, more. Jake's contacts would write with news of happy things—new engagements, babies, and jobs. Texts inviting him to watch a ball game, meet up at a bar, or asking his advice on legal matters were near daily affairs in the beginning. X-rated messages and nude photos were, too. Such explicit content was so frequent, in fact, that I warned my family and friends about the situation in case they ever found it on my phone. There was also a night close to a presidential election when, like Lizzie, I was included in a group text message about the candidates.

And then, there was the letter to Jake. I received it as a photo one day many months after having my new phone number. A large red stamp reading "Confidential" was strewn across the envelope. The return address? The Internal Revenue Service. Along with the photo, the sender included a message. *Dude, do you want me to open it?* I didn't say yes, but I could have. And so, it's a lesson for us all to be careful with the information we send via text messages, even when we've triple checked that we sent it to the correct number.

I could write a memoir twice as long as this novel about my time as a Peace Corps Volunteer in Panama. But instead, I'll highlight scenes from *Messages to Jake* inspired from my real-life experience. Let's first start, though, with what isn't real.

Almagro is a fictional village, as are the characters who live there. I expanded and played upon certain events and beliefs in order to achieve a more dramatic effect. Many scenes are also entirely from my own imagination.

It deserves to be noted that *Messages to Jake* is written from my perspective, fueled by my American upbringing. It would be fascinating to read a novel written by my Peace Corps village inspired by their experiences with me. They weren't shy about pointing out my odd behaviors and beliefs during our two years together. And because of it, we shared countless laughs.

My days in Panama were spent in *parumas* with an Emberá woman lending a hand when they inevitably became loose. Wearing shorts beneath *parumas* was cheating but, as modern-day women, they did it too. Meanwhile, the Latinas in my village were amazed that I so faithfully wore them. I'm surprised *parumas* haven't become a trend outside the Emberá community. They're versatile, colorful, easy to clean, and quick to dry.

Life revolved around the river and every year the river took life. In December 2010, so much rain fell in Panama that the Panama Canal closed. It was the first weather related canal closure since the 1930s. I'll forever be grateful for one of my community members who, on a late afternoon day, was stuck on the 'other side' with me when the river began to rise. He crossed us to our village in his dugout canoe with nothing but a *palanca* stick, instructing me to hold on tight and scoop out water with a gourd if the floor became flooded. It was dangerous, but spending the night on the other side would have been dangerous too.

My community members ate well on occasions when the river rose violently, for they filled their bellies with gigantic lobster-looking creatures. During such times, these 'shrimp' would voluntarily crawl out of the river and onto land, having made their own choice between two dangerous options. Finding such shrimp when there wasn't a major river rising was rare; it didn't happen during my two-year service, as far as I know.

My community watched over me tirelessly during my time with them. They taught me the jungle version of right from wrong and how to maintain self-care within it. With a single scream they'd come to my rescue when an extra scary spider or scorpion graced me with its presence. And they would inform me at what time I turned off my battery powered lantern the night before. As an extra sign of their watchful eye, they sometimes knew if I had gotten up to use my repurposed water bottle in the middle of the night; they would tell me so the next morning on my way to empty it in the latrine.

There's perhaps no better example of how much the villagers in my community cared about me when, shortly after my arrival, I took a cold shower after having worked in the school garden. Tears in their eyes, they explained to me how my health would suffer because of it and, if I was lucky, the cold water on my overheated body wouldn't kill me.

I made the unconventional choice to live alone, although one was never really alone in a village as small as mine. The villagers in my community built my house using fallen trees pulled from the river. They had custom made it—setting it only four feet off the ground and with a regular staircase. They had done so both for comfort and as a representation of a combined Emberá and Latino house, given that both groups lived in my village. Nonetheless, I had my fair share of experience climbing notched tree trunks, although Emma and Chuleta's grace in doing so was something I never managed to achieve.

During the rainy season, chiggers thrived in my village. Rubbing alcohol was a staple in every household. It was so effective, in fact, that I rarely covered my ankles in Vaseline to prevent the miniscule beasts from climbing up. Just as pesky for some of my community members was the term *diablo rojo*. Diehard church goers refused to refer to Panama City's bus system as such, fearing it praised the devil.

My community members savored the *tienda* for its source of gossip as much as they loved food itself. Catching food, making food, and dreaming about food were their go-to conversation topics in moments when there wasn't anything else to talk about. Politicians leaned into this and, while their gifts to win votes in rural areas were sometimes perplexing, they mostly sent rice, beans, oil, and other useful goods.

I lived in a village with cell phone reception but without electricity. Most of my community members had flip phones, although they had purchased those themselves—they were never a gift from a political candidate. They charged their phones with a communal car battery, and the *tienda* owner would recharge it when he'd leave the village to pick up store supplies. A few families in my community used generators for electricity. Eventually, the generators replaced the need for a car battery. My community members were able to purchase the generators, in part, because of income they made from small-scale gold mining at a time when gold was purchased at extraordinarily high prices in Panama City.

My community members were savvy in what was and wasn't edible. And their idea of edible was oftentimes a different version than mine. Within days of living in my village, I tucked my vegetarian ways aside and ate whatever was gifted to me with gratitude so as not to offend those who didn't always have enough food to eat themselves. The iguana scene in *Messages to Jake*—and Emma's feelings about it—were a near verbatim account of my own experience when I eventually accepted an iguana hunting invitation.

The relationship between snakebites and fruit trees was a real concept in my village. Most of my community members, however, brushed it off as an unproven theory passed down from generations. Nevertheless, everyone knew who had been bitten by a snake during their life; those people avoided picking fruit from trees that weren't theirs.

In 2016, the Panamanian government launched a campaign to offer free HIV testing in higher risk areas and free HIV treatment for everyone. At the time this novel was published, Panama's Ministry of Health

(MINSA) continues offering this free aid.

My Peace Corps service had already ended when MINSA's initiative began, so the HIV scenes depicted in *Messages to Jake* are purely from my own imagination. They were easy ones to picture, though, should testing ever arrive to my village, for my community members took pride in their preparations to welcome guests. And, above all, they had a remarkable sense of humor, even when it came to topics that would make people from outside of their circle blush.

If you enjoyed reading *Messages to Jake*, it would mean so much to me if you wrote a review and spread the word to those you know.

With thanks,

Laura

FURTHER READING: MESSAGES TO THE MULE

Join Maya in the second book of the Messages series, *Messages to the Mule.*

With her boyfriend gone, Maya is offered a choice: join a South American drug cartel or risk the cartel entering her village of Almagro. Treacherous months hiking through the jungle and lonely nights sleeping on coconut husk mattresses ensue.

Maya knows the cartel's weapon is to use relationships as a threat. Despite that, she makes a friend, visits Almagro, and develops feelings for a fellow mule—all while banking on the trustworthiness of those she encounters.

Meanwhile, scenes from the past reveal information about Maya's first love. While she struggles with loving a new man after having lost another, a revelation happens that could upheave her life as a mule.

Will Maya succeed in keeping her relationships a secret from the cartel? When faced with life and death choices, will she be able to resist leaving Almagro's residents out of the drug lords' hands?

Messages to the Mule is a story about forbidden love, the power of choice, and discovering self-worth under oppression.

Manufactured by Amazon.ca
Bolton, ON

31865875R00206